ABOUT LAST NIGHT...

CATHERINE ALLIOTT

NOSHOOZ PUBLISHING

CONTENTS

ABOUT CATHERINE

Catherine Alliott has written fifteen bestselling novels and is translated into eighteen languages. She has sold over 3 million books worldwide. Catherine lives with her family in Hertfordshire, UK.

Visit CatherineAlliott.US to get a sneak peek at Catherine's other books including:
"My Husband Next Door"
"The Old Girl Network"
"Wish You Were Here"
"Olivia's Luck"
"One Day In May"
"A Married Man"

www.facebook.com/AlliottCountry
www.CatherineAlliott.US
Catherine@CatherineAlliott.US

ISBN - **978-1-948224-21-5**

Library of Congress Control Number: 2017960712

For Susu

CHAPTER 1

I stood at the gate with my laden wheelbarrow and ran a practiced eye over my acres which stretched away in a plateau before me, rising gently to the hills beyond. I wished I felt more romantic and wistful about it – this sylvan scene and all that. I didn't, though: I felt tired, bleary-eyed and, frankly, fed up.

There was barely a paddock I could enter these days without fearing for my safety, and feeding my sheep had become a matter of high subterfuge and low cunning. If I fed the boys first, the ewes in the far field were instantly alerted and came rushing across for their breakfast. But if I fed the ewes it involved going through Buddy's field, and Buddy wanted to have his way with me – the only one who did these days – and Buddy was a big ram. So desperate – and confused, obviously – was he, he'd knocked me clean over in his lather yesterday. He'd been separated from the flock because he'd already impregnated the ewes, most of whom had lambed, and was now in solitary confinement. Whilst it was driving both of us mad, I certainly didn't want him messing with my girls again, and he was not to

1

be trusted with last year's boy lambs who were going to market soon, hopefully in one piece, with no black eyes, cauliflower ears or obvious signs of grievous bodily harm.

I pulled my hat down low, sank into my coat and set off with my mighty barrow of concentrated sheep nuts, which was darned heavy. As I, went I dreamed of a quad bike like my friend Anna's, who fed her pigs with the wind in her hair, throttle out, lipstick on. Buddy was no fool and came dashing across to ambush me, but I'd thought ahead and distracted him with a scoop of feed on the grass. Wrong-footed, he dithered, wondering which was his greatest urge, and by the time he'd decided and given chase, I'd made it to the ewes' field. I just managed to shut the gate on his indignant black nose before being surrounded by forty-five hormonal females, all desperate for my nuts.

Sometimes I wished I started the day with a pot of tea delivered by a handsome man with a charming smile. Often, actually. Instead, I sliced open the feed sack with a Stanley knife and shoved my barrow ruthlessly through the sea of moving white wool to the yards of galvanized trough lying on the ground. Nipping ahead of Nora, who was head girl and horribly bossy, I poured from one end of the trough to the other. They rushed in a veritable surge, almost knocking me over before somehow sorting themselves out to feed in two reasonably straight lines on either side. A biddable sheepdog would be good, too, I reflected, watching them, instead of two hysterical Border terriers who were more of a hindrance than a help and consequently shut up in the kitchen. At length I sighed and turned for home, mission accomplished.

To be fair, the man I'd had, my husband David, would have been brilliant. He'd be wrestling the barrow from my hands this minute were it possible, absolutely in his element out here. It was everything he'd ever fondly imag-

ined he'd be doing, in fact, before fate had so rudely inter-
vened. Always an early riser, he'd be up with the light,
feeding and tending these characters, before pottering off
to Ludlow for a few hours' gentle conveyancing in his
sleepy lawyers' office, the one he'd swapped for the City
slickers' firm he'd come to hate. David had been a partner
in a rather ritzy legal establishment in Liverpool Street, but
the strength-sapping hours and the workload had eventually ground him down.

We'd snapped up this rural idyll he'd spotted – literally
in the front of *Country Life* at the dentist's – with its pretty
farmhouse and ninety acres, and then he'd found his easy
going job a short drive away. Everything had slotted ridiculously simply into place, no doubt because David was at
the helm. We'd taken the children out of their pushy
London schools, I'd given up my job, and we'd come down
here, all ready for the Good Life.

And good it had been, fleetingly. Until, disappointingly,
one day David had taken our car to the village to get some
shopping and never returned. I paused with my empty
barrow a moment. I say disappointingly, in that ironic,
deliberately shocking way, because if I delved any deeper
into my grief I'd be back to square one. Back with my
sleepless nights, my inability to motivate myself, my weight
loss, and my three distressed children. So five years down
the track I've adopted this splendidly sort of upper class,
stiff-upper-lip approach to my husband's death, to stop
myself from gagging when his name is mentioned. And
actually, I can quite see how it got people through a war. It
certainly works for me.

I trundled my empty barrow back to the barn,
reloaded it with a bale of hay for the boys in the far
meadow – who charged me, predictably, but with less
ferocity, it being only dry grass – and then walked back to

the yard, wondering if anyone at the house was even up, had fed the dogs, or emptied the dishwasher, and by that I meant one of the lodgers rather than the children, the likelihood of the latter managing any of the above being little short of a miracle.

Actually, ditto the former. The married Chinese accountants who were currently installed in the best bedroom were delightfully smiley but permanently attached to some piece of technology, so anything practical, like letting a cat out, induced a look of panic in their eyes. It was their last day today, though, I thought with some relief, thinking of the check on the kitchen table and having my bedroom back. I didn't take lodgers as a rule, but the occasional B&B helped enormously, particularly when it had become clear that the minuscule pension David had collected from Perkins and Dawson, and the tiny one I'd paid into, were not going to go anywhere near supporting us once death duties had taken their toll.

I paused a moment before I went into the barn to dump the barrow: gazed at the row of uninterrupted hills rolling away in the distance behind the house. How he would have loved this. And how pissed off he would have been to miss it, on account of a stupid, worn-out brake pad. That had been my overriding emotion for a long time, I recollected, as I went on to feed the chickens and ducks. Anger. At how hacked off he would have been to miss all this: his dream, his reward for all those years in an over-lit, open-plan battery farm in the City. His putative gold watch.

We'd been here all of six weeks. Five and a half, to be precise. The house was still full of packing cases and two of the children hadn't even started back at school. It was the end of the summer holidays. When it happened, Minna and Nico had been on the grass tennis court at the bottom of the garden, now a sea of weeds. I remembered that long walk out there after I'd had the visit from the police: remembered them lowering their rackets as I approached and as they saw my face. I knew they'd had a flash of recognition before I spoke, before I told them that their lives would never be the same again. I remember that like it was yesterday. Lucy's face I still can't even bring myself to remember.

But as I say, that was five years ago. And however much you think life will never move on one jot, it jolly well does, at a rickety-rackety pace. And right now I had more pressing problems, like how we were going to stay here – my pledge, all those years ago to David's ghost – and how all my various concerns, the horse dealing, the lavender soap, the sheep farming and, more recently, the boxer shorts and scanty ladies' underwear business, were going to keep us afloat. How they were going to collectively re-tile the stable roof, pay the bills and, more to the point, keep my eldest daughter, who I spotted through the kitchen window looking dubiously into the fridge, in designer yogurt.

I mention this because I wanted Lucy to come down and peer in my fridge as much as possible now that she'd moved to London, and there was not a great deal to attract her these days. She was very definitely not dressed for Herefordshire today, I noticed, in tailored black trousers and a nipped-in white jacket. She wrinkled her nose as she lifted the plastic lid on a packet of curly bacon before replacing it with disdain.

'What are you doing up?' I shut the back door on a blast of air. Two clearly unfed dogs yapped in delight and hurled themselves at my legs. I took in the debris of last night's wine and fag fest with her brother and sister, which clearly no one had thought to clear up.

'I'm going back to London. Can you drop me at the station?'

Please, I thought to myself. 'I thought you said the shop was shut today?' I gathered the empty ashtrays and glasses from the table and put them in the sink to hide my face; to try not to show I cared. 'And you were going to help Minna with her project?'

'It is shut, but I still need to be there; there's loads of admin to catch up on. And it's pointless helping Minna with her project, it doesn't exist. She only said that to get you off her back in the holidays. It was a ruse, Mother. What d'you think she is, eight? Counting haystacks and coloring them in or something?'

'Right,' I said shortly.

'Is this orange juice OK?' She sniffed it dubiously.

'I don't know, darling, try it.'

She peered instead at the sell-by date. 'Fourth of March!' She recoiled in horror.

'Yes, but it's concentrate, that keeps forever.'

'Because it's full of preservatives. You should buy fresh.'

'I should,' I agreed cheerfully. 'And if I could afford it, I would.' I banged the washing-up down harder than I might on the draining board.

'The bailiff came again,' Lucy told me.

I swung around, appalled. 'Did he?' She was leaning against the dresser sipping her black coffee, unconcerned. I abandoned the washing-up and sat down at the table, clutching the edge. 'Oh God. Which one?'

'The nice one, Tia.'

'Oh, thank the Lord. What did you say?'

'I said you'd sort it by the end of the week, or at least the following one. Don't stress, Mum, she was nice. I didn't give her the silver or anything.' She ran a hand through her mane of silky blonde hair.

'I've already sold the silver,' I said abstractedly, getting up again, knowing now I'd have to sell the farm, as I romantically called our smallholding. The bailiff. *Again*.

'You haven't paid the council tax,' Lucy said gently.

'I know.' My mouth was dry. 'But I told her, I'm paying it this week. Today, in fact, just as soon as I've got a check from Lu and Sam.'

'They left it.' Lucy plucked it from the mountain of detritus on the table. 'They went about twenty minutes ago. It's precisely three hundred and eighty pounds, Mum. They were only here a week. The council tax is a deal more.'

'I know, but I'm getting loads from that chap who's buying Nutty.'

'Yes, I told her that, and she was fine about it, I told you. Although she did ask if Nutty was a relative or a horse.' She grinned. 'I rather liked her. Isn't she the one you do book club with? Maybe give her a ring?'

'Yes. Yes, I will.' I flew to find my phone on the over-flowing dresser, riffling in panic under papers and bills and soap wrappers, rotting fruit in the bowl.

'What's this, by the way?'

I turned, mid-riffle. Lucy was gingerly extracting a purple thong with a fingertip and thumb from a pile she'd found on the table.

'What d'you think it is? I'm branching out from the gents' boxers into ladies' stuff. Is my phone under there?' I dived beneath the towering pile of lingerie.

'Why so sparkly?' She peered at the encrusted sequins on the front.

'Because it excites the gentleman friend, I imagine – or maybe it excites the lady as she's trolleying round boring old Tesco's – I don't know, use your imagination. Ring my phone, would you, Luce?' I patted my pockets, glancing about the chaotic kitchen.

'And you're charging nineteen pounds fifty?' She blinked at the price tag in astonishment.

I snatched it. 'OK, so make that Waitrose.'

She dropped the thong disdainfully back on the pile. 'So the Faulkner family are flogging kinky underwear now, are they? Classy.'

'The Faulkner family will flog whatever it takes, frankly, and if you want to be kept in fresh orange juice, Lucy, I suggest you come down off the moral high ground and help me find my sodding phone. I need to ring Tia. Where the hell is it?' I swung about.

'Here.' Lucy pulled it out from under a pile. 'But my train is in twenty minutes, Mum, so maybe when you get back?'

Muttering about a child who would rather skedaddle off to London than ensure her mother was not marched from the premises in handcuffs, I seized my car keys. But I stopped short at the back door. Cocked an ear up the back stairs which descended into the kitchen.

'Who else is up?' Distinct signs of life were emanating from above.

'Oh yeah, Minna is, like, awake, but she's in deep negotiation with Toxic Ted.'

'I don't care how deep she—' I leaped to the foot of the stairs. 'Minna? MINNA!' I yelled. 'Get down here and take your sister to the station, I've got better things to do!'

Silence, obviously.

'Go and get her,' I snapped furiously. Lucy had already slunk past me. 'And please ask yourselves why your lives are so much more important than mine!'

When they came down, Minna looking thunderous

with a coat over her pajamas and Uggs on her feet, I'll admit I was going for the sympathy vote. I sat slumped at the messy kitchen table, an array of bright red final demands and the bailiff's letter spread out before me on the undies, head in hands.

'Why can't Nico?' she snarled.

'I imagine he's still asleep.'

'Golden Boy.'

I ignored her and they slunk out to the car together, no doubt discussing how impossible I was. I raised my head. Or maybe not? I was so insignificant these days they were probably already on to Toxic Ted, Minna's on-off boyfriend with whom she was in the process of splitting up, or actually, the other way round. I listened to the engine. Knew it wouldn't start first time. It didn't. They waited. The third time it fired, but only because they'd rested it between the second and third try for precisely three minutes. Which meant – I glanced at the clock – they'd now be late. I ran outside as Minna executed a smart three-point turn in the yard. 'And don't race! So what if you have to get the next train? Don't race like idiots to catch it!'

Two pairs of bored, blank eyes, one lightly and beautifully made up, the other red-rimmed and tearful, stared back at me. They roared out of the yard, scattering ducks and gravel in their wake, leaving me standing in a cloud of dust.

As I went back inside, something made me look up. A curtain twitched and fell back again. Ah. So Nico *was* up. Just avoiding the fracas. And who could blame him? Nevertheless, out of some sort of warped sympathy for his sisters, I banged around the kitchen, slamming cupboard doors and noisily putting plates in a rack, radio blaring, so that inevitably he came and sat on the stairs behind me, hunched in his dressing gown. Always his favorite spot from which to view proceedings, it had the benefit of spindles for protection, and an escape route back to his room, should the situation demand it.

I made a pot of tea for us, my mind on what to sell next should Nutty, my gelding, fail the vet. Ah yes, the transaction was subject to a vet's examination and report, which scuppered half my sales these days. Megan had only scraped through last year because the new owners had decided to overlook the laminitis and take her for a thousand pounds less, which had left me with precisely eight hundred pounds. I went hot at the thought of losing that amount on Nutty.

A huge, involuntary sigh unfolded from my wellies, which I'd yet to remove. I handed a mug of tea wordlessly to my son. His pale, bony, nicotine-stained fingers reached through the spindles like a Hogarth illustration.

'Why so gloomy, Ma? So theatrically careworn?' Nicholas, or Nico, the last of my brood, my only boy, regarded me in amusement from under a shaggy, recently peroxided blond fringe. Nothing sleepy about those eyes. He'd clearly been on Facebook for hours.

'We're going to have to move, Nico. It's final now. Lucy says the bailiffs have been back.'

'Ah.' He nodded, unmoved. 'Very David Copperfield.'

I shrugged, matching his composure. 'She says these days they don't come in and nick your DVD player, just politely ask for a check. That's certainly all they did last week.'

'And you know they have to come through the door? I Googled it. That's the only entry route available to them now. Doesn't a whole screenplay of other historical routes play out in your head? Accompanied by a seventies soundtrack from *The Sweeney* or something? Kicked-in windows? Smashing glass?'

'Thanks for that, darling.'

'And you have to actually invite them in. Even when you've opened the door, they can't just step over the threshold.'

'I'll bear that in mind. Feed the geese and the horses and the cats, would you? I need to mend that fence in the bottom paddock. Buddy's been rubbing his bottom on it.'

'Well, I'll feed the cat but I think you'll find she's very much in the singular these days. Cleo's buggered off to live with the Nelsons.'

'Permanently? I thought she just popped in and out. I'm sad about that.'

'Cleo's not. She's living on salmon and cream.'

I sighed. 'Well, feed the rest for me, there's a love.'

'And put some drugs in Nutty's?'

'Certainly not! He hasn't been lame for months. I don't sell dodgy horses.'

Muttering about a mare with a persistent cough who I'd moved on last year, and one just before Christmas who he'd test-driven out hunting and who didn't seem to have any discernible brakes, Nico nonetheless took his tea upstairs to get changed, go out, and feed what remained of our stock.

'Also, I opened a lot of your brown envelopes,' he said, pausing at the top of the stairs. 'The ones you hide down the sofa. They made interesting reading. But one was that tax rebate you've been waiting for.' He delved in his dressing-gown pocket and frisbeed an envelope down to me. It landed on the table. I fell on it. Ripped it open. A check fell out.

'You can at least get the council tax paid.'

I stared at it. Then I clutched it to my bosom and

gazed up at him, starry-eyed. 'Oh *Nico*! Why didn't you say?'

He shrugged. 'I just have. You have to open this stuff, Ma. Not all of it's bad.'

And off he went; tall, skinny and disheveled, knowing he'd delivered the best news of the week.

I instantly rang Tia and promised her that once it had cleared the money would be hers, to pay whatever bills she thought best.

'All of them,' she said happily. 'Get the lot off your back. Oh, I'm *so* pleased. But Molly, you're still going to have to think about selling. Tax rebates don't fall out of the sky every month.'

'I know.'

'Shall I get Peter to come round?'

Peter Cox was the local estate agent in the office next door to hers on the high street. Kind, avuncular and tweedy, he was no shark and would, I knew, have my best interests at heart. Get me the very best deal. I hesitated.

'Why not? It's just . . . the animals, Tia. What am I supposed to do with them all? In a cottage? In the village?'

'Who says you can't find a cottage with a few stables? And paddocks?'

'But probably only a two-up two-down if it's got land. And then what about the children?'

'They're huge, Moll, and migrating to London. Couldn't Lucy and Minna share a room?'

'They could . . .' But then they might not come back, I thought, but didn't say it. Also it was premature. Minna was still at college locally. So maybe not destined for London eventually. All her friends were here.

'And if they did decide to stay,' she went on, reading my mind – oh yes, Tia and I had shared a lot of tea and biscuits – 'they could even pay some rent. Most kids around here do.'

'Yes, but not for ages. Lucy's the only one who's got a job, and I can't ask her to send back money like some mother in the Philippines.'

'I'd say Herefordshire is the British equivalent of the Philippines,' she said darkly. 'And let's face it, your own mother would have no such scruples. I saw her just now in town, by the way. She said your uncle had died. Sorry about that.'

I frowned. 'I don't have an uncle.'

'Oh. How strange. Funny name. Custer or something.'

'Oh. Cuthbert. David's uncle. Has he? I didn't know. Not sure I even met him, actually. How sad. But he must have been ancient.' I frowned. 'How on earth did Mum know that?'

'No idea. That famous crystal ball? Perhaps for once it really did give off some information. She was on her way to see you, anyway. Perhaps she got a vibe.'

'Perhaps.'

At that moment a throaty exhaust pipe backfired in the yard, making me glance out of the window. An old black Volvo was pulling in. Ah. Talk of the devil. The woman herself was getting out and going round to open the trunk to remove some shopping.

'She's already here, Tia. The eagle has landed. No doubt come to press-gang me into lending a hand at the Hereford show, where she's taken a tent – reading palms, no less.'

'Blimey, remind me to give that a swerve. OK, I'll let you go. Come and have lunch with me next week, though, Moll. We can even splash out and try that new veggie place. My treat.'

'You're on.'

13

I put the phone down as my mother came beetling across the yard, shopping bags in hand. Her hair was piled up in a sort of mad haystack bun but then, as she said, it befitted her image as Cosmic Pam, which the children had originally called her as a joke, but which had stuck and become, God help us, her professional name. Oh yes, I was lucky enough to have a mother with psychic powers. She paused to stroke Nutty's nose over the stable door and I noticed her eyes were very bright this morning, her cheeks flushed. She turned, headed, no doubt, for the Romany-style caravan sitting in my back garden where she read tarot cards and now, it seemed, palms. I'd let her park it there temporarily a year ago as her own back garden was minuscule, but since one of the wooden wheels had rotted and fallen off last winter, I think we both knew it was moribund and permanent. I didn't mind. In fact, I liked having her close by. And I'd hazard she liked it too. It might even be why she was there. Also, we had rules to prevent the situation becoming a time-waster. She'd breeze on by with a cheery wave first thing and I'd wave back. We didn't chat and eat biscuits for – ooh, ages – although the children had no such scruples. They were in there a lot, fascinated by their fates.

This morning, however, I wanted a word, and so, apparently, did she. She came straight to the back door when I opened it, and before she'd even said hello, to the point.

'Uncle Cuthbert's died,' she told me importantly as she swept past me. She set her shopping down on the floor and jangled a veritable armful of Gypsy Rose bracelets as she reached for the mug of tea I'd been about to drink myself on the side. 'Thanks, love.' She fixed me with beady dark eyes as she slurped and settled herself down on a chair at the kitchen table.

'I know.' I shut the back door behind her. 'Tia told me. Apparently you've seen fit to spread the word around town before you even told me. And he wasn't even my uncle, Mum, let alone yours. He was David's.'

'Exactly. Your husband's uncle. And he was his only relative.'

'Who was?'

'David.' She gave me those eyes again.

I stared at her for a long moment. Then slowly I sat down opposite her. I had a nasty feeling I knew where she was going with this.

'Mum . . . if you think for one moment . . .'

She raised her eyebrows disingenuously. 'What?'

'I know the way your mind works.'

'Well, it's a thought, isn't it?'

I gaped at her in disbelief. 'Oh, don't be silly,' I snorted eventually. 'Cuthbert's an uncle-in-law, he's not going to remember a woman he's barely met! I'm not even sure I did meet him. And anyway, how do you know he's died?'

'I read it.' She reached in her bag and flourished a copy of the *Telegraph*. Cosmic Pam had some surprisingly trenchant right-wing views. 'I make it my business to know these things. After all, you never know who might be trying to get in touch.'

'How d'you mean?'

'From beyond.' She jerked her head meaningfully. 'Particularly if they've only just popped off, all sorts of things they might have meant to say. Important to read the announcements.' She set her reading glasses on her nose and peered down at the Court and Social page, which she'd already folded into a neat quarter. 'Ah – here we are.' She cleared her throat and raised her chin importantly. 'Faulkner: Cuthbert James Christopher. Died peacefully at home on April the sixth.' She removed her glasses and looked up.

I blinked. 'That's it?'

'That's it.'

'Bit sort of . . . short, isn't it? Aren't they usually much longer? Funeral details? Stuff about flowers? Donations?'

'Exactly.' My mother was making her famous face. The one with wide eyes and pursed lips. 'Interesting, eh? Sort of . . .' She contrived to look concerned, '. . . solitary.'

'No, not remotely. Just succinct. And anyway, even if he doesn't have family, he'll have left whatever he had to – I don't know – friends, a dogs' home, a charity. Something close to his heart.'

The lips became a pucker. A cigarette was placed between them, set alight and inhaled deeply. She removed it and released the thin grey line ceiling-wards.

'He might,' she agreed thoughtfully, eyes following the smoke. 'But on the other hand,' she lowered those bright eyes for dramatic effect, 'he might not.'

CHAPTER 2

I regarded her, the Wise Woman of the West Country, no less, on her metaphorical throne, my old Windsor chair. I took a deep breath. Let it out wearily.

'I despair of you sometimes, Mother. I really do.'

'Look, love, I'm just being realistic. In all probability you're right, his estate will go to a charity or something, but it could go to his nearest blood relative, and judging by this announcement,' she jabbed it with her finger, 'it doesn't look like he's got anyone else. No children or it would have said so, beloved father of Jimmy and Anne or whatever – so that's you.'

'Oh hardly,' I scoffed, turning to make more tea. 'A niece-in-law. Not much blood there. And actually, Mum, I'm ashamed of you. The poor man is barely cold and you're rubbing your hands with glee, wondering what's in his coffers. Talk about ambulance chasing.'

'I don't think you'll find it's an ambulance I'm pursuing,' she remarked, sotto voce, bending down to pull a packet of digestive biscuits from her shopping bag.

I swung about. 'What?'

'Nothing,' she said hastily, opening them and munching furiously. 'And I'm not being gleeful, just practical,' she continued, with her mouth full. 'The man was ninety-odd, for heaven's sake. Had a rich and fulfilled life. It's not like I've bumped him off.'

'How d'you know he was ninety-odd? How d'you know anything about him?' I narrowed my eyes suspiciously. 'You haven't been researching him, have you, you dreadful old druid?'

'Don't be ridiculous,' she said, feigning hurt. 'I certainly haven't stalked his deathbed or anything, if that's what you mean, but there's a great deal to be learned through esoteric channels.' She affected a vague, mystical expression.

'And from a computer, by Googling him.' I shoved the cutlery drawer in hard with my bottom so it rattled. 'Frankly, I can't think of anything more vulgar than profiting from a death, Mum. I've had one myself and the mere fact that it could be spoken of in the same breath as money is hideous. Can you imagine if David's relatives had popped out of the woodwork and clustered round? Wondered what was in the kitty?'

'They did,' she said, brushing crumbs from her skirt. 'At least, one or two godchildren did, although you were too grief-stricken to notice. Soon backed off when they realized he hadn't even managed to provide for his family – and I know,' she said quickly, seeing my face, 'that he wasn't expecting to have to do that, at his age, had no reason to think he should have made some clever investments, started a proper pension, I know that, Molly. I'm just saying you've been up the creek for five years now, and getting all pious about a tiny bit of good fortune that might finally have come your way is a bit short-sighted, that's all.'

'Good fortune. You don't know anything about him. Don't know what state his affairs were in.'

She raised her eyebrows. 'I assume you mean Cuthbert's affairs? You are now talking about Cuthbert's estate?'

'No! Absolutely not. Not in that way. I'm just saying—'

'Obviously I've no idea,' she interrupted crisply. 'But when I met him he struck me as a very grand and very civilized old gentleman.'

'You've met him?'

'Of course I have. At the funeral.'

'Oh!' I sat down. Gripped the tea towel I was holding. 'Was he there?'

'Of course he was there,' she said gently.

I'd barely been there myself. Had been in such a fog: such a mist of tears and shock and disbelief, I hadn't rallied at all. I had since. Long-term I'd been pretty good and had kept the children on track – just – making sure they'd got through school and university – well, college, and only Minna – and had kept the farm and my small businesses going, and actually, had felt better as the months and years had gone by, as the self-help books said I would. More recently, albeit rarely, I'd even sat smiling in restaurants with other men, a glass of Merlot in hand. Ghastly. But, no, short-term I'd been a mess. Which was the right way round, everyone said. None of that stoic fortitude for the first few months and then collapsing in a heap later: I collapsed first. To the extent that I barely remembered the funeral. Here, in the village, in the little church in the valley. Barely remembered who came, except that it was full.

'How far did he come?'

'He was living in London at the time.'

'What was he like?'

'Delightful, as I've told you. And very sweet and sad about David. But quite ancient, even then.'

I thought back. 'On two sticks? Sitting with a rug on his knees in the corner?'

'Er . . . possibly.' She looked shifty. 'Although that might have been Albert.'

'White hair?'

'Um, yes, swept back.'

'Oh. OK. Vaguely.' I summoned up a hazy mental vision of Cuthbert. David's own parents had died in the Boxing Day tsunami ten years ago, on a much longed-for holiday, so they hadn't been there. Oh yes, we'd had our share of tragedy in this family. And I for one would not be profiting from any of it. I roused myself: regarded her sternly.

'Get thee to thy crystal ball, you old witch; I want none of your dark side. Be gone, and get cracking on your pubescent predictions instead. How's that going, by the way?'

Mum had recently been recruited by *Just 15* website to write the horoscope page, something the children and I found hilarious, since she couldn't, in reality, predict the next five minutes, let alone a week in the life of the entire female teenage population.

'Oh, frightfully well,' she beamed. 'Although I'm a little stuck on Taurus. Their celestial circumstances are a bit turbulent this week. Venus is in ascendance and being an absolute madam. But I thought I'd couch it in terms of: "Challenging times ahead, but a great opportunity to assert independence."'

'The boyfriend's dumping them?'

'Precisely.'

She'd got into this slightly bizarre ethereal world the way most people do, apparently, by going to see a medium herself and being told she was 'extraordinarily spiritual'. She'd rushed home, fag clenched between her teeth, thinking she was the Second Coming. 'The woman literally flinched when she touched my hand!' she'd gasped. 'So much electricity, she said!' The children and I had clustered around excitedly to witness her powers and discovered the extent of them was to peer into a cupful of tea leaves which Minna had made, frown and say . . . 'You're in a crowd . . .'

Ignoring our hilarity, she'd persevered. Never one to start small, with a course, perhaps, with fellow budding psychics, or some sort of workshop, she'd gone the whole shebang instantly, buying herself a tepee in which to read palms – it leaked, hence the caravan found on eBay – and setting herself up as Cosmic Pam, so that practically overnight, there she was – ta-da! – a bona fide mystic. And in rural Herefordshire, what with the recession and unemployment and long winter afternoons, people had many gloomy moments: they needed a bit of hope. Plus Mum didn't charge much and provided tea and biscuits, so they came in their droves, mostly because her news was always cheerful. 'An unexpected pleasure is coming your way!' Vague, too, note: could be a new lover, could be a cream cake. 'Something is definitely on the rise!' Could be a promotion, could be a soufflé. They all left beaming, vowing to return again next week and cross her palm with yet more silver.

I sighed and hung the tea towel on the rail of the old Rayburn I'd never got around to replacing. 'You're a charlatan, Mum. But never let anyone suggest you don't do it with charm.'

'I like to bring a little joy into people's lives,' she agreed, getting up and replacing her packet of digestives in her bag, one of three packs, I noted. Mum lived on digestive biscuits, strong coffee and gin, and not necessarily in that order. Her eye was already wandering to the cupboard where I kept my own bottle so I pre-empted what was coming.

'No, I'm not going to join you at lunchtime for a quick one in the garden, principally because I've got a lot to do today, so if you wouldn't mind sugaring off to your own lair, I've got a business to run here. I've got a couple of hundredweight of boxer shorts to send off in brown envelopes, and that idiot Paddy Campbell is coming to vet Nutty at twelve.'

'Oh, they've chosen Paddy, have they, your purchasers? Well, you won't get a dodgy fetlock past him. Give him a bit of anti-inflammatory – I would.'

'Mum, I'm not drugging my horse to get it through a veterinary examination. I don't know what sort of person you – and Nico – think I am!'

She shrugged as she sashayed elegantly to the door. 'The sort to sell a three-legged gelding to an unsuspecting buyer, but not to take advantage of a real stroke of luck when it comes your way, in the shape of a straight-up, no-wool-pulling inheritance, which if you're not sharpish someone else will snaffle.'

'Well, if it's that straight up it'll come to me in the form of an official lawyer's letter, won't it?' I countered sweetly, to which, I was pleased to note, she looked a bit stumped.

Ah. See? Not so straightforward. Definitely some monkey business going on. There always was with Mum. Nothing downright dishonest – when she read palms or wrote horoscopes she genuinely felt she got a glimpse of the future – but just a little shading of the truth: a little blurring of the facts to work to her advantage.

As she wiggled away, hips swinging under her beaded skirt, I noticed her first lucky customer, Ena Mason from the village, already shuffling through the garden gate. I decided her last aside had been interesting: Cuthbert, in reality, probably had a whole host of relatives she wanted me to queue-barge. Mum might be the warmest, strongest, most resourceful person I knew, but she had a nose for a deal and she sharpened her elbows by night with a file. And don't let the Gypsy Rose stuff fool you. She and Dame Fortune might be in cahoots today, but tomorrow she'd be in a blue suit, hair smooth and immaculate, on the forecourt of a Volkswagen dealership in Rainsborough covering for someone on maternity leave. Then on Thursday, she'd be in a white overall stuffing sausages with my friend Anna up at her farm before flogging them beside her in Ludlow market on Saturday.

Mum was a grafter. She rolled her sleeves up and she didn't care what color they were as long as there was money to be made. She was regarded with awe and not a little terror throughout the valley, and if it was apt to go to her head, only my father, a mild-mannered man who lived solely for cricket and golf, could occasionally slap her down with a firm, 'That'll do, Pam.'

We all remembered The Great Terracotta Pot Disaster when a truckload of frost-resistant urns she'd bought from Greece and flogged locally had promptly cracked during their first winter. Dad had made her refund everyone. Likewise he'd put his foot down when she'd advertised in the local paper to give A-level History tutoring without a GCSE to her name. Her acquisitiveness baffled him. He couldn't understand why the modest amount of money he made from the academic tomes he edited for a publishing house wasn't enough. And surely if the sash windows in their cottage fell to bits when you opened them, well, don't open them. Open the door instead. Mum and Dad were surely from different planets.

Right now, though, my parents' unlikely yet successful alliance was the least of my worries. I swept armfuls of underwear from the table and shoved them into a black plastic bag. Right now, I had other things on my mind. Like how to get the men to whom I regularly sold boxer shorts to buy attractive undergarments for their wives or girlfriends – to this end I added a fistful of brochures featuring scantily clad ladies to my sack – and how to get an absolutely first-class gelding past a totally biased, anally retentive vet. I hurried with my sack and car keys to the door and thence to the village. Any suggestion that I might be a chip off the old block, incidentally, I regard as utterly scurrilous.

Coming back from the post office some time later, having stuffed and sealed and stamped countless brown envelopes, roping in my friend Lauren behind the counter to lend a helping hand, I got out of the car and encountered Nico in the yard, leading Nutty from his stable. Paddy Campbell's red pickup over by the barn confirmed my fears. Damn. He was early, as usual. I glanced at my watch. Or, OK, on time. And I'd hoped to get Nutty out for five minutes before he came to loosen him up a bit. Not that he needed loosening up, but no gentleman of a certain age wants to trot smartly from a standing start – which was what I could see Paddy was about to get Nico have him do – when they've just opened their eyes of a morning, do they? I hastened across.

'Morning, Paddy!' I cried jovially, hoping to set the tone for the next twenty minutes or so. 'What d'you think of my lovely boy, then?'

'Well, he's an old boy, we all know that, don't we, Molly?' He glanced round as I approached: tall, broad-shouldered and with tousled auburn hair and a narrow, intelligent face. He'd be attractive if he wasn't always so cross and busy.

'Oh, he's got a bit of maturity for sure, but that's what purchasers want these days, isn't it? A reliable sort who's been there, done everything, is always in the rosettes and is not going to spook at the first ditch he sees. No one wants to buy anything under ten these days.'

'He's well over fifteen,' he said as Nico brought him trotting back, jogging beside him.

'Thanks, darling,' I said gratefully, seeing my son looking mutinous.

'No problem,' he replied, dropping the head collar rope. 'Just the first two hours of my revision down the drain with all this bloody animal maintenance. Your loss, Mother.' He slouched off into the house, already rolling a cigarette as he went. *My* loss.

'Anyway, he's a fine-looking horse, don't you think?' I said, keeping a bright smile going. 'Our Nutty? Galway Nuthatch is his registered name. But he's more like thirteen or fourteen, I agree.'

He ignored me, bending down to feel his legs.

'Nothing wrong with those,' I chortled, wishing the Hiltons had asked for old Charlie Parker instead. He was much more of a pushover, almost bribable with tea and biscuits and a plea to tell his country yarns which went round and round and which we'd all heard umpteen times, before he signed the requisite form and headed off to see to someone's elderly Labrador.

'Cup of tea, Paddy?'

'No thanks. Trot him up again for me, would you, Molly? Nico barely got him out of a walk.'

I gave Nutty a smart tap on the bottom with the end of the rope and we set off briskly up the track, turning at the corner. I smiled delightedly as we came back in an effort to distract Paddy, but his eyes were firmly on the horse's legs, not mine. If he smiled occasionally it would help, I thought irritably. He was so flipping serious all the time, although Anna, with the pigs, told me otherwise.

'Oh no, he's frightfully smiley, Moll, he loves my brood. Thinks I should show my sows, and I might at the county show. He's definitely got a sunnier side. He's probably a bit po-faced with you because you're a horse dealer.'

'You mean the rural equivalent of a second-hand car dealer? The oldest profession in the land besides prostitution?'

'Something like that.'

'I'm a sheep farmer, too,' I'd reasoned.

'Yes, but you hardly ever get him out for those any more.' 'Because he's too bloody expensive.'

'Well, quite. But you can't expect him to beam at you when you're trying to get a dodgy flexion test past him.'

That bit was coming up next, I realized, when I'd come to a grinning halt. Paddy was about to pick each of Nutty's legs up in turn, hold it bent backwards for thirty seconds then ask Nutty to trot smartly off again. On the last leg Nutty faltered slightly for the first couple of paces, as anyone would, I told Paddy, if someone suspended your leg in the air for a protracted amount of time.

Again, no comment, just the pursed lips as he wrote something down on his pad, then a stethoscope in his ears as he went to listen to Nutty's heart.

'I expect that's pounding a bit, mine certainly is!' I told him, wishing I'd thought to brush my hair and put some lipstick on before this wretched man came round, criticizing my livestock. God, the Hiltons loved this horse and were mustard-keen to buy him and have young Samantha trot off to pony club shows on him. They were only having him vetted because they were new to the game and every busybody in the valley said they should. In my opinion it was entirely unnecessary unless you were contemplating Badminton. I tried this tack with Paddy.

'Did you ride as a child, Paddy?'

'Of course.'

'Ever had a horse vetted?'

'I very much doubt it. We just rode whatever was in the field, or on offer from friends. I grew up in rural Ireland, don't forget. If anyone bought a horse it was bound to be their uncle's or their cousin's. No one looked too closely.'

'Exactly!' I exclaimed, seizing on this scrap of humanity.

'But Molly, times have changed.' He took his stethoscope from his ears and looked at me squarely. Nice, steady brown eyes in a tanned face. 'The Hiltons are paying me a sizable fee to examine this horse. I'm not going to lie to them, am I?'

'Good heavens, no! I'm not suggesting such a thing. Not even suggesting there's anything to lie about,' I said as he lifted Nutty's tail and peered, suspiciously, up his backside.

'No warts. No laminitis,' I assured him and he nodded, agreeing for once. 'I'm just saying in this bureaucratic, litigious world, it's all got a bit ridiculous.'

He dropped the tail and gave me a level look.

'You mean, I'm more nervous about being sued by the Hiltons because I pass him and then he goes lame in a fortnight?'

I shrugged, kept the bright smile going. 'Well . . .' It was exactly what I meant.

'Molly, trust me, I'd love to pass your horse. And I'd love for the Hiltons to buy him and for you to get some creditors off your back and for everyone to be happy.'

'Yes,' I breathed, thinking, now you're talking. In this small valley everyone knew everyone else's business.

'But if he's in any way wide of the mark they've asked me to judge him by, you know I can't do that.'

'But he's not, necessarily.'

He packed his stethoscope back in his bag and made for his car.

'Charlie would,' I muttered as I tailed him.

'I'll pretend I didn't hear that.'

'OK. And I totally take it back. Charlie would be as professional as you are.'

'Quite.'

As he threw his bag of tricks in the back I wondered where in Ireland he'd grown up. I hadn't known that: he didn't have an accent, but I didn't like to ask. I turned to where I'd popped Nutty back in his stable, threw my head back and beamed.

'He's got the sweetest face, don't you think? A really kind eye?'

'He's not bad-looking, I agree. Not as handsome as the one Biddy Price got from the Morgans, though. You were a bit slow there.'

'I was at a bloody trade fair!' I fumed, still furious about that. Typical. When a local couple with a computer business and a yard full of hunters had gone bust overnight, where was I? 'I was in effing Newcastle, buying sodding lavender soap,' I told him.

'Not Provence?' He gave a tiny smile. 'Like it says on the label?'

'Lavender grows in Newcastle too, Paddy.'

He laughed. 'Of course it does.'

'What did she get? Biddy?' My teeth were grinding even as I asked.

'A seventeen-hand hunter out of Barley Clover. Paid

three thousand, sold it the other day to someone in the Cottismore for seven.'

Shit. I'd had my eye on that hunter. I knew exactly which one he meant, a lovely type who'd carry anyone over the biggest country. Bugger. I felt faint with disappointment. 'So you'll pass him, will you, Paddy?' I asked anxiously as he got into the cab of his red pickup and slammed the door. Paddy rested his elbow through the open window and broke into the first proper grin of the day, which caused many ruddy creases to appear.

'Now Molly, you know the rules. That's for me to tell my client, Mark Hilton, and for you to find out.'

'Ah yes, of course.' I feigned mock surprise, slapping the palm of my hand on my forehead. 'I clean forgot.' But I was encouraged by the joke and the smile. He surely wouldn't lead me on like this if he was about to fail him, would he?

'Nice to see you anyway, Paddy,' I called through the window, striking what I hoped was an attractive pose in the yard, hands in the pockets of my faded skinny jeans, the wind in my hair.

'You too, Moll.' Having smartly reversed in an arc he paused to change into first gear. His expression changed too. 'Oh, and by the way, I was sorry to hear about your uncle.'

Without waiting for me to reply, he took off through the open gate in a crunch of tires on gravel, disappearing in a cloud of dust.

CHAPTER 3

I stood there a moment in the empty yard,
watching the red tail gate disappear down the
lane. Then I turned on my heel and beetled around the
back of the house and up the grassy slope to where the
wooden gypsy caravan, painted in green and yellow swirls,
perched on the terraced lawn. Leaping the rotten steps to
the door I knocked, but only in a perfunctory manner.
Whatever I'd be disturbing could easily be resumed, and I
was bound to know whoever was inside. As it happened,
when I burst into the predominately pink, softly lit interior
– throws on the walls, fringes everywhere, candles burning
– Cosmic Pam was at her table dispensing words of
wisdom to a couple of very familiar customers. I stared.
Put my hands on my hips.

'I thought you were doing crucial Politics revision?'

'Oh. Yeah.' Nico withdrew his palm from his grandmother's grip. 'I just wondered if Granny had any
thoughts on another referendum. You know, in Scotland.
It's very topical, Mum, and we've been told to expect a

question on it.' He flashed me a grin before slinking past, off down the steps.

'And I thought you were going to help Lucy source some flowers for her shop?' I demanded of Minna, who was curled up on a sofa in the corner, awaiting her turn as she shuffled through some tarot cards, clearly putting the best ones on top.

'I am. I've got a meeting with a guy with a field later. Chill, Mum. Granny and I were just going to have a chat.'

'A field? What – you're going to grow them? I thought you were going to find a producer for next year? Doesn't Mick Turner grow daffodils?'

'What, and include a middleman? What sort of a family d'you think I'm from?'

'Yes, well, Minna, maybe I'll do your cards later,' said Mum, catching a dangerous look in my eye. Minna sighed heavily, heaved herself wearily from the sofa – still not dressed, I noticed – and shuffled off too. I rounded on my mother.

'Mum, did you tell Paddy Campbell my beloved uncle is dead?'

'I might have mentioned it when I bumped into him outside Budgens, yes. Why?'

'Because I know what you're doing. I know exactly what you're doing. You're building up momentum. Building up a head of steam so that by the end of the week everyone in the village will be consoling me about my uncle who I was apparently so close to, and then the following week, they'll be asking me if I was the nearest relative, and then the one after that, if I was the only *remaining* relative, and after that, whether he'd, euphemistically "remembered me".'

'What nonsense,' she countered smoothly, shuffling the cards Minna had deposited in a heap on the table. She adjusted the strange beaded headscarf she wore around her brow for these occasions.

'*Stop* being such an interfering old bag,' I told her sternly before turning and exiting myself, banging the door shut and falling right over Minna who was perched on the bottom step, and who'd clearly been listening at the door. I ignored her because everyone listened at doors in this family, nothing was ever private, and stalked off to the house. As I went I wished, very fervently, that I lived alone: preferably on a Caribbean island, where I'd run a beach bar, without any wretched sheep, who, having spotted me, were trailing me along the fence line, bleating piteously, because the grass was still not through and they wouldn't mind a touch more expensive concentrate if I could spare it. I couldn't. At £2.75 a kilo they'd have to wait until their rations tomorrow.

'Granny's got a point,' Minna told me, tailing me at a shuffling trot in her Ugg boots.

I ignored her and hurried on, knowing I had to get some packaging organized by Friday if I was to stand any chance of getting the soap I'd found from a cheap supplier in Gateshead – I might not have got the hunter but my trip to Newcastle had been a success – wrapped in attractive mauve tissue and off to my outlets for the summer season. Oh, and sealed with a sticker Lauren at the post office, who was also a freelance designer, was creating for me with something French-sounding on it. I might tell her to steer clear of '*Savon de Provence*', though, after Paddy's remark, and go for something a bit vaguer. '*Savon à la française*', perhaps. I didn't want to be sued under the Trade Descriptions Act, which I knew was what he'd been getting at. Bastard.

'Hasn't she?' Minna insisted as we hot-footed it into the kitchen, where Nico was on his laptop, presumably back on

Facebook, not a folder or textbook in sight. I glared at him and he rolled his eyes and dripped upstairs, like Minna, still not dressed, taking his laptop with him.

'Mum.'

'What?'

'Hasn't she got a point?'

'About what?' I countered, playing for time.

'About Dad's uncle. I mean, if we are – or you are – the beneficiary, surely it's only right?'

'I didn't know him, Minna.' I scooped up armfuls of mauve tissue paper from the dresser and moved them bodily to the table. 'How can that be right?'

'So what?'

'So everything. And, as I've told Granny, if anything's legally due, it will appear, won't it?'

'No, because you have to make a claim. He died intestate. There's no will. Granny's checked. So what you have to do is get in touch with his lawyer, say you're the nearest relative, and claim the inheritance. You'd be mad not to at least try, Mum.'

'And who, pray, is his lawyer?'

'Hamilton and Simpson, sixty-four Onslow Terrace, London SW3,' came floating down from upstairs. Nico, his Apple Mac open on his lap, was sitting in his position on the top step. 'His telephone number's here too, Mum. I'll print it all out and leave it on the kitchen table. Just give him a ring. It's an understandable enquiry under the circumstances. Where's the harm?' He smiled his most engaging of smiles through the bars, looking so much like his father it hurt my heart.

LATER THAT DAY, when I'd delivered the sticky labels to Lauren, whose house I was supposed to be returning to for book club that night – I told her it depended on how many pieces of tissue I'd cut out, and also that I hadn't read the book, and she said, so what, just come for a drink and a laugh – I wondered if I was in the wrong business. Or businesses.

What if I just chucked in all my sidelines and retrained? There hadn't been much call for PR executives in rural Herefordshire – I'd tried – which was why I'd diversified in the first place, but what if, I don't know, I became a nurse or something? Years of training, of course. But might it pay off in the long run? Or a doctor, perhaps. I turned the corner into the lane that led to my house. My fields bordered this lane and I stared forensically as I drove along, mentally checking the water, the lambs, the chaotic fences tied up with bits of binder twine. My life had essentially consisted of Getting By these past few years, but now that the children were older and possibly about to leave home, why shouldn't I be – no, obviously not a doctor – but a civil servant or something? Like Tia? I'd popped in to see her on the way home and delivered a check, and even she – whilst agreeing it wasn't her dream job, and certainly not her first choice – had conceded it nevertheless paid the bills.

'I was a court usher,' she told me as we sat huddled in her little cubicle, one of hundreds in a vast, open-plan office. 'Greeting everyone, showing in the judge and the jury, feeling really rather important. I loved it. And then I was made redundant but offered this.' She hopped to her feet to peer over the partition and see who was listening. 'It stinks,' she whispered, sitting down again. 'And I hated the very idea of it, but who am I to sniff at twenty grand a year with an unemployed husband?'

'Well, quite.'

I emptied the remains of the packet of Maltesers we'd been sharing on her desk and we ate the last ones.

'I mean, obviously reclaiming people's DVD recorders is not top of my career wish list, but most people are reasonable about it when they see it's a woman. It works in my favor.'

'A tiny one at that.' Tia was petite and blonde.

'Exactly. Some bloke carried his own stuff out to my car the other day when he could see I couldn't manage. And his son pumped up my tyre. Turns out he went to school with Tom. Thanks for this, Molly,' she said, popping my check in a drawer. 'I'll see it gets there.'

'Yes, but, um, Tia, maybe not for a few days?' My turn to hop up and pop my head over the adjoining, happily empty, cubicles. 'It'll bounce,' I whispered, sitting down again, 'if my rebate check hasn't cleared. And I was also maybe hoping to pay Ronnie for my chicken feed, he's been waiting ages . . .'

'Oh, righto. Tell you what, why don't I email the council, tell them you've come up with the money for the council tax, but there's a bit of a hold-up this end, and they can expect it from me within the next fortnight?'

'Splendid,' I beamed, admittedly part of the reason for my visit paying off, and no one under any illusions, either, I thought as we said goodbye warmly. I liked Tia, and knew from Biddy, her horse-dealing sister of the envy-making hunter, that she made the best of a shit job to keep her family on track, and I knew she liked me too and didn't want to see me disappear down the plughole of life any more than she wanted to join me, so if I popped in and used a little charm to oil the wheels, so what?

Two weeks' grace, I thought gratefully, mentally calculating in my head that I could also pay Anna for the concentrate she'd kindly lent me for the sheep, saying her husband Jim wouldn't miss it for a bit, and perhaps even get Nico's car through its MOT so there was at least some point in him having passed his test. Feeling buoyed up and happy with life, I swung into my yard, thinking I might actually put a saddle on Nutty, who I'd come to love and wished I didn't have to sell, and head off into the hills, taking a picnic lunch with me.

My mobile rang as I came to a halt and, recognizing the number, my heart lurched. I took the call. Sounding really rather upset because Samantha had so set her heart on him, Beatrice Hilton was ringing to tell me that sadly Nutty had failed the vet's examination because of the flexion test, and since they really wanted an entirely sound horse, they wouldn't be buying him. Offering him at half-price, which, frankly, was a complete bargain – this horse would jump a stable door, flexion test or not – couldn't tempt this woman who lived, I knew, like most people did, and like I used to live when I was a normal person, via sensible rules. Not by the seat of her pants and on the smell of an oily rag. I accepted her commiserations, apologized for wasting her time, and when we'd said goodbye, I moaned low and banged my head on the steering wheel three times, like Basil Fawlty.

When I raised it, eyes full, I'll admit, it was to see Paddy Campbell getting into his van around the far side of my hay barn. I stared, horrified. Then I got out and dashed across, furious.

'What the hell are you doing here?' I barked, thinking I might actually bite him. Take a chunk out of his arm. 'You are absolutely the last person I want to see!'

He shrugged. 'Minna called me. And quite right too. You've got a ewe with mastitis, Molly.'

'I know,' I snarled. 'And I've been expressing her twice a day myself. I don't need some expensive veterinary surgeon, who not only ruins my horse-dealing livelihood but charges like a wounded rhino, coming round here and—'

'She needs antibiotics,' he interrupted. 'And she'll need some more tomorrow.' He tossed me a plastic bag with a syringe and a bottle inside. 'And no, they are not on the house. I don't like treating distressed animals any more than you like paying for them, Molly, but needs must.'

Angrily, he turned on his heel, folded his long legs into his cab and, with a last black look, sped off.

When I got to the kitchen, Nico was at the computer at my desk under the stairs, pressing 'send' on an official-looking document, his phone to his ear.

'It's on its way, Luce.' He was also clearly talking to his sister.

'What are you doing looking at my emails?' I snarled, circling him like a wild animal, in no mood for anything other than a fight.

'It's the email the court lawyer sent you last week which you hadn't bothered to open. Presumably because you thought it was yet another summons, and which they sent in desperation because you didn't respond to their letter. I imagine that's *under* the sofa, rather than down the side of it. I didn't think to look there. Playing the backwater hillbilly with all these supposed strings to your bow is all very well, Mum, but try not to pass up the main chance, hm? Even Del Boy wouldn't do that.'

I stared at him for a few moments. At length I crept up behind him to look at the screen. 'What d'you mean?' I whispered, peering over his shoulder.

'Sit,' he ordered, getting up. He steered me around and propelled me to sit in the chair he'd vacated. 'And read.'

I did.

DEAR MRS FAULKNER,

We act on behalf of the Treasury lawyer and also on behalf of the late Mr Cuthbert Faulkner, whose estate we are instructed to oversee as trustees. Mr Faulkner died intestate and our preliminary research indicates that your late husband, the son of Mr Faulkner's late brother, was his only blood relative.

Consequently, subject to how your late husband left his own estate, you could conceivably be a legitimate beneficiary. We therefore invite you to make an appointment with us at the above address to proceed with enquiries into this matter and discuss it further.

We look forward to hearing from you.

Yours sincerely,

P. D. Hamilton, Esq. Hamilton & Simpson, LLP

I digested this for quite a few moments. Then I swung around.

'Oh!'

Three pairs of eyes met mine. Nico's, bright blue and victorious, Minna's the same color, smaller but just as bright, plus my mother's beady brown ones peering around the corner from the hall. I told you, listening at doors is a family trait. She took the cigarette from her mouth and leaned forward to stub it out in a dead pot plant on the dresser.

'Now will you do something about it?' she demanded softly.

CHAPTER 4

*S*ome days later, as I left Mr Hamilton's office in South Kensington under a bright blue, cloudless sky, I almost had to steady myself on the glossy black handrail as I descended the steps from the white, stucco-fronted house. I certainly paused for a moment. The rarefied London square lined with identical houses around a leafy, railed enclosure fairly squeaked with gentrification: a Porsche purred by, an elegant woman with a Yorkshire terrier slipped past, and only a discreet gold plaque beside the black front door behind me suggested I'd been anywhere remotely commercial and not just taking tea with a friend.

Not that I had friends who lived in houses like these. But neither had there been anything overtly businesslike about the conversation within; it had, to all intents and purposes, been a thoroughly convivial and pleasant affair, involving tea – Earl Grey, of course – and two tiny biscuits. Mr Hamilton, a squat, portly gentleman with grey hair swept back from a florid forehead and wearing tweed rather than flannel, had beamed most benignly at me, like a benevolent uncle, and having first expressed his sympathies had then informed me, once he'd settled himself down on the other side of his leather-topped desk, that this sudden windfall was not as unusual as I thought. Many people died without making a will, he told me, lawyers mostly, would you believe. And even though Mr Faulkner had been seventy-six – not the ancient ninety-odd Mum had clearly invented – he might not have seen it coming and quite got his affairs in order.

'Or perhaps he had,' he'd added kindly, eyeing me over his reading glasses. 'Perhaps he'd deliberately left things ambiguous, some people do. If only so that others have to sort it all out for them. Let them make the decisions. It avoids favoritism. You can see the attraction.'

'Yes, I can.' I could. But I wouldn't do it myself. Let the living have the headache of sorting it out, as I'd had to do when David had died. On the other hand, if it were a lovely surprise, as it was slowly dawning on me Mr Hamilton was suggesting it was, it could be a delightful way to do things.

'A certain amount was sitting, obviously, in a straightforward savings account . . .' He passed across a piece of paper topped with a Barclays logo and tailed with a row of numbers at the bottom which made my eyes boggle. 'And a small amount in shares. Not much, but blue-chip reliable ones like Sainsbury's and ICI . . .' Another piece of paper with nothing very small-looking found its way across. 'But I'm afraid death duties will pretty much swallow all of those, because property-wise, you have quite an asset. The jewel in the crown. The property in Lastow Mews, which you'll need to have valued, but if nearby houses are anything to go by would conservatively be worth about this amount.'

'As . . . much as that?' I'd whispered as he'd passed across another document with vast numbers on it and details of deeds of ownership to pass imminently. Plus my name, Molly Victoria Faulkner. It was at this point that I wished I had one of the children with me, just so they could verify this fairy story was really happening, and was not some fantastical dream. I'd turned them all down flatly as they'd swiftly lined up to accompany me, even Lucy who I knew would be taking notes now, asking pertinent questions, being useful, because I'd wanted to do this on my own; think about it clearly, not be taken over by them.

'But Mum, you'll want one of us, just to *get* you there. Last time you went to London you ended up in New Barnet thinking you were in New Bond Street.'

'That was a totally understandable mistake, Minna, and rest assured, I shall keep my wits about me this time. I used to live in London. I worked there, for heaven's sake.'

The children looked at me doubtfully and I knew they were thinking a lot had changed in the capital since then, particularly for a woman who mostly descaled chicken's feet and fixed barbed wire fences.

Now, as I tottered along the pavement in the sunshine, chic women sailing past swinging smart handbags rather than clutching ancient ones to their chests, I couldn't help feeling they were right. I lowered my bag. I *was* a bit out of my depth. But actually, so intensely excited too, that I could do without Lucy bossily steering me to the nearest estate agent's, or the others' excited chatter about how I should spend the money as soon as I got my hands on it. No. This gave me some valuable time to think.

This amount of real estate was much more than I'd ever imagined. It was a veritable lottery win. And far more than I'd dreamed it might be. It was too early for a drink to steady my nerves, but I certainly needed a black coffee. I found a pavement café down the road, and then sat in the sunshine dressed in my very best skirt and shoes, which, being wedged espadrilles, only just passed muster, letting it slowly sink in that, for the first time in my life, I was wealthy. Really rich.

As I sat there in the sun, I felt my old self float up to a tiny cloud, perch on it, and look down on the new me, realizing all the things I could do. Pay off the mortgage. Refence the fields. Fertilize and spray the fields instead of hoping for the best. Dredge the river which flooded every year. Repair the roof on the house and the barns, re-point the stables. Sort out the damp downstairs and the dry rot upstairs. The list was endless.

Or maybe not even stay there, I thought with a jolt. Maybe get shot of the whole money-draining shooting match and buy a lovely house in the village, with four bedrooms, and a manageable garden, or even one an hour's drive away, on the coast: put the rest of the money in the bank and never have to work, worry or wheeler-deal again.

I almost had to pinch myself to believe it could be happening to me, but a glimpse at my phone with all of my children leaving demanding messages – 'Well?' 'Any news?' 'What's the story, Mum?' – confirmed it was true. With mounting excitement I turned my phone off, paid for the coffee, and on the strength of my new-found wealth, hailed a taxi to Lastow Mews.

The taxi driver gave me a strange look as he picked me up and then deposited me no more than two streets away. It clearly would have made more sense to walk. As I paid him I gazed across to where the road ended in an abrupt brick wall.

Under an arch, though, another road began: a narrow, cobbled affair, all the little houses within painted pretty pastel shades, like the colors in an Italian ice cream parlor: yellow, pink, green and blue. As the taxi purred away I hurried across and under that arch. Across the cobbles I stole, like a thief casing the joint, passing doors flanked by bay trees standing sentry in cast-iron urns, sleek convertible motors, even a stone griffin or two, glancing at the numbers on the doors. Could it be that darling palest pink one near the end? Almost not pink at all, just a very faint blush? It was. Number 32. I almost gasped as I stopped opposite, handbag to chest again. Oh Uncle *Cuthbert*, I said instead, under my breath.

Obviously it wasn't mine yet. Mr Hamilton had told me various documents had to be drawn up and signed in probate, and then signed by him again, and that could take time, but I imagined it was empty, so why couldn't I creep a little closer and at least stand and marvel? Marvel too that we'd never known this man with such exquisite taste who clearly wouldn't be seen dead on a shabby little small-holding in Herefordshire. I gazed some more, almost at the window now, noting the dear little window boxes frothing over with something white and tasteful, the terra-cotta pots outside.

Having feasted for a moment I was about to walk away back up the mews to the pub – as luck would have it there was one directly opposite the arch where I could lurk and feast some more without looking like a total snooper – when a young woman approached, smiled, and put her key in the door of the blush-pink house. My house. She looked at me inquiringly.

'Can I help?' Only three words but within them a whole world of expensive boarding schools, a daddy in the City and a mother who'd never clipped shit from a sheep's bottom in her life.

'Oh.' I hustled a few steps towards her. Age was on my

side but little else: she was very slim, with that pale, almost translucent blonde beauty one sees in fashion magazines. She was behaving proprietorially too. As if she lived here. My heart pumped a bit.

'Well, it's just – well, this house belonged to my late uncle, you see. At least – my husband's late uncle. And, the thing is, I've just been to the lawyer's and—'

'Oh!' she interrupted, eyes widening. She lowered her key. 'You're Cuthbert's niece?'

'Well . . .'

'Oh, I'm so sorry,' she said, looking genuinely upset. 'I must have missed you at the funeral. But it was so crowded, wasn't it? You could hardly move.'

'Oh . . . er, well, I . . .'

'Unsurprising, of course, he was such a heavenly man.'

'Yes. Quite.' I could feel myself reddening.

'And so young for his age. It was so unexpected, I honestly thought he'd go on forever.'

Young for his age? So not with a rug over his knees and two sticks? The old witch.

'Well, yes. Except –' I lunged heroically for the truth, 'we didn't really know him, I'm afraid. We live miles away, deep in the countryside, practically in Wales.' I plunged as deep as possible. 'And we only heard very recently. My own husband died some time ago, you see, and I'm afraid I didn't keep up the connection. Um, and you are . . . ?'

'Oh, Camilla. I clean. Or did.' She blinked a bit, clearly upset at this use of the past tense.

She cleaned. Right. Although actually, on reflection, it didn't surprise me. I knew about how these smart girls were turning their hands to cleaning and laundering now that secretarial jobs had dried up courtesy of computers. Minna had thought about it as a route to London.

'And ironed his shirts, too, that sort of thing. But dear Cuthbert – he paid me a month in advance, always did, so no way was I not going to come in and dust and hoover,' she said fiercely. 'He'd have been horrified. He was quite particular. Would you like to come in?' She raised her key again.

'Oh, er, thank you. I don't know if I should but—'

'Oh, Cuthbert would have wanted it. After all, you're family.'

'Yes,' I said, emboldened. 'And the thing is, well, the lawyer tells me, the one I've just been to see, that because I'm the only family left, I'm inheriting his estate.' I tried not to sound too breathless or excited.

'Inheriting?' She turned. Looked shocked. She stared at me. Then quickly whipped round and opened the door.

'Does that . . . surprise you?' I ventured, following her inside.

'Oh, no. It's just I thought . . .' It clearly did, but she made an effort to compose her face as she shut the door behind us and led me, via a narrow hallway with a Persian runner, into a pretty sitting room with French windows at one end through which the sun poured.

A terraced garden surrounded by deep beds of frothy pink tulips and forget-me-nots could be glimpsed beyond. But delightful though the garden was, it was the interior that was arresting. Original modern paintings filled every inch of wall space, almost down to the skirting boards and right up to the picture rail: nudes, portraits, or simply great swathes of color I didn't understand but which looked terrific. All around the room they marched, aside from beside the fireplace, where two shelved alcoves groaned with books, all hardbacks and all improving.

In one quick glance around I understood that Uncle

Cuthbert was cultured, educated and urbane. The air was stale, though, and Camilla went straight to the French windows, unlocking them and flinging them wide, explaining that the wake had only happened the day before yesterday and she hadn't been in since, and as you can imagine it was fairly protracted – and alcohol-fueled – and the place still reeked.

'It was held here?'

'Of course, why not? What a shame you couldn't come.' She looked at me rather suspiciously now, as I might have done had I been in her shoes. It occurred to me I'd have loved to have known this man: one who could fill a house at his wake and had clearly led a vibrant and interesting life.

'Camilla, what did Cuthbert do? I mean, I imagine he was retired, but before that?'

'Oh, he was only semi-retired,' she said as she led the way out of the sitting room and into the kitchen, gathering empty glasses as she went, which had obviously been missed after the party. I seized a couple too, trying to ingratiate myself.

'He still sat on the Arts Council Committee and was a fellow at the V&A and on the board at the ICA and various other places. Everyone wanted him. He was still frightfully busy. Well, you would be if you'd been at Christie's all those years.'

'Right. I wish I'd known him. He sounds like a delightful man.'

'He was.' She raised her chin and looked at me squarely, turning from putting glasses in the sink. 'Everyone loved him.'

'I didn't really know of his existence,' I said quickly. 'Just a name. Not even a Christmas card.'

She nodded. 'Everyone has relatives like that: names rather than faces.'

'They do, don't they?' I felt comforted. It also occurred to me he hadn't rushed to introduce himself when David had died, or offered to help afterwards. Why should I be feeling guilty? Surely the onus, five years ago, had been on him to make himself known? I was about to make that excuse for myself but she was already talking.

'So when does the house become yours?' she asked casually, her back to me now as she turned on the taps and washed up the glasses. I couldn't help noticing, as I sat down behind her at the kitchen table, that there was a breakfast plate with crumbs and a marmalade jar and butter dish, both with their tops off. Was there someone living here? Camilla turned when I didn't reply and saw my eyes on the detritus. In a moment she'd removed the plate and washed it up with the glasses: popped the marmalade back in the cupboard without a word.

'Um . . . I'm not sure,' I recovered. 'When probate's been sorted out, I imagine.'

'So you've come straight from the lawyer's?'

I blushed. 'Yes.'

There was a pause. I watched her back.

'Well, if you want a cleaner,' she said, with slightly forced jollity. She wiped her hands and delved in her jeans pocket, handed me a card which read: 'The Bennett Girls: the Little Treasures'.

'My sister and I run it. We also take your laundry away and have it back the next day, water your plants, feed the cat, walk dogs, anything really. I read History of Art at Edinburgh but, hey, these days so did everybody.' She shrugged.

I smiled. 'Yes, I have a daughter like that. She's got a big brain and she runs a flower shop. I know what it's like.'

She smiled gratefully and I felt we were making progress. She nodded at the card in my hand. 'I even did some correspondence for Cuthbert.'

'Right, thanks.' I pocketed it. 'I'll, um, bear it in mind. So . . . you'll be in and out for a month then?'

'Well, as I say, he's paid me.' She gave me a steady look, as if daring me to suggest she shouldn't be in and out of this house. And I wasn't sure what my rights were. Who did own this house? If not me, and not Cuthbert any more, then who? I felt uncomfortable, though. As if the pair of us were constantly taking two steps forward and one back.

'Right, well, I'll be off. Thanks so much for letting me look around.'

As I went down the hall, Camilla tailing me, I glanced upstairs.

'I'd offer to let you look up there, but I haven't got around to tidying yet,' she said quickly as she opened the front door.

'Oh no, I wouldn't dream of it, I shouldn't even be in here. Thank you, Camilla.' I went down the two front steps, feeling her eyes on my back and not necessarily in a friendly way. Both of us, I knew, had been unnerved by that meeting. She shut the door.

Boy, I really did need a drink now, I thought, as I hurried back up the cobbled mews. The sun was high in the sky and I wished I'd thought to bring sunglasses. I wished, too, that I hadn't gone in that house. I felt as if I'd compromised myself in some way. Put myself on the back foot. I bit my lip.

London was looking at its most ravishing, though, all bright and white and beautiful, the gleam of the huge houses that surrounded the mews tall and striking against the blue sky. The blossom on the plane trees fluttered in the breeze and I raised my head defiantly, swung my bag and strode on towards the pub across the road, bound for the tables with umbrellas outside. Thinking this was the first time I'd drunk alone in public for years – obviously I'd done plenty in private – but that the situation demanded it, and a ciggy too, in the sunshine, with time to think, I went inside and ordered a gin and tonic at the bar.

As I took it outside, a group of people clustered under a parasol, heads lowered over their drinks, looked horribly familiar. I stopped in my tracks. Stared.

'What the . . .'

Lucy, Minna and Nico emerged from sun hats, caps and dark glasses and regarded me sheepishly as they sat up.

'What the bloody hell are you doing here?' I blustered, nearly dropping my gin.

'Having a drink?' Minna ventured, pulling up an empty chair.

I gaped. 'Oh. Right. At the very pub where I just happen to be having a drink too? How did you know I was here?'

'We followed you,' Nico said candidly. 'Bloody stupid to take a cab, though, Mum. We managed to nip after that on foot.'

'You followed me! What – from home?'

'Well, obviously we got the next train up, not yours. But we knew the lawyer's you were going to and what time, and we do live in London.'

'*You* don't,' I reminded Nico, sitting down. 'You live with me. So does Minna.'

'No, but I fully intend to be up here next year and so does Min. So come on, give. What's the bottom line?'

'The bottom line!' I echoed incredulously, thinking I'd like him to go to university next year. But then, actually, I couldn't control my excitement. I leaned forward. 'Well, my chickadees, the bottom line is . . .' And I told them. About the bank account and the row of zeros, and then the shares, but how these would be canceled out because of the house, which I'd just been to see. About how much it was worth. There were gasps of astonishment. Mouths fell open. Silence. Then whoops of glee.

'Bloody *hell.*'

'Fuck.'

'You are *kidding*, Mum.' Nico was out of his seat.

'No, I'm not kidding,' I assured them as he sat again, loving their shining eyes. I hadn't seen that for a while. We'd had a lot of sad eyes, a lot of worried eyes, a lot of brave eyes, but not eyes like these.

'It's like a lottery win,' said Minna slowly, gazing into space. 'Isn't it? It's like – like someone's waved a wand and gone – ta-da! Your life is going to change.' She turned to me, dazed.

'Oh Mum, you so needed this,' breathed Lucy beside me. She leaned across and hugged me, her eyes damp.

'*We* so needed this,' I reminded her, thinking it was ages since she'd hugged me. I couldn't remember when. 'All of us,' I said as we drew apart. 'It belongs to all of us. It goes to me because everything of Dad's goes to me, but it's all of ours.'

We sipped our drinks thoughtfully and I felt the ice and tonic sparkle on my tongue.

'We could go on a posh holiday,' said Nico suddenly. 'Go to Corfu, like all my mates. Hire a villa.'

'Sod Corfu, let's hire a yacht! Go to the Caribbean!' Minna squeaked.

'Well, no, I don't think we'll do that. But what we can do,' I told them, 'is pay off the mortgage.'

'Oh. Yes.' They agreed soberly, thinking, no, the

Caribbean. 'But I also think we should celebrate,' I told them, 'when it comes through.'

'God, *definitely*,' they chorused, perking up.

Then I told them about the house I'd just seen, and what I knew of their late great-uncle.

Minna whistled. 'God, who would have thought. Our only relative left on Dad's side – and we thought sweet FA – and he'd been sitting there, all those years.'

'We could have stayed with him . . .' Nico realized, his eyes wide.

'Oh yeah . . .' Minna turned to him, imagining the London scene some of their friends had experienced courtesy of relatives as they'd stood jealously by.

'How come we didn't know him?' Nico demanded.

'I don't know,' I said truthfully. 'I mean, he came to our wedding, apparently, I found the list the other day and checked, but I simply don't remember him. Also I think he worked in America for a while.' That much I'd gleaned from Mr Hamilton. 'He was at Christie's in New York. He and Dad must have simply lost touch. I mean, he wasn't *my* relative.'

'And yet he's left his entire estate to you,' said Lucy.

'Well no, he didn't, did he? He just didn't make a will. And the thing is,' I hesitated, 'well, I think there's someone living there, in his house.'

I told them about the breakfast things and not being allowed upstairs.

'Did you ask her? This Camilla?'

'No, I didn't. Because I felt she was being a bit . . . evasive. A bit mysterious.'

Lucy stared at me. 'Well, whatever or whoever it is, is no concern of yours, Mum,' she said firmly. 'If Cuthbert let a friend stay there before he died, let's suppose, they'll know the score by now. Know they have to get out when it passes to you.'

'Exactly,' agreed Minna. 'Which is when?'

'I'm not sure,' I said vaguely, remembering how heart-broken I'd been when David had died: wondering if this person, perhaps quite close to this colorful, delightful man, was feeling the same pain.

'I'm not sure you should have gone in there,' said Lucy, frowning as she cradled her drink. 'It sort of. . . compromises you. Puts you on the back foot.'

'Oh no, I disagree,' I said, coloring.

She sent me a level gaze. 'Just hold on before you do anything else. Let me check it with Robin.' Robin was her lawyer boyfriend.

'OK,' I said meekly, sinking into my gin. Luckily her phone beeped.

'Mum,' said Nico softly and urgently as Lucy read her text. 'Derek and I have got this idea, right? For a business.' Derek was one of his mates: a gnomic individual who smoked a lot of weed and as far as I knew had never had an idea, beyond rolling another joint, in his life.

'It's an app you use at festivals, right, to find out where your mates are.'

'It's been done,' interjected Minna, executing a perfect rollup and running her tongue down the paper.

'No, it hasn't, not the way we'd do it. But we do need a bit of a cash injection, like any start-up company, to get it off the ground. Set up a database, that type of thing.'

'It has been done,' agreed Lucy, pocketing her phone. 'And anyway, Mum will be far more likely to back an established business like mine.' She turned to me, looking important. 'The lease has come up for sale, Mum, on the shop, and obviously it's horrendously expensive. I couldn't possibly do it on my own, I'd have to get a loan from the bank. But I was thinking. This windfall couldn't have come at a better time, because if you could just lend me the deposit—'

'Lend?' interrupted Nico. 'Half an hour ago you were talking about *us* being the rightful recipients, seeing as how we're the actual blood relatives and Mum's only a niece-in-*law*, you said.'

'Nico!' Lucy colored.

'You *did*,' the other two chorused.

'Mum, ignore him, I absolutely did not. I mean, sure, I pointed out the bloodline but I wasn't trying to – you know – jump the queue or anything. I was just saying that we need to act as a family on this one, since a lease for sale on a shop in a desirable area of Islington is worth snapping up, as far as *all* of us are concerned.'

'You've already *got* a business!' Minna said angrily. 'I'm the one that needs to invest in something, in this field for the poly tunnels, Mum, to grow the flowers. We agreed, so she doesn't have to buy from suppliers!'

'Yes, that would be good,' Lucy conceded. 'So long as the flowers are top quality.'

'So forget buying the lease on the shop, let's start with the tunnels. We could even do it on our own land now that we can afford to get it cultivated – and also we don't have to keep sheep any more which make bugger all at market – become proper market gardeners. Get the bulbs in this autumn and then have rows and rows of gorgeous Dutch tulips coming up in the spring. What d'you think, Mum? Mum?'

But I was miles away. Or not so far, as it happened. About two hundred meters. Because from where I was sitting, opposite the arched entrance in the wall, I could see right down the cobbled mews. And my eyes had followed a tall, fair-haired man in jeans, a mint-green shirt, no socks, moccasins, brown ankles, all the way down it: past the drop-top Alfa Romeo, past the bay trees and the griffins, past the pastel yellow and blue houses, to stop at the one I'd so recently visited. He took a key out of his back pocket, fitted it in the lock, looked to left and right, and went inside.

CHAPTER 5

A few moments later, indeed almost simultaneously, Camilla emerged. She went across to a black Mini Cooper, slid the roof down electronically, reversed down the mews and into the road, and then turned left in the direction of Knightsbridge.

'Mum?'

I turned back to my family. 'Hm?'

'We said, what are your plans? What do you intend to do with the money?'

They looked rather contrite. Faces a bit pink. Ashamed of their bickering. I drained my drink.

'I don't know. I'm going to think about it. Come on, let's go.' I cast another look back towards the house.

'Where? Christ, not all the way back home, surely? I've just got here.' This came from Nico.

'You can all stay at mine, Sophia's away,' said Lucy charitably, no doubt still chastened by her niece-in-law remark. 'You too, Mum.'

'Really?' I'd never been to Lucy's. Not that she'd been there long. But I'd never been invited. She met my eye.

'Of course. Why not?'

It was cosy, to say the least, in Lucy's tiny, lower ground-floor flat in Earls Court. Once she'd allocated the bedrooms – I got Sophia's, Minna would sleep with Lucy in her double bed and Nico on the sofa – we shared a huge dish of pasta which she cooked in the minute galley kitchen, pans clattering, radio blaring, steam billowing.

I'd wanted to help but hadn't liked to: something about her purposeful demeanor had said it was her domain. I did lay the coffee table, though, and pulled the sofa and two chairs up either side – not far to pull, it was a small room – and as we ate, we commented on the footwear of the people passing by in the top of the window, the only available light space, which was a favorite game with Sophia, Lucy told us, passing round the Parmesan.

She could have rented in Holloway, I thought – Finsbury Park even, much nearer to the shop – and had much more light and space, but Lucy was all about location. All her friends were round here, she said. What was the point of going out to dinner in Chelsea, and heading back to Holloway night after night? Well, quite. The only direction Lucy was traveling was back to what she considered to be her rightful roots. Where she'd come from and where she considered she should still be now. I quietly forked up my pasta.

It was a dreary little place, though, I thought, glancing around at the magnolia wood-chip walls, even though I'd enthused about it when I'd walked in – straight into the sitting room, no hall, so junk mail constantly clattered through the letter box – and even though the two girls had done their best with huge mirrors, pictures, throws over the cheap sofa. And it no doubt cost a fortune too, so . . . could I afford to buy all the children a flat? And still have some left to do up the farm? Just how expensive *was* London? I mustn't forget the farm was mortgaged now. I'd had to do that after the death duties. Perhaps I shouldn't make promises about flats – or businesses – I couldn't keep; just wait until it all dropped in my lap?

The children, however, had no such restraints. Mouths full of tagliatelle and pesto, and getting thoroughly over-excited on the bottles of red wine we'd bought at the liquor store en route, they decided that obviously all the bills had to be paid and the mortgage and all the boring things I'd outlined, but after that . . .

'After that,' said Nico, looking at me, 'you'll be living in a tarted-up farmhouse with pristine fences and healthy, well-fed sheep and you'll never have to sell a dodgy mare or wrap a bar of soap again.'

'Exactly,' I said happily.

'In the middle of nowhere,' he added. 'With someone doing your cleaning, leaving you in an immaculate, empty house when they've gone.'

'Quite.' I looked at him doubtfully now.

'No friends,' added Minna, 'because all your real friends are in London, and you're too busy – and sad – to socialize.'

We all went quiet. 'I've got Tia.'

'Because she's the bailiff.'

'And Anna.'

'Except she's even busier than you, so you never see her.'

'My book group.'

'Which you never go to.'

I hesitated. Raised my chin. 'Granny and Grandpa.'

'Who hustled down there when Dad died so you wouldn't be lonely.'

I gazed around at them. Had a feeling they'd had a long chat before I made it to the pub.

'What are you saying?'

'What we're saying, Mum,' said Lucy, clearly the official spokesperson, 'is that there's no real reason for you to be buried deep in the country now.'

'You could sell the whole balls-aching affair,' agreed Nico.

The thought had occurred to me, of course. But I didn't let on.

'And live where?'

'Here, in London, where you used to live. Where all your friends are.'

'But I've made a life for myself down there, a rural idyll – it was our dream!'

'It was Dad's dream,' said Lucy firmly. 'You never wanted to go, you told us that years ago, although you'd never say it now. And Dad's dead.'

My eyes filled. 'But I have to finish what he started,' I said fiercely. 'Have to—'

'You don't. You don't have to do anything. Dad wouldn't have wanted that.'

'And we know why you wanted to stay, because he loved it so much, because it made you feel closer to him, but you *have* stayed. For five years. More. Now it's time to move on,' Nico insisted.

'I have moved on,' I said stubbornly, aware I was being subjected to a pincer movement.

'You haven't, you've hidden. Behind your busy higgledy-piggledy life – which you've done brilliantly,' Lucy added quickly, 'behind never sitting still. But you haven't been out with anyone or anything like that, and you're gorgeous, Mum. Everyone says so. Sophia thinks you look like Kristin Scott Thomas. It's such a waste. Dad would agree.'

This caused me to breathe in sharply. It was said urgently, but gently and sensitively too.

'I have been out with people. You made me.'

'Two suppers. Precisely two. One with Peter Cox, who, OK, is a bit dull, but one with Paddy Campbell, who is seriously hot and was seriously into you, and you're so rude to him, Mum.'

'Me? Rude to him? He's always so cross and disagreeable!'

'Because the one and only time you let him take you out you talked non-stop about Dad, and the next time, you stood him up.'

'I forgot, that's all.'

'So he was left in the pub with all his clients around, all the people whose animals he looks after, at a table for two in the window. Bummer. I'd be cross,' said Nico.

'Oh, I apologized, you're making a big deal of it. And anyway, it was ages ago,' I said airily but I remembered it well. And I hadn't forgotten at all. I had been in the car park. Unable to get out of the car. Sitting in the dark, physically unable to go in. Had driven home in tears. Pathetic. Obviously I couldn't tell the children that. Or him. Not when I'd driveled on about my deceased husband the first time.

'He's too bad-tempered,' I said, sticking to what was indisputable.

'You'd be bad-tempered if you'd been dumped and had to carry on seeing your dumper,' put in Minna heatedly. 'I'm always bumping into Ted and I just want to knee him in the balls.'

'I thought you dumped him?' objected Nico. 'You said—'

'It's beside the point, Nico,' she said furiously. 'We're

talking about Mum here and how she should move on, not me.'

'You brought him up.'

'And that includes being open to different suggestions,' agreed Lucy. 'Like possibly moving back here. We're not dyed-in-the-wool country dwellers, Mum. We weren't born in barns, we were born in Wandsworth.'

'No, I can't,' I said, almost gripping the table.

'No, we know,' the girls said quickly, in unison. 'Not there.'

I simply could not go back to Wandsworth, which I'd loved so much. Had never wanted to leave. Could not go back to my gorgeous Victorian villa, or something similar, in that lovely grid of leafy, wide roads near the common, with the wine bars and bookshops and boutiques, where I'd pushed prams, done school runs, where my best friends still lived, the ones I'd met at the school gates: Caroline, Rosie, Silvia, all with their children no doubt at clever universities now, Durham, Bristol, Cambridge, and with their lives, their husbands.

How could I go back, so bereft? I would be even more bereft all these years on. At least in Herefordshire I didn't have the comparison – right next door in the case of Silvia. And my lovely job in PR: in the old days full-time, then four days a week with small children, and at the end, when we could afford it, just three, Monday to Wednesday, which had been heaven. Leaving me two whole days to play tennis, a bit of bridge, catch up with the house, the children fully immersed in long school days, occupied. It had been an enviable life. How could I go back? I looked at them, aghast. Hurt they'd even suggested it.

'Obviously not home – I mean, in Wandsworth. But London's huge,' said Lucy.

'Where, then? I don't know anywhere else.'

'Well, why not where you actually already own a house?' Lucy jerked her head meaningfully. 'Why not number thirty-two?'

'In South Ken?' I really did gasp now. 'So smart!'

'Why not?'

'God . . . I don't know anyone—'

'Which is what you want, isn't it? Not to go backwards. A fresh start. But you wouldn't be quite so grief-stricken. Quite so . . .'

'Complicated,' said Minna softly.

Since when had my children become so wise? A minute ago they were arguing about who got what when it was sold; now they wanted me to live in it?

I tried to imagine it. Found I could. Found I could see myself coming out of the shiny white front door, tripping down the cobbled street to the little expensive shops with their shiny regular vegetables in pristine straw baskets outside, buying groceries. Maybe buying strange organic things, too: the one I couldn't say – keen-oh-ah? Studying the Otto Lenghi cookbook. Becoming frightfully grown up and civilized. And no one would know me. It was far enough away, as they said, from Wandsworth. Surely I'd done my time in the country?

I began to feel excited. Though I was determined not to show it. But I saw myself going back down the street with my lentils and my – what *was* it? Keen-ou-wiee? Greeting my neighbors as they emerged from their pretty ice-cream-colored houses, other, civilized Kensington women, off to Sloane Square no doubt, promising to pop in for a G&T later, not for soul-searching chats like I would in Bolingbroke Road, really getting to the bottom of things, roaring with laughter over a bottle of Chardonnay; those days were gone. But popping in for light chit-chat, bridge – just enough. I'd had dear friends. Bosom buddies.

Didn't want them again. I'd had a dear husband. Didn't ever want one again, or a partner, or even a boyfriend, whatever the children thought.

I could feel their eyes on me now as I turned it all around in my head. Digested it. Could feel the far-off thrill of a distinct possibility, something I hadn't felt for a very long time. For precisely five years and ten months. But a thrill of a different nature. One I was entitled to, not someone else's.

'Bound to have three bedrooms,' observed Nico.

I turned to him. 'D'you think?'

'Maybe even four.'

'No. It looked smaller.' I cast my mind back, remembering the ground-floor layout.

'So one for you, one for me, and one for the girls, when Lucy's home.'

'Yes.' I looked around. 'So we'd all be together.'

Something we clearly weren't going to be at the farm any more, not with Lucy in London having opted out of university, Minna following exactly the same path, albeit squeezing in a foundation course at the local college, and Nico in his final year at school.

'I'd see so much more of you,' I said excitedly.

'Exactly,' said Lucy. 'I'd keep this flat on, it's too much of a find not to, but Sunday lunches, midweek suppers—'

'Yes!' I breathed.

'And I could live with you, 'till I found somewhere,' said Minna. 'Maybe even for a year or two.'

'I'd love that.'

'Cool. And I'll be in London next year, Jake wants to come too. Maybe go to art college.' Nico's blue eyes shone.

'There's a garden,' I said eagerly, 'for Moppet and Flo. Or d'you think they'd be happier . . . maybe with Anna?'

'Certainly not!' said Lucy. 'People have dogs in

London! Do not re-house them. God, they're only little terriers, albeit a bit feral.'

'Right,' I agreed, no object too big suddenly, although Moppet and Flo's rampant sexuality might be. They were both loose women.

'Have them spayed,' said Minna, reading my mind. 'And don't forget we had Coco in London.'

Coco was our spaniel. A well-trained elderly dog who hadn't lasted long in Herefordshire.

'And you can walk in the park, with friends, like you used to,' enthused Nico before the girls shot him a look.

'Kensington Gardens,' said Lucy quickly. 'Not Battersea.'

'No,' I agreed equally quickly, getting up, gathering empty plates. Not Battersea. Not bumping into anyone I knew. Or used to know. With their dogs. Who we used to walk regularly there. Or on Wandsworth Common. And then drop them back at home in their baskets and race on to Pilates, or tennis, then lunch with a friend. Our lives. Our lovely lives. Until I'd wrecked it. And so we'd moved. David had decided we'd move. And then – well, then I'd really finished it off completely. Although of course, the children had no idea. They just knew I couldn't go back. As I put the plates in the sink I watched them from the kitchen, leaning across the coffee table where we'd perched to have our scratch supper, heads close, resuming their excited chatter. They had absolutely no idea what I'd done.

CHAPTER 6

*D*avid and I were married for fifteen years. Fifteen happy years, give or take the usual marital tiffs and disagreements, the occasional peaks and troughs which go with the contract, and as I say, we enjoyed an increasingly covetable life. David had made something of a success of being a City lawyer, and I'd pottered about in PR.

We'd met at Bristol University, but not until the third year, which was perfect. By then I'd almost forgotten about the dashing London boyfriend I'd beetled down most weekends to see in the first year, but not the second, when someone else had appeared on his scene, and I was ready for someone new to appear on mine. Even though David and I were on the same course, I hadn't noticed him until then, but then History was a huge intake. One morning, though, I'd arrived late for a lecture, as usual, but instead of being able to slip quietly in at the back as I normally did, I'd found the door at the top of the lecture theater locked. It meant I had to emerge at the very bottom, in front of everyone, causing Professor Henderson to pause at his lectern. In my confusion I'd dropped all my files, sending papers flying everywhere. When I'd finally picked them all up and taken a seat, crimson and mortified, the blond boy beside me had scrawled on his pad – *Smooth.*

After exchanging some banter on the way out, me defending my position on the grounds that it offended no one if I was simply allowed to creep in as usual at the back, him asking why I couldn't just get up two minutes earlier and save myself the hassle, we found ourselves going for a coffee and I remember, as I looked at his kind, intelligent face, his slightly sleepy grey eyes, wishing my tights weren't so laddered and that I'd bothered to wash my hair.

How long was it before we were going out? I don't remember. Not long. A few weeks? A month? Close proximity meant everything happened so quickly in those days. What I do remember, though, is that the fun and frivolity of the first two years dissipated somewhat: finals loomed and we studied hard. Rather sweetly we sat side by side in the library, usually writing the same essay, and because of that proximity I also knew – although I kept it to myself because he wasn't good at being teased – that I was a bit cleverer than him. My marks were always higher, which I remember surprised him.

When we left, however, he was the one who headed to a law conversion course and thence to the City and a proper job, and I was the one who dithered between advertising or publishing, or at least something fun, preferably with reasonable hours, finally joining a fashion PR agency in the West End.

Is it still like this? Lucy tells me it's better. More of her girlfriends plan to head for the money in the City after university, and Sophia's elder sister said the bank she'd applied to was bending over backwards to appear women-friendly, religiously employing two girls and two boys from its hundred and fifty applicants, even though only twenty of the applicants were girls. No doubt the sisterhood would call this progress, but I wanted to tell Lucy I thought it smacked of something else. I didn't. Lucy's her father's daughter and not that good at being teased, either.

Anyway, back then, I simply adored being in Covent Garden. I loved the fact that my girlfriends were nearby in similar PR or ad agencies, that the job itself was terrific fun – albeit badly paid – the shops were on my doorstep and the bars and restaurants a hop and a skip away. I wouldn't have wanted to be in the City if you'd . . . well, you know.

On fine mornings I'd even cycle across the river to my office in Henrietta Street, leaving first Lucy, then Minna and then Nico with a series of jolly Australian au pairs, although in the beginning I often had tears streaming down my face when I arrived, which was easier to explain if I cycled, but not if I got the tube. Gradually it got easier, and when they were at school, it was sheer bliss. I'd have hated to be at home all day and David, I think, was rather proud, as most of the wives in Wandsworth had given up by then: had stayed at home when more than one baby – certainly more than two – had arrived.

'God, I envy you now,' Caroline would wail when I bumped into her, wheeling my bike out of the front garden in a smart little suit when she was coming back from walking her youngest to school in her leggings. 'What am I supposed to do now? My lot don't come out till six by the time they've done clubs. Polish the teacups?'

'You could always have an affair,' I'd quipped as I hoisted myself on to my saddle. I cringe as I remember, and I do remember: I have a particularly vivid piece of footage in my mind, of her throwing back her blonde head and roaring with laughter as I'd peddled off down the street under the cherry blossom. Because of course, I'd been the one to do that, some years later. With her husband.

Not an affair in the sense that we snuck off week after week to a hotel – that only happened once, when we were very definitely at the end of our ropes – but an affair in the sense that we lost our hearts completely to one another. Fell hopelessly in love. And Caroline was a good friend, not just a neighbor. Our children had grown up together. Lucy and Alice were close. I can barely tell you. Barely admit it to myself. But I will.

They were not immediate neighbors, in the sense that they didn't live in our street, but around a couple of corners and up the hill, where the bigger houses were. Theirs was a particularly beautiful wisteria-clad affair at the top: detached, almost in splendid isolation, with a glorious magnolia tree in the front garden. Henri was ruggedly handsome in the dark, tousled, twinkly-eyed, craggy-face vein. Not my type at all, in that I've never really gone for the bleeding obvious, and he was also very flirty – he even smoldered when he bought his cigarettes, for heaven's sake. Flirting was a way of life to him. He said it oiled the wheels, that everyday life would be dull without it and he couldn't understand why Englishmen didn't do it. 'Surely it's like breathing?' he'd say. 'Walking the dog? Don't you girls like it?'

'We love it!' we'd assured him at one particular dinner party.

'So why your husbands so tight-assed about it, hm? Why so, David? All that boarding school at seven, you think? Too emotionally crippled, *peut-être*?' He had an outrageous French accent – not his fault, obviously – but sometimes, we thought he hammered it up. He certainly knew the English for 'perhaps'.

'Yes, we're too much the product of our upbringing to

posture away like you, Henri, but frankly if it keeps the girls smiling, we're all for it, eh Jamie?' David turned to another husband.

'Couldn't agree more,' said Rosie's husband, who was quite drunk by then. 'Henri,' he raised his glass, 'you have my unqualified permission to service my wife, in the nicest possible way, as frequently, and as passionately, as you like. More power to your elbow.' He threw back the contents of his glass.

Henri roared, pulling me and Rosie close to him at the table, landing huge kisses on our cheeks. He was very tactile like that: lots of bear hugs and squeezing of shoulders – and if two of your fingers are moving mouth- and throat-wards, I can only tell you that he could also be terribly amusing and that all the husbands liked him.

He was a terrific mimic and would have us in stitches, naughtily aping the idiosyncrasies of some of our more stuffy neighbors who felt they should be living in Chelsea and weekending in Gloucestershire, strutting around in yellow cords and Barbours at the weekends. He released Rosie and me and leaped up to give a particularly accurate impersonation of Tristan, down the road, shoulders back, tummy proud, sweeping back a few wisps of hair and looking out of the corner of his eye to see who was watching.

Henri, of course, wouldn't be seen dead in cords, yellow or otherwise, and wore crumpled shirts over skinny jeans. He always looked like he'd just rolled out of bed, where he'd smoked a couple of Gauloise and read another chapter of Christopher Hitchens – he probably had – before shuffling off for the paper, giving Tristan's wife, should he pass her in the street, a devastating smile, causing her to palpitate all day.

Although Rosie and Silvia and I laughed about this

over coffee on my days off, we all privately agreed it probably wasn't a charade: that he was probably the most tremendous Lothario, particularly in Paris, where he frequently popped to and fro on business.

'I don't know how Caroline puts up with him,' Silvia would say. 'Even for a Frog – and don't forget I worked there – he's off the scale. If he doesn't already indulge in *cinq-à-sept* he soon will, believe me.'

'*Cinq-à-sept?*' asked Rosie.

'In France they start work early – well, eightish, hardly dawn – break for a proper lunch, go back to the office till five, when a Frenchman will call it a day and visit his mistress till seven.'

'Blimey,' I mused. 'They even have a set time for it?'

Silvia shrugged. 'If you ask anyone now they laugh and say – what rubbish, that went out ages ago – but trust me, it still happens.'

'But Henri's not like that here, surely?' Rosie objected. 'Caroline would never put up with it.'

'No, no,' we all agreed, frowning and shaking our heads, outwardly loyal to our friend. Never. But wondering all the same. And we had no proof of even a flicker of infidelity. Nothing. And we all lived pretty much on top of each other, we'd probably know. It was just the way he was. Flirtatious. Suggestive. Funny. The first two risible. The last making it a fatal combination.

And ridiculously – and I know it wasn't just me – there was definitely an upping of our game around Henri. A sharpening of female wits, a flexing of argumentative muscle. He was clever, well read, and spoke three languages, but hey, so did Silvia, who'd worked for Dior, and Rosie, who'd read PPE at Oxford, was no dunce either.

'So, Henri, what d'you think of Mitterrand's Balkan

treaty?' she might toss at him as she went round to collect one of her brood, whereas she'd be more likely to ask David about his greenfly spray, them both being avid gardeners. I was also very aware that when Rosie and Silvia popped round to my house to drop off a child, remove another, return a lost book bag, borrow a recipe, it would be in tacky bottoms and not a scrap of make-up. But the moment we were dropping off Alice or Tatiana, Caroline's pair, we scrubbed up.

I'd go round to collect Lucy, who'd been at netball club with Alice, to find Rosie already in the Defois' kitchen, in a pretty Agnès B top, lipgloss on, leaning against the huge slate island, flushed and giggling, having a glass of wine with Henri. Because Henri was something of a house husband. Unlike ours who mostly went off to the City in suits, Henri was an antiques dealer, a very successful one: Greek urns and busts were mostly his thing, and vast Trojan horses, but nothing, he'd once told me, dark eyes boring into mine, after the fifth century. 'Nothing filthy modern,' he'd snarled. I'd giggled.

Encouraged that he cherished the old, I'd nevertheless pulled my polo neck up a bit further to cover the beginnings of a blotchy neck. And in my defense, I only ever reacted to Henri, never instigated; was just on the receiving end of his very direct gaze and innuendoes, but then the others would no doubt say sternly – Molly, we all were. And Caroline was so sure of him, it didn't matter.

Caroline. I shrank at her memory. A tall, willowy blonde with long legs, a ravishing smile and a heart of gold. One of those rare people one suspects is beautiful on the inside as well as out. Sick child at school needs collecting? Caroline's your girl. No one around to let the dog out for a pee when you're trapped in a late meeting? She'd be on it. When

David's parents had been killed on that terrible Boxing Day and we'd all completely gone to pieces, I'd find a lasagne or a chicken pie on my step most days. She was a brick. And these days – bored with polishing the teacups – she worked, too, helping Henri on Thursdays and Fridays in his shop, giving him time to see dealers, or to call them from home.

Henri's shop – or gallery, I'd decided, the one and only time I'd ventured inside, awed by the treasures, the rarefied atmosphere, the apparent lack of commercial transaction – was in Mount Street, in the heart of Mayfair. But he also had one in Paris, on the Rue Dauphine, in possibly the smartest arrondissement, the sixth. I hope you're getting the picture. The Defois were a cool, smart – so smart that they didn't drip around in Chanel or drive Ferraris – charming couple, much chicer than the rest of us. I was small, dark, with a slightly beaky nose – gamine on a good day – usually in an old sweater and jeans and sometimes a leather jacket.

So why me? Why, when I went round to get Minna, did he break into a particularly winning smile, leave whatever he was doing, put the phone down on whichever dealer he was speaking to with an abrupt '*Au revoir*, Christophe!', get to his feet and hasten across the kitchen to hold my shoulders, kiss me three times, smile right into my eyes, then say: 'Molly. You've come. I am so pleased. A drink, *chérie*? You'll join me in some Chablis?'

And why, on that particular afternoon, did he insist I also play doubles with him the following Thursday? He'd booked a court to play Giles and Susie, mutual friends of ours, and Caroline couldn't make it. 'Say you will?' he demanded, both hands clasped to his heart. 'Say now, or my whole week falls into decline!' I laughed, and promised not to so destroy his week. But he could have asked Rosie, who was a much better tennis player than I was: prettier, too.

'He obviously fancies you,' Rosie said when I told her the following day. 'I popped in later to get Max and he hardly addressed a word to me, was on the phone to some Christophe chappie. Just waved and pointed in the general direction of the playroom. *And* I had J'adore on, *and* I'd washed my hair.'

I grinned. 'I imagine even Henri has to be serious and talk to clients sometimes,' I told her as we swung into the bookshop together. 'And it's just a game of tennis. No biggie.'

But I was a bit elated, nonetheless. I cooked supper for the children that evening with a spring in my step, shimmied those sausages in the pan, singing along to the radio, so that teatime didn't feel like such a chore, and even David noticed when he came home as he kissed me and handed me the *Evening Standard*.

'You're perky.'

'Well I had a lovely day with Rosie. We went to that new restaurant next to the bookshop for lunch. You'd like it, we thought we'd all go.'

And tennis was a blast that Thursday. Giles and Susie were good fun, and good players, but by some small freak of the balls landing well on our side and Henri pulling faces at Susie at the net, we won, and crowed madly as the four of us, in our whites, had coffee and croissants outside our favorite watering hole opposite the common in the sunshine.

'You fluked it,' complained Giles sulkily.

'*Au contraire*, my friend, we've been practicing for months. That backhand of mine has taken years of honing, courtesy of my personal friend Andre Agassi, and

Molly's secretly been slamming balls against her wall for ages.'

'You definitely fluked it. But we should do it again, it was fun. Let's do it every Thursday. It's no good unless you have a regular slot, a commitment – you don't play. You think you will, but you never do. Come on, Thursdays at ten, what d'you say?' Giles was an ex-stockbroker, who'd made enough money just to consult these days, but he still had a way of firming things up. He also clearly wanted revenge.

'OK, we'll have a rematch, but trust me, we'll win. Molly's got some demon shots in her locker, haven't you, *chérie?*'

'I have,' I agreed. 'Possibly even demonic.'

'Come on, every Thursday,' persisted Giles.

Laughing, we acquiesced, but even then, if I'm honest, I wondered if it was a good idea. I knew I liked Henri and was ridiculously flattered by the attention. I remember going home and saying to David that night, ever so casually, as I was stacking the dishwasher after supper, that I was going to play tennis with Giles and Henri and Susie on Thursdays. Mixed doubles.

'Oh, right.' He looked surprised. 'I thought you didn't like getting tied into anything regular?'

I didn't. On the whole. I shrugged. 'Thought it might be good for me.'

'Right. So who will you play with, Henri?'

'Oh, I expect we'll swap around.'

We didn't. As I knew we wouldn't. Giles was fiercely competitive and wanted to win with his wife, who, hilariously, he sometimes got cross with, although perhaps it wasn't so hilarious for Susie when she repeatedly missed the tram-lines and Giles threw his racket on the ground.

'Susie. Concentrate.'

'He takes it so seriously!' Henri gasped to me in astonishment as we sat alone in the sunshine at the same café, Giles and Susie having declined a coffee and gone straight on to their next assignment, the gym. 'It's a game, surely?'

'Ah, but that's how come he's retired at forty-five, Henri. Unlike us.' I sipped my cappuccino.

'Yes, but unlike us, he doesn't know how to have fun, hmm?' He'd sipped too and fixed me over his cup with those twinkling brown eyes, meaning absolutely nothing, but perhaps absolutely everything.

The girls, of course, and by that I mean my girlfriends, not my daughters, were agog at this new sporting development, but I played it cool.

'It forces me to take a bit of exercise,' I explained. 'I'm not as disciplined as the rest of you, don't go for a jog before breakfast or stride round the common with dumbbells in my hands.'

'That's only Susie because Giles makes her,' Rosie reminded me. 'Likes her to be match fit.'

I leaned forward over our mint teas and told them about his appalling behavior on court. We all agreed we could *not* be married to Giles, however rich and good-looking he was.

'Anyway, as long as it doesn't become more energetic than you thought!' Silvia had joked as we left Rosie's house together, already jogging on the spot in her running gear before she set off for the common, not thinking for one moment it was anything more than a jocular thing to say. No one imagined it was the beginning of anything. Did Henri? I don't know.

Some months later when I asked him in a restaurant in Paris, 'Why me?', he'd replied that he'd seen me as a challenge. A hard nut to crack. Not that he'd genuinely wanted to crack anything, he'd gone on to say – he was very happy with Caroline – but he had known he could bowl Rosie and Silvia over, but that I would be harder. Well, he'd got that wrong. Didn't he know I'd been applying as much mascara as they had on the school runs? He clearly hadn't noticed.

'Why would you want to bowl any of us maidens over?' I'd asked and he'd shrugged. 'I told you, *la chasse* is a national sport. And not for anything extramarital—'

'Oh yeah—'

'No, *chérie*, I promise. It's just amusing to see a hitherto completely disinterested, even chilly woman' – he cast me a look – 'thaw. Sit up a bit. For a light to appear in her eyes. To think – ah, gotcha.'

'Like a fish.'

'Exactly.'

'Disgraceful,' I'd told him, removing my foot from beside his under the table in La Coupole.

'Harmless, though. Just filling in time between haircuts.'

'You could play golf?'

He made a face. 'And be completely humiliated?'

'You never think you're playing with fire?'

'I never expected to fall in love, if that's what you mean. Particularly with you, Molly.'

I knew he meant it. It was a backhanded compliment, so all the more sincere. He had fallen, as I had, and the coupling was most unlikely. I was a bit scruffy, as I've mentioned. Fancied myself as a bit edgy in my youth, with untamed locks and strange gear, a certain amount of attitude, perhaps, even a sharp tongue. I certainly didn't suffer fools. I was the least likely woman on the planet to fall for a silver-tongued smoothie who wore cashmere sweaters slung artfully round his neck and handmade Italian shoes. And yet, here I was, four months after that first tennis match, at least a dozen more under our belts, on a business trip in Paris just as he was too, having dinner, and feeling out of control in a candle-lit restaurant. And Caroline knew.

'Oh, but Henri is going next week too!' She'd turned in surprise in my kitchen. 'You can keep him company, he hates being out there alone.'

I'd paused as I doled out fish fingers, thinking, dear God, I even had permission. And she was right not to suspect a thing, because nothing had happened. Yes, we'd ditched Giles and Susie for coffee after the second or third match, or they had us, but Caroline didn't think that was peculiar. Only David did.

'You mean, it's just the two of you at Carluccio's every week? Isn't that a bit odd? Why not come straight home?' What he meant was, *I* think that's a bit odd, but he was careful not to say it. He was pussyfooting around the idea that I might be attracted to Henri because it was too awful to contemplate. So awful it hadn't even occurred to Caroline. No one, no friend, would even entertain the idea, surely? Except a glance through history tells us otherwise.

This is no mitigation, but it sets out my stall so I'll do it anyway: every Thursday, after tennis, I would tell myself I would cancel next week's match. That the butterflies in my tummy and the quickening of my heart were too strong, too persistent. That it wasn't appropriate to be in such a constant state of riotous good humor, whether I was walking Coco on the common and throwing sticks for her, buying new CDs instead of listening to Radio 4 and singing along to them in the car – particularly ones about thwarted love – or flipping pancakes in the kitchen, not caring if they landed on the ceiling or on the floor, to squeals of delight from the children. They didn't recognize the change, but David must have wondered where the short-tempered, constantly stressed woman juggling work, children and a home had gone, and who this good-tempered, well-dressed charmer was who'd replaced her. I don't think he got any further than that, though. I don't think men do. He wouldn't have thought: she's in love.

Paris had not been planned, I swear, but when it fell into place, we'd looked at each other over our cappuccinos on the common and blanched.

'The sixteenth?' Henri had said. 'But that's when the shop is re-opening. I'll be there all week.' It had been closed for refurbishment for ages, so I couldn't have known.

'Oh. Right. I've got a meeting with Hermès.' I wondered if I should get Jessica, my assistant, to go instead; knew I was in trouble.

'But I'll be very busy,' he'd said quickly, seeing me hesitate. 'I may not even see you.'

'Oh right,' I'd agreed happily, snatching at that, our smokescreen. And it had been what I'd said to Caroline in my kitchen.

'Yes, I know,' I'd said casually in response as I went round the table, spooning peas on to plates for our two sets of children. 'But he says he's going to be very tied up, and I've got wall-to-wall meetings.'

'Oh, he's so ridiculously precious. He's hardly going to be rushed off his feet, he's got Fabianne there. He can meet you for lunch if nothing else. I'll tell him. I wish I could come, but Josie's going back to Spain to see her parents that week.' Josie was their nanny.

'I wish you could come too,' I said, almost meaning it.

WE HAD DINNER, of course, not lunch. Three nights on the trot. And it was heaven. Walking along the Seine, Paris at its prettiest – though when is it not pretty, even in the rain?

– just at the beginning of summer, sitting outside restaurants as the light faded over the pink and beige buildings, laughing and joking over our rosé, his knowledge of the best places to eat, the perfect menu, the only place with a secluded roof terrace, equally seductive. But he didn't seduce me: at least, I didn't let him, for the first two nights. Tuesday and Wednesday I went back to my hotel, where he kissed me chastely goodnight on both cheeks on the steps, both of us wanting like mad to push through the double doors and go upstairs, past the night porter, but resisting, not even voicing it.

On the third evening, just off the Boulevard Saint-Germain, he asked me over dinner if I'd ever been unfaithful and I said no. I asked if he had and he said no, and I believed him. He said it was too serious a thing to contemplate lightly, that his father had been a terrible rake, that it had wrecked the family, which was why he only joked around with us girls in London. That was fun. A light-hearted distraction from the daily grind. This, though – he made a fist, placed it on his heart and leaned forward over his escargots – was not a joke. This was so serious he thought he'd burst with the portent of how he felt, how he didn't believe he'd felt for another human being. His eyes swam with tears.

'Not even for Caroline when we got married.'

'*Don't,*' I'd whispered, shocked, knowing this was the most dishonorable thing he could say, but knowing he spoke the truth, and that I felt it too. Knowing I'd felt nothing like this riot going on in my heart when I'd married David. Knowing I'd loved him, and that it definitely felt like the right thing to do, but this – this was something different. What was I supposed to do with it, this fever? What were *we* supposed to do with it?

That evening, we did, what seemed to us, the only

available thing. We paid the bill, walked silently through the Tuileries Gardens, then the Place de la Concorde to my hotel, no unbroken chatter, as there'd been on previous nights. We went up the stone steps, pushed through the double doors, past the sleeping night porter to the lift. I remember thinking, as the old-fashioned metal cage door concertinaed shut behind us, that there was no going back. Henri slid the door open on the third floor and we went down the corridor, hand in hand, to my room.

CHAPTER 7

I know for a fact from extensive research since, that for many people, for many husbands or wives, this would not be a life-changing event. Not a deal-breaker, as they say. They'd carry on as usual, picking up where they left off, shimmying the sausages in the pan and singing on the school run as if nothing had happened, only a slightly larger smile playing on their lips, a jauntier spring in their step betraying the reality. And I can't say I wasn't incredibly energized and overexcited by my few days away too, but I was also a trifle breathless. And permanently fearful. I'd flush scarlet whenever Henri's name was mentioned, even once dropping a chocolate soufflé on the kitchen floor. I wasn't very good at deception. And David wasn't stupid.

'What's wrong with you?' he said as I picked the shards of china out of the messy goo and he went to get a cloth. 'You're a bag of nerves recently and you broke the phone yesterday.'

Caroline had rung to ask us round to supper and I'd

dropped the whole contraption on the floor, whereupon it had smashed on the tiles.

'I don't know, probably the time of the month,' I'd said, but he wasn't fooled. We were very close. Knew each other's rhythms and bodies intimately, and lately, he must have been aware that I'd inadvertently been withdrawing mine. Shying away from his touch when he hugged my shoulders, or staying up to watch *Newsnight* or *Question Time* and coming to bed after he was asleep.

'She's probably menopausal,' offered Lucy, helping to pick out bits of china and who, at fourteen, thought she knew everything. 'It sends them all a bit bonkers apparently.'

'What d'you mean, "them"? You're one, too, in case you hadn't noticed,' Minna told her.

'So are you, you're a girl, you're a stupid girl,' yelled Nico, at which point, thankfully, a fight broke out at the Sunday lunch table, and David had to separate the protagonists who were prone to use fists – '*Ow! He thumped my leg, Daddy!*' '*Did not – you pinched me!*' – and underhand tactics. I was grateful for the diversion.

'Anyway, what's with the soufflé?' asked Lucy. 'You've gone all continental. We had some funny French tart last week and we like apple crumble.'

'*We like apple crumble! We like apple crumble!*' Nico chanted loudly until David silenced him with a sharp word – sharper than usual – and I threw them all a choc-ice from the freezer, glad of the blast of air as I opened it to cool my face.

We'd eventually had to go to supper with the Defois' because although I'd picked up the damaged phone and stuttered to Caroline – how lovely, but sadly we're out that evening, frantically scribbling '*theater*' in the diary in case David who was listening should query it, then hastily booking tickets to see *Noises Off* which happily we'd been meaning to see for ages and even more fortuitously tickets were available for – despite all that, Caroline had rung back with another date when I wasn't there. David had answered and put it in the diary.

So off we'd sallied, one fine summer's evening, around two corners and up the hill, my heart beating away under my new Whistles shirt, to our dear friends' house. The canopy of magnolia leaves under which we ducked, nodded, it seemed, in a knowing manner as we went up the path. No doubt Caroline would create something magical and effortless as she always did, and the rest of us – please God let it be more than just the four of us, I thought as we waited on the step – would gasp and praise as something Middle Eastern and altogether more adventurous than anything I'd ever attempt arrived on a huge platter down the middle of the table, in their expansive Chalon kitchen, originals by Gillian Ayres and Rose Hilton decorating the walls, and as Caroline, in Chloé, or something similar, wafted in the background, French windows open to the billowing garden, the air full of contented chatter and laughter.

This was indeed the scene one hour later as, after closing the oven door, she joined the rest of us – happily, Silvia and Tim and Giles and Susie were there too – at the table and we settled down to eat, and to drink delicious Margaux, and I, placed opposite Henri, tried to be as normal as possible. This moment, incidentally, in the Defois' kitchen, one of many similar ones, sometimes appears freeze-framed in my mind as I feed sheep in bitter winds or struggle under a sink to mend a leaking tap, as the pinnacle of the Good Life. The moment the scales, thus far finely balanced, became pivotal and tipped, not entirely in my favor. Although, of course, in reality, they tipped the moment I'd walked on to that tennis court with Henri.

We managed some small talk, or at least Henri did, but I could barely look at him. Up until then, which was probably a month after Paris, we'd texted constantly, and of course played tennis, although every moment, every ball played, had felt different and highly charged, but we'd never had to do this: perform in public. And I don't count being with our tennis partners, who were so introspective, so wrapped up in their own hissing and snarling – Susie showing a little mettle by then – so intent on consulting pace meters strapped to their wrists, Giles wondering if they could slip in a swim before a liquid lunch (and by that I mean a smoothie), they wouldn't have noticed if we'd kissed as we'd changed ends. This evening, however, Giles was more himself: more avuncular, the reason we all liked him. Then he ruined it by telling us proudly, as he surreptitiously pushed carbohydrates to the side of his plate, that he'd swum and cycled for three hours that morning.

'Why?' asked Henri.

Giles blinked. 'Why what?'

'Why all this exercise?'

'Oh, because it makes you *feel* so much better.' Always the response, although we knew he meant 'look', having shed his paunch.

'Caroline had a blow-dry. That made her feel better, didn't it, *chérie?*'

'Much. And I look better too, Giles.'

'And I had a manicure,' said Silvia. 'Can't tell you how much better I felt after that.'

Our mouths twitched. Giles gaped.

'Are you seriously trying to tell me you think exercise is some sort of vanity?'

83

'Well, it's certainly self-indulgent,' said David. 'You're pleasing no one but yourself.'

'Yes, but the effort is phenomenal! And I can't exactly channel that into laying a hedge or a drystone wall or something constructive, which I imagine is what you're getting at, in the middle of London, can I?'

'You're being teased, my love,' put in Susie, who, if truth be known, was much brighter than her husband, who'd employed only low cunning to get where he had in the City. 'And it's the trumpeting of your achievements, not the doing of them, that amuses them, as if it's something to be proud of.'

'It is! Bloody hell, while you were all asleep I slipped in fifty lengths!'

'Not to my knowledge you didn't,' purred his wife. 'Or if you did, I slept through it.'

We all shrieked, including Giles.

'But that's surely the point, isn't it?' insisted Henri, leaning in intently. 'You could be having a lovely time making love to Susie,' Susie pulled an appalled face, 'and going out for breakfast afterwards in the sunshine, reading the papers, strolling through the park – enjoying life!'

At this juncture I slipped away to the loo because this was what we had done in Paris. The morning after the fateful night we'd strolled beside the Seine, shamelessly arm in arm, stopped for breakfast at Les Deux Magots where Henri had read *Le Monde* and I'd flipped through *Paris Match*, then we'd headed for the Luxembourg Gardens behind the Sorbonne and spent the morning lying on the grass, kissing and gazing up at the sky like a couple of teenagers. Had it just been a figure of speech or had he said it deliberately, to force the issue? Because there was no doubt, Paris was not a one-off for Henri: he wanted to see a lot more of me; longed for me, his texts repeatedly said.

Did he want more than an affair? No, of course not. We'd only slept together once, but he definitely loved me. Had told me so. I hadn't responded accordingly in the park when he'd said it. It was too potent. Too incendiary. 'Well, we're in love.' Eyes blazing defiantly at our respective spouses, Caroline and David. As if that negated everything else.

Was that what I wanted? I thought, as I made my way back to the kitchen table, still alive with chatter, though not entirely. Two men were silent and watchful, and before I sat down, I caught the eyes of both: Henri and David.

When we walked home, David was silent. He didn't say anything until we'd let the babysitter go, Sasha, Rosie's eldest, who, at sixteen, was deemed responsible.

I quickly set the dishwasher and made to go upstairs, but David was in the kitchen doorway, his face drawn.

'Well?' he asked.

My mouth dried. 'Well what?'

'You know what. Something's going on, Molly. I've known for weeks now. Especially since you came back from Paris. You haven't been near me, haven't let me touch you. And Henri was out there too.'

There didn't seem to be a way out. That's my only excuse for hurting him. I couldn't deny any of the things he'd just said. And a tiny bit of me, Lord knows which subversive bit, wanted to tell him because it was so huge and I couldn't carry it around with me any longer. I'm told this is not normal behavior, but then I've also been told I'm not classic affair material. Certainly at that moment I felt the admission would be better than the terrible fear of constantly feeling I'd be found out: that it would be a relief.

It wasn't, of course, it was dreadful. David's gentle face was agony to watch as it contorted with the pain of some-thing he knew, but didn't want to have confirmed. He put

85

his hand out to the door frame: had to physically steady himself.

'Henri? You slept with Henri? You actually went to bed with him?'

'Yes,' I whispered as the horror dawned on me as well, not that it hadn't already, but David's articulation of it rendered it startlingly vivid and toxic.

'My friend? Our friend? The children's friends' father?'

He could not believe it, even though, as he said, he'd known, or feared. And why should he? It was cataclysmic.

He went past me and sat on the stool at the island which somehow his legs had taken him to. I turned to look. His back was to me, hunched.

'Do you love him?' he managed.

'No,' I said, knowing this was true, in that I was undecided.

Which made it a no, surely.

'And he?'

'He says he is.'

'He would.' He turned to look at me, his eyes hardening. 'Why, Molly?' He gazed at me, aghast. 'Why throw a grenade like this into our life? You've ruined everything, don't you know that? And you don't even love him. For what? Are you that stupid?'

'I – I don't know. Infatuation, I suppose.' God, it sounded so childish.

'You mean flattery,' he said bitterly. 'We all joke about it. You girls flirting with him, but to be taken in . . .'

'No, I wasn't taken in, it wasn't like that. It was much more than that, David.'

'How much more?' he asked with venom.

'I'm just saying,' I knew I had to be careful, 'I wasn't a vulnerable idiot. And I resisted – God, I resisted, David—'

'Bully for you!' he roared.

'What I mean is, I didn't just—'

'Roll over? Spread your legs?'

'DAVID!'

'Mu-um?' A voice called sleepily from the top of the stairs. We froze, appalled.

I swallowed. 'C-coming, Lucy.'

As I left, he sprang up and held my wrist. 'Shame on you, Molly,' he breathed, his eyes burning into mine. His hand on my arm was trembling. His eyes then went deliberately to the stairs and the direction of our child's voice.

'Shame on you.'

THE NEXT FEW weeks were something of a blur. I walked around as if I'd suffered a bereavement. I had, in a way, I'd lost David's love. And I hadn't realized, you see, how terrible that would be. But I also, and I'm ashamed to say this, longed for Henri. The sorrow at the demise of our hitherto happy marriage didn't, I'm afraid, quell, or even diminish, that feeling. I had to text him and tell him, of course, couldn't chance David bumping into him in the street. There was a pause – a hiatus of at least ten minutes. My hands were palsied as I waited. Naturally he'd be appalled – who wouldn't be? I'd broken a cardinal rule, not that we'd made any. The text that finally arrived said: '*It changes nothing*.' I pressed it to my heart. Knew I loved him. Knew I'd been honest when I'd said 'no' to David but knew now that I did.

David wouldn't confront him, I realized that. He wouldn't do it to Caroline, so I just had to be patient and see what he would do. I didn't have to wait long. About three weeks or so. Meanwhile, I'd made myself extremely busy at work, taking on more than I would normally, including a trip to Milan to cover the autumn collections, and one to New York, mostly to avoid seeing Caroline. When I returned, with my case, from Heathrow, David was waiting for me in the kitchen, the children at a friend's house.

'I've put the house on the market,' he said. 'Savills reckon it will go very quickly.'

I sat down carefully on a stool at the island.

'We can't live here any more, you've seen to that. And I don't want a divorce. I love the children too much to do that to them.'

'So do I,' I breathed. And yet I still wanted Henri. But a divorce? No. Unthinkable.

'I've seen a house, with a bit of land, quite a lot of land in fact, in Herefordshire. It needs some work, but it'll be a project. And I can work in Ludlow. There's a firm of lawyers who advertised in the *Gazette* for a trademark lawyer. I can do it standing on my head. It'll be a new start.'

I nodded. This was non-negotiable, I could tell.

'What about my work?'

'As I say, the house will be a project.' Ah.

'Or we can stay. You can leave me, leave this house, and set up with Henri, perhaps on the other side of London.'

My mouth felt sticky. Drained of saliva. 'No,' I whispered. 'We'll go. To Herefordshire.'

He nodded, if not pleased then relieved, at least.

'But, David . . .' I'd had some time to think about this too: about how it might happen, his dream having always been, one day, to move to the country, have a few sheep, a goat, ponies for the children. 'If we go, if we make a new life together and if I don't leave . . . well, you have to forgive me.'

He held my gaze across the kitchen. He'd had time to think too. 'Yes. I realize that.'

'Otherwise it will be unbearable.'

'I know.'

We managed to smile at one another. Not to hug, not yet, but we would, in the fullness of time. I think we both knew, though, in that sad exchange of smiles, that things would never be the same again. I'd seen to that.

The house did indeed go quickly: within three days of being on the market, and to sealed bids, which was exciting, and a distraction. At one point, as David put the phone down to the estate agent, we squealed with delight, forgetting ourselves. Then we remembered and it was back to business as usual.

Quite a lot of money went towards paying off the mortgage, which was huge, we'd overstretched ourselves, but the rest we put on a deposit on the house in Herefordshire, which he took me to see, even though I knew my opinion mattered little; it was a fait accompli.

To be honest, I was faintly appalled. The house was large and rambling, too rambling, with third-story attic rooms which were damp with crumbling sash windows and from which, when I wrenched one open, I could see only a vast, empty landscape.

'As far as the eye can see,' said David proudly, joining me at the open window.

'You're kidding. That's not a smallholding, that's a farm. Who's going to run it?'

'I will, of course. We'll have sheep. They're terribly easy to manage. Nothing to it.'

Famous last words.

The next few weeks were a blur of packing up and finding schools after the summer for the children, who were, by turns, aghast, horrified and appalled at leaving their friends, but David swept all that aside.

'But . . . don't they mind leaving?' Silvia had asked, astonished, as all our friends were.

'They'll do as I say,' replied David. And they did, because they respected him and he was always firm, but they trusted him. He was a very good father. He didn't try to sell it to them, or ask their opinion, knowing they were too young for such responsibility and pressure. That it was unfair, as we privately thought when friends canvassed their twelve-year-olds as to which school they wanted to go to. 'Be the parent,' David would mutter under his breath. And he was. A good one.

Anyway, as I say, the weeks flashed by and within a twinkling, we'd gone, or were going, the removal men having advanced ahead of us that morning. David and the children and I were poised now in the road to say goodbye to our friends: Silvia and Tim, Rosie and Jamie, Giles and Susie and, of course, Henri and Caroline. Caroline I hugged first to get it over with, feeling like Brutus, but Henri came last. His heart beat against mine as he held me tightly, but briefly.

'Never goodbye,' he said fiercely in my ear.

I couldn't reply. Was shocked he'd even dared to say this with David's eagle eye upon us and – oh dear God, was Caroline watching us too? Her face a little paler than usual? Smile a bit tighter? Perhaps I was being paranoid. I certainly hadn't had a hint of it when we'd hugged moments earlier.

At any rate, I hopped in the car and in moments we were off, with promises to come back soon and cries that they were all to come to *us*, the whole lot of them, to come and stay, we had *so* much room, all the children too, the children, who, as we purred down the familiar, tree-lined street I loved, ran along behind us as David beeped the horn and our children waved and hung out of the windows, shouting their goodbyes.

Minutes later we rounded the corner, then another on to the main road, and fell silent. I glanced in the rear-view mirror and caught Lucy's eye. She gave me a hard look then turned away. I had, of course, wondered how much she'd heard that night, but it occurred to me now that it was more than I'd hoped.

Fortunately children adapt very quickly and we were lucky in that the weather was kind and Herefordshire shone for us. We'd thrown money at the removal firm and they moved us in seamlessly. We flung open all the creaking French windows and lived in the garden, picnicking and barbecuing, David on top form waving the tongs, with excited chatter about maybe a pool, certainly the old grass tennis court could be mown and re-marked, and a trampoline, we had so much space. And despite their initial resistance, I could see the children reveling in it: exploring, running down the grassy bank to the river which snaked through the valley, certainly the younger two, and even Lucy, who'd been withdrawn when we arrived, seemed to thaw. She and I spent hours in the garden which she loved but which left me cold, but if she was out there digging and weeding and exclaiming at a new flower she'd found, I would be too, beside her, with David, I knew, passing by with a wheelbarrow, looking on approvingly.

I felt I was being a good girl. Trying really hard and behaving well. I wasn't a country girl at heart, had been brought up in suburban Andover where my most rural pursuit had been to learn to ride, but I could adapt. I admired the sixty-odd sheep we seemed to have acquired from the old owners, fed the ducks, who I quite liked, the chickens, who scared me with their flutterings and peckings, gardened with Lucy, played endlessly with the other two, helping with dens and camps, praised David for being so clever and finding this place, and we even made love, for the first time in – well, a while – and it was fine. Really fine. David would probably say it was terrific. He bounced about the house and even hummed to the radio, because although I knew a lot of him was still furious with me, he was so enamored of his new life, the one he'd always dreamed of, he forgot to be cross.

My heart ached, though. Of course the farmhouse was lovely, but it was David's dream, not mine. And it was so remote, this valley of ours. The nearest house was half a mile away, another farm. We weren't even on the edge of a village, which, when we'd vaguely discussed it years ago, he'd promised me. But he hadn't had to keep any promises, had he? And I loved people. Wondered if I'd survive without them: without my lovely girlfriends, my job, the comrades I had at work, the noise, the bustle, the being-aliveness of London. More than anything, though, I missed Henri. I'd written to him, before I left, saying this break had to be permanent, final. That I owed it to David. No more texting after 16th July, no emails, nothing. He'd written back saying he respected that and although it would drive him insane, he'd do his best. My heart longed for him, though: my funny French friend, who made me laugh more than anyone else, whose lightness of soul was so different to David's quiet thoughtfulness, whose joie de vivre just elevated my spirits. It was with terror that I felt them collapse now.

And then he contacted me. At about this time of plummeting mood, as I wondered how to rally, felt almost breathless with the effort of contemplating making yet another Victoria sponge with Minna, followed by a trip to the village fête, he sent me a text.

'*I can't do this. I miss you so much. You became my life. My spirit. Can I just talk to you? Can I ring you in half an hour?*'

I felt euphoria flood through me, almost knocking me off my feet. I was at the kitchen sink at the time, looking out to where David was overseeing a bonfire with the children, letting them throw branches on but keeping a weather eye as they pranced about. This should have been the moment to text back and say:

'*No. Absolutely not.*' No kiss.

Instead, saliva evaporating in my mouth, I texted back: '*Yes. I miss you so much too. XX* '

My breathing became desperately shallow, but I set about making the Victoria sponge on my own, without calling Minna in to help. When it was in the oven, I went outside. David was on his own now, the children having drifted off to the tennis court.

'Darling, could you pop to the shops? I've got a cake in the oven and I've just realized there's nothing for lunch.'

He looked irritated. 'I've just started a bonfire.'

'Well, I can watch that, from the window.'

He frowned. Fires were man's work.

'Can't we just have omelettes? The chickens are laying like smoke, we need to eat our produce, Molly.'

Something sanctimonious about this annoyed me. Plus my emotions were on a knife edge. 'We do eat our sodding produce. Every day I pull up asparagus, or new potatoes, or runner beans, and the children are up to here with eggs. Just occasionally I'd like some mozzarella, basil and a few lentils, is that all right?'

'London food.'

'Yes, OK, but we don't have to be so purist, such exponents of the Good Life that we become prigs, do we? Can't we just be ourselves? Can't *I* be myself?'

'Oh for God's sake, Molly, stop turning everything into such a ridiculous drama!'

'Me? I just came out and asked you to go to the fucking shops!'

It was the first time we'd rowed in weeks. Since Paris. Because David didn't argue. He kept it all in. This was big for him. It was as if one of those carefully connected fuses had popped out.

'Right,' he said, seething. 'I'll go to the bloody shops. Because if Molly wants something, Molly must have it.'

'That is *so* unfair,' I stormed as he stalked past me through the back door into the kitchen, snatching up his keys on the dresser, heading to the front drive and his car. I heard the engine rev loudly, a noisy crunch of gravel, then he roared off down the lane.

I stood for a moment, fuming. Irritated that my moment of pleasure, my first for weeks, had been spoiled. Then I felt ashamed. But not for long. I glanced at my watch. Ten to twelve. Five minutes. Tennis would occupy the children for a while. I turned and hastened inside, pulling my phone out of my jeans pocket, checking it was charged.

Up in my bedroom, he rang, and we talked and it was heaven just to hear his voice again. We didn't talk for long because Tatiana, his youngest, suddenly appeared from a piano lesson, so we quickly signed off, telling each other this couldn't happen again, but knowing it would. That it was the thin end of the wedge. That we were pretending. I pocketed my phone, feeling lighter, as if my feet could leave the floor, as if I'd been injected with steroids. I went to the window, threw it wide, breathed in deeply and exhaled. As I raised my face to the heavens I mouthed: 'Thank you, God.'

It was at that point that I heard the sirens. The wail in

the distance which got louder as a police car flashed past my yard at the front of the house. It was followed swiftly by another vehicle, an ambulance this time. Half an hour later, I would see another police car, when I was in the back garden, poking the fire. I'd spot it through the French windows, parked in the yard. Two policemen would come around the side of the house, and approach me at the bonfire. The older one would remove his hat, twist it nervously in his hands, and tell me David was dead.

*a*s I regarded my children now, nearly six years later, I wondered if I was ready for what they were suggesting. I'd told myself I'd live at the farm forever. Would never move. My mind, my heart and my soul had collectively made a pact. Yes, I'd effectively killed my husband, given reckless power to his habitually cautious foot on that pedal, sped his car too fast around the bend which he usually took so slowly and into the path of that oncoming tractor, but by golly I'd make amends. And never go back to what *I* considered to be the Good Life, the best life. Or anything similar. How could I pop to the fancy grocer's at the end of my new road in South Kensington? How could I nip to Harvey Nichols, or have lunch in Beauchamp Place? Didn't I know I had a project to finish? That I owed it to David's memory? To our love?

The children were waiting: watching me closely in the small basement flat, the pedestrians passing by in the window above, their feet clicking briskly.

'Why not, Mum?' Lucy asked in the voice she used when she was trying not to upset me.

If only she knew. How I'd upset her. Not the bit she knew about, the bit she'd overheard, the next bit. How I'd ruined her young life. Watched, as she rebelled at her new school, got into trouble, refused to work so grief-stricken was she and then at the last moment, almost in a show of defiance, studied hard for her GCSEs and, bright girl that she was, got them all with A stars. But then regressed again, as if to prove she could turn it on and off just like that. I'd had to sit by as she'd drunk too much and come home at all hours: I recalled the shouting matches we'd have in the kitchen as I waited up for her. How she'd made the wrong friends, refused to go to university and headed instead to London, with no plan and no money, how worried I'd been.

Ironically she'd found her path through her love of the country, or at least of nature and horticulture – a love so like her father's I sometimes wondered if it was a homage to him. With no help from anyone except a bank who'd given her a loan – how I wished I'd been a fly on the wall in that meeting, witnessed her giving it what for, using all the powers of her considerable persuasion – she had taken a lease on a shop in Islington and turned it into a florist. She'd never looked back. She'd made a remarkable go of her new life in London – which she'd missed, had always missed, she'd confided to me once in rare tears. Yes, if only Lucy knew.

I gazed into her beautiful blue, almond-shaped eyes, eyes full of concern for me now. 'I . . . I'm not sure,' I stuttered.

'Come on, Mum, it'd be brilliant, you'd love it,' urged Nico, who, by knowing less, was less complicated. 'Sell the farm and we'll all move back.'

Minna, I noticed, was quiet. Her heart had recently been broken and the pieces were scattered back home in the valley. Ted Forrester was the culprit, a local lad she'd been seeing on and off since she was fourteen. I wondered if she'd had second thoughts, having initially been caught up in her siblings' enthusiasm.

'What about Granny and Grandpa?' I objected, playing for time. My parents had rushed from Andover to be near me.

'G and G love it down there, they won't move,' Lucy said. 'But it doesn't mean we have to stay, they'd hate that.'

It was true, my parents were independent and having been provincial were now happily rural. Like David, and like so many people, they'd dreamed of escaping to the country – had watched endless relocation programs on the television – and were at the farm even now, feeding my flock, happily seeing to the animals, walking the dogs.

I put my head in my hands and kneaded my forehead with my fingertips. 'I don't know.'

I didn't.

'Sleep on it,' Lucy said firmly, which seemed like the best idea of the night. I nodded, not quite trusting my voice.

And so I did. We all did. In varying degrees of discomfort. Nico declared the sofa the most uncomfortable thing he'd ever slept on in his life and why did it have to be him just because he was the youngest and the boy, which we told him was precisely why, and Minna, according to Lucy, ground her teeth in her sleep. Minna retorted that Lucy slept like a starfish and was entirely selfish in bed, but I also heard shrieks of laughter coming from their room. I was pleased for Minna. She missed her sister. And although she'd never admit it, I'd hazard Lucy missed Minna, too.

The following morning Lucy cornered me in Sophia's bedroom. She came in and sat down on the edge of the bed with a cup of tea she'd brought me, her eyes full of even greater intent. Mine, I knew, almost matched them, but I lowered them, giving nothing away.

'Do it, Mum.'

I looked up at her. Took the mug she handed me and gave her a small smile.

'We'll see.'

I sipped it silently, thereby telling her I wasn't saying any more, and she left, casting me a final, meaningful look as she shut the door, disappearing to get ready for work.

Selling the farm of course would be the first step, I thought, as I quietly washed up last night's supper things at Lucy's tiny sink – Lucy had gone but Minna and Nico were still fast asleep. I raised my head from the soapsuds to stare at the wood-chip wall and allowed myself to give it a moment of serious contemplation, proper consideration, for the very first time. I realized it made me feel euphoric. I felt a huge rush of relief. To release that millstone from around my neck, that terrible weight, the source of so much pain, so much anxiety: the relentless demands of the animals, the crumbling brickwork, the constant re-patching and mending of barns . . . yes. I could say goodbye to all that. In the knowledge that I'd given it my best shot. I hadn't fled as soon as David had died, I'd gritted my teeth and done my best. I caught my breath as I sensed the far-off promise of possibility, the distant click of something quietly slotting into place, in the fullness of time, which was now. Everything turns at some point, and for me, that moment had arrived.

Wiping my hands, I left a note for Minna and Nico. Then, shutting the door quietly behind me and with a degree of stealth, I left the darkened flat. I walked up the basement steps into the sunshine and headed west along the Brompton Road. My destination was the little café beside the pub at the end of Lastow Mews and it didn't take me long to walk there. Once installed at a table outside, I ordered a cappuccino, fished my phone from my pocket, and rang Peter Cox.

Peter was a sweet man: tweedy, affable and good-natured. He had indeed taken me out to supper once – he'd gone so pink when he'd asked me outside the baker's in the village I hadn't the heart to say no – but he was a tiny bit long-winded and very preoccupied with his orchid collection, about which he'd enlightened me at great length over supper. I hadn't minded. I'd nodded and smiled and eaten my whitebait and chips, thinking there were worse things than sitting in a cosy pub with a pleasant enough man talking about potted plants.

I rang him now, knowing there would be no awkward-ness: he was far from stupid and had known I'd been going through the motions that night. There'd been no spark and he hadn't followed it up. His secretary put me through and I outlined my plan. There was a pause at the other end of the line.

'Well yes, the house itself should be fairly straightfor-ward to sell, as long as you price it right'

'You mean low.'

'I do rather, in this market.'

'OK.'

'But the question is whether you sell the land sepa-rately. Not many people want as much as ninety acres; it's neither one thing nor another. Not enough to be a viable farm and too much for most people to manage as a hobby.'

'Tell me about it.'

'Well, you do manage it, Molly, I know that, but it's a struggle. A headache. Most people want ten acres with a paddock for a pony and that's it. Or a thousand, of course.'

'So you think sell the land separately?'

'I do. The house will go much quicker.'

'But who will want the land?'

It occurred to us both at the same time. Peter cleared his throat. He'd been one of the people at the bar that night in the Fox and Hounds when I hadn't materialized.

'Well, Paddy might, obviously.'

'Yes. Obviously.' His land abutted mine, from his cottage a mile away in the valley.

'And he'd possibly even take the animals too.'

'Oh, I doubt it. He's terribly rude about them.'

'Well yes, I have no idea, of course,' he said quickly. 'Not my field. And they can always go to market.'

'Exactly.' For what, though? I wondered. Meat? I hoped not. The lambs were obviously sold for just that, but well before I'd had time to get to know them, and for all their stress-making abilities, I was fond of my female breeding flock, my ewes. Some of them had delivered lambs for me for five years now, most producing twins, and one, Rita, always triplets.

I'd been staggered in the beginning when Anna had told me her husband could tell his flock apart by their bleats but I could do that now. Particularly Agnes, who had a throaty bark, and Coochie, the oldest and slowest, who almost mewed like a cat and always came to the fence to have her head scratched. No, I couldn't sell Agnes or Coochie. So what, have them here? In the little back garden? I gazed down the road to the mews house, basking in the sunshine. Obviously not. Maybe Anna would have them? Anyway, I'd cross that bridge when I came to it.

'Tell you what,' Peter was saying, 'I'll have a little ask around and see who's interested. There's Adam and Jo Fox on your other side. They might well want the land.'

'Oh yes, try the Foxes,' I said urgently, far more keen to

talk to them than the irascible Mr Campbell. 'Try them first, Peter, would you?'

'I will. Although, they're getting on a bit . . .'

'But maybe for their children?'

We chatted a bit more and he said how sad everyone would be to see me go but I brushed that aside with a laugh, saying that it wasn't as if I'd been born and bred in the valley, and being a man, he didn't push it.

Instead he put the receiver down, promising to get on to it immediately, and as I pocketed my own phone, I realized the die was cast. I was talking to estate agents. Only Peter, but still. My heart quickened in slight panic. Well, not entirely cast. Not until a buyer was found, contracts exchanged, and that could be – God, months, a year away. No, no, nothing was decided. I'd just inched my life forward a very tiny bit. Turned the dial, the one I envisaged unlocking a safe, until something, that click I'd imagined hearing earlier, flung wide the door.

I rang my mother next, to canvass her opinion, but got my father instead, who sounded strangely delighted.

'Best decision you've made for years, love. Leave the ruddy place. It's a burden on your shoulders, or at least it's become one. Get shot of it. I say, good old Uncle Cuthbert! Don't remember the fella, I must admit, but your mother told me some time ago with great excitement. Some distant relation of David's, I gather?'

'Not that distant, actually – his father's brother. I'm so pleased you don't think I'm abandoning you, Dad. Jumping ship . . .' I paused, my eyes simultaneously following a black cab, which had turned left from the main road down into the mews and was slowing down and stopping now, outside the pink house.

'Not at all, love! I think it's a great idea. Now listen,

there's a lovely new development near Ludlow, modern houses—'

'Um, Dad, I'm really sorry.' I was on my feet suddenly, watching the cab door open. A moccasin appeared. 'I'm going to have to go. See what Mum thinks, would you?'

'Oh, she'll agree with me. We've been saying it for ages, in private. The children too. It's high time you moved on.'

'Yes, I know, I've spoken to them. Um – bye, Dad, speak soon,' I said quickly, knowing he'd hasten straight back to the test match on the telly.

I riffled in my bag and left money in my saucer for the coffee, eyes still peeled. The tall blond man, in a baggy sea-green shirt today, obviously not tucked in, jeans artistically ripped at the knee, was now out of the cab and paying the driver at the window. If I was quick, I could make it. I moved, which I can, because trust me lambing keeps you fit, across the road, under the arch, and down the little cobbled street. I had a few moments in hand because the taxi driver was obviously rooting about for some change, whilst the blond man leaned through the open window and chatted to him. So I was able to intercept him, just as he turned away and was pocketing his change. Just as he walked to the door, key in hand.

'Excuse me,' I said breathlessly, aware that he was terribly handsome with the most terrific green eyes and wishing I'd had the foresight to put a bit of make-up on when I'd left Lucy's flat.

He looked at me, surprised. A hand went up to push a flop of golden hair streaked faintly with grey out of those startling eyes and away from a tanned face. He smiled inquiringly.

'Excuse me,' I faltered again. 'I – I just wondered – could I possibly ask you something?'

'By all means.' He looked amused, smiling down at me from quite a height, as one might regard a child.

'You see, my husband's uncle lived here, in this house. The pink one. Cuthbert Faulkner. My late husband, that is, and well, obviously it was his late uncle too.' I was getting myself in a terrible tangle and could feel myself coloring. 'And – well, the thing is, I came the other day, but I wasn't aware that anyone lived here, so—'

'You're Cuthbert's niece?' His green eyes brightened, intrigued.

'In-law. Yes.'

'Ah, so you're inheriting. Camilla told me you'd popped round.'

'That's right,' I said gratefully, so pleased I hadn't had to say the 'i' word. It sounded so proprietary. So entitled. And full of cupidity.

'Well, I'm Felix Carrington. Lovely to meet you.'

He was outstretching a tanned hand which I took, another warm smile blasting down on me, loads of white teeth. Were they bleached? I wondered.

'We knew you were the heir, don't worry, and I'll have him out of here in a jiffy, I promise, before it's all official and everything. It's just, we did wonder…' He knitted his brow and looked anxious. 'Well, Cuthbert only died a matter of weeks ago and you know it's quite hard, there's so much to do. I hope you'll bear with us?' His eyes searched mine. 'Just for a few days?'

I gaped at him. 'S-sorry . . . ?'

'Oh Lord – what am I doing making you stand outside in the street? Come in, come in! You'll have a cuppa?'

He'd opened the door before I could utter a word, and was busy extracting his key from the lock when Camilla appeared down the hall, a bulging black bin bag in one hand, her jacket in the other.

'Hi, Felix, I was just off . . . oh.' Her face darkened as she recognized me. 'It's you. Back again? Give us a chance, can't you?'

'Oh – um, I—'

But she'd deliberately turned away from me. 'I'll be back tomorrow, Felix. I've done the meds and made a start on all the stuff in the desk. You just need to feed the cat.'

And flashing me another sharp look she strode past, out to the dustbins where she dumped her black sack, letting the lid fall with a defiant clatter before making for her black Mini.

'Don't mind her,' Felix told me as he shut the door behind us. He strode down the hall to the kitchen and I scurried after him. Reaching up, he unlocked the French windows to the garden and pushed them open, then turned to face me. 'She was very fond of Cuthbert and has her own views on what should happen now, which frankly she should keep to herself. Now.' He beamed, hands on hips. 'What's your poison? Earl Grey? Builder's? Mint, too . . . I think . . .' He turned and rummaged in a cupboard. 'But it could be about a hundred years old.' He discarded a few dusty packets. 'Lord, look at these, museum pieces. And then you'll have to excuse me very briefly while I dash upstairs to administer, but I'll only be a mo', and I'll make you your tea first. I might take him one too, actually.'

'H-him?' I perched on a stool, completely at a loss.

'My father. Upstairs.'

'Your father? Is upstairs?'

He turned from filling the kettle at the sink.

'Yes, in bed. He's had the flu. Quite badly, and of course it's a bugger to shift at that age.'

'Yes – but . . . why is your father . . . *who* is your father?'

'Why, Robert, of course.' He saw my blank face. 'Cuthbert's partner?'

'His partner?'

'Yes, didn't you know?'

'Cuthbert was . . . gay?'

'Yes.' He rummaged in another cupboard. 'Dad was his boyfriend. Oh, hello, ginger and lemon. That do?'

'Yes. Of course.' My head was spinning. 'So how long had they . . .'

'Been together? Ooh, about twenty years, I suppose. Not officially, of course. No civil partnership or anything like that. And plenty of sabbaticals along the way.' He laughed. 'In their younger days they fought like cat and dog, but on and off, yes, about that.'

'I – I didn't know.'

'Didn't you?' He looked surprised. Then shrugged. 'Well, no reason why you should, I suppose. The family weren't exactly close, I gather.'

'No, they weren't.' David didn't seem to have any relatives. They certainly didn't gather at the drop of a hat like mine.

'And of course, years ago it was much less accepted, so . . .' he shrugged again, 'it was less talked about, too, I guess.'

'Yes,' I agreed, wondering how he, the son, fitted in. I was about to form another question, not that one, of course, something more oblique, when Felix glanced above my head. His eyes brightened and he broke into a smile. I heard a shuffling behind me in the hallway.

'Ah, speak of the devil!' Felix cried. 'If it isn't the old man of the sea himself. I didn't expect to see you up, Pa. How are you feeling?'

'Much better, darling.' A deep, quavering, cut-glass voice made me turn. When I did, it was to see a tall, rather grand-looking old gentleman, who, despite the silk paisley dressing gown and slippers, was still managing to pull off dapper. He had a thick shock of white hair swept back from his forehead and chiseled features that I could see would have made him very handsome in his youth. He still was handsome, in fact, and his son was the image of him.

'Although I've still got this wretched cough that I'd bloody well like to get shot of. Who said old age is not for cissies? Bette Davis, I think. I say, who's this delightful creature?' He gave me a dazzling smile, his whole face creasing up as he carefully maneuvered down the step into the kitchen, holding the door frame but still keeping his eyes on me. 'Someone you haven't told me about, you rascal?' He held out a liver-spotted hand, eyes twinkling. 'Good morning, my dear, is he behaving? No? Didn't think so.'

Felix laughed. 'Oh no, Dad, this is – I say, I'm so sorry, I don't even know your name.'

'Molly Faulkner,' I breathed.

'Molly Faulkner,' repeated Felix. 'My dad, Robert Carrington.' He gave his father a gentle look. 'The clue's in the name, obviously. Molly is Cuthbert's niece,' he told him carefully. He handed me a mug of tea but his eyes were still on his father. 'She's inheriting his estate.'

CHAPTER 9

*R*obert's manners were as impeccable as his appearance. He didn't miss a beat.

'Of course it is, and naturally you are! Well, how lovely to meet you, my dear, I hope you'll stay a while. Have you been offered some refreshment?'

Ever since I'd met these delightful people, all I'd been offered was tea, hospitality and warmth. I felt shabby in comparison.

'I have,' I said, jumping up to take the hand he'd extended across the table. 'And I'm so sorry to be here at all, disturbing you like this. It's just – well, I couldn't resist another peek at the house even though I popped round the other day and met Camilla and then I saw Felix going in and – well . . .' I felt myself reddening. How *awful*. Was I a stalker? I certainly sounded like one.

'Naturally, naturally!' he broke in, rescuing me. 'Who wouldn't be intrigued? I certainly would! Would you like to look around properly, pop upstairs? Happily I've made the bed but believe me, that's not always the case!'

'No, no!' This was beyond embarrassing, but to explain

that I was more curious than covetous would be fraught with difficulties too, given the circumstances. 'I'm intruding quite enough as it is and – and I am so sorry about your terrible loss. You must be devastated.'

Robert's face collapsed briefly and he momentarily lost his composure. He regained it quickly enough, though, nodding.

'Thank you, my dear. Time heals, of course, but he was my very greatest friend. Naturally I miss him dreadfully.'

'We all do,' said Felix sadly.

'Do you . . . have any pictures of him?' I asked tentatively. If only I'd known him, this man who'd engendered such warmth and tenderness. 'Only David and I never really knew him, I'm not sure why . . .'

'Do I! Masses of them. Come with me, my dear, nothing would give me greater pleasure.' He turned and led the way, shuffling with alacrity in his slippers back down the hall to the sitting room. I made haste.

'Dad, shall I make you some tea?' called Felix after us.

'Please, darling,' he called back.

Loving the way he called his son darling, I followed Robert as he crossed to a mahogany bureau at the far end of the room beside the French windows. The top was crowded with photographs but he carefully selected a large studio portrait. It was of a handsome man in his sixties, wearing a velvet jacket and a floral shirt. He regarded it fondly for a moment before passing it to me.

'There he is. You'll see a resemblance, I think.'

To David's father, he meant, and I spotted it immediately. They were both handsome men, but this one looked more genial.

'He and your husband's father fell out years ago, of course. Money, I believe. It usually is. To do with their father's will, I think. David tried to heal the rift when he was quite a young man. He was fond of Cuthbert. It didn't work but Cuthbert was grateful. And then of course your husband's loyalty essentially lay with his father and the two families drifted.'

'I didn't know that,' I said, surprised. About David stepping in to help. I was taken aback that I hadn't known.

'I wonder why he didn't mention it? I suppose I never knew Cuthbert, but even so . . .' I studied the strong jaw, the ironic smile as if on the verge of something much broader. 'What a shame. Although, hang on.' I lowered the photo and gazed into space, racking my brains. 'I do vaguely remember some drama, about David's relatives, when I first met him. But we were very young and totally preoccupied with our own lives.'

'Not those of boring older people.'

'Well, quite. Yes, perhaps he did mention it, but I hadn't taken much notice?'

'They did keep in touch, you know.'

'David and Cuthbert? I didn't.'

'Wrote and then emailed, when Cuthbert got the hang of it.' He smiled. 'He was something of a Luddite. Had lunch about once a year in the City, too. Christmas time. Wheelers, I believe.'

I stared at him, astounded.

'Are you sure? He certainly never mentioned that.' Never said – off for my annual jaunt with old Cuthbert. Why?

Robert shrugged. 'Perhaps it was one of many at that time of year?'

'Even so . . .'

'I met him once, David. He came to the house.'

'He came here?' Now I really was staggered. 'When? Why didn't he say?' Obviously Robert didn't know the answer to that either, but such was my astonishment I couldn't help but voice it.

'Well . . .' he hesitated. 'There was our sexuality, of course.'

'Yes, but David wasn't like that!'

'No, but . . .' Robert picked his words carefully. 'I gather his father might have been. And from Cuthbert, I also understood that your husband feared his disapproval dreadfully. I believe Michael was frightfully old school.'

'Yes, he was. He was a nightmare, if I'm honest.' My late father-in-law made no secret of his homophobia, his intolerance of immigrants, or even women working full-time. I'd had a hard time over that. And he was scary, too. I realized Cuthbert's name had never been mentioned in my in-laws' house.

'David was terrified of his father, as you know,' Robert told me gently. 'He probably got so used to keeping his uncle's secret, he felt it easier to withhold it from you, in case it slipped out. To his parents, inadvertently. Not that you would deliberately, but you wouldn't, perhaps, ascribe it so much importance? People never do when the secrets aren't their own. Or – I don't know – if you'd told one of the children and it came out that way, over lunch, or something.'

'Yes,' I agreed, knowing that sharing a confidence made it uncontrollable, and that David liked control. Not in a horrid way, he wasn't domineering, he just didn't like anything messy and chaotic, but still, it was odd. I didn't think David and I had secrets. Well, except my socking great one, of course. And this was tiny, in comparison, so I shouldn't mind. I did, though. I replaced the photograph.

'But then . . . when his parents died . . .' I was thinking aloud now.

'Yes, I agree.' Robert frowned, thoughtful. 'Some sort

of warped loyalty, perhaps, to his father's memory? It was that dreadful tsunami, wasn't it, not so long ago? I believe the lunches had tailed off by then, both men were so busy with their careers, so maybe . . . I don't know, my dear.' He looked anxious, as if worried he'd upset me.

'Heavens, no, why should you know? And it's no big deal, a man having a quiet lunch with his uncle, it's just . . . well, you never really know someone, do you? I mean, completely?'

He smiled. 'Never. But surely that's what's so interesting. Not having it all on a plate?' He chuckled. 'Cuthbert certainly kept a few things back from me, I'm sure. I know I did too.'

I sighed. 'Yes, that's probably where I go wrong. I have a nasty feeling I'm dripping off the sides of the plate and all over the table too.'

He laughed. 'Well, that can be equally disarming.' He picked up another photo, this time of him and Cuthbert together. Gazed at it a moment then passed it to me. 'But we'll never know, will we? They've both taken those Christmas lunches to the grave.'

I looked at the picture of Robert and Cuthbert, smiling broadly, arm in arm in the sunshine. It was clearly taken abroad: southern France perhaps, with cypress trees behind.

There was so much I wanted to ask David now. To be honest, I'd never taken much interest in his family. His father had been cold and aloof, but his mother was lovely, if a little quiet. Bullied, I'd always thought. I should have asked her. Would she have told me? Possibly not. A tiny bit of me wondered whether David had been embarrassed by his uncle's set-up. Yes, he was modern and broad-minded, but . . . perhaps it was different within his own family? He definitely had a streak of his father's conformity about him. It wouldn't be that he'd disapprove, but it might have made him uncomfortable. Yes, that was it. Particularly with the children. Who he believed in shielding from things which they didn't need to know. Gossip about our friends, for instance, which some parents shared – mothers who sat smoking with their teenage daughters sharing tidbits about the locals – he thought that appalling. Heavens, how the girls would have loved it, though, if he'd included us in the lunches. A gay uncle? How cool was that.

Felix had joined us now, with a proper pot of tea on a tray, fresh cups and saucers – I realized I'd abandoned my mug in the kitchen and he'd clearly had to wait for the kettle to boil again. Robert motioned for us to sit at the other end of the room, where the creamy sofas were under the bay window, amongst the books and the art. I perched and sipped my tea when Felix had poured it and looked around at the crowded walls. Robert had eased himself into what was clearly a familiar old armchair and put his feet on a faded footstool. I could feel Felix's eyes on me.

I turned to Robert. 'This is your house,' I blurted out suddenly. 'Not mine. You and Cuthbert were as good as married. It's not my inheritance, it's yours.'

Robert gazed in surprise. Then threw his head back and laughed. 'Nonsense, my dear! It's not remotely mine. I never expected it and Cuthbert never intended it.'

'You talked about it?'

'No, but—'

'Well then, how do you know? How do you know, if he hadn't died as suddenly as he did, that he wouldn't have left it to you?'

'Because it wasn't in his will.'

'He didn't leave a will.'

'No, so in a way, he did, didn't he?' he said calmly, smiling still. 'He left it to the will of the country. The law of the land. I believe he didn't want the responsibility. That was very Cuthbert.'

Felix was very still.

'Anyway, I don't want it,' said Robert firmly, wrapping his dressing gown tighter over his lap and crossing his ankles; a regrouping gesture. 'I'm off to Felix's studio, to be surrounded by lovely paintings in my dotage.'

'Oh, you're an artist?' I turned to Felix.

Felix smiled. 'Yes, but there's less paint these days. Dad's remembering the old days with a bit of wishful thinking. I do installations now, that sort of thing.'

'I see.' I didn't. What was an installation? I racked my brain. 'Like a Tracey Emin bed type of thing?'

'Well yes, that's rather old hat now, but in a way. Fine Art, or the practice of it. Turner Prize territory.'

'Oh Turner! I love him. All blazing sunsets and ships at dawn.'

Father and son smiled and Felix began to talk about the great room in the attic he could give his father, at which point I remembered the Turner Prize was about people standing stark naked in buckets with rubber ducks in their mouths, but it was too late to retract my gaffe. I also felt I'd offered up the house in a rash moment but that it had been equally swiftly refused, so I'd surely done my bit – made the gesture? I could see my children's horrified faces; hear their shrieks – what are you *doing*, Mum? We're the only blood relatives, it's the law! I quaked silently at my narrow escape and concentrated on my tea.

Felix chatted on a bit longer about an artist called Jean Pasteau, whom he much admired, whilst I admired his brown ankles between his jeans and his moccasins. I nodded knowledgeably all the while, trying to concentrate on what he was saying, about the way contemporary art was heading today and how it filled a gap in an increasingly mechanized society, brought people together through discussion, but if I wasn't looking at his elegant ankles I was gazing into his sea-green eyes in his tanned face and that was distracting too, so I went back to the ankles as if deep in thought, scalding my lips on the hot, strange-tasting tea in an effort to drink it quickly and take my grubby presence more rapidly from these rarefied, cultured people, the like of whom one didn't stumble across much in the lanes of Herefordshire.

I thought of Peter, blushing his way through supper in a tweed jacket he clearly hadn't worn for years, bursting out of it as he described, in detail, exactly how he'd extended his greenhouse for his plant collection. Of Paddy flinging a dead chicken at my feet, the life of which I'd apparently mismanaged, before roaring rudely off in his pickup. I realized it didn't have to be like that. That there was another life. Here. One with sunlit antiques and paint-ings in elegantly curtained rooms; thoughtful, engaging people who dressed well and talked of literature and the theater before popping to the latest exhibition at the Tate Modern. I wanted this new life so much it hurt.

I'd have to shape up, of course. I sat up. Lose a few pounds, get some new clothes – I tucked my old espadrilles under the sofa, aware that bits of rope were coming adrift from the wedges – have some highlights, that type of thing. But I'd done all that before in my other life, albeit juggling small children madly so always slightly frayed at the edges – look closely when I flew back from the agency to make supper and supervise homework and you'd see egg down the front of the Nicole Farhi shirt, or find bits of Nico's Lego in my handbag – but it wasn't complete anathema. I could do it. And now I had more time, I could do it prop-erly. I really could become, not the yummy mummy I'd aspired to be in Nappy Valley, but one of those truly leisured women in SW3, the ones we south-of-the-river-dwellers scorned but secretly envied, with their manicured nails, their lunches in Daphne's, their flits to the Saatchi gallery before tea in Peter Jones with friends.

Ah, yes, friends. Silvia and I had originally kept in touch, but only via email. And only because she was so persistent. I hadn't answered her calls. Rosie had tried hard too, left loads of messages on the answerphone, and Caroline also, although she'd abruptly gone quiet. I'd often wake in the small hours, wondering how much she knew.

All had eventually given up, assuming sadly I'd gone into my shell after David's death. The last time I'd seen them had been at the funeral, which was a blur, although Rosie had driven down unannounced once afterwards, had a cup of tea. But I hadn't made her very welcome. I'd been so terrified to see her, feeding the hens in the front yard as her convertible BMW drove in, my hand frozen on the grain in the bucket as I recognized her smiling and waving at the wheel. Speech had deserted me as she got out in smart jeans and long leather boots with a huge bunch of flowers. I couldn't get rid of her fast enough, and it was a long drive from London. I'd been so scared she was going to say something about Henri or Caroline, which I knew would send me shooting back to square one in terms of guilt and remorse and depression, that I'd manufactured an appointment with a lawyer to get rid of her. She'd known, though. I'd seen her sad face as she got back in the car. Knew she'd tell Silvia: 'I did my best, Silv, honestly. But she doesn't want to know.'

'Maybe we remind her too much of what she had?'

'Maybe.'

But I could find new friends here, I thought, spotting, out of the corner of my eye, a beautiful coiffed woman of about my age through the window, heading off down the mews. I had friends at home, of course: Anna, enormous fun and jolly but ten years older than me, and Tia, of course, and—

I realized with a start that my tea was cold and the room very quiet. Robert and Felix were looking at me.

'Are you all right, my dear?' Robert looked anxious, his face coming closer to mine.

'Me? Yes! Gosh, sorry.' My cup clattered down into its saucer. 'Don't know where I was for a moment. Well, I do, but—' I got hurriedly to my feet, putting my cup on the side.

They rose instantly as one, Felix's long legs unfolding and straightening.

'I must be away,' I said, beaming. 'You've been more than kind and I've intruded on your time for far too long. I can't thank you enough for telling me about Cuthbert, and please, um . . .' How did one say take your time, don't rush to get out, I'm in no hurry without sounding like a patronizing landlord?

Predictably, Felix came to my rescue. 'And we'll be in touch about timings,' he said with easy grace, walking me to the front door. 'I've already organized a small removal van next week to take Dad's stuff, but there's hardly anything, most was Cuthbert's which stays put, so—'

I stopped. 'You mean . . . the art? The furniture?'

'Of course. He was a great collector. Always at the auction houses, and Pa was his greatest supporter. They had such fun trawling, but it was all Cuthbert's.'

Lordy. I felt a bit faint at this news. Could imagine the children saying – sell it! Must be worth a fortune! But I wouldn't. I would love to be surrounded by it.

'So perhaps if we swap emails . . .' Felix was saying.

He drew his phone from his back pocket and I was equally quick on the draw. I'd swap anything with this man. Was he married? I wondered. He hadn't mentioned a wife, but why would he? Or perhaps he was gay, too? No, I didn't think so. He was way out of my league, of course, and if he was married, completely out of bounds. I was never going there again. But close up, which I was now, he was older than he looked. Definitely older than me. By a few years. Just incredibly well preserved. Which I wasn't. But I would be bloody soon. Oh, you betcha.

I shook hands eagerly with Robert, who'd followed us down, agreeing it had been absolutely lovely to meet, and if *only* we'd met before, and in an effort to match them on the manners front, assured them the house was completely gorgeous, which was probably the crassest thing I could have said. Even Robert was nonplussed.

'I'm so glad you like it,' he murmured as I flushed to my roots.

With a smile he took his leave, letting his son see me off, but as I stepped outside I turned. I saw him go back down the hall, his correct military stance drooping a little. The figure I recall, as he put his hand on the banister to steady himself and go on up the stairs, was not of a proud, stately gentleman, but an old man, still suffering from flu and grief, and worn out now by conversation, going back to bed.

Felix joined me in the street. He turned to me, his eyes slightly anxious.

'Now that Dad's out of earshot, I wonder, would you mind terribly meeting me on my own? For lunch perhaps?'

For a mad moment I thought he was asking me out. My heart leaped right up into my throat. Already? Then, in a nanosecond, I realized it was about his father.

'Of course.'

Father or not, there was no way I was turning that down. His eyes practically matched the faded sea-green shirt he was wearing – did he know that? He was an artist, after all.

'Shall we say next week? I have to judge a prize on aesthetic relations in Venice this week, it's the Biennale. But I'll be back on Tuesday. May I take the liberty of booking a table somewhere?'

May he . . . blinking heck. He could book a *hotel* somewhere. No, of course he couldn't, I didn't mean that. But I realized it was the first time in five years I'd actually been attracted to anyone. I felt something dry and desiccated unfurl deep within me: felt tiny new green shoots appear beneath the withered brown husk, pointing their delicate pale tips to the sun. I smilingly took my leave, agreeing he jolly well could, and turned down the street, hearing the door shut softly behind me.

Ridiculously, I felt as if I were being carried along on a carpet of air as I tripped lightly across the cobbles. I knew I had a lot to do. And precious little time to do it. I had to dash to Earls Court and collect my things, then I had to get to King's Cross and trundle back down to Herefordshire to hassle Peter pronto. That depressing, energy-sapping farm had to go. I *would* have my new life. I clenched my fists excitedly. Before I went back to Lucy's, though, I headed up to the King's Road to make a few purchases. One was a shed-load of new make-up from the department on the first floor at Peter Jones, and the other was a large, shiny book which I found in Waterstones, entitled *Contemporary Art and Relational Aesthetics*.

CHAPTER 10

On the way home I made two discoveries. One was that it doesn't matter how much ruinously expensive Touche Éclat you slather on your face in an effort to cover the red thread veins on your windblown cheeks, they still shine through, and the other was that my hunch about Fine or Contemporary Art had been right. It is not fine at all. Not in the way you and I would imagine. It is not glorious oil paintings of damsels in crinolines or strutting cavalry officers in tight breeches à la Gainsborough, it is indeed naked men in buckets, and the rubber ducks are not necessarily in their mouths.

I stared at a photograph of an array of shop mannequins flying upside down around a maypole, the ribbons tied to their feet. How did one go about viewing that? I wondered. Not that I'd necessarily be leading the stampede. Did the gallery lay on coaches to a field? Cart punters off to see it? Maybe I should have staged something similar at the farm, charged for entry. Diversifying was all the rage these days, although I couldn't necessarily see the good burghers of Ludlow beating a path to my door to see that. I turned the page to view another color plate, this of a naked woman curled up inside a grand piano and fondling a piglet. I turned the book sideways to get a better look. Right. I just didn't understand it, that was all. I needed to be educated. But I'd have it under my belt in no time, I decided, snapping the book shut. Oh yes, this wouldn't be a problem. I hastened off the train at my stop, feeling better than I had done for years.

I'd rung Peter from the train and he'd agreed to come and value the farm properly.

'Today?' I'd asked.

'Er, well, yes, OK. If you like.' I did. 'When are you back?'

I told him and he agreed to meet me. He said he'd put some feelers out already and that the feedback was encouraging.

'Oh *good*, Peter,' I breathed happily. 'So you don't think it'll take long?'

'Well, we'll see. We don't want to give it away, do we? Can I ask what the tearing hurry is, anyway, Molly?'

He could, but I wouldn't give him a straight answer. Instead I mumbled something about it having been on my mind for a long time, ages in fact, but now I'd finally crossed a line and made a decision, which was rubbish, of course. I'd decided in the space of about a day and confirmed it over a pair of green eyes.

Two pairs of brown ones, one more hazel – Peter's – the others darker, like hard, chocolate chips, were waiting for me in the yard as I sped in, scattering chickens. Oh Lord, Paddy Campbell too. What was he doing here? Ah, of course. Sizing up my land already.

'You don't waste much time, do you?' I cried as I got out of the car and went across towards them, swinging my handbag jauntily.

'What d'you mean?' he asked stiffly.

'Well, I imagine Peter told you I'm leaving? Offered you the land?'

'No, I didn't know that.' A muscle went in his cheek.

Annoyance, no doubt, at not being the first to know.

'No, I hadn't mentioned it,' Peter said quickly. 'Thought we'd discuss it first. Decide which paddock you want to keep with the house. As we said, the long meadow is the obvious one, but I wanted to make sure.'

We turned as one and gazed at the daisy and buttercup strewn meadow at the back of the house: long and lush, it was looking particularly enchanting today with my goat, Monty, grazing it. In fact the whole place looked magical, floating with early cow parsley whose heads bobbed like little clouds in the faint breeze, the woods beyond speckled with creamy wild garlic, the sun, on this glorious day, glistening on the river which meandered through the valley.

It reminded me of the day David had first brought me here, and of course I'd patched up the house since then, so it was in a much better state with newly painted windows, reappointed eaves, mown lawns. Even the fencing was looking good. But I knew the reality: the eccentric plumbing, the galloping damp, the leaky basement, the mice – rats, even – the cold, depressing winter months, trudging across rock-hard fields at six in the morning with my axe to crack ice on troughs, my hands frozen with cold. April was definitely the cruelest month in that it was surely the most deceptive.

'I think the long meadow,' I said firmly. 'It's the obvious one. The rest we'll parcel up and sell separately. Might you be interested, Paddy?'

'Depends. Where are you going?'

'I'm off to London!' I said gaily, for all the world like Dick Whittington, sailing off to the gold-paved streets.

'Back home, really.' I was aware that my eyes were shining and that Paddy's were like flints.

'Bully for you.'

'I've come into an inheritance,' I went on, knowing it was nobody's business but my own but unable to contain myself. 'A relative of David's has died.'

Paddy shrugged. 'Well, you know what they say. Where there's a will, there's a relative.'

I frowned, unsure how to take that.

'So, um, I was thinking,' Peter broke in, aware that sparks were about to fly, 'that there's no rush then, surely, Molly? It's not as if you have to sell the farm in order to buy in London, is it? Why not take it more slowly? Get the best price?'

'Oh no, I want to be shot of the worry. And you know when you've made a decision, you just want to be there? In that place in your head you've decided you want to be?' Since, in my head, I had a cosy supper with Felix in my new kitchen, sharing a bottle of wine, eyes locked over a dish of pasta – vongole, I'd decided, I was good at that – the two men in my front yard looked understandably blank. But then neither was particularly in touch with their feminine side. Or had much imagination either.

'So what are you doing here, Paddy?' I turned. 'If not sizing up my acres?'

'Your mother called me. One of your ewes can't get up, she's grazing lying down.'

'Oh no! Which one?'

'I don't know which one,' he said irritably. 'A Hampshire, in the far field. Two lambs at foot.'

'Oh. Damn. OK, let's go and see. Peter, d'you mind taking a look round the house on your own? Mum's gone, she texted me.'

'I was going to suggest that anyway,' he said. 'And your

mother said the same, I saw her leave. I just thought I'd wait because she said you were on your way. I won't poke around too much.'

'Oh, I wouldn't worry, no secrets in this house!'

'It's easier, actually. Don't have to ooh and ah.'

'Well, quite. Give the dining room door a good shove – it sticks – and watch the last few steps down to the cellar, they're completely rotten. I usually jump them.'

'I stand warned.' He turned and went around towards the front door, which the dogs had pushed open.

'Hang on,' I told Paddy. 'Back in a mo.' I darted round to the back door, found some boots and a puffa jacket, ditched my handbag and came back to meet him.

'Molly sports her country wardrobe,' I told him with a grin, striking a pose.

He didn't answer and I added 'no sense of humor' to my list. In fact I could tell he was in a filthy temper. We walked in silence through the bright spring grass sparkling with jewel-like dragonflies, down the slope to where the ewes were, beyond the stream. Usually I made conversation to jolt him out of his mood but today I couldn't be bothered. I'd wait for him, I decided. It would be interesting to see how long it took. It was interesting. He didn't bother either. Nor did he seem uncomfortable with the silence.

We crossed the stream at the narrowest part via the stepping stones and went in amongst the sixty or so ewes grazing quietly with their lambs or sleeping in the sunshine. The twin lambs we'd bottle-fed since their mother had died came rushing up for more at the sight of us, but I could see their tummies were still full from Mum's efforts and they were just trying it on.

'They won't need much more anyway,' said Paddy as

one of them nudged his leg hopefully. 'There's almost enough nutrient in the grass.'

'Good. That would be one less thing to do.' Making up powdered milk every morning with that smell, so redolent of SMA for babies, took me straight back to David and Bolingbroke Road in the very happy early days, when he often did the feeds, leaving me to sleep. I could do without that jolting memory.

'The novelty's really worn off, hasn't it?' Paddy said dryly.

I looked at him angrily. I actually really liked feeding the orphaned lambs – who wouldn't? It was one of the very pleasurable springtime activities, and even the children helped: he had no business thinking me a dilettante. He couldn't know my sad thought associations, of course, but he didn't half jump to conclusions about me, and I was about to have a go, when he surprised me.

'Sorry. You've worked hard here, Molly. No one's denying that.'

Wrong-footed, I closed my mouth. Was about to come back with something snappy but more even-tempered, when, over his shoulder, I realized who it was on her side, trying to graze uncomfortably.

'Oh no – it's Rita!' I darted across. Paddy followed. 'Typical!' I cried as I sank to my knees.

'It's never the ones who are crap mothers and drive you mad, always the ones you care about.' I scratched her head and she looked up at me with unusually bleary eyes. 'Oh, thank you for coming, Paddy. She's feeding triplets, not twins, and she's one of my absolute favorites.'

'Well, I've given her a shot of steroids and some antibiotics,' he said, squatting beside me, 'but I can't promise anything. She's a mystery, actually. I've lifted her up repeatedly, but she collapses again, and there's no mastitis.'

'Should I feed the lambs?' I watched as one nudged her teats quite hard to suckle. She'd been amongst the first to lamb and they were big brutes now.

'No, she's managing, I should leave her to it. It might distress her more to have them taken away.'

'Oh, I'd leave them here, I just meant as supplement.'

'Then she'll bag up and get swollen. I'd leave her. Just check she's not worse in the morning. But to be honest, Molly, she can't get to the water like this and although they don't drink much, she'll need it if she's feeding.'

'Can't I bring a bucket to her?'

'How's she going to get her head in?'

I licked my lips. 'I could bury it? In a hole.'

He gave me a withering look. 'This is a sheep, not a household pet. No, if she can't get up tomorrow, put a bullet in her. Or get Nico to. Cheaper than getting me out again.'

I swallowed. I knew this was right, but it was the problem I had with farming. No other farmer got the vet out as much as I did, not for sheep. Cows were different, more valuable, but by the time I'd paid Paddy's bill, it was the same as I'd get for a decent lamb at market at the moment. About fifty pounds. And I'd get much less for Rita. Not that I'd ever sell her. She was special. Yes, I had three special ones, I realized. Agnes, Coochie and Rita. I looked up and saw Milly with her twins. She was lovely too. Don't look any more. Over there was Gloria. Instead I tickled Rita's ears and crooned to her. She laid her head on the grass and looked resigned. As if she knew. She was far more accepting of her fate than I was.

I took a deep breath. Let it out shakily. The farmers round here all thought I was soft. None of them could believe I'd kept Maggie, the chestnut mare who'd been dumped in my field in foal, no doubt by the gypsies. Ken at the hunt kennels had told me he'd take her, shoot her and feed her to the hounds, but I'd kept her. Paddy had told me most hunts charged for this service and I was a fool not to take up the offer, but Maggie and Freckles, as Minna had called the foal, which had arrived amid much joyous shrieking on a freezing January night, had stayed, and I'd lost my heart to them. Together with a great deal of money. Yes, the pair had cost me dearly in injections, as no doubt Rita would, I thought, trying to harden my heart and get Paddy to do the deed now, as I knew he thought he should. But then she bleated. And I'd know her bleat anywhere, throaty and low. All sheep have different voices, but hers was distinctive. I stood up.

'Thanks, Paddy. I won't put a bullet in her. I'll call you out again if I may, but it'll be the last of my vet's bills, so that's something.'

He shrugged, but didn't say anything. I gazed around at the undulating emerald-green meadows, the hills rising gently beyond, tinged with blue in the hazy mirage from the sun.

'Do you want this, Paddy? My land? That's what Peter was referring to. He thinks it's too much, with the house. Says people only want a pony paddock.'

'I might well,' he said cagily, following my gaze. I looked at him, knowing he was playing it cool. No countryman ever turned down adjoining land. 'OK, yes. Definitely. Don't offer it to anyone else.'

'Please,' I said teasingly. I gazed into those dark eyes, wondering why it was so hard to force pleasantries out of him.

'Please,' he added grudgingly. Oh, he was all charm. 'What is it, eighty-six? Eighty-seven?'

'Eighty-eight. D'you want to walk round it?'

'I might.'

I knew he was dying to. I shrugged. 'Suit yourself.'

He did. He strode off, taking his cast-iron ego with him, in the direction of the river and the fields beyond. I watched him go. No questions about drainage, or troughs, or fencing, my opinion being woefully inadequate. No enquiries as to boundary ownership, or whose responsibility it was to maintain the hedges or the drystone walls. He'd clearly be coming to his own conclusions. I watched until his dark head disappeared down the dip in the land that flanked the river.

Inside, Peter was infinitely more polite and solicitous of my opinions. Were any of the chimneys capped? Was the septic tank emptied regularly? How much damp actually came through that north wall and had I had it seen to? Obviously not, unless you counted the occasional lick of paint. All in all, though, he agreed it was in pretty good shape, but appreciated it was a mammoth task to keep it that way.

'Every time I finish painting one set of windows, there's another broken sash to fix, or the heating system breaks down again. It's like the Forth Bridge, and I don't want to spend my days being a maintenance man. Let someone else do it. Someone with a husband, preferably, who can go up into the loft in the middle of a January night and bang the relevant pipe to stop it hissing. There are bats up there too, and whatever people say, they're not sweet. They're mice with wings.'

He nodded. 'I know. It's been a Herculean effort. But we'll miss you, Molly.'

We were at the kitchen table now, where we'd been discussing prices and glossy sales brochures, a pot of coffee and a packet of Hobnobs between us.

'Nonsense, I hardly know anyone! Apart from you, and

Anna, and the Frenches. And Tom and Pam, and the Pipers. And Biddy. Well, the Foxes, I suppose.'

'That's pretty much everyone in the valley.'

I wanted to say – yes, but don't you see how *limiting* that is? How can you *bear* it? But I knew it was his much loved life.

'You should have come hunting, Molly. Gone out with the Teme Valley. That's what people do for society in the winter.'

'No thanks. All those arrogant tossers in tight breeches who think because they wear a red coat, they can bark orders and roger every woman in the county . . .' One such tosser put his head around the door.

'You've got ragwort in most of the fields. They all need sorting out. And you haven't sprayed for months.'

'I sprayed in January!' I roared.

'Well, that's a bloody stupid time to do it. Nothing would have germinated. If you're moving the ewes I'd spray again next week.'

'Why don't you mind your own business!' I bellowed. 'These are not your fields yet and, frankly, they may never be!'

He shrugged, unconcerned. 'Suit yourself. I'm just saying, if you want the best price, you'll want them in good order. It's only like Peter telling you to put a course of damp proof on that wet patch.' He nodded at the north wall behind the stairs where there was indeed a large tell-tale stain.

'Yes, but Peter's an estate agent – you're a ruddy vet! If you're not interested in the land, mind your own business, Paddy.' He really did bring out the worst in me.

'Oh, I want it. Just pointing out its imperfections before you try and put an inflated price on it. Let me know the damage, Peter.' And with that, and a rare grin, he withdrew.

I fumed for a moment as Peter diplomatically drained his coffee and got to his feet.

'I'll be away too, Molly. I'll send a photographer round and have the brochures out by next week, I promise. I'll pop one through your door first, though.'

In the event, however, we didn't need the photographer. Or the brochures. Peter rang that evening, a bit breathless, to ask if he could show a couple round in the morning. I assured him he most certainly could, simultaneously plumping cushions and kicking a magazine under the sofa. They came as promised, a lovely middle-aged couple, who I only met briefly: I was out checking on Rita, who miraculously seemed a bit better; she was even on her feet, which I felt was one in the eye for the know-it-all vet.

Anyway, the delightful couple promptly made an offer the following afternoon which was so stratospheric I had to put the phone to my chest a moment to shut my eyes and breathe. It was light years away from what we'd paid for the place. I thanked Peter profusely and said I'd accept. Then I rang the children to enthuse. They were delighted, particularly at the price, but I could tell there was something in their voices that was wistful and a little nostalgic.

'So it's really going,' said Minna.

'Yes, darling, it is.'

'Which means I'll never see Ted again.'

'Well, that's what you wanted, isn't it, my love? Remember how you said you never wanted to see him? Listen, I must go, I've got to ring the others,' I said cravenly, knowing from experience she was about to dissolve and, for once, wanting to protect myself. Not to be brought down, as I always was when Minna cried. I spoke to Nico, who said, 'Yeah, OK, whatever,' which was a bit rich considering he'd been so keen, but naturally the one I lost it with was Lucy.

'You were the ones who bloody told me to!' I snapped, when she said something about how much she'd miss the orchard, and the apple blossom every year.

'I know and it's brilliant. It's just a shame we can't keep both, really.'

'Well, we can't,' I said shortly. 'Stop being so bloody spoilt. Some people don't have a home at all.' And then, to change the subject, and also because I couldn't help it and had to tell someone, I told her about the divine Felix Carrington. She was quiet a moment.

'Well, I certainly don't think you should have lunch with him, Mum.'

'Why not? You're always telling me to go out more. Always trying to fix me up with someone, and for the first time in five years I've met someone I actually wouldn't mind sharing a lunch table with!'

'Yes, but it's obvious. He's going to lay the guilt trip on you. Cuthbert and his father were to all intents and purposes married, from what you've said. He'll try and make you feel bad about having the house.'

'Oh, don't be silly! I'm sure he just wants to ask me to be sensitive to his father's wishes. Not to change the décor or something.'

'How's his father going to see the décor?'

'Or – I don't know – maybe ask if Robert can come back and visit? Who knows? Perhaps he fancies me, Lucy.'

'Who, the father?'

'No! The father's a relic. And gay. Felix.'

'Oh. Right. I thought you said he was a complete dude? Ripped jeans, brown ankles, moccasins?'

I was speechless. '*I* have ripped jeans, Lucy!'

'Yes, but only because you tear them on barbed wire.'

'And very soon' – I fished in the bag of goodies I'd bought from Peter Jones, brandished a bottle of fake tan at the phone – 'I will have brown ankles, too!'

'Right. OK. Well – you know . . .'

'What?'

'Don't make a fool of yourself, Mum. Peter Cox is one thing, but some hunk nipping off to Venice to judge the art Biennale is another. What were you wearing?'

'What was I . . . you saw me! My best blue dress, very smart, and my white jacket!'

'Oh, shit, yes. Right. I rest my case. Just . . . tread carefully, Mum, OK? He clearly thinks you're some hick from the sticks, foaming at the mouth at all the glamour and sophistication of London. He might try to sweet-talk you, that's all.'

My mouth opened and shut at her gall. I was dumbfounded. Didn't she remember the days when I'd flit back from my office in Covent Garden, head to toe in Agnès B?

No, of course she didn't. No more than she'd remember the charming little cashmere tunic I'd worn over black Capri pants which I'd taken to Paris – and understandably never worn again. But she could mock all she liked. I had once been a sophisticated woman, and given a pair of tweezers, a tub of St Tropez, a crash diet and some mustache-bleaching cream, could quite easily be that woman again.

She'd already gone, though. With barely a goodbye, as apparently her other mobile – her *other* mobile – was ringing and it was Robin. I snapped my ancient phone shut. Yes, well. *I* was busy too. Had things to do. Masses, in fact. Seizing my purchases – and of course my new book – I headed upstairs to lay it all about me, to run a foaming scented bath, and to make preparations for the forthcoming campaign.

CHAPTER 11

*M*y lunch with Felix took place in possibly the most exquisite restaurant I'd ever been to, and although my children would dispute it, I've been to one or two. It was in Chelsea, naturally: all white and light with sparkling floor-to-ceiling mirrors, a glass floor – lethal, I took it gingerly – and vast tropical plants. It even had a parrot, called Hortense, in a gilded cage, and a myna bird too, in the corner. It was full of people who looked as if they'd never done a day's work in their life but spent a great deal of time maintaining the fiction.

Outside, where we ate, since it was yet another beautiful day, and because it was even more enchanting out than in – a leafy, walled enclosure with spreading plane trees providing dappled shade, the tables laid with the thickest, whitest linen I'd ever seen set around a tinkling central fountain complete with frolicking cherubs – were yet more of the elegantly dressed, lightly tanned, bejeweled, be-coiffed gentry I'd observed within, murmuring to one another over their Bellinis. What was the phrase I was groping for? The beautiful people, that was it.

Most were women lunching à deux, I noticed, as we threaded through the tables led by the waiter, although they barely seemed to be eating, just picking at rocket and Parmesan salad, but there was a smattering of suave, handsome men too, not in suits, but colorful, open-necked shirts and linen jackets, who didn't seem to have a care in the world, laughing heartily – OK, braying – and looking as if they were more involved in managing their property portfolios and trust funds than the real world.

Trying to look as if these were the circles I mixed in on a daily basis, I waited as our chairs were pulled out. The maître d' greeted Felix like an old friend and they marveled at the continued, unseasonably warm weather.

'Does it mean a terrible summer for us, Carlos, d'you think?'

Carlos spread his hands despairingly. 'Ees so often the way in this country, no?'

'I'll take it, anyway,' said Felix with a grin as we sat down. 'It would be churlish to quibble. Now. What d'you recommend? I saw some langoustine as we came through.'

As they discussed the menu I had a quick look round and realized that whilst I didn't begin to match up sartorially, I hadn't entirely let the side down either. Obviously nothing in my wardrobe had been remotely suitable, not even the flimsy blue shirt and white jeans I wore on my occasional forays out with Anna or Tia in Ludlow, but I knew I had treasures in the spare room closet which hadn't been worn for years.

As I'd eagerly pulled out my erstwhile working girl wardrobe, hustled it back to my room, piled it on the bed and tried it on, enthusiasm turned to dust and ashes in my mouth. I regarded my reflection in dismay. Surely that little pigskin jacket with the black Capri pants had been positively cutting edge back in the day? Why, then, did it suddenly look so shapeless and dowdy? And wasn't the collar a bit large? I stepped forward to peer. And how on earth had the trousers shrunk so dramatically? I couldn't even do them up. I hadn't washed them, had I, instead of having them dry-cleaned? I tried them on with a larger top, to hide the gaping zip, this time of the palest dusty pink, the cashmere tunic, in fact, of that fateful visit to Paris. So tight. Not a tunic at all. More of a body-con. But perhaps it always had been thus? Perhaps I'd just forgotten?

I threw on some gold jewelry and high heels and minced uncomfortably downstairs to canvass Minna, who was with Nico in the sitting room, both horizontal on a sofa apiece, dogs asleep all over them, curtains drawn, positions which had been adopted three days ago on their return from London and aside from brief forays to the fridge or the lavatory hadn't been relinquished. Naturally they didn't look up from their screens so I finally coughed and struck a pose in the doorway.

'What d'you think?'

They glanced round. Stared. Then Nico fell off the sofa, holding his stomach. Minna looked aghast.

'What are you going as?'

'Oh, it's fancy *dress*,' gasped Nico from the floor. He got up and resumed his viewing position. 'Shit. I thought it was for real.'

'It is for real, it's for this lunch I've got with Felix Carrington.' I held my stomach in then realized it was already in.

They both looked horrified.

'Oh no, absolutely not,' said Minna. 'You look like a pregnant prawn. What about your blue shirt?'

'Too parochial,' I said, letting my tummy out with relief.

'Well, you must have something else.'

'I haven't. Have you got anything?'

'That would fit you? I sincerely hope not.'

'Minna!'

'Joke, Mother. Come on, let's go see.'

She leaped up and led the way upstairs, taking the stairs two at a time, secretly liking the idea of a bossy mother-daughter makeover. She hadn't quite lined up with Lucy on the cynical approach to my lunch either, and was even prepared to agree it was practically a date when I'd filled her in earlier.

'OK, so what's he going to be wearing?' she demanded, folding her arms and surveying the discarded clothes littering my bed and decorating my floor.

'Suit?'

'God no, he's arty.'

'Linen jacket?'

'Mmm . . . not even that. I'd say . . . silky shirt? Jeans?'

'Oh right. He's cool.'

'Yes,' I said happily. 'He's cool.'

'Don't say it like that.'

'Like what?'

'I dunno, you just say it wrong. Too much ooo in the middle.'

She swept a practiced eye around the assorted garments already on display, then plunged her head in my wardrobe, foraging like a pig for truffles. She emerged empty-handed, looking flummoxed. Undeterred, we headed for fresh hunting grounds and eventually found a long blue floaty top of Lucy's which Minna said would work if I didn't eat until Tuesday, my white jeans and a denim jacket of hers which she told me was edgy but I thought made me look like *The Lady in the Van*.

'And wear your hair up,' she commanded, holding it up at the back. 'It's less like a doormat then.'

'A door . . .'

Stung, I hastened into Ludlow the following day and had my hair cut, highlighted and blow-dried, then, in a sweet little boutique down the road, happened upon a simple grey silky shift dress which was neither mutton dressed as lamb nor mother of the bride.

Minna raised her eyebrows when I brought it home and said something about *Prison Break*, but I felt more comfortable in it.

Sitting here, though, looking at Felix's wafer-thin, collarless, dusty pink Indian tunic – think Imran Khan – I wished I'd added the denim jacket. He was bohemian. An artist. Or an artistic judge anyway, I wasn't sure which, but then, I didn't need to know everything yet, did I? I wasn't at an interview.

'How was Venice?' I asked with a dazzling smile when the waiter had withdrawn, determined there wouldn't be an embarrassing silence to kick off with.

'Venice was good.' He turned his full attention on me, leaning in and folding his arms on the table. 'Very good. Warm, like this, and absolutely stunning. Venice at its best, in fact. And in terms of art, it was thrilling.' His face lit up suddenly, with a brilliant, blowtorch smile. God, those *eyes*. 'Sebastian Malpass shone, of course, but then you probably saw his installation in the papers, a very deserved winner.'

I hadn't. Hadn't realized the news would cover it, which was annoying, and I didn't always manage to read a paper, but I'd done so much research otherwise I wasn't going to let that stop me. I knew the sort of thing it would be.

'Yes, I thought it was sensational. Particularly in terms of conceptual interaction. Phenomenal impact.'

His eyes widened. 'You got that? So many people didn't.'

'It was the first thing that struck me when I saw it. The, um . . . conceptual interaction going on.'

'How intriguing.' He leaned forward eagerly. 'You're the first non-artist I've spoken to who understood. What convinced you?'

My mouth dried a bit. 'Well, um . . . the, sense of scale?' I hazarded. 'And . . . grandeur.' All of these installations, I'd noticed, were enormous: most didn't fit in galleries, no wonder they were out in the fields. Felix's eyes were narrowing and not necessarily in a good way. He frowned.

'But not, if you see what I mean,' I said quickly. 'Not grandeur at all. In fact, the sense of . . .' I swallowed. 'I'm not quite sure how to express it . . .'

'Nothingness?'

'Exactly! Nothingness,' I agreed happily. 'It wasn't really about anything at all, was it?'

That frown again. 'Well, I'm not sure I'd say that—'

'Or everything,' I interrupted, feeling a bit sweaty. 'Maybe, in fact, it was about everything? How did you interpret it?' The waiter brought a bottle of white wine and poured it. I took a huge gulp. Half a glass disappeared. 'I mean, when you first walked in, what was your first impression?' Good, Molly, much better. Inspired, in fact.

'Well, initially I thought a pea in a vast white room lined with egg boxes was novel but not entirely original – Maurice Chappelle did something similar in Copenhagen, if you remember.'

'Yes, of course. And Mae West used peas too,' I added

brightly, recalling a picture I'd seen in my book of loads of peas in a pile at Tate Modern.

'You mean May Weston?'

'That's the one.'

'Really? I don't recall.' He looked confused.

Crikey, quite famous. All those peas in a great big – suddenly it dawned. Damn. Wrong artist. Not May Weston at all, Ai Weiwei, and it was sunflower seeds, thousands of porcelain ones.

'But – but maybe this was an allegory?' I said quickly. 'Just the one pea, so – a bit like the princess and the pea? All those mattresses and amazingly she still felt it? Perhaps it was all about heightened sensitivity and how we're never sensitive enough to each other's feelings? Too self-obsessed and shut off from one another. Not enough – conceptual interaction.' Brilliant. Bloody fucking brilliant, Moll. I sat back, delighted.

'N-no,' he said slowly, shaking his head. 'I think the opposite, actually. I think territorial. So thinking selfishly.'

'Yes, yes, I see.' I nodded, leaning in. *What?* I licked my lips. 'You mean . . . the idea of a tiny pea taking up so much space? In one's head?'

'No, I mean the concept of a urination being territorial. Claiming ground. In war zones. In Syria.'

Oh, *that* sort of pee. Blimey. I was exhausted. And rather repulsed. Was it fake? I sincerely hoped so. Lemonade or something. Well, let's face it, that could be interpreted as anything, couldn't it? Someone who'd been a bit desperate taking a leak, a dog raising its leg – what were these people on? Talk about the Emperor's New Clothes. I drained my glass and wondered if we could move on, hopefully to safer ground.

'But you're more of a traditional artist, aren't you, Felix? Your father mentioned paint, so . . .'

He laughed. 'He's harking back to the good old days, which he liked, although to be fair, I'm still not afraid to get a canvas out. It's more commercial. Paint sells and I've got to make a living. Political commentary, though, is something I prefer to be involved in; it's what everyone's doing these days, but it's obviously harder to get punters to buy. At the moment I've got seventeen alarm clocks going off in a freezer. I've set them to go off on the hour at five-minute intervals as part of a commentary on the government's blurring of the lines in the Nigerian atrocities – muffled, cushioned wealth at the helm, obviously, but with insistent subjugation.'

'Yes, I see.' I didn't, really. And he was right, not a hope in Hades of selling that. Who'd want that racket going off in the middle of dinner?

'But enough about me.' He picked up his wine glass and gave me a twinkly smile over the rim. 'Tell me, Molly, what do you do? Do you work?'

'I did,' I said carefully, opting for scallops and a salad when the waiter came and went, not wanting to look greedy. 'In PR. And I still do, but not in an office. In fact I work harder than I ever did in London, but it's all odds and ends. I have a soap business – tiny, but I do OK at country fairs, that type of thing – and I have a mail order underwear business. And I buy and sell horses. And I'm a farmer.'

'Oh, cool.'

'Really? Which bit?'

'Well, all of it, but farming in particular. Agriculture is the only tangible interaction we have left with the natural world, otherwise we're just spectators. People can ponce around making art out of gardens, of course, but the real meaning is in the toil of sweating in the soil. And production, naturally.'

'I'll second that.' I grinned, on firmer ground for the first time since I'd put my bottom on the chair.

He put his head quizzically on one side. 'And yet you want to give it all up. Move to London. Why is that?' The green eyes were faintly flecked with gold, I noticed, and they were kind.

'I told you, it's too much like hard work. It's much harder than any office job in London. People like you, Felix, purists in the city, romanticize it, but it can be bloody grim. All slopping buckets and mud up to your knees and acres of emptiness and a Land Rover that breaks down and machinery that doesn't work. It's remote and it's lonely and it's through gritted teeth most days. And at the end of the day, you think you're going to be baking cookies at the Aga but you don't. You just slide your bottom down it and sit on the floor and smoke and get depressed.'

He looked startled and I realized this was not necessarily the most seductive of portraits. I rallied, shoring up a winning smile.

'The thing is, I *want* to get back to potting around in a garden like most people do. Hopefully just a roof terrace, actually. Something small at any rate.' I reached for my wine glass and went on casually, 'I noticed Cuthbert's has a rather sweet space at the back?'

Lucy was wrong. I could be steely. And I sensed why Felix was advocating the rural life. As long as I didn't look at his eyes, or his tanned neck with a hint of chest, I'd be fine. Absolutely fine.

'Yes,' he said carefully. 'A very sweet garden. Which they both loved. Dad was – is – an extremely keen gardener and did most of the work. He designed it, you know. He's pretty talented like that. It took him about two years.'

'Right.' I swallowed. The scallops arrived. Suddenly I wasn't terribly hungry.

'His great love is amaryllis. Well, you'll see why when they come up later in the summer. He always planted ten more each year to accommodate the natural decline. That and lily of the valley. I hope you'll keep the garden up?'

'Yes. Yes, I . . . definitely will.' I chewed hard on a scallop. 'But he'll be very happy with you, won't he, Felix?' I said anxiously. 'Surely at his great age, and not so well these days, it'll be nice to know he's not on his own?'

'Except I travel so much – and I live alone, obviously.'

'Oh? Why obviously?' The wine had emboldened me.

'I'm divorced,' he said simply. 'Two kids, but they're mostly in America with their mum.'

'You must miss them.'

'Yes, but they come across for holidays when they get time off work, and I go there quite a lot too. Actually my son's working here at the moment. Has been on and off for the last ten years, he flits back and forth.'

I glanced up. 'Ten years? You don't look old enough to—'

'Have grown-up children?' He laughed. 'I'm older than you think, Molly.'

Good. Excellent. Although he clearly wasn't going to tell me how much older.

'And do you miss her?' I asked cautiously. 'Your wife?'

He considered this. 'I miss family life. But Emmeline and I came to the end of something many years ago.'

'And you never found anyone else.'

'I never found anyone else.' He regarded me pensively over his wine glass. 'You ask a lot of questions, Molly. Most people pussyfoot about.'

'Most people?'

He inclined his head, conceding this with a small smile.

'Yes, OK, when I say I haven't found anyone else, I've obviously interviewed.'

'Are you interviewing now?'

'Are you?'

Things had indeed moved on apace. Here we were, having met only very recently, gazing away at one another over glasses of Chablis in a sunlit courtyard, cherubs tinkling away behind us pouring water from their urns. But I knew I'd felt something when I first saw him. And I'd been round the block enough to know I'd sensed an attraction to me, too. I might be self-deprecating at times in order to protect myself, but I wasn't so much of a fool as not to notice when I'd got a flicker out of a man. We both had our agendas, of course. I was aware of that. But the more he liked me, the harder he'd find it to implement his, surely? I decided to address it full on since he liked my direct approach. Also I was quite drunk. I put my glass down.

'My daughter, Lucy, who is the most sensible member of our family, says you've only asked me here today to make me feel guilty about inheriting a house that your father has lived in with his partner for twenty years.'

I saw a glimmer of surprise in his eyes: a certain wrong-footing, but he held my gaze.

'And do you?'

'Feel guilty?'

'Yes.'

'A bit, yes. Quite a lot, actually. But I'd be a fool to act on it. I have a crumbling remote farmhouse and a life I've come to hate. I've got no husband and three children who I want to give a decent start in life, since their father isn't around to do it for them. And they're determined to live in this city, where barely anyone can buy their own house any more. Whatever my latent sensibilities and sensitivities are,

I can't let a pair of green eyes and a delightful pink shirt put me off my stride.'

He looked even more astonished. Then a slow smile developed.

'You like to call a spade a spade, don't you?'

I shrugged. 'I wield one enough. Mostly on the muck heap. I have a lot of time to think.' I looked at him steadily. 'We're both grown-ups, Felix. We can level with each other. I had lunch with you today because I liked the look of you and it's a long time since I had lunch with a man in a ritzy London restaurant. But if you're having lunch with me to twist my arm, you're wasting your time.'

He played with his scallops, quite a few of which he hadn't eaten either. Then he put his fork down.

'I was,' he admitted. 'That was very much my aim. My agenda, as you put it. To charm the figurative pants off the ingénue up from the country and then to prick her conscience a bit. See what happened. I didn't expect you to hand over the whole shooting match, but some sort of compromise. I could see you were a nice person just from chatting to you at Dad's. I thought it might play well.'

I nodded. 'And now?'

He looked at me a long while. Suddenly he sat back in his chair. His mouth twitched then a broad grin broke over his face. He ran a rueful hand through his thick golden hair.

'To be honest you've put me off my stride, Molly. You've disarmed me. I don't know what to think. Don't know what to think at all!'

CHAPTER 12

*T*he afternoon sailed on. In fact it eased into a gloriously idle, sybaritic golden haze, the like of which I hadn't experienced for years. Having paid the bill – I tried but he wouldn't let me share – and since it was such a lovely day, Felix suggested a stroll by the river.

We walked for miles, deep in conversation, this comparative stranger and I. Heads bent, smiling down at our feet pacing the pavements, we navigated the street artists and passers-by, parting periodically to accommodate them and glancing occasionally to smile at one another as we made our way under a canopy of blossom along the Embankment. The river glistened beside us, bridges stretched across it proud and invincible – and beautiful, in Albert's case – and pleasure boats cruised by at a leisurely pace whilst more commercial crafts sped busily past.

As we chatted, I found myself telling him about David, and about how his death had left such a hole in my heart and a void in my life. About how you don't appreciate someone solid and dependable until they're gone.

He told me about Emmeline and how he'd met her

when she was modeling in New York. Very young, very naive, thrown in at the deep end in a flat full of much older, more savvy models who took drugs to stay thin, she'd sought refuge one afternoon in the Museum of Modern Art. He'd spotted her huddled in a huge coat staring at a Hockney, and when he'd asked why, she said it reminded her of home. Of Yorkshire. They'd struck up a friendship. Then a relationship. Later a marriage.

'But it wasn't destined to be,' he said sadly. 'I thought once she had a family and a home she'd give up the modeling, but she didn't. She became even more addicted to it and desperate for work. And of course in that world there's a law of diminishing returns: there's always a beautiful, skinny sixteen-year-old coming up on the rails. It made her a bit desperate. She had a lot of work done.'

'On her face?'

'Everywhere, really. Became someone I just didn't recognize. In so many ways.'

'It's a cruel world. Lucy thought about it because she was scouted so many times, but luckily she decided against it.'

'Lucy the sensible one?'

'And the beautiful one.'

'Picture?'

I took out my phone and showed him my screensaver of the three of them. He pointed her out.

'That one. Just like you.'

I laughed. 'I should be so lucky. Anyway, she's a florist now.'

'So men come in to buy flowers for their girlfriends and linger just a little longer than they should?'

I smiled and pocketed my phone. 'Perhaps. She has a beautiful shop in Islington and on sunny days she sits outside doing her arrangements – all very rustic, tied up with straw and hessian. There was a piece about her in *Country Living* last month. I'm very proud of her.'

'Didn't do university?'

'No, she had a place at Bristol, but David's death put her off her stride. She said she couldn't be getting drunk at freshers' parties and waking up in strange beds and living a hedonistic life in return for two measly essays a term when there was so much crap going on in the world. She wanted to do something more constructive.'

'Serious-minded.'

'Only by default. She was much more light-hearted when she was little. But yes, she's always campaigning about something. She was on that Stop the War march last week.'

Felix smiled down at his feet. We walked on. 'And the other two?'

'Students, lolling around at home in a *totally* hedonistic manner with absolutely no qualms about it at all. I think they even eat lying down, like Greek gods. Hopefully they'll do a bit of revision and some animal husbandry while I'm away but I doubt it.' I turned to smile. 'And yours?'

'Octavia's a lab technician in San Francisco and Daniel's a sculptor.'

'Ah. One like you then.'

He shrugged. 'A bit. More talented, I think. You can see some of his stuff, if you like. We're quite close to the gallery he's exhibiting in at the moment.'

'Oh, I'd love to!'

We'd crossed the river by now and Felix led the way down a quiet, narrow side street which led in turn to another. Many of the old Victorian warehouses around here had been converted into bars and galleries, and he stopped outside one such tall, red-brick affair very near the Tate Modern: looked proudly at the poster by the door.

Daniel Carrington was writ large, together with a photograph of his work. I stepped forward to inspect it.

'He's the real deal,' I said, impressed.

Felix glowed. 'I think so.'

In we went. We wandered around the exhibits, alone apart from one other couple in the three cavernous rooms with whitewashed brick walls and high, echoing ceilings which made me tread quietly in my clippy-cloppy heels. Daniel's sculptures took my breath away. Enormous sleek bronze leopards and crouching tigers full of sensitivity and menace were dotted sparingly on plinths around the rooms.

'Right,' I said, surprised. 'Traditional.'

'Extremely. You like?'

'Very much. They're very me.'

We strolled around some more, and I read with interest the captions beside the sculptures, learning he'd been out in Africa for years, but now moulded mostly from instinct and memory.

'Any idea who this is?'

Felix had stopped beside a life-sized head, not of an animal this time, and on a small table, not a plinth. I knew immediately.

'Oh.' I came up beside him. 'It's your father!'

'Exactly. Daniel's grandfather.'

'How lovely.' I reached out and stroked the Roman nose gently with my fingertip, admiring the crinkly eyes, the noble forehead. 'He's caught him just exactly.'

Felix smiled. He stood back to admire, his head on one side. I joined him, realizing the perspective was better from a distance. We looked on in silence. At length I spoke.

'Is he very fond of him?'

'Daniel? Very. We all are. You know that special, solid

person you were talking about, the one you need in a family and won't miss until they're gone? That's Dad.'

I nodded; moved on to the next piece, a lioness asleep with her neck stretched out. I gazed at it distractedly.

'He's eighty-six, right?'

'Yes, this year.'

'And apart from flu at the moment, he's fit?'

Felix turned and narrowed his eyes beyond me, out of the huge floor-to-ceiling windows that gave on to the river. 'It's not flu. He calls it that but he has emphysema. It comes and goes, but it's debilitating.'

'Emphysema. That's serious, isn't it?'

'Can be.'

I swallowed. 'So he's in his room a lot?'

'A bit. He always gets dressed, though, no matter how rough he's feeling.'

'What do the doctors say?'

'They say . . . that it could be months. Or it could be a few years. They just don't know.'

A few years. At most. Not many. I licked my lips. 'Felix . . . this . . . compromise you were talking about.' I turned to him properly, away from the sleeping lioness. 'What did you have in mind?'

He smiled. 'Nothing. It was stupid. A delusion. Forget it, Molly. And I didn't mention Dad to wear you down. Come on. Let's stroll back down the river.'

'No, I'm interested. Go on, what was it?'

He took a deep breath. Hesitated. 'Well, I just thought, in a crazy moment, and it really was a bonkers one, that you might let him stay. End his days there. In the house he's lived in for twenty-odd years. Surrounded by the things he's known and loved, surrounded by . . . Cuthbert.' He paused. 'But it was a madness. A fantasy.' He glanced down at his shoes. 'Come on, let's go.'

'No, wait.' I stayed his arm. 'You mean I'd still own it?'

'Of course. You probably own it already.'

'And your father would . . . lodge.'

'And pay rent.'

'Oh well, no, I couldn't . . .'

Suddenly I realized what I was considering. Letting an old man I didn't know, while out his days in a house he'd once lived in: put on hold my own dreams for someone I'd only met the other day? I shook my head. Fell in step beside Felix as he'd moved towards the door.

'No,' I said in a low voice. 'No, you're right, it couldn't happen.'

We walked away.

THE FACT that the afternoon stretched into the evening was purely through coincidence. Purely by dint of the fact that, as we were walking back along the river, me destined for Lucy's flat in Earls Court, him to a tube to transport him to his studio – a converted town house in Docklands, he was telling me – a cyclist was knocked off his bike in front of us on the Embankment. We didn't actually see the crash, just heard a horrid bang, and then there was this young lad, thrown, mercifully, on to the pavement and not in the path of the traffic, and wearing a helmet, but in a tangle, a heap, his bike on top of him. All the traffic stopped and car doors flew open, but we moved fast. We were the first to reach him, this lad of about nineteen, white-faced, staring up at us with huge grey eyes, his leg through the spokes of one wheel, the other wheel still spinning. Felix was brilliant. He knelt right down on the pavement beside him and kept him calm while I phoned for an ambulance. As I waited for the operator, I heard Felix's low, soothing voice, telling the lad he was absolutely fine and that help was already on its way. He asked his name.

'Tim.'

'Tim. Just keep holding my hand. Keep looking at me. You're going to be absolutely fine.'

He didn't try to move him, but draped his jacket over him for warmth. The boy shook violently but kept his eyes firmly on Felix's face, drinking in his eyes, his voice, until the ambulance arrived, which, thank goodness – we heard the siren blaring – was relatively soon.

'He's fine,' the paramedic assured us as they lifted him carefully on to a stretcher and covered him with a blanket.

'Just gone into shock. And the leg's not broken, neither is anything else as far as we can see. Well done, mate.'

'You'll let us know?' asked Felix.

'We'll take him to Thomas's. You can ring A&E.'

'Thanks.'

The doors closed and they were off, lights flashing. Moments later a police car arrived amid more sirens. Two policemen got out with notebooks and asked us if we'd seen the accident, which we hadn't, so they spoke to a driver who had, and who'd also seen a truck trundle away, oblivious to the fact he'd clipped a bicycle. We were told we could go. As I stood there hugging myself, I realized I was shivering. It had all happened so quickly.

'Come on.' Felix threw his jacket round my shoulders and gave them a quick squeeze. 'Let's have a drink at the Savoy. We deserve it.'

He took my arm and at the next lights we crossed the main road and walked around the back of the hotel, then up a side road to the front. The familiar art deco exterior, backdrop to so many films and Poirot episodes, with top-hatted, long-coated doormen and black cabs drawing up, was a comfort. Inside, we made our way down the steps to the piano bar and the banquette seating in the corner. A large, strong cocktail, cold and sweet, worked its magic. I could feel it pumping into my veins.

As I leaned my head back on the plush, buttoned velvet, I took stock of the day. I realized it had been rather a special one. Not the last bit, of course, the cyclist – although mercifully he was fine, we'd checked – but this bit. It was such a far cry from my life. Next week, when I was hosing down the stable walls, or turning sheep upside down with Nico to clip their toenails, I'd remember this day, and this man – I felt Felix's smile rest on me – for a long time to come.

BACK AT LUCY'S flat that night, I cooked for her and Robin, her boyfriend, to give them a night off, before getting my train back home in the morning.

'This is nice of you, Ma.' Lucy came into the galley kitchen to peer into the pan I was stirring. 'What is it, some kind of ethnic concoction?' She ate a forkful then passed another one to Robin, who'd followed her.

'Oh, yum. Delicious, Mrs Faulkner.'

'Molly,' I corrected, as ever, with a smile.

He'd recently been caught in a compromising position with one of Lucy's more attractive friends and was desperate for a toe back in the door. Robin adored my daughter, but Lucy, never one to commit, often pushed him away. I'd seen her do it: heard her being foul to him at the farm when they came down for weekends, bossing him about, picking on him. Everyone has their saturation point and when he finally reached his, he split up with her. Lucy pouted and flounced and claimed to be unmoved, but a few weeks later, he'd been seen kissing her friend in a nightclub. I'd thought it was inspired and had even wondered if he'd done it deliberately. It had certainly had the desired effect. She was incandescent with rage, but also grief-stricken. Minna even whispered, awestruck, to me when Lucy was upstairs, that she'd seen her crying, which was unheard of. More recently the two of them had got back together, which pleased me, because personally I liked the boy, but the scales, bizarrely, still seemed to be tipped in her favor. Why? Surely she either forgave him, or she didn't? I held my tongue on this, though, as wary as Robin was of hers.

I looked at her now, carrying plates of stir-fry to the coffee table while Robin brought the glasses and a bottle of wine. In one elegant motion, she settled, cross-legged, on a sofa, like a ballet dancer, slim and lithe in an assortment of grey and white vests, skinny black jeans ripped at the knees. As she forked up her supper her silky blonde hair draped around her angelic face with those high cheekbones and almond-shaped, pale blue eyes. She tucked her hair behind one ear and I saw Robin looking at her. She'd always looked like that, like an angel, and when she was little David and I would stare at her in her sleep, wondering if it was because she was our firstborn that we found her so lovely, but realizing, as she grew, that others thought so too. Her brush with Robin's so-called infidelity – *They were on a break!* Minna would shriek indignantly – was the first time a boy had ever given her trouble. Personally I thought it had been terribly good for her but I wouldn't have dreamed of voicing it. Any more than I could quite believe what I was about to say next.

'Lucy.' I put my fork down. 'I've been thinking about this house.'

'Which house?'

'Lastow Mews.'

'Oh?' She glanced up.

'And I think I might rent it out. Just to begin with.'

She continued to eat silently. Took a cool sip of wine and replaced her glass on the table. 'Sudden change of heart, Ma? How come?'

'Well, I just think,' I felt a bit sweaty under the arms, 'it would make sense. Just for a few years.'

'A few *years*?'

'Maybe.'

'Right. And where would you live?'

'Well, that's just it,' I said eagerly. 'I've practically sold the farm, Peter's seen to that, to a lovely couple, so I thought I could buy something smaller up here with what I get for it.'

She raised one perfectly groomed eyebrow. 'Two houses in London. Quite the property magnate.'

'Oh no, just – you know. A little flat.'

'Which would cost?' She turned coolly to Robin who was a property lawyer, so knew. He cleared his throat.

'In what area?'

'Oh, anywhere really, I—'

'Mum wants to be in South Ken. She said so.' She turned to me firmly. 'Didn't you?'

'Well, I—'

'Three bedrooms,' she added. 'So we all have a base.'

Robin glanced up at the ceiling to consider, then mentioned a sum of money so huge I thought for a moment he must be talking in drachmas.

'Right,' I said faintly. 'Well no, obviously the farm won't cover that. What about two bedrooms?'

Lucy's eyebrow went up again. 'Two?'

'Well – Minna and Nico won't mind sharing—'

'I think there's a law against that, at their age.'

'Or – or a sofa bed, in the sitting room, for Nico. And you've got this, so . . .' I felt myself reddening.

'My, he must be attractive,' she murmured as Robin suggested something a bit lower for two bedrooms, but not much.

'Or maybe around here?' I suggested.

'Yes,' he agreed, 'around here would be cheaper.'

'I know, perhaps we could all crowd into my basement flat and Felix and his father could come and feed us bowls of gruel? Poke them through the bars?' She nodded at the window.

'Lucy, don't be like that.'

'Like what? Reasonable? You're honestly suggesting we put on hold Dad's rightful inheritance to accommodate some family we don't even know – I imagine that's what this is all about? Letting them stay there or something? Tell her, Robin.'

Robin flushed, horrified to be called on thus. 'Well – heavens – I don't know. Um, it does seem a little rash, Mrs – Molly.' I was clearly going to be Mrs Molly forever. I narrowed my eyes at him. 'O-on the other hand I can see,' he groped about for what he could see, caught as he was between a rock and a very hard place, 'I can see that – well, if you do just rent it out, as you suggest—'

'How much would that set them back?' demanded Lucy. 'This remote, bizarre family we've never heard of.'

'Well . . . a three-bedroom house in South Ken – about a thousand pounds.'

'A month?' I hazarded.

'Um, no. A week.'

'A week! Good God. Oh, I'm quite sure he hasn't got that,' I said faintly. 'Cuthbert was the one with the money.'

'Exactly,' said Lucy grimly.

'I was thinking more like . . . well, I don't know—'

'No, you don't,' Lucy broke in. 'You don't have any

idea. Taking pity on an old man is one thing, Mum, but being taken for a fool is another. Isn't that right, Robin?'

'Well – gosh – um, I wouldn't say a fool, exactly.' Lucy glared. 'I mean – yes, in a manner of speaking . . .' My turn to raise an eyebrow. 'But – as a – a figure of speech, only. But Mrs – Molly, why not – why not get a buy-to-let? One bedroom, bought with the farm, and rent it out to him, at a reasonable rate?'

'Yes, why not?' demanded Lucy. 'Good idea.'

'Oh, but that's not what he wants. He wants to be surrounded by the things he knows and loves, by the man he loved, his memories.' I realized I was echoing somebody. 'To end his days there. And it may not be long,' I said eagerly. 'Felix says it could be months, weeks. He has emphysema.'

'Well golly, let's hope it's hours, eh?' Lucy looked at her watch. 'Let's hope he's expiring as we jolly well speak. I could rustle up the flowers. I love a coffin top. Lots of work space. All that mahogany. It could be our gesture, then everyone will be happy. If you don't mind me saying so, Mum, it's pretty unseemly sitting around twiddling our thumbs waiting for an old man to die.'

'I am not sitting around waiting for him to die and I am *not* unseemly,' I said hotly. 'I'm just trying to think of a fair and practical solution.'

Lucy seized the pepper pot and ground it on to her stir-fry as if grinding her foot on someone's face. Robin looked fearful.

'Firstly,' she spat, 'there is no solution needed, because there is no problem. Secondly, had there been a problem, which there isn't, nothing you've suggested has been either fair or practical. Isn't that right, Robin?'

Robin seemed to have got his tongue wrapped indefinitely around his tonsils, so puce was he becoming. 'Well, I must say . . . I certainly think . . . what I mean is—'

'Oh shut up,' she said, banging the pepper pot down hard on the table and making us both jump. 'If you can't say anything constructive, don't say anything at all. Sometimes I think I'm just surrounded by idiots.'

And with that she picked up her plate and barged into her bedroom with it. She turned and kicked the door shut and then a few moments later, we heard the television.

Robin and I raised our eyebrows at each other, bonded by our common fear. He didn't go after her, though, which impressed me. We ate silently and companionably – and, it has to be said, rather thankfully – for some minutes, and then I initiated a conversation about the theater, which I knew he was keen on. We actually had a rather pleasant meal as he told me about the latest David Spence production at the Haymarket, the unusual stage setting, and the spectacular performance of a young actor friend he'd been at Cambridge with, in an amusing cameo role. Nice boy, Robin. Shame about his girlfriend.

CHAPTER 13

$\mathcal{B}$ack at the farm the following day it was as if the previous one had never happened. It was as if London didn't exist at all, had been a figment of my outlandish imagination: a ridiculous, phantasmagorical dream that had taken place only in my head as I temporarily inhabited cloud cuckoo land, whilst in reality Herefordshire, or more specifically my ninety acres of it, was the only place on earth. In other words, it was business as usual.

Water was dripping from the kitchen ceiling via a damp patch where Minna had let a bath overflow and under which she'd placed a bucket which was now also overflowing. The tap water had tasted so vile that Nico, stirred from his habitual inertia, had gone up to the attic to investigate and found a dead rat in the tank: he'd thoughtfully left it there for me to deal with and bought bottled water instead. The septic tank in the paddock had backed up and overflowed because I'd forgotten to have it emptied and, consequently, effluent of the most repulsive nature was oozing, even now, into the back garden en route to the house.

All this Nico informed me of, in a laconic, detached voice, in semi-darkness, horizontal in his dressing gown on a sofa, eyes never leaving a repeat of *Top Gear*. Although to be fair, the overflowing bucket I'd already encountered in the kitchen.

'And have you even bothered to do anything about it?' I screamed, flinging off my jacket, throwing my bag on a chair and lurching to the window to yank apart the curtains with one hand while simultaneously scrolling down my phone for Stuart the Septic Tank Man's number with the other.

'Can't you even make a phone call?' Nico clearly considered this a rhetorical question and, anyway, I'd run back to the kitchen to empty the slopping bucket into the loo, phone wedged between shoulder and ear, replaced the bucket and run back again.

'Stuart! God, Stuart, I need you!' I plunged a frenzied hand through my hair.

'Like I said,' Nico said flatly, in response to my earlier question when I'd finally talked Stuart into coming, 'I went up into the attic. Took me ages. Had to find a ladder and everything. It's a real mess up there, Mum, needs sorting.' He wrapped his dressing gown around his skinny torso in disgust. 'There's, like, crap everywhere.'

I was bent double now, scooping up pizza boxes, crisp packets and other detritus such as fetid yoghurt pots, mugs and spoons which decorated the carpet. The dogs, who'd initially thought an enthusiastic waggy-tailed greeting in order, had slunk back to the kitchen to their baskets, sensing the mood.

'Yes, and you bloody well left the rat up there too! In the tank! That won't add to the ambience, will it?'

'It was gross. Enormous. Sort of . . . bloated. You'd be better. I don't do dead things. Oh, speaking of which, Rita took a turn for the worse so Minna rang Paddy again. He's out there now. Oh – *epic.*' These last words addressed, not to me, but to Jeremy Clarkson, leaping a ravine in a white van.

'Paddy? Is he? Where? Help me, please, Nico, why the bloody hell should I pick up your lemonade cans? In the field?' I paused to glare at him, mid-stoop, guiltily aware that I'd rather blithely assumed Rita was better; she'd been on her feet and drinking, after all.

'No, he drove out there in his pickup and brought her back to the barn. That one's still live.' Nico reached down to retrieve a can with lily-white, consumptive-looking fingers. 'Minna's out there too, bawling her eyes out.'

'Dear God, she's *hopeless* with sick animals, why didn't you go?' I staggered to the kitchen, arms full of rubbish, to the bin, which naturally was overflowing. Seething, I dumped it all on the table instead, picked out the yoghurty spoons, shook out a new black sack and swept it in.

'Nah, it's not that. It's Toxic Ted.'

I turned. 'I thought that was over?'

'Well, if you believe that . . .'

But I was already on my way outside, through the back door, pausing only to kick off my shoes and plunge my feet into wellies, experiencing yet more guilt. A bit of me had known Minna had her own problems before I left. I'd heard her on the phone to a girlfriend. But I'd shimmied off to London nonetheless to conduct my own romantic liaison knowing, from experience, that talks about Ted Forrester could be endless, tortuous and circuitous. But she didn't need Rita on top of that. I cursed Ted under my breath and his predilection for, when he felt like it, taking sabbaticals from their seesawing relationship in order to connect socially with other girls.

'Nothing sexual,' Minna would assure me, eyes wide. 'Just having a break.'

I'd nod, keeping my counsel. Knowing, again from experience, it was wise to say nothing.

'He says we're too young to have a long-term relationship,' she'd say, blinking away – unlike her sister, tears were never far from the surface. 'And also, that being apart makes us appreciate each other more when we get back together.'

'Ah. Right.'

Currently there'd been just such a hiatus; however, no obvious local diversion had materialized – and Minna was forensic in her enquiries. Perhaps she'd unearthed one while I'd been away? Perhaps Ted was back with – who was it last time? Round-the-Block Becky? I shuddered. I could see that Ted was a very fine specimen – tall, blond, broad-shouldered and extremely fit in both the modern and traditional sense of the word – but the trouble was, everyone else could see it too. He was a farm laborer who did a lot of ditch-digging and hedge-laying in various states of undress. Stripped to the waist in the summer I could understand, but I'd once driven past him dredging a river in wet boxer shorts, everything rippling and flexing away to the obvious delight of a gaggle of girls, hiding behind a dry-stone wall. Biddy at the livery yard, who was also his aunt and lived next door, told me local girls took convoluted routes past her house just to catch a glimpse and she was thinking of selling tickets in the summer to view him sunbathing over the garden fence.

'It's Minna's fault, she's punching.' Nico would tell me when I canvassed his opinion.

'I don't think so,' I'd say doubtfully. Loyally.

'She is. He's way out of her league.'

I wanted to say *not socially, Nico*, but knew this would land me in trouble of the most heinous kind.

'Perhaps he likes a bit of posh.'

Ah. OK from his mouth, then. But he didn't seem incensed by such behavior towards his sister when pressed.

'What does she expect? He's young. He's a player. And don't say "your sister" like you're expecting me to run off for some bare-knuckled, eighteenth-century fight.'

Lucy, though, agreed with me.

'Just tell him to fuck off!' she'd roar down the phone to Minna when her sister rang her in tears.

'You didn't say that to Robin.'

'Oh yes I did. For a good six months. And Robin got with a girl in a club, Minna. Toxic Ted is laying more girls than he is hedges.'

'Don't say that!' Minna would gasp, flinging the phone down and then flouncing hysterically from the room. Minna could be very eighteenth century herself when she felt like it. If we were in the midst of such a drama now, I thought nervously as I hurried across the yard and round the back of the stables to the barn, we were in for a protracted period of histrionics. A season of emotional discontent. I wasn't sure my nerves could stand it. At least Ted always had the decency to suspend relations when he was playing away, I reflected grudgingly, which exhibited a degree of decorum, but I had to encourage her to finally end it this time.

I flew into the barn, shutting the bottom half of the stable door behind me, and, once my eyes had adjusted to the gloom, found her and Paddy in the straw, a moribund Rita between them, two lambs bleating piteously at her side. Rita was horribly bloated and her fleecy sides heaved gastrically as she struggled for breath. Minna stood sobbing with the third lamb in her arms, shaking piteously, tears pouring down her cheeks, whilst Paddy, crouching, removed his stethoscope from his ears, his bag open beside him.

I hastened across.

'Oh Minna, darling. I'm so sorry you had to deal with all this. Go in.'

'She's dying,' sobbed Minna as Paddy shot me an incredulous look, clearly having been party to this for some time. 'She's literally taking her last breaths, Mum, with her three darling babies watching. It's tragic!'

'Minna, I've told you, the lambs are bleating because they're hungry, they couldn't care less,' said Paddy. 'And she's not taking her last gasp, but she is in a lot of discomfort. I seriously think we need to put her out of her misery, Molly. This is terminal anyway, but she could be in agony for days.'

Minna's wail filled the barn as she dropped to her knees, abandoning the lamb, hugging the smelly sheep fiercely to her E cup breasts, which made Rita's already bulbous eyes pop further.

'There must be something we can do!'

'Minna, go inside,' I commanded crisply, the cacophony of wailing and bleating really too much now. 'Blow your nose and have a cup of tea and calm down.'

She shot me a tortured look but released the sheep and fled, her shoulders shaking as she went.

'Sorry about that,' I said, crouching down opposite Paddy. 'She's quite emotional.'

'Can't think where she gets that from.'

'Plus she's got boyfriend problems.'

'Ah yes. Ted Forrester. Well, she needs to get rid of him. He's shagging his way round the county as we speak. Sheep shearing's come early this year with the hot weather and he's helping Freddie Fallon. They're going from farm to farm stripping the ewes and then the daughters. Wives too, sometimes.'

'Oh dear God,' I said faintly, putting a hand to my heart. 'I didn't know it was that bad. You mean . . . *famous* Freddie Fallon?' I breathed in horror.

'The very same. A legend in his own shearing leathers. He can't keep it in his trousers any more than Ted. You need to tell her.'

'How?' I yelped. 'She'll dissolve!'

'What, more than that?' He jerked his head housewards.

'Much. She won't come out of her room for days.'

'Well, you still need to address it. She'll be a laughing stock. Quite apart from anything else, she'll catch something.'

'Do you mind!'

He shrugged. 'You need to hear it.'

'Not from you I don't, you're – you're my vet, for God's sake, not my – my – I don't know – my – whatever!' I blustered as Paddy calmly filled a large syringe.

It hadn't escaped my notice, though, that this sort of straight talking was possibly what my children needed. I was all too aware that often I fell into the classic single parent trap of being a bit too easy on them because they'd had a tough time. But someone surely needed to tell Minna to find some steel, Nico not to be so lazy, and Lucy to be softer sometimes?

David would have done that. He hadn't always been perfect, but he'd been a brilliant father. I wondered how Felix had brought up his two. Rather well, I imagined, since both seemed to be thriving, with good jobs, and he spoke fondly of them. How old would he have been when he had them? How old *was* Felix? Five, ten years older than me? Ten would be good. Eleven or twelve even better.

I was conscious, like Minna, that I was not necessarily fighting my weight bracket, and a bigger age gap would play to my advantage. I remembered his face gazing down at mine in concern in the Savoy and felt a frisson of excitement. I imagined us there again, in the future, for dinner this time or – no, some- where a bit trendier – mustn't say that . . . cooler. Covent Garden, perhaps. A buzzing, happening place, like that club where all the stars went – um – yes, the Groucho. He was probably a member. And I'd get the look right this time: be much thinner, too. Sexier. Head to toe in black, which was hard on a woman of a certain age in daylight, but fine at night in a place like that, in a dimly lit corner, drinking champagne, heads close, all snuggly and giggly on a leather couch, as a waiter leaned over and said:

'Shall we get this effing show on the road?'

I blinked. 'What?'

Paddy's cross face was in mine.

'I said, shall we get this over and done with?'

I swallowed. Gazed down at Rita.

'You're going to do it now?'

'Well, I'm not going to come back tomorrow and mop her brow again, am I? There's no point.'

'Oh, Paddy, wait. Rita's so special, couldn't we try stronger antibiotics?'

'No, we couldn't. She's in great discomfort.'

'Oh, my poor girl!'

I laid my cheek on her smelly fleece, which was heaving horribly.

'Wait,' I instructed. I shuffled around and positioned myself at her head: picked it up and laid it gently in my lap. Bowing my own head I said a silent prayer, lips moving, then I crossed myself. Finally I looked up at him gravely. Nodded. 'OK. Go on then.'

Paddy picked up a hind leg, found a vein, administered the syringe swiftly, and in moments Rita's tortured eyes had shut and her labored breathing stopped. Her sides collapsed right into her ribs. I lowered my head in sorrow and felt tears well, but managed, heroically, not to spill them.

'Well, that's the first time I've had to do that.' Paddy packed the syringe away in his black leather bag with a snap.

'What?'

'Put down a sheep. I told you, any normal farmer would have slotted it.'

'Yes, well I'm not normal, am I? And I don't have the wherewithal for slotting.'

'Nico's got a gun, and a license. Hopefully.'

'For rabbits!'

'Which he leaves in the field. I've seen him, lamping at dusk with those scruffy mates of his, then leaving the rabbits all scattered about. It's disgraceful. If you kill an animal for sport you skin it and eat it. Make a stew.'

'Who says?'

'The unwritten law of the countryside says.'

'And since when did you become such an oracle for the countryside? Just because you were born and bred in a barn – and what gives you the right to be such a vociferous judge of my children?'

'Since it seems to me that every time I come here they could do with it. Now help me put this ewe back in the barrow and I'll take it to the kennels on the way back.'

'You will not!' I gasped. 'I will not have her eaten. I shall bury her.'

'Oh, don't be pathetic, Molly. You'll need a hole as big

as a trench and the foxes will dig her up. It's not even legal.'

'So report me,' I spat across the dead sheep's carcass as we crouched opposite one another, nose to nose.

'This one's special. Report me to Defra if you like.'

'I don't like, but I will. I'm not having my professional reputation sullied by your sentimentality.'

I affected a mincey voice:

'I'm not having my professional reputation – *bollocks*,' I roared. 'You don't give a stuff, you're just picking on me. You're a sanctimonious, holier-than-thou, small-minded, egotistical—'

'Everything all right in here?' Nico's head appeared over the stable door, eyes wide. He blinked. 'What's this, some funky, postmodern nativity scene? Not pregnant, are you, Mum?' He spotted Rita. 'Ah. Right. She's a goner then.'

'Nico.' I stood up: realized I was shaking. 'Dig a trench,' I commanded.

'What?'

'A hole. A big one. Under the oak tree at the top of the hill. Beside Jeremy.'

'Shit, Mum, that's got to be huge. Jeremy was a hamster.'

'Just do it,' I seethed. 'It will do you good. Stop you lazing around guzzling lemonade and eating pizza in front of the television. Now get dressed, dig a trench, and *stop killing poor, defenseless rabbits for fun!*'

He blanched, taken aback.

'Oh for fuck's sake! Keep your wig on.'

'And stop *swearing* so much!' I roared as he turned and sauntered away, albeit plucking a spade up as he went.

'Right.' I turned back to Paddy, chin raised, still trembling. 'Now, if you would be so kind as to help me put her in the barrow, I will take her up the hill for a proper Christian burial.'

'Sorry. No can do. I told you, it's illegal to bury fallen stock.'

'You know as well as I do Clive Burns gets his digger out and buries sodding great cows! He's got mass graves up there!' I pointed a quivering finger up the valley.

'Yes, but I'm not party to it and neither do I care about Clive Burns's reputation. The man's a charlatan.'

'Right. Well if you won't help me, I'll do it myself.'

An unseemly struggle ensued. Between a huge woolly sheep, a small, inappropriately dressed woman and a wobbly barrow. My long dangly necklace didn't help and somehow, Rita got her head stuck in it, which forced our faces cheek to cheek. I tried to pull away and naturally it broke – no matter, it was only River Island – and I would *not* be beaten. Snaking out a foot I tipped the wheelbarrow up on its prow and dragged Rita panting and heaving – me, obviously – head lolling, tongue hanging out – both of us – into it, then set it upright.

'There,' I panted, victorious. 'But that was very undignified for her,' I gasped as Rita lay flat on her back, legs in the air.

'Oh, I don't think it's Rita's dignity you should be worried about. Here, you dropped some beads.'

'Stuff the beads,' I snapped, tossing his offering in the straw. I felt a bit like that girl who takes over the farm in *Far from the Madding Crowd*, Bathsheba whatnot, all feisty and blazing.

'Open the door for me, please.' I was poised with the barrow now, flicking hair from my eyes, a triumphant gleam to them hopefully.

There was more of a quizzical gleam to his dark, faintly amused ones. He raised his eyebrows, mouth twitching. I waited. He clearly wasn't going to move. Wasn't going to help me one iota.

'Oh, you wretched man!' I roared. Incensed, I ran and flung the stable door wide. I ran back and, trying not to look as if she weighed a ton, which she flaming did, I wheeled her, unsteadily and wobbling, through the straw and out, staggering a bit and flinging a haughty 'send me the bill!' over my shoulder as I went.

I heard him laugh but I didn't look back.

A few minutes later, after I'd trundled through the yard and down the track, and as I began pushing her up the grassy hill, crouching very low, almost to my knees under the weight, I heard the welcome roar of his pickup as he drove away.

In the event, we didn't bury her. When I finally reached Nico at the top, he'd dug a hole about the size of a packet of cigarettes, and was sitting down beside his handiwork, smoking a roll-up.

'It's hopeless, Mum. The ground's like concrete. You try.'

'*Why* do I always have to do *everything* myself? Didn't you see me struggling up here?'

'Oh no, sorry. I was on the phone.'

I seized the spade and made a sterling effort but, naturally, I couldn't do it either. It hadn't rained for weeks, and the ground was solid. I sat down exhausted beside him and smoked one of his roll-ups which he'd thoughtfully made for me. We sat there, with our dead sheep in the barrow, puffing away and mulling over the predicament. Eventually we settled on snipping off a chunk of her fleece, emptying out the last grains of tobacco from his Golden Virginia packet, and stuffing the wool inside. Then we popped it in the hole and covered it over again. I said a little prayer as Nico looked bored. Then I found a couple of sticks, bound them together in a cross with what remained of my string of beads – it looked like a rosary actually, gave a rather pleasing, devotional look – and stuck it in the ground over the grave.

We turned and headed for home. Nico, at least, carted Rita down the hill, but it was quite a steep hill, and she was heavy. The barrow began to run away with him, until they were racing down.

I followed, shouting, 'Nico! Careful!' as he shrieked with laughter.

'Can't stop, Mum!' he shouted back when, all at once, the barrow overturned. Rita fell out, Nico fell headlong on top of her and, unable to stop, I fell on him, unable to keep from shaking with laughter too. Weeping, actually.

Ultimately, too, of course, we had to do exactly what Paddy had instructed, and Nico took Rita off to the kennels. Naturally it was humiliating, but Paddy would never know.

'Let him report me to Defra,' I told Nico when he came back with the receipt and handed it to me in the kitchen. 'I almost hope he does. Then I'll wave this in his face and have the last laugh.'

'Yeah, whatever,' Nico said wearily. He plucked a lemonade from the fridge and headed on through to the sitting room to adopt the position again: the horizontal one, tin can balanced on his chest.

'Whatever presses those neurotic old buttons of yours.'

CHAPTER 14

*T*he following morning I rang Peter. I had a cigarette poised and lit it nervously the moment he answered: highly unusual before midday and without a glass of wine.

'Morning, Molly, how's tricks?'

'Pretty good, thanks, and you?'

'In peak condition.'

'Peter, can you just remind me, how much are those people offering for the farm?'

'The McDonalds? Asking price, as agreed.'

'But I haven't agreed, have I? I mean, not absolutely.' There was a pause.

'Well . . . you've accepted their offer.'

'But isn't it more usual to get a few rival bids going?'

'Well, it depends. It's certainly not terribly ethical to renege at this stage, Molly.'

'Peter, I need more money, that's the thing. Much more.' I felt a bit breathless.

'I can't go and get a better offer now.'

'No. Right. Yes, I can see that.'

'And they're a lovely couple. They'd be devastated.'

'Well, quite. No, I do see. Paddy, then.'

'Paddy?'

'He wants the land.'

'Yes.'

'Can you . . . get more from him?'

The line went silent.

'Paddy's buying it at market value.'

'Which, as we know, is a snip. No wonder he's so excited, snooping round my fields, spying on my children. I think I can get double if I advertise it properly. Hasn't it got development potential?'

'Hardly. It's farmland, not industrial brownfield, thank God.'

'I think we should look into it anyway. Maybe get some competition going? I can't just sell it off to the nearest neighbor, can I? I owe it to the children to get as much as possible for it.'

'The children?'

'Yes, you know, for their – inheritance.' Golly, who was I, some Greek shipping heiress?

'It's just – I might need to buy in London, Peter, that's all. And that's a pricey exercise, as we know.'

There was another pause. His voice when it came sounded weary. Sad, even.

'I'll see what I can do, Molly.'

I felt crummy, obviously. Really crummy. But not for long. Heavens, not for long, because this was business, wasn't it, for Pete's sake? I couldn't just give away my only asset, could I? David would be horrified. Actually – no. Don't think about David. Instead I legged it upstairs, taking the stairs two at a time, which I can still do when I feel like it, and, in the privacy of my bedroom, logged on to Zoopla on my iPad to look at flats, whereupon an almighty row broke out downstairs. Wishing there was still a point at which all teenage children had to do a spell of National Service, I dashed back down to separate the warring parties. I found Minna, pink with fury, cheeks wet with tears, shrieking at Nico, who lay prone and unconcerned on his sofa, eyes on the television.

'*What* is the problem now?' I roared.

'Nico has only ruined my entire life, that's what!' she screamed, fists balled.

'Minna is employing ridiculous hyperbole as usual,' said Nico, who liked to run verbal rings around his sister. 'I simply told Ted she wasn't at home when he came to the door with his dick out, which is what any responsible brother would do for his *sister*.' He flashed me a look. 'And she's gone shouty-crackers.'

'He lost his phone and he came to ask me to the pub and now he'll probably take Gemma Parker!' she sobbed.

I sighed and perched on the arm of the sofa. 'I think Nico's right, Minna,' I said gently. 'You do need to be a bit more unavailable. A bit less eager.' A text vibrated in my pocket. I couldn't resist taking out my phone but didn't look at it. 'If you play a bit harder to get, he'll be less interested in looking elsewhere.'

'She needs to tell him to piss off,' muttered Nico.

'You know nothing about love!' shouted Minna as I glanced at my message.

'*So loved our day. Can we do it again? Next week? Felix.*'

I went hot. My heart leaped right out of my throat, bounced around the room across the furniture then popped back in again.

'Doesn't she, Mum?'

'What?' I whispered, glancing up, my face hot.

'She needs to tell him where to go. You don't just jump

if he says jump,' Nico said forcefully. He swung his legs around and sat up. 'Guys don't like that.'

'Don't they?' I said, unthinking, glancing at my phone again.

'No, of course not, Mum. You need to be a bit mysterious.' Minna perched on the other sofa arm. We sat silently by, absorbing the wisdom. 'Jesus, it's lesson one. Don't make it too easy, be unavailable, and then they'll start eating out of your hand.'

My fingers had been itching to text back: '*Yes! I loved it too! How lovely! Any day at all!*'

'Ted will just forget me if I do that,' Minna gulped. 'And find someone else. And don't say – well then he's not worth it, he *is* worth it!' she said fiercely.

'OK, I won't say that. And I'll admit it's a gamble, he might go and shag Gemma Parker, but trust me, Minna, he looked a bit disappointed when I said you were still clubbing in London with Lucy.'

'You *didn't*,' we breathed in unison.

'I did. He needed it. That shook him a bit. He probably hasn't been further than Worcester. He muttered something about letting him know on Facebook when you were back.'

Minna and I were silent.

'So . . . what should I do? Tell him I'm back?'

'No, get the next train to London and *do* some clubbing with Lucy. Put the pictures on Facebook and then come back.'

She swallowed. 'I'm not sure he'll like that.' She scratched inside her arm where her eczema was flaring up. 'He doesn't like me flirting with other guys. He's quite possessive. I mean – sensitive.'

'Well, a lot of guys are, that's standard. But trust me, Minna, if you want to stand any chance it's your only option. Otherwise join the line with Gemma and all the other bucolics.'

'I don't think she's got that,' she said doubtfully.

Nico rolled his eyes in despair. Minna gave an almighty sniff but she looked a little calmer.

'I'll think about it,' she muttered before slinking from the room, pausing only to grab her moth-eaten rabbit from down the side of a chair, whose ear she still stroked in extremis. Still scratching her arm, she went up to her room.

'Thanks, Nico,' I breathed when she was out of earshot.

'My pleasure.' He picked up the remote, changed channels, and lay down again. 'Anything I can do for you, Mum? Any little creases that need ironing out in your life?'

I stood up quickly. 'No. Thank you.' Nico was remarkably perceptive; something I often forgot. He was surprisingly in touch with what the *Daily Mail* would be pleased to call His Feminine Side.

Very much wanting to follow more basic instincts, I nonetheless steeled myself, went into the kitchen and sat down at my desk. I looked at my soap and underwear emails on the computer. A smattering of orders had come in. Dutifully I turned and packed up the requisite items from the pile on the kitchen table into Jiffy bags. Halfway through packing a sparkly thong I did take out my phone and read the message again. But I resisted texting Felix back for at least an hour. I even made a phone call to Twinkly Andy, my underwear supplier, who sometimes got a bit carried away on the glam- our front, and who promised to tone the sequins down a bit. Then I went upstairs to sit quietly on my bed and reply. I wrote:

'I enjoyed it too. Can't do next week, I'm afraid, but possibly the following one?'

I pressed my knees together, shut my eyes tight, crossed myself and pressed 'send'. A few seconds later, a text came back.

'Following week I'm in Vienna – shame.'

I shot up from the bed and paced around the room, appalled. I went cold. Then I felt dreadfully hot and sweaty. I licked my lips and before I could allow myself to think further sent back:

'Oh – hang on – just realized, I have to come up on Tuesday to deliver something to Lucy!'

In a flash he was back:

'Great. Let's have dinner Tuesday night. I'll be in touch nearer the time.'

I gazed at my phone as if it were a devotional icon: kissed it reverently, pressed it to my cheek, then pocketed it guiltily. Not very smooth. Not at all classy. But still, I had my date. Nico would strongly disapprove, I thought, cringing. I crossed to my dressing table and feverishly rearranged bottles and creams with a nervous, fluttery hand. But on the other hand, I thought as I sat down and looked at my reflection which was flushed and bright-eyed, I didn't have all the time in the world, did I? As a middle-aged woman? It was not on my side as it was on Minna's. I wasn't convinced a week or two would make a spectacular difference to my laughter lines and eye bags – I leaned forward and studied my face closely in the mirror – but still. Apart from anything else, *how exciting!*

Next door, I could hear Minna opening and shutting drawers, packing to go to London and escape the object of her desires, whilst I, of course, was flinging myself at mine. I picked up my precious Touche Éclat: raised it to my dark circles. No – no, I wasn't. Not flinging. I lowered my concealer and eyed my reflection. Just . . . accommodating a busy man's very demanding schedule. That's all. Any

unfortunate juxtaposition with my teenage daughter's
newfound restraint was purely coincidental. I painted away
with my magic wand, covering up all sorts of inconve-
niences.

THE FOLLOWING TUESDAY, almost to assuage my own
conscience, I cut it rather fine. Minna was, to her enormous credit, still in London with Lucy and had asked for a
bag of clothes to be brought up in case she stayed longer,
which was encouraging. It also meant I had a genuine
reason to go to the flat and deposit her bag, and of course
mine. I'd intended to arrive in the afternoon but at the last
minute a buyer suddenly materialized for Nutty, the iron-
grey gelding I'd bought at auction some time ago and
failed to sell, and the woman was offering the asking price
if she could see him today. Also, she was coming with a
trailer, she told me, which was a frightfully good sign.

Naturally, Mrs Pritchard was late. One o'clock became
two o'clock as I waited anxiously in the yard. Minna's and
my bags were already stashed in the car and although I
was dressed in jeans and a T-shirt, I had smart London
clothes laid out on the bed upstairs for a lightning change.
The make-up was already in place, the hair blow-dried
courtesy of the local salon – I was all ready to catch the
three o'clock train. She'd sounded so excited, Mrs
Pritchard, when she'd rung: thrilled to have found exactly
what she wanted, the ad on *Horse Quest* reading so
marvelously. 'I hardly need to get on him!' she'd gushed.
'He sounds completely perfect!' Please God, let her be
quick. Let her buy the completely perfect horse in seconds
flat so I could be on my way to London, with four thousand pounds in my pocket.

Half an hour later and with no reply from her mobile,

I realized she wasn't coming. I ran upstairs, changed, and ran back down, bringing my jeans with me to throw in the wash, when all of a sudden, a silver Range Rover swept through the gate into the yard. I quickly shed my London clothes but got in a terrible muddle putting my jeans back on, which were inside out, so that as, not Mrs Pritchard, but Mr, strode directly towards the kitchen window, I was still hopping around in my pants trying to get a leg in.

It wasn't ideal. But neither was the fact that Mr Pritchard, when I finally burst out flustered to meet him, was a lean, bald, tight-lipped man whose bandy legs looked as if they'd been hugging top-class eventers all their life. Wearing what looked like pre-Raj breeches, he had a clipped, military manner that suggested he knew exactly what he was doing. Indeed, as I hurried him across the yard and opened the stable door, he told me he'd seen six or seven eventers already that week and had rejected all of them. He also told me his wife didn't know what she was talking about and that it was much better for him to buy a horse on her behalf as she tended to get emotionally swayed. My heart sank deep into my boots. Particularly when I led Nutty out and Pritchard felt his legs.

'He's got a slight lesion on his left hind,' he said, straightening up.

'That's an ancient injury,' I told him. 'He's never lost the bump, but he's as sound as a bell. Trot him up, if you like.'

'Yes, please.'

Right. That meant *I* had to trot him up, which wasn't entirely in the script. I was rather hoping Pritchard would do it in the absence of Nico, who'd suddenly made himself annoyingly scarce. It was another warm day and my make-up would glow and I'd get sweaty if I wasn't careful. I was careful. I trotted Nutty very, very slowly, jogging gently beside him, barely getting him out of a walk and keeping my arms right away from my sides, like an ape.

'OK,' he said doubtfully when I'd jogged back. 'Although I wouldn't have minded an extended trot. Can I see him ridden?'

This was a standard request and one I was totally prepared for but totally unprepared to carry out, since a riding hat on my freshly coiffed hair was out of the question.

'Ah, well, you see, both of my daughters are away – he belongs to my daughter Lucy' – always better to claim a family pet than a horse bought at auction – 'and I can't find my son and I'm afraid I don't ride any more. So if you wouldn't mind just hopping on yourself,' I beamed charmingly. 'He's perfectly safe.'

'I don't doubt it, but I'd like to see his paces.'

'Yes, I appreciate that, but—'

'Isn't that your son?'

I swung around. There was no denying that the lanky, barefooted, hunched adolescent could probably fit the profile. Nico dripped out of the house, in communion with his mobile, trailed by the dogs.

'Yes. But he might not—'

'*Excuse me!* ' Mr Pritchard's glass-shattering, commanding tones pierced the air. Nico stopped as if he'd been shot. 'Excuse me, can I have a word?' Definitely ex-Army.

Nico looked as if he'd been turned to stone. At length he turned: stared. Then he came across, very, very slowly.

'Um, Nico, I'm selling dear Nutty here, as you know,' I said breathlessly. 'Or showing him, at least, to Mr Pritchard. Darling, would you be an absolute angel and hop up for me? He'd like to see his paces.'

Nico squinted at me incredulously. 'I haven't ridden for months, Mother. Why don't you?'

'Because – I've lost my nerve, remember?' I stared at him hard, willing him to twig.

'Since when?'

'Since I fell off, remember?' I made my eyes very large.

'But you were riding yesterday. I saw you get the tack out.'

'Yes,' I gasped. 'And that's when I fell off.'

'You fell off this horse?' said Pritchard, frowning.

'N– no.' I gulped. 'I fell off . . . Tufty.'

We all looked doubtfully at Tufty in the adjacent stable. He was the children's beloved first pony and the size of a large dog.

'Why were you riding Tufty?' asked Nico incredulously.

'To – to try and get my nerve back.'

'But I thought you said you fell off him and lost it?'

'Yes, for the second time,' I hissed, totally losing track of my web of lies and feeling a bit faint. 'I fell off him twice. Now, Nico, are you, or are you not, going to get on Nutty and show Mr Pritchard his paces?'

'Not,' he said firmly. He turned on his heel and sloped off. I watched him go, wishing, actually, that Mr Pritchard would do the same. This was not an in-the-bag sale. This was not a done deal. This was a protracted sale and I knew all about these. Subsequent visits would follow – two or three sometimes – complete with trainers and other, so-called equine experts and, four thousand pounds or not, I needed to catch my train.

'Very well, in the absence of a rider, I'll take him round the paddock myself. But I'll be back another day when perhaps one of your daughters can ride him.'

'Yes, another day, another day,' I said happily. 'And tell

you what, why don't you ride him then, when they're back?'

'No, since I'm here, I'll ride him now,' he said firmly.

Plucking the saddle and bridle from the stable door where I'd handily placed them, he tacked him up himself in seconds flat. Then, taking the reins, he sprang athletically into the saddle. Nutty's eyes flickered imperceptibly but recognizing he had a pro on board, he immediately found his manners. In moments he was off, on the bit, neck arched, chin on chest, at a showy walk, through the open gate and into the paddock.

Pritchard walked then trotted endless circles and figures of eight whilst I stood at the fence glancing frantically at my watch, calling, 'Lovely! That's probably enough, isn't it?' whilst he totally ignored me. Instead he barked orders as he passed at a canter now: 'I'd like a small jump please, a cavalletti.' Or: 'Could you put up a double?'

All of which meant I had to dash around in the heat, putting up poles and crossbars while he hopped over them and then adding tricky colorful fillers to see if Nutty shied, which he didn't. It took so long I thought I was going to be sick.

Finally I strode into the middle of the paddock and roared, '*I think he's probably had enough now!*'

Pritchard pulled up beside me. Glared down. 'Why? Is he unfit?'

'No – no. But I have to catch a train. I'm going to London.'

'Oh. Right. You should have said.' He dismounted in one fluid movement.

The truth. So simple. Why hadn't I lunged for it earlier?

'He's a nice horse,' he said, giving him a quick pat. 'I'll come back and have another look.'

'OK, goodbye,' I breathed, snatching the reins from him.

'Oh. Right.' He looked startled. 'You are in a rush.'

'Yes, terrible rush,' I said, swiftly unsaddling Nutty and pulling him to the fence, where I left the tack. Yelling for Nico, I raced away with the sweaty horse beside me, running now, full pelt through the yard. I popped him smartly in his stable, yanked the bridle off, and flung it over the door.

Mr Pritchard followed slowly. I felt his eyes on my back as I dashed back into the house. As I glanced through the kitchen window, I saw him shrug and go towards his car.

'*Nico!* ' I yelled in the direction of my ever prone child as I took the stairs two at a time. I tore into my bedroom, ripped off my jeans and T-shirt, and was about to don my London clobber when I realized I couldn't possibly and hopped in the shower to hose myself down. I concentrated on pits and parts and avoided face and hair but, inevitably, caught disastrous sprinkles. I hopped out, dried myself hastily, and had just got my underwear and skirt on, when Nico finally appeared.

'What?'

'I'll give you twenty pounds if you hose Nutty down, feed him, and tip him out in the paddock.'

His eyes popped. 'Twenty quid?'

'Yes, twenty quid. That sale's in the bag subject to Lucy or Minna riding him, so I'll be flush.' I reached for my deodorant. 'Oh – and clean the tack.' I blasted away under my arm. Froze. 'Shit.'

'What?'

I stared at the can of aerosol. 'Fucking hairspray!'

He blinked. 'Well, at least you'd shaved. Otherwise you'd have, like, rigid bush under your arm. Nasty.'

'Bugger, I'll have to *wash* again now. Just do it, Nico,

OK?' I seized my purse and flung the money at him, knowing if I'd gone for less, he might dither.

Nico turned to go.

'God. He must be hot if you're flinging twenty-quid notes around,' he muttered.

I swung about. 'What did you say?'

'Nothing.'

He disappeared, trousering the cash.

Minutes later, as I turned my car smartly round in the yard, aiming now for the twenty-two minutes past, I saw him lead Nutty out. He tied him up and picked up the hose. I gave him a cheery wave and yelled the usual stuff about keeping an eye on the sheep and the chickens and the dogs and then I was off, but as I plastered on a smile and told him there was a pizza in the freezer he gave me a very old-fashioned look. I had a horrible feeling he was about to say, 'Just watch yourself, Mum' as Lucy had done, so I shot off through the gates before he could.

Happily the lanes were clear: no ponderous tractors to seethe behind, no heaving hay lorries to lurch dangerously past. And happily, too, I had ten minutes in hand, I realized, since my watch, according to the clock in the car, was slightly fast. Sighing with relief, I sank back in my seat and tried to relax. Breathe, Molly. Just breathe. I turned on Classic FM for karma. As I was slowing down to approach a junction, I was honked suddenly from behind. I glanced in my rear-view mirror. Bloody hell. Bloody *hell*. Wretched Paddy Campbell. All I needed. I stopped, stuck my head out of the window and glared back at him.

'What?'

'Pull over. I want a word.' Flaming cheek.

'I haven't got time, I'm catching a train.'

I realized, to my horror, he was already out of his pickup and striding towards me. Plunging the car into first,

I shot off, seeing his shocked face in the rear-view mirror. I grinned. Arrogant twat. I drove on. Some minutes later, I rounded a bend and came to another junction but there was Paddy's red Jeep, right in front of me, sideways on, blocking the road. *Bastard.* I screeched to a halt. I knew exactly what he'd done. He'd gone through the ford, which was a short cut through Jim Baker's land, through his farmyard, in fact; a route only to be used in extremis. Paddy was standing waiting in the lane. Livid, I leaped from my car. I strode up to him.

'Get out of my way, Paddy, I've got a train to catch.'

'Not until I've had a word with you first. What d'you mean by putting up the price of your land?'

'I'm putting it up to the market value. I'm not giving it away, I'd be mad to do that. I'm getting what's fair.'

'You know damn well I'm the only one who's going to buy it – who else would want eighty acres in the middle of nowhere without a house attached?'

'The Foxes might.' My other, elderly neighbors.

'I've already asked, as apparently you have too, and they don't. You're just forcing my hand way above what's fair.'

'I'll tell you what's fair. You getting out of my way and letting me through and talking about this some other time.'

'Some other time that suits you, I imagine.'

'Yes, Paddy, that's right. My land, my rules, and if I were you I'd be a little more obsequious.'

'Oh I'd like to—'

'What?' We were facing each other now, inches apart in the middle of the road, glaring fiercely.

'What would you like to do? Put me over your knee and spank me or something, like you'd like to do to my children?'

I have absolutely no idea where that came from. It had

appeared in my head from space, and employing no filter whatsoever, I'd said it.

Paddy blanched, taken aback. Then, in his eyes, I saw something arrive in his head too, and just as impulsively he acted on it. In the middle of the lane, in the middle of nowhere, he took me forcefully in his arms and kissed me, very thoroughly, on the lips.

on't ask me why I didn't pull away immediately. Perhaps I was too shocked. Too completely and utterly wrong-footed. I did pull away but, if I'm honest, it was a second later than might have been appropriate, under the circumstances. In fact, if I'm being totally truthful, we parted at exactly the same moment, when a car horn sounded abruptly behind us.

Appalled, we pulled apart like deflecting magnets. Paddy's eyes were still full of something extraordinary, but when he glanced over my head at the car, whose path we were blocking, they instantly became guarded. Without giving me another look he turned on his heel and strode to the cab of his truck. In one seamless movement he was in, executing a smart three-point turn in the road, and roaring away throatily in the opposite direction, splashing back through the ford and the farmyard, scattering chickens and ducks. I turned and hastened back to my own motor vehicle just as Mr McCarthy from the Spar in the village stuck his head out of the window of his stationary blue

Ford Focus behind me. A huge grin split his desiccated, weather-beaten old face.

'Tha's nice, luv. I didn't know you and veterinary were like that.'

I froze, my hand on my door handle. Then I hurried over, bent down to his open window.

'No. We're not. Not remotely. In fact, I don't even like him.'

He looked taken aback.

'Right you are, luv. None of my business, I'm sure.'

'And he doesn't like me, either. He really doesn't.'

He gazed at me, astonished. Then he threw back his grizzled old head and roared with laughter, revealing an unusual dental arrangement.

'Does he not? Is that so? Don't you worry, luv, your secret's safe with me.'

'Oh, I do hope so, Mr McCarthy, I sincerely hope so, because there's absolutely nothing in it, OK? Nothing whatsoever.'

I gave him a searching look. He grinned at me again, revealing those terrible teeth. 'I have to dash,' I told him and with that I raced back to my car, fired up the engine and plunged it into first. I swung a left at the T-junction before roaring away down the hill.

At least it had been Mr McCarthy, and not Mrs, I thought, raking a frazzled hand through my hair and glancing in the mirror as he trundled after me at a more leisurely pace. She was a dreadful gossip. Mr, I felt sure, would be as good as his word and keep it to himself. Men did, didn't they? But it wasn't ideal, in a small place like this.

What had he been *thinking*, Paddy, to – to kiss me like that? So – you know – *roughly*. No. No, that was wrong. I swallowed. *Rudely.* Yes, that's what he'd been, plain rude. And I would tell him so. I straightened up decisively behind the wheel. The very next time I saw him. Tell him he was out of order. I drove on through the lanes towards town.

After a bit, I touched my lips. My fingertips stayed there a moment. It was odd, though. I felt . . . rather extraordinary. Well, of course, who wouldn't? I was bound to feel peculiar. Not excited, which I'd been about to say; more, well, dislocated. Because let's face it, I hadn't been kissed for five years. And certainly not like that. Ever, really, like that. Well. Perhaps Henri. Definitely Henri. I felt my mind crouch, ready to spring to Paris with effortless propulsion, but I halted it immediately in its tracks. Oh yes, I knew how to do that. Knew which buttons to press.

Fortunately, anyway, I was on the cusp of a complicated roundabout and then the dual carriageway which required concentration, and then, in moments, I was hanging a left into the station forecourt and going around the back of the building to park.

Once on the train – the next one *again*, of course, the forty-eight, and by now, horribly late – I took out my phone and read a text.

'Sorry about that. Can't think what came over me. Thought you needed teaching a lesson, I suppose. It meant nothing. Paddy.'

Fury raged. I texted back. *'You were totally out of order and I'm appalled. I hope you're thoroughly ashamed of yourself. Too right it meant nothing.'*

'Stupid of me to imagine you could read. Can't help noticing my initial text contained the word "sorry". Are you one of those people who likes to milk an apology?'

'I'm one of those people who knows a genuine apology when I see one, and yours had all the sincerity of a rat in a trap.'

'Having trouble with the rat analogy. Tends to apply to a person

of dubious moral integrity with a propensity to double-cross. Anyone spring to mind?'

'Are you calling me a rat?'

'Your word, not mine. This is childish and I have a calf to deliver.'

'Oh, suddenly it's childish and you have a calf to deliver, aren't you the big grown-up man with an important job?'

No response. Which was annoying. Because I'd wanted *him* to be last, not me, and then I'd ignore *him*. But now he was ignoring me. Although I did check my phone occasionally. Twat. I pocketed it, wishing my final text had been a trifle more dignified. No matter. He could go to hell as far as I was concerned. I rummaged in my bag and concentrated instead on my latest find in WHSmith, which was far more exciting, and far more accessible than anything else I'd discovered so far. It was a reassuringly slim volume entitled *Contemporary Art for Beginners*.

LUCY AND MINNA were getting ready to go out when I arrived at the flat, and I have to say, Minna looked fantastic. Having let me in she hopped back up on the sofa to finish her make-up in front of the only good mirror in the place, Lucy presumably in the bedroom from whence I could hear music.

'Darling.' I dropped my bags in the middle of the room, which looked like a changing room at Topshop, littered with clothes and overflowing ashtrays and bras on radiators, doing my best to ignore what wasn't my business. 'You look amazing. You've lost weight.'

She had. Minna wasn't fat but she could run to a tummy and chunky thighs if she wasn't careful.

'Thanks, Mum. I haven't eaten at all since I've got here, just drunk loads. And I've had so much fun.'

I wasn't sure I should condone such an admission but her smiling face told me to let it go and I wondered if drinking vodka and dancing for several nights on the trot would do the same for me.

'I've brought your stuff.'

'Thanks.'

'But I've got to hurry or I'm going to be late. Obviously I'm going to need a key – where's Lucy?'

'She and Robin are going to a drinks party.' She carefully applied mascara to her upper lashes.

'And you're seeing them there?'

'Oh no, I'm going somewhere different and I've got Sophia's key, she's still away. Luce and I don't always do the same thing so I need it.'

'Oh. OK. Leave it under a pot for me?'

'In London?'

We exchanged a worried look.

'Yes, but don't tell Lucy.' We exchanged another guilty, complicit one and I opened the door and located a handy geranium.

'Except I'm bound to be later than you,' she said, frowning, as I shut the door, 'so why don't you take it? We'll probably end up at a house party.'

'We?'

She slipped the key from her jeans and I pocketed it gratefully.

She colored. 'Oh, just this guy I've met. Friend of Lucy's.'

'Oh *good*, darling. *Good.*'

'Easy, Mother. I'm going for drinks. Not marrying him.'

'And he's taking you out to dinner?'

'No, we're going to this bar.'

'And does he have a name?'

'Sadly not, his parents forgot.' She gave me a bolshie grin. 'And yes, I am still in love with Ted so don't get any big ideas.'

'Has he been in touch?'

I joined her standing on the sofa and began dabbing my face with yet more powder to soak up the shine so that I began to resemble a French courtesan.

'Yeah, a bit.' She lowered her mascara brush and picked at her nail varnish. Her mouth drooped. Why had I asked that? Why?

'Minna, shall I take it all off and start again? The make-up?'

She peered, brightening as I knew she would, at being style-counseled.

'I would,' she said firmly. 'You've obviously been slathering it on and it's gone a bit gloopy.'

This had me speeding to the bathroom in seconds flat, whipping a towel around my head and washing vigorously.

By the time I'd reapplied the works, I was seriously late. Shouting a last goodbye to Minna, who'd disappeared into the bedroom to change into something I'd brought her, I grabbed my handbag and fled. I tottered down the road in heels, hoping, praying for a taxi. For once, God was in his heaven and a black cab rolled up right beside me just as I'd swung around to look.

'Where to, luv?'

Felix had been at the restaurant for literally ten minutes, he assured me, as I hastened to take the seat beside him at the zinc bar of some super-cool, buzzing Chelsea restaurant. It only took me two attempts to achieve the high bar stool and he shot out a hand to ensure I didn't tumble off the other side as it spun but, other than that, it was seamless.

'You look lovely,' he told me, resuming his seat, having dismounted to softly kiss my cheek when I'd arrived which had caused an electric current to fizz through me. Only one kiss, which I always felt was far more intimate than two.

'I took the liberty of ordering some champagne, is that OK?'

'How lovely. Yes, please.' I raised the glass he'd already poured me greedily to my lips. 'What are we celebrating?'

'Oh, nothing. I just thought . . .'

Calm down, Molly. Just calm down. This is how urbane, sophisticated people behave of a Tuesday night in SW3. Do get a grip and try to behave as if you're awash with Bolli at home and you've been to a sushi bar before, which, I had a feeling, this was.

'Are you a fan of these fishy crustaceans?'

'*Love* fish.'

'Excellent, I assumed you would be since you didn't demur at my choice of eatery. I've ordered twelve.'

To my horror, a vast platter of oysters appeared in their shells from beneath the zinc bar in front of us with a murmured 'bon appétit' from the smoldering garçon. Not a sushi bar at all, an oyster bar. *Yuck.*

I composed myself and there was a bit of preliminary chat about our respective weeks, his far more exciting than mine, and then I asked after his father, watching, mesmerized, as he expertly squeezed a dash of lemon then Tabasco on to a wobbling, translucent . . . *glob* . . . and popped it in his mouth.

'He's not so good, I'm afraid,' he said sadly when he'd rolled it around enough and swallowed. 'He's back in bed this week. The emphysema's flared up again. Camilla's being a brick, though, she's stayed on to look after him.'

'Oh. Poor chap.' I tentatively picked up a shell. Only once. In France. Not a huge success.

'He insists on getting dressed, and she finds him sitting on a chair beside his bed, fully clothed. He's better lying down. It makes him cough to sit up. With a bit of gentle persuasion she gets him back in his pajamas and into bed again.'

'Oh *dear*.' I put my shell down.

'I can't really pay her, but she says it doesn't matter.'

'*So* sweet.'

'I know. Dad adores her. He'll miss her. Anyway. Hey ho.' He rallied, straightening up on his stool and popping another oyster. 'The decorators are coming next week and I've got grand plans for his new accommodation. I've decided to shift my studio to the top floor and move him downstairs, which will suit him better.'

'Golly. What an upheaval. All those easels, paints . . .'

'Oh, it's not too bad. Don't forget, I don't do much of that stuff. And to be honest, I don't think it will be for long.'

'You mean . . .'

He shrugged. 'Who knows. The doctors say they're surprised he's still with us.'

I nodded. Thought of him being helped by Camilla from his chair back to his bed. His marital bed, really. Of twenty-odd years.

A hand covered mine. 'Molly, I am absolutely not trying to make you feel guilty in any way; in fact I was determined not to mention it, it's just you brought it up.' Felix's eyes were soft and kind. 'It's already arranged. I felt so bad about what I can see amounted to emotional blackmail last time we met and I don't want a repeat of that. It's all organized. He's moving in with me in two weeks' time.'

'Right. But no Camilla.'

'No, it's too far. You see, she lives in Chiswick. But I'll find someone else. He'll be fine, don't worry.'

'And you'll have to walk through your aged father's apartment to get up to your studio as will all your clients . . .' I shook my head. 'No, Felix. *I've* got it all organized. I've been thinking about this. In fact I've already decided. I'm going to use the money from the farm to buy a small flat near Lucy's and your father can rent the house for as long as he – well. As long as he needs it.'

He smiled. 'Molly, you have no idea what the rental on a house like that would be. He couldn't possibly—'

I raised my hand. 'I do know. I've been into it. And I don't expect it. I'd only ask for a fraction of it, a pepper-corn rent. Cuthbert's inheritance is a totally unexpected windfall as far as I'm concerned, one I'm not even convinced I'm entitled to, if I'm honest, and this would go a long way to making me feel better about it. It would assuage my conscience. And actually, I don't want to hear any more about it.'

And with that I joyfully popped the last remaining oyster which he was clearly leaving for me, got it as far as my throat, realized it had the consistency of a large blob of phlegm, gagged horrifically, twice, eyes boggling, looked desperately for a napkin and, finding none, slipped none too elegantly from my stool and fled to the ladies. Happily I didn't throw up when I disgorged it into the basin but it was nip and tuck. A couple of girls in there were sweet; I'd pushed right past them as they washed their hands, the loos being occupied, and they told me they couldn't bear the bloody things either. When I finally tottered out, white-faced, Felix was hovering, looking concerned.

'Golly, what happened?' He escorted me back to the bar. 'I thought you were about to puke.'

'No, no, just went down the wrong way, that's all.'

I took a large glug of cold, refreshing, totally gorgeous champagne, climbed back on to my stool again, which would insist on revolving – how *did* people do this? – and then sat, like a child, still spinning, waiting for whatever came next.

Felix was sweet and so grateful in his appreciation. He insisted continually that if I was to change my mind at the last minute, I was to shout. He was also touching in his deeply felt happiness for his father.

'He'll be beside himself,' he said softly, his eyes filling.

'Shall we ring him?' I asked gleefully, having drunk most of the bottle of champagne. Was Felix even drinking? He was more of a sipper, I'd noticed. I must try to cultivate that.

'Oh Molly, I don't know. It casts it in stone, rather.'

'Come on, let's cast. The sooner the better.'

I made him get his phone out and after a really rather playful – and quite sexy – charade about him putting it away again and me digging it out (jacket, not trousers, although I wouldn't have minded), he laughingly agreed and found the number. The landline didn't answer and he looked a bit anxious and I suddenly panicked Robert was already flipping *dead*, but then he answered his mobile. Felix relayed the news and his beaming smile told me how much it was appreciated on the other end. For some reason David sprang to mind as he was grinning, and I couldn't imagine why. It shook me a bit. Indeed I had to have another drink and regroup on the stool to shed the image of my husband's face. Was it because I was having supper with a man five years after his death? No, it wouldn't be that. It wouldn't be that at all.

'Was he up and about?'

'Just coming back from the pub,' Felix said happily, pocketing his phone. 'He's thrilled.'

'The pub?'

'Oh – he – occasionally joins a quiz team there, on a Tuesday. Thought he'd better – um – pop in, and tell them he couldn't make it.' Felix licked his lips. 'Typical Dad, doing the right thing. Hobbling down with his stick.'

'Oh.' I nodded. Somehow I hadn't imagined him going further than the loo.

'Someone helped him home. Put him back to bed. The old devil. He sneaks out occasionally. Such a worry.'

'Ah, right.' I sank happily into my champagne. Gosh, these elderly parents. More trouble than children some- times. I made a mental note to ring mine; I hadn't seen them recently. I also realized, rather guiltily, I hadn't seen my friends. Anna. Tia. Who'd called, left messages. I wasn't quite sure why I hadn't rung back. I'd do it when I returned. Tell them all my news. Or no. Better still, listen to theirs.

The evening rolled on in a delightfully languorous manner. Felix was concerned I hadn't eaten much and ordered some delicious garlic prawns and then later, after a few more drinks, suggested a club. I didn't argue. The only clubs I ever went to in Herefordshire were for books or bridge, and even those I never managed to get to more than once a month.

I climbed eagerly into the taxi Felix hailed outside, assuming Annabel's or somewhere similar, where David and I used to go occasionally with Giles who'd been a member. I was therefore surprised to find myself in a much younger environment: still in Mayfair, but in a tall white town house. Inside it was very dark, supremely sultry and extremely chic. The walls were clad with black velvet and there was a great deal of zebra skin on the floor; indeed animals were clearly a theme here, there even appeared to be a giraffe at the bottom of a flight of stairs. Stuffed, obviously, but life-size. There was a lot of smoky black glass and subdued lighting and girls with dresses falling off, and lithe, beautiful men. It was clearly very much private, members only.

'Oh. OK.' I smoothed down my tired black dress from Coast. 'Not sure I'm dressed for this.'

'You look gorgeous. Come on, through here.'

Felix led the way through a dimly lit corridor of rooms, some lined with books and paintings and some with more animal skins, all freckled with the beautiful people. Although it was quite hard to see in this light, the clientele appeared to be both expensively and scantily dressed. A dark Italian-looking man in a cerise silk shirt was talking to a beautiful young actress I recognized but couldn't put a name to. He was peering down the front of her tiny gold dress seemingly made entirely out of chains. She raised his chin with her finger to avert his gaze, took his glass, drained it, and walked off.

On a fur rug in a corner, a couple were curled up, talking earnestly, nose to nose. Two very beautiful black men dressed identically in turquoise Nehru jackets were holding hands on a sofa, whispering intently to one another, gazing rapturously. I was glad I was with Felix, whose casual grace, even in this glamorous menagerie, set him apart somehow. He led me to a red velvet sofa draped casually with a pony skin over the back, in possibly the darkest, most secluded corner of the room. We sat and we chatted and when a waiter passed by, Felix ordered a couple of Cointreaus.

He sweetly asked about my family. I couldn't really take my eyes off the room, but I told him about Minna, and how I'd been worried, and how well she looked now, and he was kind and sympathetic.

'She'll learn.'

'I know.'

'You have to fall for at least one shit in your life. It's the rules.'

'Exactly.'

Although, as I watched the two black men kiss, I realized, rather thankfully, I never had. Neither David nor Henri; and before David, I'd spent a year with a lovely boy called Will. I'd been lucky.

The Cointreau arrived and was sweet and strong, giving me the kick I needed if I wasn't going to feel sleepy with all this soft lighting and music. At one point Felix took my hand which I liked very much. We were close now, proximity-wise, because a gorgeous red-headed creature in a tiny green dress had smilingly raised her eyebrows to ask if she could sit on the end of the sofa and we'd happily shifted along to accommodate her. Her boyfriend had perched on the arm, a slim blade of a boy in an immaculate suit, gazing down adoringly at her.

The music got louder and, in front of us, not exactly on a dance floor, more a Persian carpet, a couple swayed rhythmically, lithe and mysterious, pressed close together but with their arms by their sides, feline in their movements. A few more couples got up to join them. I watched, entranced. The lights became dimmer and the music thumped with an insistent bass note which seemed to throb right through me.

A husky French chanteuse crooned a love song over it. Felix whispered something in my ear about the lack of expression on the face of the not so young blonde woman who was dancing closest to us, with a beautiful young Asian boy. I giggled. Our faces were very close now. Felix put his finger under my chin and turned mine towards him. His eyes flickered with something thrilling. Before I knew it, his lips were on mine and he was kissing me. Properly. And I was kissing him back. And it was sublime. On and on it went, his hands never touching me, just his lips, which somehow was terrifically exciting. I felt like it would never end, and that I might actually pass out before it did. I didn't pass out. Instead, I froze, as a horribly familiar voice hissed:

'Mum! What are you *doing*?'

CHAPTER 16

'*L*ucy!' I gasped.

My daughter's eyes were huge, her face frozen with horror. I saw Robin behind her, looking almost as shocked and blinking rapidly, his mouth ajar. Felix got to his feet and I clambered to mine.

'Darling, what a surprise! Who would have thought?' I managed, flustered, smoothing down my dress with a fluttering hand. Felix raked his through his hair sheepishly.

'Mum, I am appalled. What are you *thinking* of, snogging in a club at your age? And with someone you hardly know?' She was pale with fury, towering over me in her heels, her tiny yet voluptuous figure encased in a minuscule black dress, blonde hair piled messily on her head and falling in disheveled ringlets around her face like Medusa.

'Felix Carrington.' Felix proffered his hand so that Lucy had little choice but to take it although she almost didn't. 'And if I might interject on your mother's behalf, we know each other really rather well. And I don't think there's any age restriction on kissing.' He smiled pleasantly.

'You can't know her that well because I've never met

you before,' she snapped. 'And you know as well as I do it's a cheap and tacky way to behave in public.'

'Lucy, that will do,' I said, jerked from shame to fury. 'Felix and I are adults and how we conduct ourselves is absolutely none of your business.'

A few people were turning to look now, catching our tones. I saw the beautiful black boys whispering to one another behind their hands.

'It is my business if it reflects on me and, frankly, I don't want to stumble across my mother in a compromising position in a regular haunt of mine!'

'Oh, so it's about you, is it?'

'Shall we . . . continue this discussion somewhere less public?' enquired Felix as Robin muttered, 'Luce . . .' and put a restraining hand on her arm which was instantly shaken off.

'No, we won't carry it on because no more discussion is necessary. I've said all I have to say.' She turned to her boyfriend, tall and immaculate in a dark suit.

'Robin, let's go to Kitty Fisher's. We should have gone there in the first place. I know exactly who you are, by the way.' She shot this at Felix before she turned to go.

Robin, hopping from foot to foot and unable to control his innate good manners, lunged back to kiss me goodbye, murmuring, 'Mrs . . . Molly.' Then he quickly shook hands with Felix before, with an acid look from his girlfriend, they departed.

We watched them go. Felix rummaged through his hair again, looking abashed. He cleared his throat.

'Your daughter, I presume.'

'Yes, my eldest, Lucy,' I breathed, watching her slim back stalk out through the corridor of rooms, rake straight.

'Not the one who's escaping the rural Lothario then?'

'No. The one who has all the men in London panting after her and has settled on poor Robin.'

'Poor?'

'Well, I'm not sure he's up to her. She's . . . you know. Feisty.'

'I can see that. Here.' He passed me my drink as we sat back down on the sofa again, perched, though, on the edge.

'Shame,' he said ruefully as he sipped his drink. 'I was enjoying that.'

'Me too,' I agreed quietly.

'But I imagine the moment has passed.' He turned and gave me a quizzical little smile.

'Yes,' I said, recalling Lucy's blazing blue eyes boring into mine. I cringed. What *had* I been thinking? 'I'm afraid it has.'

He nodded. 'What did she mean, I know who you are?'

I sighed and gazed bleakly into my drink. 'She knows you're Robert's son. She thinks I'm mad to even consider letting him stay on.'

'Ah, I see.'

'Which is none of her business and, anyway, I've already decided.'

'I know.' He paused. Swirled his drink around in his glass. 'What's Robin's surname?'

'Farringdon. Well, until his father dies, then it's Dashbarton.'

'The Earl of?'

'Yes.'

'I thought I recognized him.'

'Oh really? Where from?'

'Society pages. Photos in *Tatler*, that kind of thing.'

'Oh. Why d'you ask?'

He shrugged. 'Well, it just seems to me . . . you know,

nice enough chap, but as you say, not really up to her.'

'No. Lovely boy, but tiny bit . . .'

'Wet?'

'No, not wet. Accommodating, perhaps.' I frowned. 'So what are you saying?'

'Well, why's she going out with him?'

'You're saying she's after his money?' I said, bridling.

'Not money, necessarily, but possibly . . . the whole package.'

I made myself consider this. 'Maybe. But then of course, that makes him who he is.'

'Exactly.'

'Just as' – I waved a hand at the lithe Asian boy dancing with the heavily lifted blonde – 'his upbringing makes him who he is.'

'Quite.'

No conclusion seemed to have been drawn but I realized he meant Lucy had no right to the moral high ground. And that she'd been finger-pointing, which was wrong of her. Felix wasn't after anything, I knew that. Just a few more weeks, or months, in familiar, comforting surroundings for his father.

Suddenly I felt confused. And the lashings of champagne and Cointreau which had felt like such a splendid idea so recently were making me feel awfully light-headed and dizzy. I put my glass down on the little table beside the sofa, feeling decidedly foolish. What *was* I doing snogging a man I barely knew in a nightclub, but also . . . why ever not? Which?

I hoped Lucy, en route to her next venue, would be racked with guilt at embarrassing her mother so, but somehow I knew she wouldn't. She'd still be fuming, whilst Robin tried to soothe her, falling over his words a bit as he did. He had a slight stutter which didn't improve when he was stressed. I frowned, pulled my dress down over my knees. Surely Felix couldn't be right? That couldn't be why she liked him?

I shook my head and declined another drink as a waiter approached. Felix asked for the bill, which came almost immediately and for which he signed: no money or credit cards changing hands. Why did he come here, I wondered? And who did he usually come with? Women? Not men, surely? All at once, it was out of my mouth before I could harness the flow. Felix looked surprised.

'Oh, clients mostly. Or dealers. It's quite convivial to have somewhere civilized to bring them and talk business. Thank you.' This, to the waiter.

'Yes,' I said, relieved. 'Yes, I can see that.'

'I mostly use it for lunch or drinks after work. There's a very good dining room. And the food's excellent. This is the first time I've been here so late, actually. Bit of an eye-opener, if I'm honest. Shall we go?'

He flashed me a lovely smile and as we got up, I saw a couple of women closer to my age sitting with their dates on clubby leather sofas, surreptitiously watching as we left. He really was a very attractive man. I straightened my back and tucked my tummy in. And I'd had my moments, I thought, as a man on the way out gave me a smile. OK, he was the cloakroom attendant, but I'd definitely had them. Not recently, of course, but I still could, surely? It was never too late. Never.

WHEN I AWOKE the following morning – Felix having dropped me back in a taxi, then, with a chaste kiss, asked if I'd stay one more day so he could see me the following night, to which I'd readily agreed – I got out of bed, went to the galley kitchen and put the kettle on. As I crept around being quiet, making a cup of tea, getting dressed, making the bed, and a mental note to put fresh sheets on and wash these when I left, I took my mug to the kitchen to rinse it and turned at a noise behind me. Lucy and Minna appeared through the front door. They slammed it shut behind them.

'Thanks a bunch,' said Minna, glaring at me.

I gazed back, astonished. They were still in their evening clothes.

'You forgot to leave me the key,' Minna snapped.

It took a moment. Then: 'Oh!' Both hands flew to cover my mouth in horror. '*God*. So what did you do?'

'Well, obviously I had to stay at Adam's, which wasn't entirely in the script.'

'Oh my God! Adam who?'

'Exactly. I've only seen him three times and I end up sharing his fucking bed.'

'Oh *Minna!*' I was horrified. I clutched my heart. Felt faint.

'Don't worry, it wasn't actually a fucking bed. He was a perfect gentleman. But it's not ideal, Mum. Not quite what I had in mind. Puts me on the back foot, rather.' She barged past me in the kitchen, snapping on the kettle. She swung back, folding her arms and looking at me mutinously. 'So how did you . . . ?'

'Lucy collected me this morning. She was at Robin's because she was so upset about last night. And then of course Nico rang, so we got the whole story.'

'What whole story?'

'About you snogging Paddy Campbell in the lane.'

I gasped.

'Nico was in the Spar and heard everyone talking about it. It has really, really upset him.'

'Oh!'

'Sit down, Mum.' Lucy's voice, which had yet to be heard, was stern and low. I perched, horrified, realizing she looked pale and determined. She sat down beside me.

'Do you have a problem, Mum? Would you like to talk to us?'

'No, of course not – don't be ridiculous!'

'It's not unusual, you know. A friend of Robin's has got it.'

'Got what?'

'A sex addiction.'

I gaped at her. '*Sex* addiction? Blinking heck, I haven't had that for six years!'

'Oh, so it's not that then?' They exchanged a relieved glance. 'Just . . . what? Snogging? Attention? How many, Mum?'

'How many? None!'

'Well, two we know about. And as Nico says, it's the local ones who are the worry. After all, he's got to go to school. Face his mates. He says you were very flirtatious with the man buying Nutty.'

'Flirtatious with . . . oh don't be absurd!' I stormed. 'I was selling a horse! Turning on the charm!'

'Taking your clothes off in the kitchen?'

'No! I mean – I changed, quickly, but not for him, because I was late, so I—'

'Nico says you were running round in your pants.'

'What rot, no, I—'

'Mum.' Lucy held up her hand, palm in my face like a traffic cop. 'Enough. We understand. Or at least,' she put her head on one side and gave me a sort of caring, counsellor look, 'I think I do.'

'Well, I bloody don't!' snorted Minna. 'She gets all eggy with me for getting with Ted, and all the time she's taking her clothes off for some guy buying Nutty!'

'Oh, don't be ridiculous! Mr Pritchard – and I am *not* in a courtroom – surprised me when I thought *Mrs* Pritchard was coming, Paddy Campbell is an odious man who forced a kiss on me to teach me a lesson or something fatuous, and Felix and I are grown adults enjoying each other's company and an evening on our own, which frankly is none of your business!' I directed this last comment at Lucy but she was up, suddenly, on her feet, glancing around, eyes darting. She strode into her bedroom, crossed the room and yanked open the wardrobe.

'No, he is *not* here,' I stormed. 'What on earth do you think I am?'

'We'll talk about that later, Mum,' she said, shooting me a grim look. She kicked off her heels, threw her evening bag on the bed and seized a T-shirt and jeans.

'Right now, I have to go to work. But please, no more dramas, OK?' She shimmied out of her dress. 'Rein in. This is my patch and I'd ask you to respect it. If you need help, we'll get it for you.'

'Ooh, I could—' but she'd already kicked the bedroom door shut in my face.

A moment later, Minna, holding two mugs of slopping tea, threw me a last dirty look before opening the door with a crooked little finger and going in to join her. I heard a muttered, outraged exchange through the door, but I was pretty livid myself.

I decided the only thing for it was to slam out and leave them to it, before either of them could slam out on me. And let them calm down a bit too, of course. No one likes to arrive back at their flat wearing what they had on the night before, I could see that. And Minna would be hugely enjoying the moment of camaraderie this engendered with her sister, who didn't always let her in. My younger daughter could usually be relied on to be sweet and biddable, but if the wind was blowing Lucy's way . .

Resisting the temptation to barge in and have a flaming row with both of them, I got my nightclothes together, stashed them in my bag in a corner of Sophia's room, then found my handbag and left.

I'd have breakfast in the café round the corner, I decided, in peace. As I clattered up the iron steps from the basement to the street, a sash window flew up from below. Minna's face appeared at the window, behind the bars.

'The key, Mother.' She held out her hand.

'Oh! Yes.' I fished it from my bag, scurried back a few steps and proffered it through the bars. 'Or shall I leave it under the—'

'I will.' Minna snatched it. 'Since I presume that means we have the pleasure of your company for another night?'

'Well, I—'

But she'd gone, before I could finish my sentence, slamming the window shut, which frankly left me *incandescent* with fury. I stomped noisily up the steps again and turned down the street.

The number of times I'd forgiven them *their* little foibles and peccadilloes, their countless acts of thoughtlessness, their falls from grace! The times I'd overlooked *their* glaring indiscretions and downright bollock-dropping, and in one night, I'd made a few minor, cosmopolitan errors – and I was demonized! Ganged up on. Called names. A sex addict, for crying out loud! Minna, glaring at me, her mouth disappearing like a cat's bottom. Lucy, speaking to me in that ghastly tone of voice, like some sort of pious therapist – she'd even rested her elbows on her knees and regarded me over interlaced fingers. Oh, I'd show them. *Really* give them something to talk about. I strode on. Well, no, obviously I wouldn't do that. That would be silly.

I'd reached the café now and I pulled out a chair at a table on the pavement in the sunshine and sat down. A waitress appeared and I ordered a cappuccino and a croissant. But I certainly wouldn't be 'reining in' as Lucy patronizingly put it. I would certainly be keeping my date with Felix tonight, oh yes.

I fumed into the drone of traffic for a bit, then fell on my coffee when it arrived. It was boiling hot and I burned my lips. Irritated, I put it down, the cup rattling in the saucer, coffee sloshing all over the place, which I hated. The morning was not going well.

Felix texted me a few times throughout the day, though, which was lovely, and my spirits, ever mercurial, rose like a hot air balloon. The first time I was in Tate Modern, which I'd never been to, skirting the perimeter of a room containing a sea of blown-up, blue plastic bags.

'Are you still on for tonight?' I read.

'Yes, of course.'

'In light of your daughter's disapproval, would completely understand if you changed your mind?'

'Certainly won't be doing that!'

He said he'd meet me at six. He suggested a drink in a bar first, and then he wondered if he could cook me dinner.

I caught my breath. Golly. His place. Before my thumbs could stop themselves I'd texted back:

'Why not?'

Oh yes, I was playing very hard to get. I pocketed my phone guiltily. But at least I'd deleted 'SUPER!!' which had been my initial response. I made my way back around the room full of blue bags and into the next one, full of yellow ones. I blinked when I saw a pink room, further on. That might be a bag too far.

In the event, Felix couldn't get away as early as six

because he became immersed in a series of meetings with gallery owners, but he kept up the contact throughout the afternoon, and let me know it would be more like seven. Perhaps we could rendezvous closer to his gallery meeting? he asked. Might that not be easier for both of us, particularly since I was shopping in the West End? I'd told him I was doing that, even though I was now on more familiar territory, pottering in and out of the boutiques in the Fulham Road in the hope I might find something affordable to wear tonight. Stupidly I'd felt Bond Street sounded smarter, although it probably wasn't. What was wrong with me? I felt myself flush, embarrassed for my usual self. I was behaving like a ridiculous teenager.

Nevertheless, I hotfooted it over to Bond Street for the rest of the afternoon and, resisting the gravitational pull of the Topshop of my youth at Oxford Circus whose Hieronymus Bosch-like depths I still felt I could plumb with my eyes shut, I acted age-appropriate and embarked on Fenwick's. In actual fact it yielded a host of pretty outfits to choose from. They were all reasonably priced, too, and I settled on a pale blue linen dress and a pair of wedged sandals.

As I paid, my jeans and shirt now in the stiff carrier bag, linen dress and heels on, I eyed the bag guiltily. I couldn't turn up with an overnight bag, obviously. And I wasn't even sure I was going to need one. But my day clothes were now stored in a very understandable way, without my needing one. And since I was walking through the lingerie department on my way out, I bought some knickers. Because I was short of them at home. But I put them at the bottom of the bag. A pack of three. I added a toothbrush from Boots, then hurriedly threw it in a bin in the street. That really was going too far. And anyway, I could always . . . no. Don't be ridiculous, Molly. *Do* calm down.

At seven, I set off for Mayfair. I walked there, not too fast – I didn't want to work up a disastrous sweat and it was warm – but nevertheless enjoyed the saunter through the very solvent streets, window-shopping as I went. Berkeley Square was bathed in dappled, dancing light: its tall, ancient plane trees filtered the sun's rays but it was quite dark and terrestrial too in places.

A thick canopy of green spread over the center and I enjoyed its cool and shade, taking a moment to sit on a bench. This was what I missed, I decided, following with my eyes a couple of smart businesswomen in dark suits. They strode past in heels, deep in conversation, both with terrific legs – one a barrister, I realized, noticing the white bands at her throat. Yes, the sense of purpose, the buzz. The hum of ideas. I'd been asleep too long. Five years now, nearly six. Six years selling lavender soap, sparkly pants and horses, and not very many of those, either. It was time to move on. Time to put my penitential days behind me.

On a branch high above me, a bird trilled an accord; not a nightingale, but I'd swear I'd heard a cuckoo earlier, through the honking of horns, the hum of traffic round the square. First one of the season. Would the good burghers of Mayfair notice that? I smiled. I fancied not.

I smoothed down my new dress and crossed my freshly waxed legs. Weirdly, I'd missed that a bit, too. The maintenance: something the sisterhood railed against. But so many people in the countryside let themselves go – me included. Who was going to see my legs under jeans and wellies? But here there was none of that. And appearances *were* important, I decided, sitting up a bit: they defined one.

I thought of Felix with his trim figure, his light tan. He'd mentioned he went running in Hyde Park. Could I still run, I wondered? Jog, perhaps. Happily I'd always been reasonably slim, but I'd go to the gym, I determined. Lose those extra pounds, get more toned, although horses and sheep did that for you: kept you in shape. And of course, a dress like this helped too, I thought, getting up and smoothing it down. Amazing what a spot of tailoring could do, that and an expensive blow-dry – I'd nearly passed out when the receptionist in Fenwick's had asked for fifty pounds; Wendy, at home, charged fifteen. Yes, I'd been asleep too long. I needed to rejoin the real world. I walked on through the square with its flickering, changing light, and out through the gate on the other side.

As I turned into Mount Street, with its wide pavements and classy street lamps, I wondered if I was starting at the higher or the lower end of the street. I glanced at Felix's text. Marscho's, number eight, was all I'd been given. Ah, here was number two, so it was this end, rather than towards Grosvenor Square. I was surprised to see quite a few people gathered ahead of me on the pavement, sipping drinks, and realized there was something of an opening-night exhibition going on, perhaps even in Marscho's, the gallery to which I was bidden. No, it was next door, at number six.

As I threaded my way through the expensively dressed, chattering throng, a huge dark Bentley purred sedately past. I happened to glance up at the name on the front of the gallery, in discreet and exquisite gold lettering, because of course somewhere around here – yes, how stupid. It was precisely here. Lafitte and Defois, which meant . . . my eyes came down and around. The very first person they came into contact with, standing ahead of me, with a glass of champagne in his hand, his eyes like lasers over the shoulder of the elderly, foreign-looking woman he was talking to, was Henri.

CHAPTER 17

I stopped still in the street. We didn't speak, just stood staring at one another. He was exactly the same. Never tall, but compact and wiry; a presence, despite his lack of stature. His hair was still very dark with just a few flecks of grey, his eyes brown and penetrating, his face unchanged. But then it had only been five years. Not a hundred. I gazed at his familiar, craggy features, that Roman nose and creased face, his slightly shabby yet expensive clothes. I felt as if a spear had dropped vertically from the sky and skewered me to the pavement.

It was the elderly woman who moved first. She turned around at her companion's evident distraction and, with her maturity, put a couple of things together. She gave me a small smile and with a discreet murmur to Henri, moved back into the hub of the party.

Henri walked towards me, never taking his eyes from mine. He stopped a few feet away.

'Molly.'

'Henri.'

There was a silence. After a moment, he spoke again, gentle and low. 'How have you been?'

'Oh, you know.'

'David . . .'

'Yes.'

'I'm so sorry.'

'I know.'

I felt a huge well of emotion threaten to surge up inside and overwhelm me. Something I'd kept a very firm lid on for a good many years was churning away deep down like molten lava, but I kept it low.

'I wanted to come to the funeral, but I thought...' He made a hopeless gesture with his hands.

'No, definitely not,' I said quickly. 'We were . . . on the phone.'

'Who were?'

'We were.'

'When?'

'When . . . you know.'

I watched it dawn. Watched that terrible penny drop. He looked as if he'd been shot.

'Oh mon dieu. I had no idea.'

'I know, and I shouldn't have told you that. I don't know why I did.'

'No, you must tell me. I was the other party. You can't shoulder all that burden, all that guilt, on your own.'

I gulped, nodding. Knowing he'd understand. But at the time I'd felt any sort of contact with Henri, even to tell him what had happened, was diabolical: it made me feel sick. I loved him for understanding now – no, not loved, but . . . you know. I gave myself a moment: needed a thousand more. Instead I took some good, deep breaths. He waited for me.

'And Caroline?' I glanced around, blinking, expecting

her to bear down on us at any minute, glass in hand, smiling broadly, blonde and glamorous as ever in something silky and wafting. Henri looked confused.

'Caroline?'

'Yes.'

'Molly, don't you know? She left me soon after.'

It was my turn to rock as if I'd taken a bullet.

'*Left* you?'

'Yes. For Giles.'

'*Giles.*' Now I really did gawp. 'You're kidding. Giles and Susie Giles?'

'Yes. I can't believe you didn't know. They'd been having an affair. For nearly a year, according to Susie, who found all sorts of emails, texts, the usual. Then she dug and found even more.'

'Good God.'

'Right under our noses. Caroline, it seems, was not working quite as much as she made out and certainly not late into the evening. And Giles was not pumping iron and getting in shape for Susie. All the time she was helping him, timing his laps on the common, being his doubles partner, going to the gym, it was for someone else. She was unwittingly facilitating his love affair with my wife.'

'Oh, poor Susie. And poor you, Henri. I'm so sorry.'

He shrugged. 'Maybe in my head, I knew. Perhaps. I don't know. Things hadn't been good for a while.'

'You never said.'

He shrugged again. 'I thought it would be disloyal. And such a cliché. My wife doesn't understand me. You never complained about David either, except . . .'

'Yes – I know I told you about that.' I glanced down at my feet. Then up again. 'But you never said a single word, Henri.'

'A bit of me thought perhaps it was my fault. That I

was the one losing interest. Well I was, obviously, we both know that – I certainly thought I was the only guilty party. I never imagined it was her, too.'

'But with *Giles*. Such a . . .'

'Handsome man?' he ventured with a wry smile.

'No!' I said vehemently. 'I mean, yes, OK. Smarmy good looks if you like that sort of thing, but such a *twat*!'

He laughed. 'Thank you for that, Molly. I have to say I never thought I'd lose my free-spirited wife to such a crashingly conservative stockbroker.'

'A very good one, though,' I reminded him. 'And a very rich one.'

'Very. A man obsessed with money. I think that was the thing he resented most. Paying Susie off. Giving her the house.'

'You mean they're still together?' I asked incredulously. 'Giles and Caroline?'

'Oh yes. Still together. In Battersea.' He gave me a curious look. 'Lucy knows. She never said?'

I caught my breath. '*Lucy*? H-how does she . . . ?'

'She and Alice keep in touch.'

I was flabbergasted. Rocked, almost more than seeing Henri. 'I – I didn't know that.' Henri's eldest. The same age as Lucy. I tried to assimilate it.

'Just Facebook, probably,' he said quickly. 'That sort of thing.'

I knew he was protecting me. 'Right,' I nodded, hustling the information to the back of my brain, to chew on later. 'And – and you, Henri? Did you ever . . .'

His eyebrows shot up like a flying buttress. 'Ever?'

'You know. Re-marry?'

He broke into a broad smile at hearing me say it, not helping me out. 'No, I never did. Never even found a significant other, as I believe it's called. Except, of course, that's not true. I did.'

His eyes held mine and I felt the breath leave my body.

'And you?' he asked. 'Did you ever find anyone?'

I glanced down, shook my head: was about to try to explain about the terrible crushing guilt that had folded me in its rocky crease, squeezed the very life out of me, when, from behind a few heads, Felix appeared. He looked very tall and bronzed next to Henri, whose olive skin hadn't seen the sun for a while. His face broke into a smile of relief as he came around the throng to put a hand on my shoulder.

'There you are!' He kissed my cheek. 'I was beginning to worry, thought you couldn't find it.'

'Oh – n-no. I'm sorry. I just – I'm sorry, Felix, I bumped into an old friend.' I licked my lips, which were exceedingly dry. 'Felix, this is Henri Defois. Felix Carrington.'

The two men shook hands with seeming bonhomie but I sensed a slight frisson: a vague wariness on both parts.

'We know each other, don't we?' asked Felix.

'I think so. Art fairs, perhaps . . . ?'

'And I see a bit of Pascal, next door.'

'Ah yes,' Henri agreed. 'You exhibit there? I know the name.'

'My son does.'

'Of course.'

'I was there just a minute ago, having a meeting with him. Daniel tends to get a bit flummoxed with the commercial side.'

'Ah. Well, that's what fathers are for.' They smiled at one another.

'Well, Henri, it was lovely to see you,' I said, breaking the silence. My heart was pounding.

'And you too, Molly.' He gave me a steady gaze. 'Perhaps we'll see each other again?'

'Perhaps,' I breathed.

'You know where I am.' He inclined his head back towards his shop's façade. He gave me a last, searching look and, with that, he turned and walked back into the heart of the party he was clearly hosting, no doubt to launch his latest finds, all exquisite and critically acclaimed. I wondered if I'd read about them in the arts pages of the *Sunday Times*. It wouldn't be the first time I'd sat at my kitchen table and devoured a review of one of his exhibitions. I watched him go.

'So,' said Felix jovially, taking my arm. 'Shall we go?'

I nodded, finding myself unable to speak. From the direction of Grosvenor Square a taxi appeared, yellow light shining, heading towards us. A doorman at Scott's further down made his way towards it but Felix was quicker: he shot his hand in the air and walked to the curb, keeping his eyes on it, making sure it had seen us. It gave me a few moments. We climbed aboard, and inside its black leather depths – like the inside of a camera, I always felt, windows like eyes on to the world – I steadied myself, listened to Felix's chatter about his day, and smiled and nodded appropriately.

London passed by. Within moments we were purring out of the quiet, prohibitively expensive world of art and antiques housed in grand, red-brick former homes into the bustling and more transparently commercial streets of Piccadilly. From there we headed south, down towards the river, to trundle along the Embankment and across a bridge and beyond.

At length I joined in the conversation, and we kept up a light social chit-chat. I even threw back my head and laughed on occasion. But I was badly jolted. Seeing Henri had knocked the stuffing out of me. Blown out my flame. So many latent emotions, buried deep, had been stirred. Emotions about him, Henri, to be sure, about how I'd felt back then, but also about David. I opened the window for some air. Felt the breeze cool my hot cheeks and ruffle my hair.

I wondered what he'd think of me, my husband: sailing off to have my supper cooked for me quite a long way from home – the unfamiliar surroundings of Brick Lane, the warehouses, the edgy and alternative shops flashed by – tomorrow's knickers in a carrier bag.

I gulped and for a moment was transported back to a time when, at this stage of the year, the Easter holidays, we'd be at Daymer Bay in Cornwall, in a rented cottage on the cliffs overlooking the beach. We found it too crowded in the summer so always went then, and sometimes had blissful weather, like we were having now. At the fringe of the beach David would have Nico on his shoulders, negotiating sharp rocks to find the best pools where he knew there'd be crabs – he'd already found them on our stroll along the beach together the previous evening whilst the children had been asleep but would pretend he'd found them with them. I'd be holding Minna's hand and Lucy would be running ahead. Very happy days. Days before I'd taken all that for granted, played the bored housewife, taken another man, soured our love until it curdled badly, and suddenly, he wasn't just lost to me in my heart – we both knew it wouldn't be the same again, hadn't he said so in our Wandsworth kitchen? He was dead. David was dead.

Perhaps I hadn't done enough time, I thought with a lurch, clutching the taxi-door handle and sucking in the fresh air. Perhaps six years wasn't sufficient for what I'd done; maybe I hadn't completed my penance. I glanced at

Felix's profile as we drew up outside an austere grey terraced house. He leaned forward to open the taxi door. On the other hand, all I was doing was having supper with a very nice man – something I knew David would thoroughly approve of after years on my own – calling a taxi, and going back to Earls Court. To our daughter's flat. Yes, of course. I felt a bit better, calmer. I even gave a genuine smile as Felix helped me out of the cab. I felt my equilibrium return.

Inside the rather dark, narrow townhouse, Felix got us both a drink and I glanced around the sitting room while he was in the kitchen. I knew I'd normally pay much more attention to the canvases on the walls, the huge swathes of color and the dramatic lighting, the minimalist décor, the plain white brick walls, the spiral staircase, the fresco at one end, the studio across the hall which I barely even poked my nose in, just glimpsed all sorts of strange and wonderful creations divined from what looked like copper piping and black tubing. I'd dreamed of drinking in every detail, every nuance, comparing and contrasting later with my books at home, but my thirst, together with my curiosity, had dissipated. Temporarily, of course. It would return. I was just a bit out of sorts, that was all. A bit *bouleversée*, as someone, not a million miles away, would put it.

Felix returned with two glasses. Champagne again, I noticed, although I determined not to drink too much. We sipped and we smiled and we chatted. After I'd asked a few polite questions about the fresco on the back wall and we'd walked across to study it – one of his, obviously – I followed him into the kitchen and sat on a stool whilst he chopped garlic and sliced chicken breasts. I even did a bit of chopping myself and together we assembled the wherewithal for a stir-fry. Nothing too fancy, I was pleased to note: no three-course meal complete with candles and mood music, just something simple to eat at the small island, side by side, together with a bottle of red wine.

'You're distracted,' he said eventually as a pause ensued for longer than might be deemed entirely comfortable.

I came to. 'Sorry.'

'Since you saw Henri Defois?' he ventured gently.

I thought for a moment, then nodded. 'Yes. Henri and I were lovers. I haven't seen him for five years. I nearly broke up my marriage for him. In fact . . . I did break up my marriage. Indirectly.'

Felix didn't say anything. He watched me with interest. At length he spoke. 'And his marriage?'

'Well, that's the strange thing. I learned tonight that his wife has left him. Long ago. For a friend of ours. I never knew.'

He nodded, pensive. 'Ah. So he is single. Is that what you were thinking in the taxi, and now, as you sit having supper with me?' His eyes were kind: teasing, almost. Beautiful green eyes flecked with gold. Like a tiger's.

I smiled back. 'Of course not, Felix. It was years ago and I'd never go back. I genuinely wasn't thinking that. For complicated, personal reasons I could never go back, but it certainly jolted me.'

'Seeing him, or hearing his wife had left him?'

I considered this. 'Both. I'd always felt a huge amount of guilt about Caroline, but it seems it wasn't necessary.'

I remembered how it had threatened to consume me at times: my betrayal of my dear friend down the road. I wondered how consumed Caroline had been for her dear friend Susie? No less than I was, for certain. Caroline was a sweet girl. God, we'd all been at it, I thought with a stab of horror.

An evening at our house in Bolingbroke Road sprang to mind: a barbecue, at the height of my infatuation with

Henri, just before Paris. Susie and Giles, Caroline and Henri – they'd all been there. I remembered tripping back and forth from house to garden with salads and sauces, feeling both on fire and terribly guilty. So Caroline had been feeling the same. With Giles beside her. Had she guessed about us, I wondered? About me and Henri? And did it suit her to ignore it? Or did she have absolutely no idea? I recalled the six of us, laughing around a candlelit table at the bottom of the garden in the long grass under the two cherry trees, the ones I'd hung with tea lights and laughingly called The Orchard, where I'd sown wild flowers and placed an old white beehive I'd found on eBay: empty, of course, the beehive, just as the laughter had been around that table. Empty friendships. Rotten lives.

'Well, as you saw, I don't know Defois well, but I know *of* him and I can assure you he hasn't been that lonely since she's gone.'

I returned to the present: glanced at Felix, startled. 'Oh really?'

Felix made a face and shrugged expansively. 'For sure, why not? Your wife leaves you, you're a good-looking Frenchman, you have a point to prove. There are lots of very attractive women in the art world.'

'Anyone in particular?' I thought of his purported lack of Significant Other.

'Well, Françoise Courbet for a bit, but listen, I'd be spreading gossip to say I knew more than that. Jemima Warburton too, very glam, but hey, he's a single man. What d'you expect? Five years of sackcloth and ashes?'

I smiled. 'Of course not.' I resumed my meal, although I wasn't terribly hungry. As I ate, I caught sight of a bundle of papers on the island, tied with a familiar pink ribbon like the ones that habitually bound David's cases. A brief ribbon.

'Got a court case?' I asked with a smile, changing the subject.

'Hm?' He followed my eyes. 'Oh, that. Lord, no, it's just a document. I had it drawn up about the house.' He looked serious for a moment. Put down his fork. 'I want it all to be signed and legal for your sake, Molly. I don't want any loose verbal agreement that you suddenly feel panicky about. I want you to know exactly what you're doing, what you're letting yourself in for, with no bullshit.'

I smiled, touched. 'That is so kind.' I reached out and drew the document towards me, turning it round so I could see: it was indeed headed '32 Lastow Mews'.

'And also you need to know that you can change your mind at any moment. But now is not the time.' He pushed it away.

I pulled the document back. 'No, now *is* the time, actually, Felix.'

I knew why, too. Suddenly I was feeling a bit shabby. I wanted to do something good. Prove to myself I was a decent person, not one of those philandering adulterers in the moonlit back garden with their false smiles and their treacherous laughter, as artificial as the *rus in urbe* I'd created. I thought of Susie and David, neither of whom would have dreamed of being duplicitous. They just didn't have it in them. They were good people. Decent people. I wanted to be like them. And now that I knew David had been fond of Cuthbert, had supported him despite his father, I absolutely knew he would have wanted me to do this.

'Where do I sign?' I flipped through.

He laughed. 'Nowhere, until you've read it. You really want to do this now? Tonight?'

'I really do.'

He shrugged. 'OK. You win. I'll make some coffee and

you have a perusal. If there's anything at all you don't understand, just shout.'

He slid from his bar stool and went to administer to some complicated, hissing machine in the corner, the like of which all urbane folk seem to possess these days. No doubt I'd have had one too had I stayed in London, but instead, like a lot of life, it had passed me by. Time to catch up. I turned to look at the document.

It wasn't long, only about six or seven pages, and not hard to understand. It just rambled on about how the house was only to be rented at such a low rate during Robert's lifetime, and how I, Molly Faulkner, had authority to call a halt at anytime to the arrangement, should I so wish.

There was nothing terribly binding at all, and it was all very much slanted in my favor, which was sweet of him. Naturally the pen I managed to find in my bag didn't work and as I rummaged for another, I drew out the tampon case Lucy had given me years ago. Embarrassed by her mother producing items of an intimate nature instead of pens, she'd given me the plastic cover. My sensible daughter.

Hm. Perhaps she should take a look at this? Robin, even. He was a clever boy and I knew he drew up loads of contracts. This wouldn't be a problem at all. And perhaps, I wondered cravenly, I could ask Robin, without alerting Lucy? No, that would be going round her. I couldn't do that. I remembered the tweedy, convivial lawyer in South Kensington and narrowed my eyes thoughtfully.

'Pen not working?' Felix turned from the cafetière in the corner.

'Oh – hopeless, no.' I flourished the broken one. 'But—'

'Here.' He tossed me another one from the side.

'Thanks.' I looked at it doubtfully. 'But actually, I was thinking . . . do you mind if I take it away? Show my bossy daughter, perhaps?' I rolled my eyes and grimaced.

'Of *course* not. God, there's no rush at all, I was only thinking of you.' He came across and stood close to me, a coffee in each hand. He put them on the island then ran a fingertip down my cheek. 'You look lovely tonight, Molly, did I even manage to mention that?'

I felt my heart pump like a teenager. 'Not . . . in so many words.'

'Well, you do. And don't worry about the document. I'll run through it with you later, if you like. Why don't we take our coffee next door?'

He picked up the tiny mugs and led the way through into the drawing room, where, opposite the fireplace, a huge, claret-colored sofa loomed under dim lights. This, I supposed, was more what I'd expected, but by now I'd drunk quite a lot of champagne and more red wine than I'd intended and I wasn't going to object. Anyway, it was only coffee.

We sat very close on the sofa and sipped our espressos and talked in low voices, almost as if people were listening. At length he slid an arm around my shoulders and pulled me close. I turned my face up to his and he kissed me, gently, as he'd kissed me in the club, pausing occasionally, as if to register my reaction as he looked into my eyes, which was sweet and considerate, but as I say, it was exactly as he'd kissed me in the club. And somehow, because of that, it felt slightly practiced. A bit like a routine. Certainly it had none of the urgency and passion of . . . *damn*. I drew back a moment. Felix smiled.

'Something wrong?' he breathed.

'No, no.' I went back for more. But there was that routine thing again, the pause between the soft, fluttering kisses to gaze into my eyes, and there was that man again. Cropping up when I didn't want him. With none of the urgency and passion, I'd been thinking, not of Henri, and certainly not of David, but of that irritating incident back home, when I'd been clasped so fiercely and kissed so very comprehensively by that bloody man in his bloody pickup truck. *Bloody Paddy Campbell.*

CHAPTER 18

elix regarded me quizzically, his green eyes very close to mine. 'Something wrong?' he murmured.

'Sorry,' I breathed. 'Something – just came to mind. It will go.' I willed it away, or rather them away. Paddy Campbell's eyes. Dark and intense.

Felix nodded understandingly. 'Your husband?'

It seemed prudent to lie. Not say no, another man, to which Felix would say 'Henri Defois?' and I'd have to say, no, another one. So many men. An embarrassment of menfolk. What was the collective noun, I wondered? Not a harem, obviously . . . a machismo?

'Yes, that's right,' I gulped.

'It's too soon,' he said gently; he stroked a line down my cheek with his fingertip, which was nice, but again, a bit considered. He'd done it in the kitchen. Well for heaven's sake, he was bound to have his share of moves, wasn't he, at his age? Even I had some moves. Couldn't quite remember what they were right now, but I had some. Up my sleeve. For later. Yes, later, because disappointingly, and all my fault of course, the moment seemed to have passed. Certainly for Felix. He was disentangling himself from our embrace and leaning forward towards the coffee table from where, on top of a pile of glossy art books, he plucked the document, which seemed to have shed its pink ribbon and made its way through from the kitchen to join us. He sank back into the sofa with it and smiled.

'Tell you what, let's look at this instead, and you tell me anything you don't understand.' He drew a pen from his top pocket. 'If there's anything at all, I'll put an asterisk by it for you.'

'OK,' I agreed, rather relieved by the lack of pressure on the seduction front. God, he was a nice man. No rush. In no hurry to get me into bed. We might not even make it there tonight; might take it much more slowly. So subtle. Lovely. Obviously I hadn't had sex for five years, but what was one more night?

He put his arm around me and I curled up against him on the sofa, which was delightfully cosy and quite homely. And I mean, who knows, we might get friendly again later: plenty of time.

'Incidentally, did I tell you I've had this looked over by my lawyer?'

'No, you didn't.'

'Oh yes, it's all kosher.'

'Oh *good*. That's excellent, Lucy will like that.'

'Here, here's his card, you're welcome to ring him.' He drew a business card from his pocket and gave it to me. I felt embarrassed.

'Oh no, I won't do that. If you've had it checked, it's fine.'

'OK. Well, you read it through. I'm just going to bung those plates in the dishwasher.'

'Oh – d'you want me to . . . ?' I made to get up.

'No, no, you stay here.' He kissed my forehead, smiled and got to his feet. 'I'm a bit anal like that, on the domestic front.'

As he withdrew and started clattering around in the kitchen, my phone buzzed in my bag on the floor. I retrieved it and glanced at the message. It was from Nico.

'Any danger of you coming home so I can resume normal teenage life or should I resign myself to being a farmer?'

I texted back quickly. *'So sorry darling, I'll be back tomorrow.*

Anything particular you'd like to do?'

'Get shit-faced with my mates.'

Presumably he meant tonight. Nico only thought in the moment. And presumably he meant at Derek or Jake's house – neither boy had transport – which meant he'd be too drunk to drive home and have to stay over, and then wouldn't wake up until tomorrow afternoon and none of the animals would be fed or watered. Although actually, it was just the dogs, I thought: the livestock were fine at this time of year, no hay or concentrate needed, and although Nutty and Tufty usually came in during the day, they wouldn't mind staying out. And surely the dogs could cross their legs until I got back? Let's face it, they'd had enough practice.

I texted back. *'OK it's just the dogs really, but if you take them out before you go they should be fine. Maybe you could be back by midday tomorrow?'*

'Maybe you could, Mother.'

I went hot. That was cheeky. What did he know? Oh yes, of course, everything. I went hotter. I'd forgotten about Mrs McCarthy at the Spar. And no doubt his sisters had spilled the Felix beans, too. I compressed my lips. Tapped away.

'Just going over a document for the new house. It's quite compli-

cated Nico. Back tomorrow when I've seen a lawyer,' I added importantly.

'Ah so you're seeing a lawyer. And a vet and an artist.'

'I'm doing nothing of the kind!'

'My ass.'

I gasped. Then turned my phone off with an exasperated flourish. Threw it in my bag. Felix reappeared and saw my face.

'What?'

'Wretched children. They think their lives are so flipping important and can't imagine why they should keep the home fires burning for more than one night. Anyway, I've told him I'm seeing a lawyer and can't come back, but they don't half answer back,' I fumed.

'Oh, I don't think we ever get it right.' He sank down wearily beside me on the sofa. 'Mine were the same at that age.'

'Really?'

'God, yes. Answered back continually, and if I so much as mentioned another woman after I'd split up with their mother they wanted her name, age, rank and serial number. Particularly Octavia. She even came on a date with me once, to check out someone she claimed I never brought home. I did bring her home, Octavia just wasn't there. Out on her own dates, probably.'

'Quite normal, then? For us single parents?'

'Totally. They're just being protective.'

'Yes. I suppose.' I sighed. That was nice of him. He could have said – God, what needy children you've got, always on the blower, just tell them to sod off.

'I'd tell them to sod off, if I were you.' I blinked rapidly. 'So I take it you would like to see my chap? Changed your mind?'

'Sorry?'

'You told your son you were seeing a lawyer.'

'Oh, no.' I flushed, embarrassed. 'No, I absolutely haven't. I was just saying that to get him off my back. Just a teeny white lie. No, I totally trust you, Felix.' I hesitated. 'I suppose I thought I might put it in front of Lucy's boyfriend, though; he's a clever chap, draws up loads of contracts, or there's this chap in South Ken . . .'

'Ah, I see.' Felix went a bit quiet.

'But I don't have to,' I said quickly.

'Oh heavens no, good idea. Always worth a second opinion.'

'That's what I thought.'

'Although I will go through it with you very, very thoroughly, Molly.' He turned and regarded me earnestly, picking it up again. He flipped over the first page. 'OK, let's see. I, Molly Faulkner, do hereby declare . . .'

He started to read it aloud to me. Explaining clauses he thought might be complicated or open to misinterpretation. And the trouble was, it was longer than I'd originally thought, which surprised me for a rental agreement, quite a few pages. Or perhaps that was standard?

Also, rather inconveniently, my head was beginning to swim. It felt terribly heavy. Which was odd, because I hadn't had that much to drink. A couple of glasses of champagne, probably the same of wine. Which didn't sound an awful lot. But perhaps it was?

I certainly wasn't used to drinking much at home. After David had died I'd sunk a bottle of wine a night, which had horrified me, so I'd knocked it on the head and stuck to two glasses, one at seven by the Aga, another with supper. Obviously I drank more if I went out, but I didn't go out much, and certainly not on consecutive evenings. And this London life was relentless, wasn't it? Maybe I was constantly and unwittingly topping up my alcohol levels? *Was* two nights on the trot a lot? What was the trot? What did it mean? God, I felt weird. Why was I coming over all existential? I put a hand to my head.

'Concentrating?' He smiled down at me, seeing my eyes glaze over as he rambled on.

'Of course,' I murmured, and then he leaned down a bit further and kissed me gently on the lips, which was lovely. Then again, for longer still. Gorgeous. I wouldn't have minded a bit more of that, but he was talking again. Murmuring in my ear.

'Tell you what, why don't you text the kids if they're concerned about you? Tell them where you are and what you're doing.'

I stared. Managed to concentrate enough to say: 'Oh no, I don't think they'd like that at all. Lucy can be a bit . . . prim.' Was that the word? So hard to find any words just now. All a bit confusing.

'I didn't mean that.' He laughed, squeezing my shoulder. 'I meant to tell them you're signing the rental agreement.'

'Oh I see!' I laughed. 'Well, I've already mentioned it to Nico, but yes, maybe a family text.' Good idea, actually. Give them all the heads-up so there was no argument later. Why hadn't I thought of that? That was presumably what he meant but hadn't liked to say. 'You mean, so there's no argument later?'

'Well, no, I meant in case they have any strong objections now.'

So sweet. I'd totally misread that. God, he was nice. I lurched forward for my phone in my bag on the floor, which was a mistake. I experienced a terrible head rush and had to steady myself. I took a few moments, gripping the coffee table. Then, when I was upright, it took me longer than usual to text, and I'm generally a bit of a whiz on the keyboard. Eventually I tapped out:

Just so you know am signing document which as discussed gives Cuthbert's partner the right to live at Lastow Mews for rest of his life.'

I showed it to Felix. 'Only fair,' he said.

'Yes, I agree.'

'No, I would add that. In case, like you said, they do question it. I'm just thinking of you.'

'Brilliant!' I added – *'Only fair'* – and then for good measure because I was feeling quite punchy and actually quite peculiar: *'I also think it's the Christian thing to do.'*

Felix frowned. 'Are you born again?'

'Oh. No. I just thought . . .'

'So won't they think that's a bit odd?'

I deleted it with difficulty. To be honest, I just wanted to get rid of the wretched phone, and the words, and the whole concentrating palaver, and send the blinking thing. There. I snapped my phone off. I knew he'd said to see if they had any objections, but I was bored with them now. Irritating children.

'Done.' I smiled, sinking back into the sofa.

'Perfect. Right. Now I'll read it to you.'

I groaned loudly. 'Oh Felix, must we? Can't we get back to that nice sleepy snugly thing we were doing earlier?' My eyelids honestly felt as if they had lead weights in them. I could barely open my eyes. He gently lowered my head to rest on his shoulder with his hand.

'That?'

'Yes.' I purred. 'That.'

'In a sec. And much more. But first, let me finish this, I'm only on the second page.'

I moaned low. 'Felix, we'll be here all night! Why don't I just sign the wretched thing?'

'Are you sure?' He produced the pen again.

I hesitated. 'Well, why not? I'm going to sign it anyway, when Robin or whoever's seen it, aren't I? It's only a formality.'

Felix appeared to consider this. He shrugged. 'I suppose.' He pulled the coffee table towards us and spread the papers out. 'OK, well, if Robin wants to amend anything afterwards, we can always put a sub-clause in. It's not a problem.'

'Oh *good*.' I picked up the pen. 'What, even though I've already signed it?'

'Why not?'

'I don't know.' I didn't. I tried to remember. Could you change a contract once it was signed? To my addled knowledge I'd never actually signed one like this. Or had I? Well, obviously years ago when I was working, but they were standard contracts with clients which barely needed reading they were all so formulaic, but since then . . . I racked what remained of my brain.

I'd signed something with Twinkly Andy once, but literally on the back of an envelope over a pile of knickers across my kitchen table: shaken hands and opened a bottle of cider on the strength of it. Horses too, of course. But more bills of sale than contracts: a scrap of paper scrawled on the bonnet of a horse truck in a howling gale with some other bellowing, horsey woman.

All the proper stuff, houses, et cetera, David had done. David. Only very recently I'd thought he'd thoroughly approve of this, but now I wasn't so sure. I leaned forward and rested my head, perplexed, on the glass table. Or was it Perspex? Which was so like perplexed? God, what was *wrong* with me? My head was so fuzzy. So heavy. I raised it with difficulty, slowly bringing it to a vertical position. The room was spinning.

'Molly, I think I *am* going to read it to you,' Felix said gently. He went to take the papers from me.

'No!' I held on tight, tenaciously. 'God, we don't want that fucking reading lark again, actually I think that's the problem. I think I'm going to pass out with boredom.'

He laughed. Then he waited. I picked up the pen. And then I don't remember much else, because my brain, which had been behaving very strangely anyway, behaved in an even more peculiar manner and sent a sharp message to my eyes to shut immediately, which was rude. I wrestled with them. So rude. Particularly since poor Felix, who'd already gone to so much trouble this evening, clearly thought I needed more reassurance, and was reading again. Mid-sentence, would you believe, further on, something about the dotted line . . .

'Here . . .' he was saying, 'at the bottom . . . and then the date . . .'

Which was the twenty-fourth, he told me as I gripped the pen and as he moved the paper closer, and basically made it all so easy for me, explaining so sweetly, that I'm afraid I don't remember anything else. Except that finally, everything was taken care of most beautifully, most thoughtfully, and most delightfully. Phew.

CHAPTER 19

The following morning I awoke in a strange frame of mind in a very strange room and in a very strange state of undress. I managed to open my eyes just enough to see light pouring in through French windows at the end of the bed: the bed which, I realized, slowly swiveling my eyes around without moving my head, must be in Felix's bedroom. All white. No carpet. White floorboards. Barely any furniture. One huge mirror propped against the wall. Very chic. Very understated. Very minimalist. So minimalist, in fact, that the occupant – my eyes traveled left to the empty space in the bed, white duvet thrown back – wasn't even in situ. My eyes returned but my head stayed resolutely immobile and I had a feeling it would have to remain so for the rest of its days: it felt so peculiar.

'Good morning!' Felix appeared through the open doorway in a tasteful white waffle dressing gown, bearing a breakfast tray. 'Coffee, orange juice, croissants – for Madame.' He executed a little bow with an exaggerated flourish of the hand. Carefully placing the tray in the middle of the bed, he slipped in beside me, taking care not to spill anything. Then he leaned across and kissed me languorously on the lips.

'How are you, my darling?'

I stared at him as if seeing him for the very first time. 'I'm . . . fine. I think.'

'Good. I thought a little restorative coffee might be just the ticket. For both of us, actually. A much needed pick-me-up.' He smiled as he began to pour from a percolator. I gazed as if not only had I never seen him before, but I'd never set eyes on a coffee percolator either.

'Yes, it . . . might.'

Under the duvet, my hands traveled surreptitiously and tremulously over my body. I swallowed. Right. Naked. Definitely naked. Lordy. I licked my lips, which were unaccountably dry. I managed to dredge up a soupçon of saliva to moisten mouth and tongue. I also managed to inch up the pillows a wee bit. Only a wee bit, my head was fit to combust.

'Felix, about last night.'

'Hm?' he murmured. 'Sugar?'

Did he mean me?

'Oh, no thanks.'

'Juice? It's from this new state-of-the-art machine I've got. I've never used it before so you can be guinea pig. You literally throw in about ten oranges, wait a few seconds, and out it all comes, no peel, no pith. I'm rather pleased with it actually.'

'Right. Um, Felix, last night, did we . . . ?'

He paused from his pouring. Looked up.

'What?'

'I mean, did we . . . you know.'

'What?'

'Do it?'

He put the jug of juice down. Looked a bit shocked. 'You're kidding?'

'Er . . . no.'

'You don't remember?'

'Well, I mean, obviously, a bit. Snogging in the sitting room, on the sofa.'

'But that's all? Not in here?'

'Not . . . really.'

He blinked in astonishment. 'Good grief.' He ran his hands through his hair. 'That's terrible. Molly, you were sensational!'

I gasped. '*Was* I?'

'Amazing. All your incredible ideas – so athletic!'

I inhaled in horror, pulling the duvet right up to my chin and clutching it tight. 'No! God. Really? In a good way?'

'Oh my darling, in a *very* good way. The very best. In fact, I feel something a little similar – although perhaps not quite so energetic – coming on right now.' He smiled and leaned across to kiss me again. I waited until he'd finished.

'Right. Except, the thing is, Felix, I can barely move my head. In fact, weirdly, it feels like a solid lump of concrete.'

'Well, you did have quite a lot to drink.'

'*Did* I?' I had fully intended to stay sober.

'Well, I've just put two empty champagne bottles in the recycling bin.'

'No!' *Two* bottles. And Felix mostly drank wine. I really shouldn't be allowed out. And what a shame I couldn't remember anything at all of my big night when by all accounts I'd been sensational. I wondered if I could possibly rise to the occasion and raise the requisite energy to . . . no. Out of the question.

'Maybe later?' I bleated.

He laughed. 'Hey no, fine. You put me through my paces last night, don't you worry. And I've got to meet a dealer at ten, so maybe later later, as in when I'm back.' He helped himself to a croissant and some jam.

'Back?'

'Yes, I'm off to Vienna, remember?'

'Oh. Yes.' Vaguely. 'And I must go home. Poor Nico. Holding the fort.'

Felix's mobile beeped. He sighed and made a long arm to the bedside table to scroll down through his messages. I, meanwhile, managed to snake a hand to the other bedside table where my bag was – I have absolutely no idea how it got there – ferreted around and found my own phone: another message from Nico.

'Half a hundredweight of lavender soap has arrived. Apparently you said put it on the back step which means no one can get in or out. I'm using the window. Also that weird guy rang again about the horse. Wants it vetted.'

Oh Lord. I really needed to get back. But I literally couldn't move. I felt truly dreadful. And apparently I'd been a veritable sex machine last night. Extraordinary.

'Felix, this sounds so pathetic, but you couldn't just, sort of, help me up a bit, could you?'

He laughed. 'Come on, old girl.' He heaved me bodily up in the bed as I clutched the duvet, tucking a couple of pillows in behind.

Old girl. Right. He passed me a glass of juice.

'Want me to help you drink?' he joked.

'Yes, please.'

Felix looked startled but he held the glass to my lips as I sucked.

'Molly, is this sort of hangover usual?'

'No. It's not. At least . . . I don't really remember. Haven't been this drunk for years. I don't drink that much as a rule, and certainly not two bottles of champagne.'

'Ah, that'll be it then. Hang on, I'll get you a Berocca and some Nurofen.' He slid lithely off the bed in his waffly thing and into the en suite. I heard him rattling around in there. God, this was beyond embarrassing. I badly needed to get out of here. Not to be the creaky old lady billowing dog breath all over him and needing to be hoisted up. And what on earth did I look like? I riffled in my bag for my powder compact and flipped it open. Error. I snapped it shut, horrified.

When he returned I took the pills and drank the potion and told myself that in twenty minutes, when they'd kicked in, I'd be up, showered and in a cab, having kissed him a lingering goodbye.

In the event, it was more like an hour and twenty minutes. The pills did kick in but they took a good long while, by which time Felix had gone to meet his dealer in Cork Street, promising he'd ring very soon for a re-match, which hopefully, he grinned, I'd remember. I'd smiled wanly, hoping I wasn't going to throw up as he leaned over to kiss me goodbye having showered and then got dressed in front of me, and no, I didn't remember that lithe, tanned body I'd so recently grappled with. What a waste. Did he sunbathe naked? He didn't appear to have a shorts mark. Or any trace of a tummy. Had I held mine in? Unlikely, I felt, in my sensational abandonment. Anyway, Felix left, but unfortunately he forgot his wallet, and when he popped back for it, he found me sitting up in bed with my sunglasses on. Luckily he roared and asked if I liked the River Café, only it had to be booked well in advance. I assured him I did, even though I'd never been there, and he took his leave again.

So then I really was alone to . . . take stock. Consider. I

rummaged gently in my brain. Not too brusquely. No nails. But I tried all the files, present and past. Then I tried trash. No. Nothing. Absolutely zilch. I shook my head slowly: another mistake. After a bit I got gingerly out of bed and tottered to the shower, making it long, but not too hot. Then I dressed very carefully, not bending over when I put my pants and jeans on for fear of head spin, keeping my back straight, which is harder, when you're older. I made the bed in the same position, head erect, looking into the distance, and ordered an Uber taxi on Felix's account which he'd told me to do: then I shut the door behind me and put the key in a pot, which surprised me, but apparently his cleaner had lost hers and came Mondays and Wednesdays, and then, holding myself together like a piece of broken china, I sat on the back seat of a rocking, smelly, low-slung, vomit-inducing vehicle and was transported away across the river.

When I achieved Lucy's flat, which thankfully was empty, everyone being at work – or play, in Minna's case – I fully intended to consult the train timetable, pack and clear out. Strangely, though, I found myself straying into Lucy's bedroom. I looked longingly at the bed. That cosy Moroccan bedcover. Those ethnic cushions. Just five minutes. With my eyes wide open, I decided, so I didn't nod off. Then I'd be away. I kicked my shoes off, lay down in the fetal position and within moments, Morpheus had claimed me.

Sometime later I heard the doorbell go. Or was it a dream? It was faint. Distant. Perhaps it was my head still buzzing, or perhaps it was a subconscious clarion call summoning me back across the oceans of sleep into which I'd plunged. Happily it stopped and I went back to my sea bed.

At length, though, it resumed in a more intrusive

manner. Louder. More persistent. Impossible to ignore. I glanced at my watch, realizing I felt almost normal, like a proper human being, but then that was hardly surprising considering I'd been asleep for five hours. It was four o'clock in the afternoon. Shit. *Bugger.* Four o'clock. Nico, the dogs – so *stupid* to lie down like that. I sat bolt upright. Thankfully my head was mobile and my brain alert and such boldness could be accommodated. Why had I awoken? Oh yes, the doorbell. I darted to the door. Yes, I could dart too. I pressed the intercom machine, but whoever it was had been waiting too long and had gone away.

Thanking the Lord I'd at least been roused – how galling would it be for Lucy to discover me fresh from work – I set about collecting my things, smoothing down my daughter's bed, and even had a piece of toast and a cup of coffee since irritatingly, my timetable informed me I'd missed one train and had an hour to wait until the next. In an attempt to adopt a philosophical approach to life's vicissitudes – which broadly involved me not looking at my phone in case it was Nico – I gave the kitchen a thorough clean. Then, just as I was making ready to leave, bag in hand, I saw feet descending the external staircase through the bars of the basement window. The doorbell went again. It occurred to me that this was the third time of asking. It was impossible to get much of a view of the persistent caller in this subterranean basement, but I'd seen enough to spot smart jeans and expensive Italian loafers. One of Lucy's admirers, no doubt. I pressed the intercom machine.

'Hello? Who is it?'

'It's Henri.'

I stared at the machine on the wall. Stepped back from

it. Blinked at the red light still flashing. Then I moved forward again.

'Henri?'

'Yes. Can I come in?'

'Um . . . just a mo.'

I leaped up on to the sofa to peer in the mirror. Found a brush nestling on the back of it and flew it through my hair. Then I found a lipstick – this was clearly the girls' dressing room – and slicked it on, but it was too dark, too young, so I rubbed it off. I jumped back down, realizing that had taken a few moments and he might have gone, interpreting the pause as a subtle message to withdraw, a disinclination on my part to see him, but as I opened the door, there he was. Henri Defois. Stepping into my daughter's flat. Second sighting in as many days and before that not for five years.

As he shut the door behind him I absolutely knew the previous calls had been his. I thought how this was the last thing in the world I needed right now, but also, the very best. It had been so lovely to see him last night. Until Felix had come along and. . . well, claimed me.

'Henri.'

'Molly.'

In that moment as I waited for him to signal what to do next and how to react I was flooded with irrepressible thoughts. He was such a mnemonic for my old life, my old days: here, in the seclusion of a small room, rather than in the open, crowded street of last night, I was almost knocked over by the force of the memories. My heart banged for my old self in that moment. His too, I believe, as I held his eyes. Not only had we been so much to each other, we represented so much, too. A different family dynamic, a different way of being, of living. Sunny, happier times.

'How did you know where I was?'

'Forgive me, I asked Alice. I had a hunch you'd be staying with Lucy.'

'And she knew where?'

'She did.'

It struck me anew that Lucy had been very secretive about her friendship with Alice. She'd never mentioned it. Or the fact that her parents had divorced. I remembered that young girl in her nightdress, listening, at the top of the stairs. She had her memories. Her reasons for keeping things to herself. For keeping Henri and me apart.

'I just had this terrible feeling that last night was a one-off and I wouldn't see you again for another five years,' Henri said. 'I couldn't bear that.'

'You could have found me earlier, through Alice, at the farm.'

'I didn't want to instigate anything. Burden you with more guilt. I didn't think it was my place.'

At the mention of guilt, an ancient roll of terror came loose and unfurled in my head like a blackout blind. I remembered not being able to walk: literally staggering from side to side down a long corridor in that terrible building in Worcester, after I'd identified David. Realizing, as I swayed from side to side, what I'd done, each unsteady step ramming it home.

For a moment I wondered what I was even doing in this room with Henri and glanced behind him at the outside staircase, desperate for escape. Then something steadied me. His eyes perhaps. Telling me it was OK. Not to give credence to the demons in my head, which weren't real. I took a breath to balance myself. He waited. At length, he reached out and took my hands in his.

'Moll,' he said softly. His eyes were very tender. It rocked me again.

'Henri, don't say it like that,' I whispered. 'You can't still feel like that. Not after all this time. After everything that happened.'

'I can. I do. I can't help it. But I do also know it didn't happen to me. It happened to you. So it's easier for me.'

'Yes. It was my husband who died.'

'Exactly.'

'So . . . because of that . . . I may as well say it right now, I could never find it again, Henri. Could never feel it.'

'You mean you could never act on it.'

'No.'

'Which is different from feeling it.' He led me gently to the sofa and we sat down together; perched on the edge. 'We didn't kill him, Molly,' he said softly. I inhaled sharply at the vocalization of it. Felt my breathing become very shallow.

'We did. We as good as did. Or I did.'

'*He* lost control and drove his car into a tree, not you.'

'Yes, but . . .' I covered my face with my hands, remembering leaving the morgue, driving home. A brick wall at the side of a building had presented itself and for a split second, I'd thought of heading the car straight for it. I withdrew my hands slowly.

'Henri, I could never do it to David's memory, you know that. You know *me*.' I clenched my fist and thumped it to my heart. 'That's why you haven't called in five years. Because you absolutely know that about me.'

Henri stared sadly down at his hands, limp between his knees, in recognition. Hands I knew. Loved. Creative, yet capable. The sort you'd trust the care of your children to. On swings in the park. In a Mirror dinghy in Cornwall, where they'd sometimes join us.

He nodded. 'I know. But then last night, I thought – it's fate, seeing her out of the blue like this. It's a sign. Why else would we bump into each other? It's as if someone,' he jerked his head to the heavens, 'up there thought, enough time, enough pain, enough sadness. Time to—'

'No,' I interrupted softly.

He took a deep breath. Let it out shakily. 'David wouldn't want you to be on your own forever,' he said stubbornly.

'True. But he wouldn't want me to be with you. I'd see his face every time I saw yours. See you both walking home from the station after work together, having a quick pint in the pub, in our back garden doing the crossword.'

'He's dead, Molly! That's got to be bollocks. We're the living!'

'My children,' I said brokenly. 'Lucy. Particularly Lucy.' He nodded as tears flooded my eyes. I took a shaky breath. 'She'd never forgive me.'

'She knew?'

'She found out. Heard us rowing.'

He sighed. 'I often wondered.'

I cleared my throat; a regrouping gesture. Then I crossed my legs. 'Anyway,' I said, trying to change the mood, the tempo. 'I'm seeing someone.'

'Oh?' He jerked his eyes up from the floor, alert.

'Is that so strange? It's been five years, Henri. And as you say, David wouldn't want me to be alone.'

'Who?'

'You saw him last night.'

Henri blanched. 'I did?'

'Yes, Felix Carrington.'

He stared at me. 'Felix Carrington? Oh, don't make me laugh.'

'What? Why shouldn't I be seeing him?'

'Felix Carrington? Felix Carrington is *un salaud.*'

'A what?'

'A cad. He'd sell his own grandmother. You certainly *shouldn't* be seeing him if you are. And anyway, he's been with the same girl for years – although apparently he cheats on her.'

I went cold. 'Don't be ridiculous. You mean his ex, Emmeline. He broke up with her ages ago.'

'So he says. But anyway, no, I don't think that's her name.'

'Yes, it is, she lives in America,' I insisted. I was cross now.

He stared at me as the full horror dawned.

'Oh God, Molly, seriously, don't fall for Felix Carrington. That way madness lies.'

'I haven't fallen for him, I've just been on a couple of dates with him.' I went hot and then cold in quick succession.

'Well, thank Christ for that. Keep it that way. You certainly don't want to end up in his bed.'

'Why not?' I gasped, clutching my pearls.

'Because you'd just be another notch on his belt, that's why not. Shit, you haven't already . . .'

'No! *No.* I absolutely have not.' My mind flew to last night's lurid antics, gaudy highlights of which, for all I knew, included me dancing naked with a lampshade on my head, or doing my interpretation of Anna and me at Zumba class, which the children found hilarious when I played to the gallery in the kitchen, but which might not translate so well to a cool dude's Docklands bedroom.

'Anyway, yesterday you said you barely knew him!' I retorted.

'True. I don't really. Only by repute.'

'Which often stems from jealousy.'

'Oh, I'm not jealous of the man, Molly.'

'No, I meant the rumors. They could have originated from people who are.'

We regarded one another angrily, both hurt. Two pairs of pained eyes. At length I took his hands. 'Don't let's argue, Henri, it's so lovely to see you.'

He nodded. 'And it's beyond lovely to see you.' He opened his arms and I moved easily into them. We held on tight. I felt his heart beating under his shirt; inhaled his smell: good soap, cotton. At length we drew apart but I knew he'd wanted to hold me for longer.

I looked into his dark, liquid eyes. 'I don't like to think of you living alone.'

'I don't. I've got Alice and Tatiana with me.'

'Oh! They didn't stay with Caroline?'

'They didn't want to.'

'Gosh. Quite a compliment.'

He shrugged. 'I didn't take it too personally. They would have had Giles knocking around as a stepfather and his abandoned wife and children down the road.'

'Bloody hell. No shame. Is that how it panned out? Caroline and Giles in your house? I thought you said Battersea?'

'They moved there recently.'

'But you left, not her?'

'Once I knew, I couldn't bear to stay. I rented across the river and the children wanted to come with me. Caroline agreed to it for a bit to let everyone calm down. They just never went back. It all happened by accident, really. The luck falling with me, I suppose.'

'You make your own luck.'

He shrugged. 'Maybe. I dare say if I'd left their mother and went off with another woman they'd have stayed with her.'

I gave him a long look. 'And would you?'

'Have gone off with you? Yes, I would, Molly. I didn't think for a moment I would when we first started to see each other. Or should I say, play tennis together. You weren't my type at all.'

I laughed, despite myself. 'Not pretty enough.'

'I didn't say that.'

'You didn't have to. You thought I was safe.'

'You grew on me.'

'Like bindweed.'

'No, like another skin.'

I was taken aback.

'And now I'm going to ask you the same question, Moll.'

'Would I have left David for you?'

'Yes.'

I gazed at him. Shook my head. 'No. I'm sorry, Henri, but I wouldn't have left David for anyone. Not that I didn't love you more than him. I believe at the time I did. I was certainly infatuated with you. But I couldn't have left my children. And I have a feeling they might have done what yours did.'

'Voted with their feet.'

'Exactly.'

'And you wonder how Caroline could have done that – left them?'

I didn't answer. He held my eyes. 'OK, fair enough, so you couldn't have left them five years ago, but your kids aren't children any more. They're young adults.'

'I know.'

'And you can't live by their rules forever.'

'Why not?'

'Because it's unrealistic. And after a while, there's a funny smell.'

'What d'you mean?'

249

'Like burning martyr.'

'Oh, for heaven's sake.' I went to get to my feet but he seized my wrists.

'I mean it, Molly. You can't live in purdah forever, drifting round Wales with a burning cross in your hands, flogging soap and three-legged—'

'Herefordshire, and don't make fun of my business! Who told you—'

'Alice. Or Lucy, on occasion.'

I gasped. 'You *see* Lucy?'

'I told you, I live with my children. Their friends come round.'

'You said Facebook . . .' How could she even bear to see him? For some reason this seemed incredibly treacherous of my daughter. I didn't know why.

'Well,' I fumed. 'Bully for her. Bully for all of you. How very cosy. How perfectly lovely in – where is it these days, Henri, Chelsea?'

'Pimlico.'

'Pimlico. Splendid. Lots of kitchen suppers, lots of trendy food from fancy cookbooks—'

'Hardly.'

'Lots of chat about poor old Mum, up to her eyes in mud and soap and horse shit—'

'Only when I ask, and then only some throwaway line in response which I have to turn away to hear so she doesn't see my face and which makes my heart pound if she did but know it. And she's only been round twice, if I'm honest. And on both occasions I was supposed to be away, but turned up unexpectedly. Alice knows Robin. His sister's her best friend.'

'Oh. I didn't know that.' So much I didn't know. So much Lucy had hidden.

'And the only reason I'm telling you—'

'Yes, why are you telling me, Henri?' I rounded on him.

'Is to prove to you she'd be all right with it. Lucy. Eventually. She didn't stalk out when I arrived back at the flat, she behaved herself. Even talked to me. Because she's an adult, Molly. And because people change. Grow up. They have to. I know you think it's an insurmountable hurdle, always have done, but the fact that she can even set foot in my house when she knows what happened all those years—'

Whatever else he'd been about to say was lost as a high-speed jet roared overhead, seemingly inches above us, making us both duck in reflex and certainly drowning words. As its sonic blast filled our ears he pulled me close to him, as if the unearthly noise was our cover, as if we could enter another world. I buried my face in his shoulder. Found his ear.

'It's been five years, Henri. Five whole years.'

'Tell me they don't just roll back.'

He'd taken my face in his hands and then I couldn't reply because a whole host of jets – a fleet, even; was it the Queen's birthday? Were we being invaded? – whooshed overhead so that it seemed as if we really were in some strange parallel universe, in another country, or another life, a long time ago. He rested his forehead on mine and we both shut our eyes. The noise also, of course, drowned anything local, anything proximate, like footsteps down a staircase, or a key in a door. Voices, even. What it didn't mask, however, was the flood of light pouring into the room, which made us spring apart. At first all I could see was white light and dark figures, silhouetted in the doorway. But in a heartbeat, my eyes adjusted. There, on the threshold, shopping bags in hands, eyes wide, faces aghast, stood my daughters.

CHAPTER 20

*H*enri and I froze, transfixed in the glare of their horrified faces: caught, like a couple of Nico's doomed rabbits in a hunting lamp, their eyes round like the barrels of his gun. Eventually Lucy found her voice. It was ominously quiet.

'I just do not believe you, Mother. The other night I find you getting with some man in a club, then Nico tells us you've groped our vet in the lane, and now this. With him!'

Henri looked slightly horrified at this news. He shot me an askance glance as he collected himself and got to his feet.

'No!' I spluttered, getting to mine. 'You've got it all wrong, it's not like that, Lucy!'

'What is it like then?' she demanded. 'Why were you kissing him?'

'I was not kissing him!'

'Why were you so close?'

'Just – just for – old times' sake.'

'For *old* times' sake? Well, excuse me, but for *fuck's* sake. You are literally outrageous!'

'Lucy, that's enough,' Henri said sharply. 'You've no call speaking to your mother like that, this is none of your business.'

'In *my flat* it most certainly is my business. And who do you think you are to tell me anything?' She rounded on him, furious. 'Isn't it enough that you ruined our lives? Forcing us to move, which if we hadn't, Daddy would still be alive – ruined *my* life by never going to university—'

'What d'you mean, Daddy would still be alive?' Minna's eyes were huge. Scared.

'Nothing. She means nothing by it. Lucy, stop it.' I was trembling with emotion, but Lucy had already pushed past us and run to her bedroom. She slammed the door behind her and burst into noisy tears. There was a ghastly silence. Minna looked stricken.

'I'll go,' said Henri softly at length.

'Yes,' I whispered. 'I think that's best.'

He turned sadly and went to the front door; opened it and then shut it quietly behind him. I stared at the door a long moment. Suddenly, in a flash, I'd crossed the room, wrenched it open and flown after him.

'Wait! Just a minute!' I cried. I ran up the basement steps and down the street to join him as he turned back.

'Henri,' I gasped, catching his arm, 'it's not just Lucy. You can see how difficult that would be, but I would over-come her feelings if I had to. It's what I said to you just now. *My* feelings.' I put a hand to my heart. 'Of guilt. I'd never overcome those.'

He gazed at me as I panted, searching his face earnestly with my eyes.

'I know,' he said. He did. His face was eloquent with pain.

'And however euphoric we were to find each other again, just now,' I went on, my breath coming in short bursts, 'and be together again, they'd already come between us, those feelings, even just back then, in that room. And they'd return with a vengeance, I know they would. For me at least.' I gulped at the thought. 'Nasty stabs in the gut in the early hours. Waking up with my eyes wide open. A horrid taste in the mouth.'

He hung his head. I took his hand. Shook it. Tried hard to explain.

'It's *me*, Henri, it's not you. It's how I am. Don't look so ashamed. What we did wasn't so terrible. It happens every day. Having affairs – it's part of normal life. It's just that in our particular case, its effects were catastrophic.'

'Only if you believe in cause and effect.'

'I do.'

He nodded gravely. 'And a greater power than us over-seeing things, judging us?' He jerked his head skywards.

'Yes. As you do too, Henri.' I knew he did. I'd lit candles with him. Knelt beside him. His mind flew there too. To Notre Dame.

'So all we have are our memories.'

'Yes. But at least we have those.'

We regarded one another, two pairs of eyes searching out the other. At length, he held out his arms. I walked into them. For the second time in as many minutes we held on tight.

'Paris,' he whispered in my ear.

'I know.'

The traffic rumbled past: a pedestrian sidestepped us. I felt I was barely conscious. In time we drew apart. His eyes were full. Then he kissed his fingertips and placed them gently on my lips. With a last sorrowful, crooked smile, he turned and walked away. I watched him go, my eyes brimming as his familiar figure went down the street. I wondered if he'd turn when he got to the corner but he didn't. I stared at the empty space for a long time. Felt myself rock slightly. After a bit, I collected myself. I turned and walked slowly back to the flat. Back to my life.

Lucy had emerged from the bedroom when I shut the front door behind me. She and her sister were sitting side by side on the sofa, waiting for me in silence. I wondered if she'd told Minna about Henri. Her eyes told me that she hadn't. And never would. I thanked her silently with mine and took a seat opposite them. She was in no mood to be conciliatory, though, and I knew I had to suffer the consequences.

'Where were you last night?' she began, tight-lipped.

For one surreal moment I was transported back many years ago, to when I was younger than her, about Minna's age, at the breakfast table with my own parents.

'With Felix,' I admitted. The truth, I'd decided, was my best policy, although I might temper it occasionally: the same ploy I'd used all those years ago, although I had a feeling Lucy was going to be a tougher adversary than Mum, who was always a pushover.

'And is that what you were wearing?'

I glanced down at my jeans. 'No,' I conceded.

'So where's your dress?'

'In my bag.'

Minna seized the carrier bag from the floor and rummaged through it with all the thoroughness of the Drugs Squad. She pulled out the offending article – a crumpled linen dress – plus a pair of wedged heels and placed them on the coffee table between us, like exhibit A.

'She's got a pack of knickers in here too,' she reported, peering in. 'And some Berocca.' She tossed them both at me accusingly and I caught them. If this was good cop, bad cop I wasn't quite sure who the good cop was.

Lucy's lips tightened. 'So you stayed the night.'

'Yes, I did actually, Lucy. And that, as I've told you, is my affair. I'm a grown woman.'

'So you're sleeping with three men.'

'Of *course* I'm not sleeping with three men, don't be ridiculous. Henri and I were close because' – I glanced quickly at Minna – 'because we're old friends.'

'He had your *face* in his hands!' Minna said furiously.

'And Paddy kissed me to annoy me, probably, and make me late.'

'Again, unusual,' Minna retorted.

'And Felix is my own business, and frankly—'

'Frankly, Mother, your behavior reflects on us, and as Lucy so rightly says—'

'All *right!* ' Lucy cut through the squabbling like the parent.

We were silenced.

'So it's just this Felix jerk, right?'

'Who says he's a jerk?'

'Everyone. Well, Robin, who knows him. By repute. Bit of a player, apparently.'

'Oh.' I clutched the pack of knickers on my lap. Suddenly I went hot. 'Oh *Lord.*'

'What?'

'No – n-nothing.'

The document came flooding back, with all the force of a tidal wave. The wave broke and crashed right from the back of my brain where I'd rummaged tentatively only this morning, and on that tide, as the sea came in and then shrank away again, there it was, beached on the sand, marked 'Lastow Mews'. I gripped my pants tighter. Had I signed it? I couldn't remember. Did it matter if I had? What *was* that document? I felt Lucy looking at me.

'What's up, Mum?' she asked sharply.

'Nothing, nothing.'

'You've gone all pink.'

'No, I haven't.'

'Yes, you have.'

'I haven't.'

'Shit.' Her eyes sprang wide suddenly and her jaw dropped. 'You're not on the bloody Pill, are you?'

'Oh! No.' I blinked rapidly. 'Well, at least . . .'

'You are?'

Christ. I really *was* back at my parents' breakfast table, but hang on . . .

'Did he use something?'

'Oh yuck!' From Minna.

'Lucy!' I was equally horrified, but *had* he used something? I rummaged in that addled old brain again. Couldn't find anything. Couldn't remember. Not a thing.

'God, is it possible you're pregnant?' Minna said incredulously. 'Is that why you've gone all red? Aren't you much too *old*?'

'Yes, she is, but still. Here. Go get. Just to be sure,' Lucy said tersely, reaching for her bag. She handed Minna twenty pounds from her purse. Minna got to her feet and left, casting me a last appalled look.

'Where's she going?' I asked, bewildered, as the door slammed.

'Morning after pill. Just in case.'

'Lucy,' I licked my lips, 'you didn't tell her . . .'

'No. You know I didn't. I never would.'

'Thank you.'

'One life in bits is enough.'

'Darling, you can't—'

'What?'

'Blame me forever.'

She swallowed. 'I don't. As a rule. Only in my darkest moments.'

I nodded, ashamed. 'But you knew Henri's marriage had broken up and didn't trust me enough to tell me.'

'No. I didn't. And it seems under the circumstances I was right not to.' She was very pale.

I leaned forward. Gave her the steadiest look I could.

'Lucy, I give you my word. He held me like that purely for old times' sake. To say goodbye. We'd already agreed nothing could ever happen. What I said was true. I would never be with Henri, not now.'

I saw a flash of trust flit across her eyes. A small light.

'Thank you,' she said in a much smaller voice. Like a little girl. She took a deep breath. Let it out shakily. 'It would break my heart.'

'I know.' I leaned across and took her hand. 'I know that, but, Lucy, mine too.'

She gulped and nodded. I knew she believed me now. But her beautiful face was white and contorted with grief. The long pent-up emotion which she hadn't always shown me was there, undisguised. Lucy was the eldest. She'd known her daddy the best. Had easily been the closest to him. I moved to sit next to her on the sofa and put my arm around her shoulders. She put her arm round my waist and I almost cried with relief. I said nothing, though. After a bit, she sighed, dredging it right up from her red canvas high-tops and from the depths of her soul. We uncoupled. She turned to look at me properly.

'I'm really sorry I said what I did about this Felix guy. You have every right to some happiness, Mum. It's just what Robin said, and I'm sure he was only trying to make me feel better. You go for it. Have a lovely time. If you feel he's the one.'

'Yes. Thank you, darling. I will.'

I was uneasy, though. And a little unsure. Two people now. And Robin was a really good egg. Lucy knew as well as I did he was unlikely to make something up to appease her. She stood up.

'Take the pill when Minna gets back. I'm going to have a bath. And get yourself sorted out, Mum. Chloe Frowbisher's mother got pregnant and it was beyond embarrassing. Apparently the eggs can have some sort of horrific last hurrah even if you're ancient, so it's possible even you could get pregnant.'

Even I. This washed-up, desiccated old bag. The thought was terrifying, though, and I gratefully gulped down the pill with a glass of water when Minna wordlessly handed it to me on her return, her eyes cold. And then I took another one for luck. It occurred to me, as she stood over me, that I hadn't got a grip on Minna's life. I had no idea what she was up to or with whom, but didn't quite feel in the position to ask. Who was Adam? Had she been staying with him since that night when she'd had to, or was she back here now? At least she wasn't with Toxic Ted.

'Nico's under quite a lot of pressure, Mum,' she told me sternly. 'I think you'd better go home.'

'Yes – yes, that's the plan. Although – it's so late now, I might just ring him and stay one more night. There's something I need to—'

'*No*, Mum. You've had quite enough fun. Go home.'

I gulped. 'I wasn't going to see any more – you know. Men.' Well, I was. 'At least, not for – you know.' I badly needed to see Felix before he went to Vienna.

'Sex?'

'Minna!'

'Just behave, OK? Is that too much to ask?' She walked into her sister's bedroom and shut the door behind her. She didn't slam it, though. That was something.

I sat on the sofa, knees clenched. Obviously I really needed to go home. But I also really needed to see a man about a house, too. I wondered how much time I'd got. I quickly texted Felix.

'*When are you off?*'

'*Off where?*'

'*Vienna.*'

'*Oh, right! Imminently, my darling.*'

I stared. Imminently. Did that mean in ten minutes or this evening, or tomorrow, even? Hating my lack of cool, I asked.

'*Just en route to the airport now. So sorry not to see more of you but back in two weeks.*'

Two weeks. I thought he'd said next week. Damn. I lifted my eyes from my phone and sat staring at the botanical prints covering the cream wood-chip wallpaper. I could hear one daughter running a bath and the other's muffled tones, presumably on the phone. I got to my feet. Noiselessly I put all my things back in the carrier bag, found my overnight bag in the corner, plumped up the cushions, and left.

Outside, I only had to walk a few steps before I saw a taxi. I hailed it, climbed in and off we trundled, my mind racing. Five minutes later I arrived at a familiar street corner and a familiar Italian café. I got out, paid the driver and took a seat on the pavement at my habitual spot under the green umbrella. The waiter recognized me and greeted me like an old friend. He offered me my usual cappuccino and I agreed that would be just the ticket. Then, feeling like a member of MI5, I put my sunglasses on, plucked an abandoned newspaper from an adjacent table and pretended to read it whilst simultaneously shooting surreptitious glances over it, down through the familiar brick arch to the cobbled mews beyond. At the end, on the right, a little black Mini was parked opposite the pink house but I knew if I sat here long enough, it would move.

Sure enough, two cappuccinos and a slice of cheese-cake later, a slight blonde figure in white jeans and a black T-shirt appeared through the front door of the pink house carrying a bin liner. She dumped it in the dustbin, stuck her head back through the door, called a cheery goodbye and left. She sashayed across the cobbles to her car, keys swinging from her finger. I gazed determinedly at my newspaper, heart thumping. The car came slowly up the mews towards me. In my peripheral vision I saw it pause under the arch, waiting for a gap in the traffic. Then, dark glasses on, and music playing through her open window, Camilla drove right past me, just feet away as I doggedly studied births, marriages and deaths, heading west.

When she'd gone I raised my head. I left some money in a saucer and got to my feet. I was wearing soft ballet-style pumps through the soles of which, as I tripped across the road and under the arch into the exclusive cloisters of this expensive mews, I could feel every cobble. But I was glad of them. They added stealth, and since I was on a mission, I needed stealth. I also needed as much guile, subterfuge and tact as I could possibly muster, none of which, if my recent behavior was anything to go by, were necessarily in my repertoire. But I could dig deep and find them. Oh yes.

CHAPTER 21

With all the clear-headed, cognitive grey matter I could muster stacked between my temples and with one last exhortation to my mind to resemble a steel trap, I stepped up to the front door of the pink house and rang the doorbell. Robert answered after just one ring, which surprised me. I thought it would take him longer to potter from wherever he'd been malingering, reading in an armchair perhaps, dithering in the kitchen, to get to the door. He blinked a bit in the sunlight as he took me in. Did a slight double take, then the penny dropped.

'Ah – of course! It's Polly, isn't it?'

'Molly.'

'Molly! That's it.' He smiled and stood aside, swinging the door wide. 'Come in, my dear, come in.'

He was wearing a well-pressed cornflower-blue shirt, a rather natty paisley cravat and red corduroys. His hair was freshly washed and slicked back.

'You look well,' I told him, as he shut the door behind me.

'Oh I am, I'm in peak condition. Threw off that ghastly cold I had when you last saw me but, boy, it laid me low. That's the trouble these days, anything I used to shake off in a jiffy hangs around like a bad smell. Now, I was just making some coffee.' He bustled ahead of me, leading the way down the hall to the kitchen. 'You'll have a cup?'

I'd already had two but it seemed rude not to so I agreed, determining to sip only a tiny bit or I'd be bouncing off the walls.

'I'd love one. And I'm really sorry if I'm intruding, Robert, I just wanted to ask you a couple of things about the house.'

'Absolutely, absolutely, no problem at all. Ask away. Hang on, I'll just get to grips with this machine.' Yet another state-of-the-art cappuccino maker whirred into action in a corner of the kitchen and he gave it his full attention. 'Still up in the bright lights, eh?' he called over his shoulder and above its grinding din. 'Not being seduced by them, I hope?'

Luckily his back was to me.

'Hopefully not,' I said nervously, thinking this might rather neatly encompass things. I sat down at the table. 'Um, Robert, I thought you had emphysema?'

'Emphysema?' He turned in surprise as he waited for his gadget. 'Good Lord, no, just a touch of flu. Emphysema's a hospital job, isn't it? Whoever told you that?'

'Felix.'

'Heavens, what a fuss he makes! You'd think I was decrepit the way he talks.'

'But you're not?'

'Decrepit?' He turned again. 'I should hope not, my dear. I still play bowls at the Hurlingham twice a week. I'm in the team, I'll have you know. And until last year I swam in the pool there most days.' He made a face. 'I must admit, I find it a bit chilly now, even though they claim it's a piping eighty-two.'

'That's amazing,' I said as he put a cup of coffee in front of me. 'I bet not many eighty-six-year-olds could say that.'

'Eighty-six!' he squealed. 'Whatever gave you that idea? I'm seventy-eight!' He looked aghast. 'Good God, do I *look* eighty-six?' He swept a horrified hand through his snowy locks.

'No, you really don't. As a matter of fact, this morning you look about sixty. I was totally joking, Robert.' I sipped my coffee thoughtfully.

'Pulling my leg, eh? Why didn't I get that? Too slow.' He tapped his temple. 'Now that's not good. More Sudoku needed.'

'Except I gather you do the pub quiz?'

'Never missed a week, not even when I had that wretched cold, still made it to the pub.' He frowned. 'I say, I do apologize for my poor form that day, no wonder you thought I was past it. Believe I even retired to bed.'

'You did, but then that happens to the best of us,' I assured him, my mind whirring. 'I retired there with a hang-over only this morning.'

He sat down opposite me and we sipped our coffee together. I could tell he was wondering why I'd come but was too polite to ask. I pondered how to broach this: wished I'd thought through all the possible ramifications more thoroughly in the café. Above all, I thought, looking at his fine, gentle face, I didn't want to hurt him. I put my cup down in its saucer.

'Robert, forgive my nosiness, but you and Cuthbert were terribly happy, weren't you?'

He looked surprised. 'Extremely, my dear. Why do you ask?'

'I don't know.' I flushed. 'I suppose I just wondered . . .'

He set his cup down. 'Why he didn't leave the house to me?'

'Well, I know you said before he didn't want the responsibility of sorting it all out, wanted to leave it to fate and let others handle it, but – I can't help feeling . . . he was a highly intelligent man.'

Robert sat quietly a moment. 'He was,' he agreed eventually. 'Extremely. And in my heart I believe he might have done, had things been slightly different. But I'm not saying that to put any pressure—'

'No, no,' I interrupted hurriedly. 'I know.'

We were quiet a moment. I sipped my coffee, waiting.

'Had things been different . . . in what way, Robert?' I asked, eventually.

His eyes came up from his cup to meet mine. 'Have you made a will, my dear?'

'Me? No, I haven't. Keep meaning to.'

He shrugged. 'Exactly.'

'But I'm a bit – you know. Younger.'

'And yet your husband died tragically young, so one might imagine it concentrates the mind.'

'True.'

'And Cuthbert didn't think he was old. Thought he had years ahead of him. I suppose he was rather . . .' he hesitated, 'not arrogant, but in denial about it. Which happens.'

'Sure. I can see that.' I wasn't fooled, though. I waited some more.

'You're not going to give up, are you?' he smiled.

'Not really,' I agreed, smiling back.

He nodded. 'OK, you're right, there was another reason.'

I sat very still.

'Felix and Cuthbert didn't always see eye to eye. So perhaps Cuthbert felt if he left the house to me...'

'It would go to him.'

'Well, of course it would.'

'Right. Why didn't they get on?'

He sighed, sat back in his chair. 'Just different personalities, I suppose.' He shrugged. 'Cuthbert and I led a very laid-back existence. We ambled on through life in a slightly shambolic, or as we liked to think, bohemian manner.' He smiled reflectively. 'Back in the day we were both hippies of a sort, you know. Glastonbury, that type of thing.' He straightened up. 'Whereas Felix is more, well, determined, I think. Like his mother.'

'Right.'

'Lovely boy, don't get me wrong.'

'No, no, I won't.' For determined read ruthless. And I'd *slept* with the man. My heart began to bang and my tummy churned. But he'd been so sweet, so charming. And of course he was *so* bloody handsome. But perhaps I was jumping to conclusions? Determined didn't mean complete shit. Or even ruthless, actually.

'And of course, you're a blood relative – well, your children are – and Felix isn't. So naturally in that respect, it makes sense, the inheritance. Not so peculiar.'

'No. But Robert, as I'm sure Felix has told you, I want you to live in it for your lifetime,' I said firmly.

'Yes, which is more than kind, and no rent either, although I insist on paying something.'

No rent. I held my tongue. And my breath, for a moment. And he was only seventy-eight. Not that I wanted him dead.

'Robert, how long is Felix in Vienna for?'

'Vienna? He's not in Vienna.'

'He's going today.'

'No, no, you're mistaken, my dear. I'm having lunch with him the day after tomorrow.'

'Right.'

'And Camilla's going to the theater with him tomorrow tonight.'

'Camilla . . .'

'His girlfriend. You've met her. Helps me here. Runs a cleaning company. Doing brilliantly. Got six girls working for her now. Sweet girl. Hope they get married.'

'Yes. Yes, of course.'

'Molly, are you all right? Only you look a bit pale and you've hardly touched your coffee.'

'Yes. No, I'm – fine. It's just . . . well, it is a bit warm, isn't it?'

'It is indeed. Stuffy, too. Just a tick.' He got up and went to open the back door. He struggled a bit with the mortise locks at top and bottom and whereas normally I'd leap up to help, I didn't, because it gave me a much needed moment. Eventually he flung the door wide and resumed his seat.

'Robert, do you know anything about a document Felix has had drawn up to make things a bit more – you know – official?'

He frowned. 'I don't, I'm afraid. But I can see that might be necessary. From your point of view, actually. Not a bad idea.'

'No, quite. But you haven't signed anything?'

'Lord, no.' He looked perplexed. 'Molly, why don't you ask Felix? I'm sure if he's drawn something up he'd be happy to go through it with you.'

'Yes. I might. Thank you.' I drained my coffee and stood up. Robert looked worried.

'My dear, if you've had a change of heart I would completely understand. My sister lives in Broadstairs and would be only too happy to accommodate me, I know. We get on famously and I love the sea.'

No relatives, he'd said. Felix. His whole house to be reorganized and turned upside down so his father could live with him. But hadn't Robert said that too? I turned.

'I thought you were originally moving in with Felix? Thought that was the plan?'

'Yes.' He looked embarrassed. 'At one stage. But he changed his mind. And I can quite see why,' he added quickly. 'It wouldn't really work, an old boy like me in that trendy Docklands environment, not my patch at all. And having to move his studio up to a bedroom.'

Which was why Robert had jumped at my supposed offer. He looked awkward. 'But Broadstairs would suit me tremendously well, so really, my dear, have another think. You know, we don't even know each other, and—'

'No. No, Robert, it's fine. I just have to sort a few things out, that's all, but I'll be in touch.'

'Right you are.'

I made for the door, my heart pounding, and he followed me down the hallway. He reached past me for the doorknob to let me out and I turned back on the step to say goodbye.

'Molly . . .' he hesitated. 'Don't sign anything, will you? Without a lawyer being present. Or reading it properly first.' He was looking beyond me into the street as he said this, not at me.

'No,' I gulped. 'No, I won't do that, Robert.'

He nodded and we pecked each other on both cheeks as befitted the friends we had become and then I was gone. Down the cobbled mews in my thin-soled shoes, feeling every bump, every jar, with ever more heightened sensitivity. I'd fully intended to get a train home but waiting for Camilla had made me late and the next one wouldn't deliver me until the small hours, so instead I went back to the flat, my mind still racing. Happily it was empty, a key thoughtfully left, and cravenly, I didn't ring Nico, just sent a text, to which he didn't reply.

The cogs of my brain were whirring furiously as I lay down on the sofa with just a lamp on: no television, no radio, too many speeding thoughts to accommodate any other distraction. So. Felix and Camilla were a couple. Cuthbert disliked Felix enough to cut his partner out of his will. Felix had told many, many lies. Round and round they raced, these revelations, like cats chasing each other's tails, and my shock, of course, was great. But also, strangely, not tremendous.

Indeed, when I analyzed it properly, I was shocked, but not surprised, if that's possible. I also felt incredibly enlightened. Energized. When I did get into bed an hour or so later, I fell asleep quite quickly. In fact, as I turned my face to the wall, I dropped off almost immediately.

Two pairs of abandoned high heels in the sitting room the following morning were testament to the fact that the girls had arrived home as I slept, but I was up very early, before they stirred, and away across London. I got the tube to Paddington and hurried through the crowded concourse. Luckily a train was waiting on my platform so that in no time at all, I was clutching my handbag on my knees and rattling back on the long journey to Herefordshire.

The cogs of my brain seamlessly resumed the furious activity of the night before but with more drawing together of strands now: more conclusions.

So. Felix was indeed a complete shit. So complete that even his own father had warned me against him despite the fact that Robert clearly adored him. And would you effing believe it, after five years of abstinence, this was the man I'd chosen to go to bed with. Splendid. I swallowed as I gazed out of the window at the hurrying countryside. But I couldn't help but be sad, too. I'd liked him so much, you see. I recalled our day together by the river, barely drawing breath as we talked our way along it, so much in common it seemed, and then in the art gallery, too.

I'd thought he'd liked me. Had been so flattered. And foolish, I realized with a jolt. A foolish, naive old woman. Why on earth would someone as attractive as that be drawn to a hick from the sticks like me? I'd thought a few years on my side might be enough, but Camilla was much, much younger. Early thirties at most. He'd reeled me in like a huge, wriggling fish. I squirmed when I thought how apposite that analogy might be in Felix's bed but shut my mind to it. That wasn't important.

What *was* important was whether I'd signed the bloody document. I actually, as I strained to remember, didn't think I had. I had a vague recollection of resting my head on the glass table, pen in hand, pre-signature, but as I say, it was vague. I really couldn't swear to anything. Instead, I leaned my head on the window of the train as we flashed through open countryside, and as acre after acre of rolling green meadow sped past, I subconsciously indulged in the game I'd played since childhood, jumping every hedge on an imaginary horse, until my eyes closed and I fell into an uneasy sleep.

When I awoke, fortunately within twenty minutes of my stop, I felt loads better, but surprised. How extraordinary. *More* sleep. So early in the morning too. I was clearly sleep deprived, I decided, as I got off the train with my bags. I made my way to the car park. That's what I'd been lacking all these years: not men, not hot sex, just a bit of shut-eye. It was something of a eureka moment, if I'm honest. What a blessed relief. All that man stuff was so *messy*. So complicated. And look at the trouble it had got me into! For the love of God, be gone. All of you. Just leave me to my bed. Alone.

Coincidentally, Tia was leaving her car not far from mine in the car park to get the train to Ludlow. We exchanged a hug and a cheery word.

'We're all going to miss you so much!' she wailed. 'Peter says you're definitely selling – I can't bear it!'

'Come and see me, Tia, come and stay.'

'In London?'

'Why not?'

'D'you know, I might just do that. Tell Mike to get his own bloody supper, rustle up his own toad-in-the-hole. But it won't be the same without you, Molly – our lovely cosy lunches! Quiz nights at the Firkin!'

I thought of some of the hilarious, raucous nights we'd had in the village pub and realized I'd miss her too. But I'd be having civilized bridge evenings with my new friends, if I could remember how to play the wretched game, not celebrating being on the winning team in the saloon bar, punching the air and yelling '*Yes!*' after too many ciders, roaring with laughter.

'And what about the fête? Who am I supposed to do the White Elephant with? Not bloody Wendy Armitage, she morphs into Oberführer given a stand and a clipboard. I swear she was goose-stepping last year.'

'Well, you never know, Tia, they might promote you to second-hand books – without me as a disruptive influence, of course.'

'Always the dream. Except they know I'll just sit there reading. Speaking of which – the book club, Moll! We were going to do the steamy ones next!'

'I know.' I felt a pang at this. 'You'll have to do them without me. Ask Biddy, she loves a good bodice-ripper.'

'God, far too much. She'll probably bring sex toys or something hideous.' We giggled at the alarming prospect of Biddy, possibly still in her jodhpurs, bustling in with armfuls of well-thumbed paperbacks and who-knows-what-else in a plastic bag, getting thoroughly over-excited.

I'd be joining a different book club, of course, I thought, getting into my car as we said goodbye: where they read improving books like A. S. Byatt and Fay Weldon, not the commercial fiction Tia, Anna and I gulped down. Yes, just the three of us. Plus Lauren sometimes, when she could. But no one else. We certainly didn't want anyone like Wendy pushing their choices on us for next month, and we liked lots of food and wine. And gossip. Not much chat about books at all, if I'm honest; we just agreed we'd loved the last one – Marian Keyes, Sophie Kinsella, whatever – and moved on to who'd been doing what to whom at the Terriermen's ball.

I pulled out of the car park with a bit of a lump in my throat. Tia wouldn't come and stay, I knew that. She didn't get much further than Cheltenham these days. Too busy. And Mike wouldn't like it. He couldn't cook toad-in-the-hole to save his life. But I'd come back. Of course I would.

I drove down my lane, the verges billowing with butter-cups and cow parsley, and was about to pull into the yard, only the gate appeared to be shut. I got out and opened it at which point a film set straight from *The Darling Buds of May* met my eyes, lacking only Pop chewing a straw.

All the ducks and chickens we possessed seemed to have chosen that moment to congregate in the yard, together with both dogs who were chasing their tails, the geese, who were forbidden due to their propensity to emit revolting green excrement but who were honking and strutting merrily, and even Buddy the ram was there. And there were too many cars, too many *people*, I thought nervously, leaping out to shut the gate firmly behind me as Buddy eyed the lane. He gave me a truculent I've-been-here-for-ages look as he plucked the only remaining pansy from my terracotta pot.

Nico and his two mates, Jake and Derek, were up by the house in the front garden, fast asleep and stripped to the waist in their jeans, surrounded by tins of tobacco, beer cans and flies. In the far corner of the yard Nutty was tied up outside his stable. Paddy Campbell, with his back to me, was bent over his front hoof, peering at it in a nosy manner. Bloody man – what was he doing here? Who did he think he was, the RSPCA? I ignored him as he did me and hurried through the bestial melee and up the slope to the garden. I stood over my sleeping son and his snoring buddies.

'Nico. Wake up.'

He roused, but only briefly. Dozed off again. I nudged him gently with my foot. He blinked. Peered up.

'Huh? Wah? Wha's up?' He shaded his eyes with his hand. 'Oh, it's you.'

'What's *he* doing here?' I hissed, jerking my head eloquently. He followed my gaze.

'Buddy or Paddy?'

'Both.'

'Buddy kept escaping and shafting the ewes, so I thought he was safer in here, and Paddy's come to vet Nutty.'

'Really? How come?'

'I told you, they're buying him, that Pritchard lot, subject to Paddy passing him.'

'Oh! So soon. Gosh, that's good.' I crouched down to duck out of sight, realizing suddenly that Pritchard was over there too and that must be his rather sleek silver convertible beside Paddy's truck. 'I thought he wanted to see him ridden?'

Nico shrugged. 'Changed his mind. Thinks he's a bargain and needs snapping up. And by the way they've done the fetlock test. He passed this time.'

'Oh! Excellent.'

'Exactly. Excellent. And all down to me. How about ten percent commission if you're trousering four grand?'

'What have you done?'

'Talked to that bald bastard endlessly on the phone, made up stories about competitions Nutty's won, gave him some happy powder this morning, got Paddy round to vet him – what more d'you want? I'm not bloody riding him for the fitness test, though. You can do that, now you're here.'

'We'll cross that bridge when we come to it,' I muttered, pretending I hadn't heard that Nico had slipped Nutty a little something in his morning feed. 'Perhaps Paddy will do it.'

'Oh, like that's going to happen.'

'Good morning, Molly.'

Jake raised his handsome dark head from the daisies, always charming, always on the ball, despite the alarming tattoos, whiffs of illicit substances and liberal piercings.

'Good afternoon, Jake. Do you have all that you require?'

I asked pointedly, regarding the litter of burger boxes, crisp packets and beer cans that surrounded him. 'Working hard, I see?'

'Oh, it never stops. And Nico here has been a more than generous host. Must be his upbringing.' He grinned cheekily and I grinned back and mock-clipped him round the ear, always our routine, before heading inside. Derek snored on moronically, mouth open, catching flies.

Suddenly I stopped in my tracks. 'What the . . .'

Nico followed my gaze. 'Oh, yeah. Like I told you. The soap.'

Masses of large cardboard boxes had been piled on top of one another in the back porch, precluding entry.

'But that's *far* too much. I ordered two boxes, not—'

'Twenty, I've counted. But it would be a pleasure to shift them on for you, Molly.' This from Jake, who was something of a budding entrepreneur. 'There's a bloke down the pub—'

'Thank you, Jake, I'll shift them.'

'Oh, and Twinkly Andy's been round,' said Nico. 'He's a bit stressed. Apparently some woman was wearing those pants you sell, you know, with the metal balls in the crotch for extra stimula—'

'Yes, yes,' I said quickly, seeing Jake's face light up.

'And she got too close to her Waitrose trolley. Got attached. Apparently the balls are very magnetic.'

I gaped. 'No.'

Jake guffawed.

'Andy's worried he's going to be sued, he wants to recall them all. Said he was worried about zinc bar stools or something.'

I felt my eyes widen in horror at this vision. Rows of stuck women.

'I'll ring him,' I muttered, hurrying on house-wards. 'Andy catastrophizes.'

I climbed in through the open kitchen window, resisting the temptation to wonder aloud why three strong boys couldn't have moved the boxes to the barn, whilst they resumed their horizontal positions, pausing only to put beer to their lips or light another fag, should they have the energy to roll it.

In the kitchen, every cupboard door swung wide in

welcome, every drawer hung out cheerfully, and no surface remained uncovered, so thoroughly had every plate, mug and glass we possessed been utilized. The sink, likewise, was piled high with baked bean and bacon pans. I gritted my teeth and moved quickly through to the sitting room where the curtains were drawn, the television blared, and the carpet was covered with dog-licked plates and mugs from previous meals. In a nod to civilization the waste-paper basket overflowed with yoghurt pots and folded pizza boxes, but the kitchen bin was clearly a bridge too far: too much of a hike.

A putrid smell of boys' feet, trainers, stale booze and smoke, heavily laced with chips, prevailed. All animals, however, appeared to be alive, albeit pretty much in my front garden, so I couldn't really complain. I turned off every appliance and light, flung open the curtains and windows, carried the plates and mugs through to the kitchen and balanced them on the already tottering pagoda in the sink, then I fled upstairs to change. When I came down in my old jeans, still doing up my shirt which seemed to have shrunk in the wash, Paddy was in the kitchen.

'Ah. Good. You've changed.'

'Why good?' If he wasn't going to say hello neither was I. We regarded one another coldly. I put my hands on my hips.

'Well, obviously you're here to ride this horse. I need to see its paces before I can pass it.'

'Can't you do it?'

'Don't be ridiculous, I'm supposed to observe; you know that as well as I do. But hey, if you don't want this sale to go through, that's fine. I've got a heifer with a twisted gut in Barrowbridge and I should have been there ten minutes ago. I'll be on my way.'

'No, wait. Hang on.' I flew to my purse on the dresser,

found twenty pounds and climbed outside through the sash window. Paddy followed, simultaneously answering his phone. I glanced around the garden. Two sleeping boys.

'Where's Nico?'

Jake raised his head. 'Gone to see a man about some business.'

'What sort of business?'

'Gone to see a dude about some grass,' muttered Derek, eyes still closed.

I gasped. 'What did you say?'

'He said there's a man in Potterham wants his grass cutting. Paying good money,' said Jake, kicking his mate. 'Nico thought he might earn a few extra quid. You know how driven he is.'

'Oh. Right. Well, Nico will be hopeless at that, he's never mown a lawn in his life. How long will he be?'

'As long as it takes, man,' intoned the gormless Derek. I ignored him. I had a nasty feeling that boy took drugs. Either that or he was phenomenally stupid. When I'd asked Minna, she'd said a bit of both.

'Right.' I bit my lip, annoyed. Jake lay back and shut his eyes again. After a moment, I crouched down beside him. 'Jake,' I murmured. 'Can I ask you something?' Jake remained prone but his eyes snapped open sharpish. Biddy had told me he'd already serviced one or two yummy mummies in the neighborhood, which I felt sure was a thumping lie, but he nonetheless had a twinkle about him.

'Absolutely, Molly,' he murmured. 'Ask away.'

'Um, Jake,' I whispered. 'Do you ride?'

He gazed at me a long moment. Then he propped himself up on one elbow, turning his back on Derek. Happily Paddy was still on his mobile, pacing round the garden.

'Ride? You mean . . . euphemistically?'

Clever boy, this Jake. Bound for Oxford, apparently. I tried to remember what euphe-thingy was.

'Yes,' I agreed. 'Throw a leg.'

His eyes held mine. He licked his lips. 'Well, I've broken in a fair few fillies, if that's what you mean.'

'It is indeed, Jake. Splendid. Would you do it for me?'

There was a long silence as he gazed some more, his eyes widening. He sat up properly, his back firmly to his friend whose eyes had flickered. He cleared his throat.

'Here?' he whispered. 'Now?'

'Yes, I'm afraid I'm a bit desperate.' He stared.

'And you don't mind an audience, do you? I'll pay.' I proffered my note. 'Twenty quid?' I fluttered my eyelashes mock wantonly. Jake liked a bit of banter. He looked a bit alarmed.

'Hey. There's no need for that.'

'Nonsense, I'd like to.' I straightened up as Jake did too. He got to his feet with alacrity. He looked frightfully keen. Good boy. I liked Jake. He had a bit of backbone. Unlike that dopey Derek. He strode towards the house and the open window, casting his friend, who was now all eyes and ears, a very cocky look.

'Oh no, I'll get you a hat, Jake. You go and meet the horse.'

He stopped in his tracks. 'The *horse*?'

'Yes.' I sprinted past him. 'Over there, in the yard. The grey.' When I returned with Nico's hat, which had taken ages to find in the gun room, Paddy had put the tack on Nutty and was looking dubiously at Jake.

'You're riding?'

'Yeah.' Jake grinned sheepishly, scratching his ear. 'Apparently.'

'You do this much?'

Jake shrugged. 'Like riding a bike, isn't it?'

'Well, hardly.' There was a pause. Mr Pritchard and Paddy were looking at him skeptically.

'Well, get on,' said Paddy impatiently. 'I haven't got all day.'

'Right.' Jake put a foot in the stirrup. He didn't have the reins, though, just a hand either side of the saddle, and he swung himself up with such gusto . . . that he promptly went straight over the other side and landed on the concrete.

He moaned, clutching his leg. 'Crap. Man. That hurt.'

I stared down at him, aghast. 'I thought you said you could ride?'

Jake got to his feet, rubbing his thigh. 'Yeah. Years ago, though. Bit out of practice. Mostly ponies at the village fête.'

'Oh, for heaven's sake,' snapped Paddy, looking at his watch. 'I've got another appointment. Hop up, Molly.'

'But I—'

'Oh, just bloody well get on.' He seized my leg, yanked it backwards and legged me up.

This really wasn't in the script, I thought as I landed in the saddle. I hadn't ridden properly for ages. Wasn't riding-fit. But there was nothing else for it and, silently cursing Jake, I gathered up the reins and rammed on Nico's hat which Paddy had passed me and which was horribly small.

'Right. Take him into the paddock and walk him around a bit. Then trot, and when I say so, canter.'

So bossy. 'Is that what you'd like to see, Mr Pritchard?' I pointedly asked the bald head that was walking along beside me, like a huge egg. Had he even greeted me? Or I him? I couldn't remember. He might have clicked his heels and I probably should have saluted. 'After all, you're the client, and my vet here is known to be over-rigorous.

You're a very busy man. Shall I just walk a few circles and call it a day?'

'No, of course not, I want to see his paces,' Pritchard said testily, barely glancing at me. He'd lost none of his charm. 'I'm paying for a five-stage vetting here. At vast expense, I might add.'

Five-stage. Blimey. Usually my horses were vetted to the two-stage, and all that meant was a fetlock test, a peer in the mouth and a trot up in hand. Five-stage was the works. Also, I always rode in a sports bra and I had on a rather tiny balcony bra, a recent acquisition for Felix, plus a tightish shirt, the buttons of which were prone to popping open at the best of times, and this was the worst of times. None of it was ideal. Nutty, too, had quite a bouncy trot, which hadn't escaped Paddy, or Jake, I noticed, who appeared to have recovered his equilibrium and come to the fence to watch. As I circled and passed them on the right-hand rein at a brisk rising trot, only Mr Pritchard was looking at the horse.

'Right, change the rein,' ordered Paddy. He leaped the fence in one deft bound and strode to the center of the circle like a bloody ringmaster. I could tell he was enjoying this. Jake and Mr Pritchard looked on from the side. Jake was grinning from ear to ear as I got bouncier and sweatier and more and more breathless and jiggly, and even dopey Derek had ambled across to join them, sniggering. I wished I could put one hand across my chest to steady the buffs but the buffs were doing their own jaunty thing, and Paddy was making me trot for what seemed like an eternity, a huge grin on his face, before he yelled 'Canter!', which was equally bouncy. Worse, in fact. Nutty was very fresh and leaped with every stride. Round and round I went, all eyes on me.

'OK, gallop!' Paddy yelled, which was, frankly, unkind.

'Really?' I yelled back. 'Is that necessary?'

'All part of a five-stage vetting,' he assured me. 'Mr Pritchard wants his money's worth.'

Mr Pritchard got it. As I pushed Nutty into a gallop he couldn't believe his luck and bucked with delight. I kept my seat – just – but not my buttons. As I landed with a bump in the saddle, they flew open, to reveal my scanty balcony bra, which was aptly named, as a great deal was spilling over the railings. Glancing down, I shrieked in horror, which spurred Nutty on to greater speed, despite my yanking on the reins. It was at this point that a throaty old white Fiesta roared into the yard and pulled up at the fence. Nico had arrived, just in time to see his mother galloping around in her bra – just – to roars and whoops of approval from his two best friends, a hugely grinning Paddy Campbell, and an aghast-looking Mr Pritchard.

CHAPTER 22

'What the fuck . . .' Nico leaped from the car *Miami Vice*-style, only just pausing to switch off the engine, but not to shut the door.

I couldn't stop. Couldn't breathe either, such was Nutty's speed. It was all I could do to stay on board and sit the next fly-buck he'd decided to throw in for good measure as we careered around the paddock. He hadn't been out for a good long while and this was the most fun he'd had in ages. In desperation I yanked the left rein very hard, putting all my strength into it, turning him straight for the hedge on to the lane, which was a good four foot, and which I knew would stop him in his tracks.

It didn't. He locked on to it as if he were in the Grand National, ears pricked, hooves pounding, mouth like iron as I pulled for all I was worth. When he took off it was with an almighty, unseating bound and we parted company mid-air. Pegasus flew on whilst I soared vertically, as if propelled by a 007 ejector seat, before landing, luckily in the field and not in the lane, and thankfully on my bottom, which was well padded, and not on my neck or my back.

Nonetheless, it completely knocked the stuffing out of me. I sat there amongst the daisies, seeing stars. I wondered if I was also going to see my breakfast. As I staggered to my feet, Nico rushed up, not an iota of concern on his face.

'You are so out of control it's not fucking true!' he roared. 'What the fuck are you up to, galloping around with no clothes on in front of my mates?'

'I wasn't – wasn't galloping with no clothes on,' I gasped, feeling for my shirt which was right around my back. I dragged it back across my overflowing bosoms and with trembling fingers did up the buttons. 'Just flew undone,' I panted. 'Bit tight.'

'You're a fucking disgrace!' he bellowed. 'Derek took pictures – have you any idea what that's going to look like on Facebook?'

I felt faint. Really faint. In the unhappy pantheon of terror, pain and mortification, this seemed like the worst blow so far. What would I do? Change my identity? Where would I go? Australia? But Facebook was everywhere. Should I kill myself? Yes, definitely. What a shame my neck hadn't broken in the fall.

'He wouldn't do that, would he?' I quaked.

'He won't now,' said Jake, who'd joined us, snatching Derek's phone from him and speedily pressing a few buttons before tossing it back.

'Oi!' objected Derek loudly. 'I could have sold those!'

'Are you all right?' asked Mr Pritchard, also making it over to us with his bow-legged, military gait. He was looking deeply embarrassed and everywhere except at me.

'Yes, fine, thank you,' I gulped, still breathless and rubbing my coccyx. I noticed Paddy hadn't put in an appearance except – oh yes, there he was. Coming back down the lane having gone after Nutty. Typical bloody vet, not even as concerned as Pritchard was about me. He was leading, I noticed as he came in through the yard gate, a badly limping horse.

We made our way back towards the house but Nico hung back. I heard him talking on his phone.

'I swear to God,' he hissed, 'she got her tits out. She was like Lady fucking Godiva – in front of my friends!'

Lucy. Or Minna. But most likely Lucy. Oh *God.*

'She is like totally out of control. We need help. Professional help.'

'Don't mind Nico,' Jake murmured comfortingly in my ear, ever the gentleman, but walking just a bit too close. 'He's always been a bit prudish. My mother always tears around in her bra. So what?'

'Thank you Jake,' I said, knowing this was extremely unlikely. His mother was a tight-lipped, prim-looking matron who worked at County Hall and was buttoned up in every sense. But I was grateful for the solidarity. Grateful for anything, frankly. I'd take what I could get. And actually, you never knew with those librarian types. They were often the worst.

By now we'd reached the yard and Paddy was approaching, leading Nutty, and still grinning from ear to ear.

'Ah. You've recovered your equilibrium, I see,' he said jovially. I hadn't seen Patrick Campbell so happy for a very long time. Generally he went around with a face like a wet weekend and a mouth like a cat's ass. I told him so. He threw back his head and roared.

'Ah, but then I haven't been so royally entertained for ages. Your horse is lame, by the way,' he told me cheerfully. 'Strained tendon.'

'I can see that,' I snapped, snatching the reins possessively. 'All your bloody fault for making me gallop. I'm so sorry, Mr Pritchard, it seems you've had a wasted journey.

Due to my vet's recklessness, my valuable horse has sustained what I'm sure will be an expensive injury, but then that suits him tremendously well. No doubt he'll charge like a wounded rhino for the treatment and obviously send you a bill too for this wasted visit.'

Paddy laughed. 'Oh, naturally I'll charge. I've been here bloody ages, and I charge by the hour these days. Had to get someone else to do the heifer.' He turned. 'Oh – goodbye, Mr Pritchard!' he called, and we all turned to see the rapidly retreating back of a man in a hurry, desperate to escape this madhouse with barely a thank you or even a backward wave.

'I'll be in touch, Mr Pritchard,' I called, hastening after him, but he was already in the driving seat of his swanky convertible, in which he looked ridiculous. 'When Nutty's better, no doubt you'd like to come back? I'm sure once he's had a bit of box rest he'll be absolutely fine, and then why don't you bring your wife next time and—'

'If you think I want my wife anywhere near that uncontrollable animal you've got another thing coming!' he spat at me, his bald head going a bit mottled. 'You're lucky I'm not having you up under the Trade Descriptions Act. Bomb-proof, you said. Snaffle mouth. Lovely controlled paces. There was nothing remotely controlled about that!'

'I think you'll also find I described him as a "fun ride", and I for one had a ball. Galloping and jumping are meat and drink to me, and who cares about the occasional little tumble. But if that's all too adventurous for your wife she'd probably better stick to dressage and ponce around in circles.'

'Good day, Mrs Faulkner!' he spluttered, thrusting his expensive machine into first gear and speeding off towards the gate.

'And goodbye to you, you old fart!' I bellowed after him.

'That's it, Mum. If all else fails, resort to the language of the playground.' Nico walked past me with his friends towards the house. Jake cast me a last, admiring glance.

'Leave it out, mate, your mum's a legend,' I heard him say, to which Nico responded: 'She's a fucking nutter.'

I took a deep breath, exhaled it slowly and gave myself a moment, standing in the dust that still gently hovered in the wake of Pritchard's car. Then I shut the gate on Buddy, who was inching sideways towards it, and stalked back to Paddy, who was untacking Nutty. He was whistling in a rather irritating way, still smiling broadly.

'My grandfather used to say only window cleaners whistle,' I told him, snatching the tack as he handed it to me.

'My, what a classy family you must have been. What a shame you've been reduced to horse-trading, the oldest and shadiest profession bar—'

'Prostitution, yes, I know. And which, according to my children if you'd care to ask them, is pretty much what I've resorted to anyway these days, so hey, why not combine the two?'

Paddy caught something in my tone and glanced up. He'd been about to hose Nutty down. 'What's up?'

'What d'you mean, what's up? Everything's up,' I muttered, stalking off towards the tack room with the saddle and bridle, tears unaccountably pricking my eyelids. I lifted the saddle on to its rack and hung up the bridle. Then I leaned my forehead on the saddle and shut my eyes.

Just for a moment, I wished Paddy and I could stop sparring with each other. Stop this relentless verbal volley-ball, and get back to how we were a few years ago, before

I'd stood him up in the pub in front of all his friends and before he'd never forgiven me. Back to when we were friends, and when David had just died, and I'd been left with all these ruddy animals. He'd been a bit of a brick, if I'm honest. Something of a rock.

I remembered him coming round regularly when all the ewes were giving birth in the fields and I was running round in circles like a crazy woman, screaming at all the afterbirth, repulsed and anxious at the same time. He'd arrive unannounced and calmly deliver any that were in difficulty, not sending a bill, just saying he'd been passing. At night, on occasion, I'd scream down my mobile to him, crouched in the barn with a ewe I'd brought in who was bleating in agony, her sides heaving horribly: I couldn't bear it. Triplets, it had been that particular night: two safely delivered but not the third, and the first two incapable of surviving without the mother, I'd thought. Two tiny, wet black things in the straw, the third breached. And I couldn't deliver it. Couldn't bring myself to stick my arm up and turn it. Now, of course, I could. I've stuck my arm up more ewes' fundaments than I've had hot dates, but not then. Then I was terrified. And in deep shock from losing David. In the middle of the night, Paddy had come. Those days were long gone. But I could do with a friend right now. Not a man. Just a friend.

I took a moment, in the quiet hush of the tack room, inhaling the reassuring smell of leather and tack cleaner and all things horsey. Then I raised my head, gathered myself and walked back to the stable. Nutty was being led into it, having been washed down and given a feed, and Paddy was just filling a water bucket and delivering that, too.

'What's up?' he said again, and I wished he hadn't. My lip was quivering.

'Nothing,' I said. He waited. 'Except . . . oh God, Paddy.' I sat down heavily and rather abruptly on a hay bale outside the stable door. Put my head in my hands. 'Everything, actually. I've been a bit of a fool, I think.'

He sat down beside me and I waited for him to say, 'So what's new?' or something equally pithy, but he didn't. After a bit he said, 'Well, that happens to the best of us.'

I looked up, gratefully. 'It does, doesn't it?'

'Course it does,' he said gruffly.

I thought of him kissing me in the road the other day, no doubt to make me miss my train. Perhaps he was regretting it. It had been a bit childish. And Paddy was so resolutely grown up. Weirdly, despite its undoubted satirical intent, it had come back to me the other day, in a strangely erotic manner, but I couldn't remember when. I racked my brains. Oh yes, when someone else was kissing me. Who? I couldn't remember now. So many men. Perhaps they'd put that on my tombstone? The children. *So many men.* Probably. Except, if I lived till I was about ninety, maybe they'd forget these last few indiscreet weeks? Or maybe not, I thought soberly, heaving up a great sigh from my boots. My children couldn't remember which buttons to press on the dishwasher, but their mother enjoying herself for the first time in five years? Oh boy, they'd remember that all right.

'Define fool,' said Paddy, breaking my reverie.

I turned to him. 'Hm? Oh. Yes. Right.' I cleared my throat. 'Well, amongst many other things, many idiotic, thoughtless, stupid things I've done recently, I think I might have signed a document which relinquishes my claim to a very valuable property I've inherited, until such time as a healthy man of seventy-eight keels over and dies, which could be in about twenty years' time. That's what I think I might have done.'

Paddy frowned, clearly having trouble with this supposition. 'Right,' he said slowly. 'Would you care to be a tiny bit more specific?'

I was, in that I told the story, but I kept it clean. Without any funny business on the Docklands sofa, or any hot sex afterwards in a minimalist bedroom. I skipped over all of that – which took some mental dexterity – and moved smartly on, until I woke up dazed the following morning.

'In the spare room?' asked Paddy.

'Er . . . yes.' I licked my lips. 'No. In his room. But nothing happened,' I said quickly, flushing to my roots.

'Clothed?'

'Sorry?'

'I said were you clothed?'

I knew what he'd said. My flush deepened to a vintage claret.

'Of course I was clothed!' I spluttered. 'What d'you think I am, Paddy?'

'That ancient profession – I'm joking. No, I'm just checking, because from what you've said, it sounds like you might have been drugged, so it might not have been your fault if you were undressed.'

I leaped to my feet. Stared down at him, appalled.

'*Drugged?* Do you *think* so?'

'Well, I don't know. Were you sleepy afterwards?'

'Yes! Massively! Loads of times! In Lucy's flat all afternoon and again on the train – oh Paddy, loads. So bloody sleepy. Drugged!' I clutched my throat. 'Paddy, I was naked!' I gasped, sitting down again. 'Completely starkers. Do you think he . . . ?'

'I don't know,' he said more curtly. 'I said that. But anyone can get hold of things these days, and it doesn't take much to knock a horse out, so a slip of a thing like you . . .'

I was very definitely not a slip of a thing, but I loved him for that, even if it was in comparison to a horse.

'Oh Paddy, what are we going to do?' I whispered, realizing I'd rather brazenly included him in this. 'No one will believe me. And if I have signed it . . .' I cringed, 'the children will kill me. Really kill me.' Unless I did it first, I thought. Took some pills. Evidently these things were readily available.

'Well, I believe you,' he said thoughtfully. 'But, on the other hand, I know you. Others might not. Let me think about this. Felix Carrington, you say? An art dealer?'

'No, artist, really. But . . . I haven't seen much of his own work. He always seems to be judging competitions, abroad, that Venice bipolar thing, so I'm sure he's huge.'

'Biennale. Have you looked him up?'

'What?'

'Googled him.'

My entry into some areas of the technological world had been somewhat sluggish. 'Oh. No.'

He whipped out his phone and did just that. Shrugged.

'Well, he's got a website, and there's lots of pictures of his stuff, but he's not exactly Jackson Pollock. No Wikipedia. And not much in the way of endorsements either, except from himself.'

'Oh.' I had a thought.

'Paddy, look up Cuthbert Faulkner.' He did.

'OK, so his testimonials go on forever. Patron of the Arts Council, on the board of the National Gallery, associate professor at the Slade, director of Christie's, not an artist as such but a jolly revered art historian. Generous, too, loads of charitable institutions he's chaired, and there's a Wikipedia page.'

'Right.' My mind was quietly ticking over for once. 'Paddy, I have got to get that document. Have to see what it says, and if I've signed it. And I've got to do it quickly. Like now, before he does something with it.'

'OK, where is it?'

'In his house. In Docklands. A terraced house near the river.'

'Right. So, what – we break in?'

'We?' I seized on this, and his wrist, hard. 'Oh Paddy, would you? Come with me?'

'Well, you can't do it on your own, you're not to be trusted. You'll end up dangling from a drainpipe with no clothes on.'

'Drainpipe. OK. Then through the window. But Paddy – you'd go all that way—'

'I have been to London before,' he said testily. 'Spent my teenage years in Kensington and went to Westminster and Imperial College. I wasn't entirely born in a cowpat.'

I sat back, amazed. 'No! I never knew that, Paddy – how cool! I thought you lived in Ireland?'

'Only as a child.'

'Where, exactly, in Kensington?' I crossed my legs and if I'd had a cigarette, I'd have lit it.

'Molly, can we get back to the matter in hand? Getting that document? Now what we've got to do is discover when he's out.'

'Yes. Good plan. But how the devil are we supposed to . . . oh!' I had a sudden lightbulb moment. I seized his wrist again. 'Oh Paddy, he's out with his girlfriend tonight, at the theater, and at lunchtime tomorrow – his father told me! He's having lunch with him. He's lovely, by the way, Robert. I don't want him to get a flicker of this.'

'Right. Well, tonight's out of the question, but—'

'*Oh!*' I was shaking his wrist now with a shriek. 'Oh

God – oh *God*, Paddy, we don't even have to break in! His cleaner's lost her key and she comes tomorrow, he'll leave one out – we can just walk in!'

'Except the cleaner will be there.'

'Oh. Good point, good point.' I sobered down.

'But not all day.'

'No, *not* all day.' I turned, excited.

'But we don't know when.'

'Probably not in the afternoon?' I hazarded. 'Most work in the morning, and she'll put the key back.'

'Yes, but he might be back from lunch by then.'

'True.' I narrowed my eyes into the distance.

'So maybe we have the key copied and use it when we know he's out.'

'Brilliant! You're brilliant!' I seized his poor bruised arm again. 'But isn't that illegal?'

'Of course it's effing illegal but so is breaking and entering in the first place.' He looked worried. 'Have you got any better suggestions?'

'No. No, I haven't. Oh, thank you, Paddy. And you're so straight, so law-abiding, I know you wouldn't do this lightly. Thank you, thank you, thank you.'

'Tomorrow it is then.' He whipped out his phone and started texting.

'Yess,' I breathed happily. 'Tomorrow it is.' I watched his fingers move like lightning across the keyboard. 'Can you really disappear at such short notice? Will someone cover for you?'

'That's what I'm doing. It's not ideal, but Poppy will have to. Actually it might do her good to be thrust in at the deep end.' Poppy was his new assistant, young and slightly nervous.

'Right.' I leaned back on the stable wall as he rearranged his diary. 'Gosh. Quite exciting, really.' I was immensely bucked, particularly at having Paddy's help. 'Paddy, I am so grateful. I'd take one of the children but they hate me at the moment. All of them.'

As if on cue, Nico's bedroom window flew open at the front of the house. Some very weird, very loud, thumping garage music pumped out and I caught a glimpse of Nico, puffing away on what I hoped was a very large roll-up. He glared pointedly at me and disappeared from view.

More music joined the unsteady rock beat, but from a different direction this time, and a different era. I turned. Coming down the lane and approaching the gate was a familiar ancient black Volvo. The windows were open and Boney M. blared as smoke billowed from the passenger side. Why did my family smoke so much? A tent and a battered suitcase were tied, rather precariously, to the roof. My parents, back from some whacky psychic festival in Wales, loomed into view. Mum, incongruously dressed in heart-shaped sunglasses and a headband with feathers sticking out of it, waved both hands madly from the passenger seat, whilst my father smiled weakly from behind the wheel, looking rather drained and tired. As I got up and walked across to open the gate it occurred to me that with no compliant children on my books at present I was going to need these two rather badly. And really quite rapidly. I smiled broadly at my guests. Never had I been so pleased to see my mother.

CHAPTER 23

*T*he car came to a juddering halt in the yard and the doors opened, disgorging its exhausted occupants. Looking like aging hippies with back problems, my parents staggered from the car at an angle. My mother was definitely looking the part in yellow flares, an ethnic waistcoat, beads and what looked like tampons dangling from her ears, whilst my father looked like a man who'd reached his journey's end. I went round and gave him a hug and I believe he almost sniffed the air as he released me, already scenting his old armchair, the *Racing Times* and a large whisky. I decided I'd leave him firmly out of tomorrow's equation. He'd had enough fun for one week.

'Darling!' My mother and I hugged too and then she puffed hard on her Consulate Menthol, throwing her head back to release the smoke to the sky. 'We popped by to drop off Nico's tent, which was an absolute godsend. Although you might like to tell him it's got the most terrific holes in it. Luckily it didn't rain but if it does he'll get drenched. I'll patch it for him if he likes.'

'You can tell him yourself,' I told her as the boy himself

climbed out through the kitchen window, followed by his disciples. Nico had his overnight bag in his hand and a defiant, truculent look on his face.

'We're off to Jake's,' he announced, as if my heart would break. 'I've had it with you, Mum. I'm out of here.'

'Oh dear, what a shame,' I said, thinking, yippedy-doo-dah. 'How long for?'

'At least a week. No more animal husbandry for me.'

Why hadn't I thought of this before? Obviously he'd been useful whilst I'd been away, but on a more general basis, want a clean, tidy house with no teenagers in it? Just strip to the waist and frighten them all away.

'Er, well, mate, I think just tonight with my mum. Then to Derek's,' said the ever alert Jake.

'Uh? Wha'?' Derek somehow came to life, his eyes clearing. 'Not sure . . . my mum can be a bit – you know . . . funny.'

'She'll come round,' I assured him. 'Don't forget, I'm funny too.' I smiled winningly. Turned back to my son. 'Got all your dirty washing, Nico? Make sure you make a present of that for Mrs Harper. After all, Derek is quite welcome to bring us his. Try not to be sick, though, the Harpers don't have dogs to clear it up like we do.' Derek was prone to vomiting when drunk, usually outside, but on one famous occasion down my curtains from a top bunk, which had challenged even our terriers. Waiting until Nico had at least had the grace to greet his grandparents, I jerked my head towards his bedroom.

'Don't suppose you could have turned that thing off before you left?' The walls were still throbbing, a relentless bass note pumping out.

'What? Oh, no, I left it on for Ted. He's still up there.' I stared at my son for a very long time.

'*Ted* is?'

'Yeah.'

'*Toxic* Ted?'

'Yeah. He came round last night, looking for Minna. Brought some booze.'

'Quite a lot, actually,' Jake put in. 'Bottle of Gordon's and a six-pack. Seemed rude not to ask him in. Nice bloke.'

'Nice . . .' I resumed my contemplation of Nico.

'Yeah, he's all right actually. But we had a bit of a session, so I thought I'd let him sleep it off. Don't worry, I didn't use the spare room, he slept on my floor.'

'Darling, we'll be away, we're a bit bushed,' called my mother as Dad, having removed the tent from the car and set it down in a corner of the yard, dusted his hands down wearily. 'Thank you, Nico, frightfully useful.'

'Glad to be of service, Granny,' grinned her grandson. 'How were the mystics?'

'Oh splendid, although a little alternative for your grandfather's tastes.'

My father rolled his eyes meaningfully at Nico. 'And not that psychic either. We followed signs to the festival – why? Why do they need signs?'

Nico sniggered.

'Tutty-bye, darling, speak soon,' warbled Mum.

'No – no, don't go, not yet. Yes, *you* go, Nico – but Mum, could you possibly wait one sec? I won't be a mo.' I turned to my veterinary surgeon, whose skills I was testing in all sorts of ways. 'Paddy,' I hissed, 'chat her up. We need her.'

I dashed inside, rolling through the kitchen window commando-style, and took the stairs two at a time. I flew down the corridor and through the open door at the far end into the loudly pulsating room. Sure enough, there on Nico's floor was a comatose Ted in a sleeping bag, mouth open, blond hair tousled. The music was deafening. I snapped it off.

'Ted!' Nothing.

'*Ted!* ' I shook him. Then I shouted in his ear. In desperation, I poured a handy glass of water from Nico's bedside table on him. Not much, but I did.

'Eh? Wha'? Wha's happening?' Ted spluttered and sat up, fine young torso dripping.

I put my face close to his.

'Ted, you have precisely five minutes to get your things together and to get out of this house, do you understand?'

He gazed at me uncomprehendingly through half-closed, heavy-lidded eyes.

'TED!' It was no good. Moments later those eyes had given way to gravity and he'd lain down again, snuggling into his bag. Glancing out of the window I saw Paddy talking to my parents, who were being polite, but clearly keen to be away. Dad was very much on the back foot, reversing towards his car. I flew downstairs, thinking 'priorities' and rejoined them in the yard.

'Mum, Dad, I know you're exhausted, but would you do me the most humungous favor?'

'Depends,' said my father warily, up to here with favors.

'Actually, not you, Dad, but Mum – could you possibly house-sit for me from tomorrow? Just for one night? Paddy and I have to go to London.'

'Paddy and . . .' My mother looked from me to Paddy. Her face cleared and the sun came out. 'Oh darling, of course!' She became wreathed in delighted smiles as she puffed excitedly on her ciggie. She loved Paddy Campbell. Let's face it, she loved all vets, medics, doctors, lawyers, professional men. For an aging hippie she had remarkably bourgeois views on what would suit her daughter.

Valiantly resisting giving her a withering look, I ploughed on. 'I know it's horribly short notice, but we have to be there by lunchtime tomorrow.'

'Lunchtime! Of course! Where are you taking her, Paddy? For lunch?'

'Oh, well—'

'Mum, Dad wants to go home,' I said firmly, cutting through any more embarrassing chit-chat. I hustled her firmly away and she complied, although she couldn't resist throwing over her shoulder, 'Stay as long as you like, Paddy, Frank and I will be fine.'

'Shall I ring you later and talk you through who needs what on the animal front?' I said as she got in the car. 'The sheep are fine, and the chickens and ducks you know about, it's just Nutty who needs a bit of TLC at the moment.'

'Do that, darling.'

'Just wait until I've had forty winks, though, I'm on my chinstrap,' warned my father as he got in the car. 'And remind me never to escort your mother to a psycho-whatsit festival again. Words cannot describe the tedium, the exhaustion and frankly bonkers people.'

'Quite right, Dad. I'll go with her next time.'

'Oh, would you, darling? There's a marvelous American mind-reader appearing at Wembley in September, he's filling stadiums in the States. You'll love him.'

'Er, well, yes. I expect so. We'll see.'

'And I'll get going in the caravan again while I'm here, shall I? I'm rather inspired by my week away.'

'Yes, but, Mum, please don't keep telling Gordon Butcher he's coming into a fortune – his wife told me he spent practically all his wages on lottery tickets last week. And after you told Brenda Smyth she'd meet a tall, dark, handsome stranger in Budgens they had to escort her from the premises. She loitered all day, accosting any man with dark hair, or, as the manager put it, any man at all.'

'Anyone would think I make it up,' said my mother tartly, snapping her seat belt on. 'I can only tell them what's written in the stars.'

'Yes, I realize that,' I said in a placatory fashion. 'And of course get the caravan going and pop your sign out in the lane. I'm really grateful to you for holding the fort.'

'No problem, my sweet.' She patted my cheek. 'Have fun, you two!' She glanced past me and gave Paddy an annoying wink. My father raised his eyebrows in sympathy at me and then they drove away.

'On second thoughts I think we should go tonight, actually,' said Paddy as they chugged out of the drive in a cloud of messy exhaust fumes. 'If we go in the morning we'll never get there in time.'

'Do you?' I turned. 'Yes, you may be right. And the dogs will be fine if Mum's here tomorrow. I'll text and ask her to come first thing. But where will we stay? Well, obviously at Lucy's, but it's tiny and they are *so* cross with me at the moment. I don't know if I can impose much long—'

'No, no, we can stay at my place. I told you, I grew up in Kensington. I'll see you on the five thirty-six, and try not to miss it, Molly.'

'As if I would! Golly, will they mind? Your parents? What will you say? Won't they—'

But he'd gone, striding away in the midst of my babble of questions, no doubt keen to escape and to check on the difficult calf delivery up at Baldwin's farm. I watched him go. Stood, a moment, feeling strangely unsettled. There was quite a lot I felt I knew about that man, but then again, more recently, quite a lot I clearly didn't. My reverie was interrupted by Buddy, who gave me a friendly butt from behind which nearly sent me flying. He was far too familiar, I decided, staggering a bit, he'd be in the kitchen soon. I watched him saunter arrogantly away to have a word with Nutty over the stable door. I had to do something about that ram, he was becoming a problem in so many ways. My eyes strayed nervously to last year's ewe lambs in a distant field which Nico said he'd broken into. And done what, exactly?

I hurried inside. The five thirty-six. Crikey – I glanced at my watch – I'd have to get a wiggle on. I didn't have much time. Or much money left, I thought queasily. All this back and forth to London was taking its toll. As I got to the landing, Ted's snores had reached fortissimo level. I dashed in to have another go. It was only when I unzipped his sleeping bag to try and shake him bodily to his feet that I realized he was naked. Shit. I stepped back, dropping the bag in horror. Oh no, I couldn't be grappling with that. And knowing my luck, one of the children would appear again and accuse me of interfering with minors. Although there was nothing minor about . . . anyway. He'd have to sleep it off. I'd try again before I left. At least he'd turned over and stopped that dreadful racket. I hurried from the room and along the corridor.

I realized, as I glanced in the mirror in my room once I'd repacked a bag with clean clothes, that I looked an absolute sight. I peered. Never mind, it was only Paddy. And it wasn't as if I was ever going to see Felix again. The thought both stilled and saddened me as I added a clean shirt to my bag. I paused as I recalled how, very recently, I'd been up here in my room, preparing myself, sartorially speaking, for him. Then my core stiffened as I thought of him with Camilla. At the theater. Living together, probably. Where? There hadn't been any sign of a woman at his house, but perhaps that had been deliberate. Was he really such an arch fixer? Such a Machiavellian schemer, removing all traces? Hard to imagine. And yet the signs were not in his favor.

At any rate, I thought, zipping up my bag and seizing the handles, it was a relief not to squeeze into Spanx or camouflage the brown age spot on my cheek, or shave my legs to within an inch of their life, and also to be able, I thought, racing downstairs and opening the larder door, to eat a whole packet of Jaffa Cakes on the hoof. I threw the empty packet in the bin, munching hard. Not being in thrall to a man definitely had its compensations.

Paddy read his newspaper on the train and then *Farmers Weekly* and then *The Field* and then he did some work on his laptop and then he slept. For someone who was coming to my aid he showed remarkably little interest in me and I wondered if he owed his parents a visit or something. I asked him when he woke up.

'Yes, definitely. They don't make the journey to Herefordshire much and I rarely get to London.'

'So this is a good excuse?' I didn't mean it to sound as snide as that and wished I hadn't said it. He raised his eyebrows.

'Well, I could do without it, if that's what you mean. I've had to cancel appointments and get Poppy to stand in for the rest.'

'I didn't mean it like that. I'm incredibly grateful. I just mean it would be good to see them, from your point of view.'

'Of course.'

'And who will you say I am?' Those eyebrows went up again. He wasn't remotely meeting me halfway. 'I-I mean –' I stammered, 'just a friend?'

'You are just a friend.'

'Yes, but – won't they think it's odd? I've come to stay?'

I could feel myself coloring, damn it. I wished I wasn't sitting opposite him.

'Well, you can stay with Lucy if you prefer.'

'No,' I said quickly. 'No, my children are sick of me.'

'Don't worry, they're used to me bringing home all sorts of people. They won't bat an eyelid.' He picked up his copy of *The Times*, folded it efficiently into quarters and started doing the crossword.

Right. That told me, didn't it? All sorts of people. I watched his pen fly over the puzzle, really rather briskly. And it was a broadsheet, not the easy one I sometimes managed in the *Mail*. It occurred to me this man was very clever. Well, vets were, weren't they? It was well known. Apparently it took longer to train to be a vet than a doctor. Which made sense, because animals couldn't talk. Couldn't tell you where it hurt. I was on the point of asking about this, if it was a problem, and stopped myself. How inane did I want to sound? Usually I didn't care with Paddy, but something about his detached manner silenced me. Made me almost shy. I pulled my skirt down to cover, what I realized, were slightly bristling knees. I wished I'd shaved my legs.

The train rattled on. After a bit, I cleared my throat and contrived to look intelligent.

'Paddy, can I ask you one more thing?'

'Ask away.' Without looking up.

'Is it OK for Buddy to be in with last year's ewe lambs? I mean, they're too young to be – you know – susceptible, aren't they?'

'To what?'

'To becoming pregnant.'

He looked up. 'Of course they're susceptible. And apart from anything else, he was the sire, wasn't he?'

'Oh. Yes.'

'So we wouldn't want him having his way with his own daughters, would we?'

'No! Of course not.'

'Which is why you borrowed one this year, if you remember.'

'Yes, Bob Fisher's. And he had Buddy.'

'Quite. To guard against incest.' Incest. Golly!

'Why, has he broken in?'

'To where?'

He eyed me. 'To the ewes' field.'

'No! Of course not.'

More of that wretched blood to my face. Paddy regarded me a long moment then resumed his crossword. I bit the inside of my cheek. What would happen, I wondered? Would the lambs run round in small circles? Be a bit – you know . . . simple? But they were simple anyway. Mine certainly were. Thank God the mothers couldn't speak, I thought, cringing down into the lapels of my jacket. Couldn't tell the whole story, point the cloven hoof at Buddy and cry, 'Rape! He raped me!' Did Paddy mean the lambs would have deformities or something? I went a bit cold. Had a nightmare vision of ghastly monstrosities being born next year: Paddy's cold eyes as he came round to view the five-legged, one-eyed flock. Would that happen? I couldn't ask Paddy now, of course, he'd know I was guilty. Except, actually, Nico was. I'd have to pin that boy down, I thought grimly. Discover just how comprehensively he'd taken his eye off the ball.

At Paddington, we got a taxi to Kensington because Paddy said it would be quicker and as it was we were late.

'For what?' I asked.

'For supper.'

'Oh. Yes, of course.' A cosy supper with his parents in the kitchen. How lovely. And how *intriguing*. I perked up no end. He must have rung them. Well, of course he rang them, Molly, don't be an idiot. Or texted them.

The taxi rumbled across London, weaving in and out of the traffic, and then eventually it purred down Kensington High Street, up the hill, and stopped outside a tall, white, stucco-fronted house in Essex Villas. Essex Villas. Blimey! The streets fairly creaked with money round here. It was all you could hear.

As Paddy paid the driver I got out and gazed around. There was no bustle of pedestrians, just the purr of an expensive, smoky-windowed four-by-four as it stopped opposite. It deposited a child in a straw boater and blazer from the back seat. The man who opened the door for the girl was clearly not the father but a paid retainer, and the girl ran up to an enormous house, the door of which was opened by a foreign-looking woman in a white apron. Every window box frothed with tasteful white flowers and every front door was shiny and black to match the railings that enclosed the immaculate front gardens. Paddy's parents' door was no exception.

Paddy led the way up the path and fished around in his pocket for a key, but before he could retrieve it, the front door flew open, and a ravishing-looking woman with a beautifully coiffed mane of ash-blonde hair and stunning cat-like green eyes in an extraordinarily well-preserved face, gave a beaming smile, which reached her eyes and beyond.

'Darling!' Dressed in a black wrap dress, she held out slim, graceful arms. She smelled divine.

Paddy grinned and walked up the steps to hug her. 'Hi, Mum.'

I gaped. Mum? This gorgeous creature?

She beamed. 'Oh, I'm so glad you made it, you're in

time for supper. I hoped you would be. Although we've polished off the scallops, I'm afraid.'

'No worries. Mum, this is Molly Faulkner, who I told you about.'

'Oh yes! You poor thing, with the farm and the soap and all those wretched animals and now those tenants in your house! Virginia,' she told me, as I took her hand which she extended, smiling. 'Come in, come in, you must be exhausted. Such a long journey and you've been back and forth quite a lot, I gather.'

'Um, a bit,' I admitted, 'but glad to be here.' She ushered us inside.

'What have you said?' I asked in an undertone to Paddy when she was out of earshot and leading us under a vast curving staircase and on down a lofty, chandelier-lit hall. My eyes were on stalks.

'Only that you've got a tenancy problem with your house in London and that we're here to sort it out,' he said. 'But actually, there's nothing we can't say out loud, is there?'

'No. I suppose not. Within reason. How *old* is your mother, Paddy? She's beautiful.'

He shrugged. 'Dunno. Sixty-something? She had us quite young.'

The most beautiful sixty-something I'd ever seen was heading towards a room filled with noise and laughter, and as we turned a corner, it was into a dark red candlelit dining room full of people chattering and laughing, clearly mid-supper at a long mahogany table groaning with silver and crystal.

'Paddy!' An aristocratic-looking man with silver hair swept back from a high forehead got to his feet at the far end then came around the humming throng to hug his son, the likeness between them unmistakable. 'Well done, you made it!'

'Hi, Dad, this is Molly. My father, Jack.'

Oh, how I wished I'd not only shaved my legs but my armpits too, so that I could be wearing a little black sleeveless dress like the majority of the gorgeous women around this table. They gazed up at me with interest. Although the possession of such a dress, gossamer-thin and floaty over slim brown limbs, was of course out of the question.

'So kind of you to let us invade when you're clearly busy,' I told Jack as he shook my hand heartily. His dark, penetrating eyes were spookily familiar.

'Not at all, we don't see nearly enough of Paddy. I'm delighted you've dragged him up. Now, Paddy, pull up a couple of chairs, one here, and one at the far end, next to Claudia, and you sit here, my dear.' He indicated beside him at the head of the table as Paddy went down the other end.

The woman I was usurping gave me a welcoming smile and politely shifted around a bit, not looking in the least put out as I apologized profusely. Jack clasped her shoulder warmly and introduced her as Regine, declaring her an absolute poppet.

'Now,' he said, resuming his seat and beaming at me. 'I've put you opposite Willem for a reason.' He nodded towards an attractive blond man deep in conversation with his neighbor on the other side of the table: meanwhile cutlery and a place mat appeared magically before me, courtesy of a discreet maid.

'Paddy says he's essential to your plan, but we won't go there yet, first things first. Red or white, my dear? It's game, I think.'

Everything seemed to be happening very quickly. I wanted

to glance around the room, at the exquisite oil paintings on the deep red walls, the antiques, the other guests, to have a closer look at their faces. Paddy, I noticed, was sitting between two women of extraordinary beauty, who both kissed him warmly, looking inordinately pleased to see him. But the genial Jack was asking about my farm, my children, and as well as answering, I suddenly had a guinea fowl to contend with.

'We barely see Paddy, he's so immersed in his practice. Do they not have any other vets in your neck of the woods, to take the pressure off him?'

'He's the best,' I said honestly. 'So everyone wants him.' For some reason this made me blush. 'I mean, to see to their livestock. There is another practice in Ludlow, but the chap who runs it is a known alky and he doesn't always get the diagnosis right. Then there's a woman called Sarah Harris who's absolutely terrifying and insists your animal always needs clinical attention – particularly horses – so the bill is astronomical. No, Paddy's the one everyone wants to get hold of.' There I went again. 'But he's horribly busy, as you say.'

I glanced down the table. It hadn't escaped my notice that the blonde beside him had turned her chair at an almost ninety-degree angle to talk to him, her tiny pink dress riding high on her slim brown thighs as she crossed her legs. She chatted away excitedly. Paddy threw back his head and laughed.

'Yes, well, he considered doing it here, of course,' Jack went on, filling up my wine glass. 'But only for a nanosecond. The idea of a surgery stuffed with pampered Kensington ladies and their equally pampered pekes did not appeal.'

'He'd have made a fortune, though,' observed Regine in a French accent beside me and I shifted my chair back to include her. 'Imagine the line of lonely old women in *his* waiting room?' She laughed.

'Not so old, either,' laughed another gorgeous creature, sitting opposite. 'He'd have all those It Girls with chihuahuas in baskets lining up!'

This was extraordinary. It struck me abruptly, and with some considerable force, like that of a runaway train, that Paddy was a catch. A huge one. Even in London. Especially in London. Why hadn't I spotted it?

'That's Claudia,' murmured Regine with a conspiratorial smile, seeing me look down the table again. The blonde in pink was even closer now, her guinea fowl abandoned. 'Because I know you're wondering. I would be.'

'Claudia?' I asked.

She looked confused. 'Oh, I'm sorry. I assumed you two were together. Thought you'd know about . . .'

'Oh – no, we're not together. Not at all. We're friends.'

'Ah, right.' Her face cleared. 'Well, Claudia's his ex. He broke her heart disappearing like that.'

Inexplicably, my own heart lurched. 'You mean, to Herefordshire?'

'Yes. She just assumed they'd be in London, or the home counties at the very least. Guildford, perhaps. Kicked up quite a fuss.'

'But he went anyway.'

'He did. And she sulked like mad and finally said she'd come and join him, at which point he told her not to bother.'

'Oh! But they were in love?'

'Engaged.' She looked surprised that I didn't know this, as I too looked surprised to hear it. I would have liked a moment to accommodate this news, assimilate it, but Jack was interrupting, his hand on my arm.

'Now Willem here is an art dealer from The Hague.

And I hope he won't mind me telling you he has some serious commissions under his belt.' He smiled conspiratorially. 'He places artwork in the reception halls of all those mighty City institutions – Chase Manhattan, UBS – you know the sort of thing?'

I didn't, but I could imagine, and nodded knowledgeably, my mind still on Paddy and Claudia.

'And I gather you have a problem with Felix Carrington,' said Willem, leaning across the table towards me and speaking with a slight accent. I was taken aback as the Dutchman's blue eyes met mine, a slight smile on his smooth, tanned face.

'How did you . . . ?'

'Paddy emailed me from the train. Thought I might know him, which indeed I do, in a professional capacity. As a slightly disreputable artist-cum-dealer, albeit perfectly charming.'

'You like him?'

He inclined his head. 'On a superficial, convivial level, I get on with him. But I wouldn't trust him as far as I could throw him. He'd sell his own grandmother. Now. I gather there's a document you're keen to get hold of.'

'Yes,' I said breathlessly, wondering how much of this Jack was listening to, but happily he'd turned and was engaged with the waiter chappie standing beside him serving the wine, giving him some instruction, and Regine had turned to her other side.

'But your plan is shot with holes, if I may say so,' Willem went on, 'if you even call breaking in a plan. I'll come up with something much better and more legitimate. Leave it to me. You don't want to do anything illegal if you can possibly help it, stay as squeaky clean as possible. Also, my plan will be more fun.' He smiled.

'You have one?'

'Not completely, it's definitely embryonic at present. But leave it with me. I owe Felix a little payback. He slipped a Renoir drawing right from under my nose at an art fair in Istanbul a few years ago. I've been waiting for my chance.'

He grinned good-naturedly as he sipped his wine, eyeing me merrily across it, as if wheeling and dealing art and large amounts of money was a mere bagatelle to him.

As I glanced around the table, I saw that it probably was to all these people. This was a moneyed, international, cultured set, very different to my Wandsworth crowd. Quite a few were foreign, I decided, drinking in the exotic mix: the beauty in the sari halfway down, her husband perhaps opposite, in his silk Nehru jacket. The sultry South American-looking woman beside him. And it was a set Paddy was clearly part of, I realized, watching as he rocked with laughter at the far end at something his neighbor said. He saw me and raised his eyebrows to check I was OK. I nodded then he immediately went back to listening to Claudia's anecdote, a rapt expression on his face.

I wondered if she'd known he was coming. If her heart had leapt when she'd heard, last minute, that he'd be here? Or even if she'd been invited last minute? If Virginia had got on the phone immediately: 'Darling, you'll never guess, Paddy's coming up! Yes, for supper! Claudia, *do* come . . . Yes, he is bringing someone, but only a friend. A client he's befriended, poor thing. At a bit of a loss, it seems. Helping her out.' And of course I looked dreadful. She'd barely glanced at me as I'd walked in, had written me off in a heartbeat.

My own heart began to pump. It came to me, in a blinding flash of hideous white light behind my eyes, that I felt ridiculously jealous. And yet I didn't fancy Paddy. I stared at him. As I gazed some more, the feeling didn't dissipate; it grew. I felt more and more horrified. Oh God, I *did* fancy him. Or did I? No, I couldn't. It was just this environment, surely? Seeing him in civilized, urbane surroundings, not in his beaten-up jeans, striding through the cowpats. Was I that shallow? Oh God, I *was*. I clutched my pearls. I had the most awful, sinking feeling. I'd been around this man for years. I'd argued with him, stood up to him – stood him up too – had never put a jot of make-up on for him; why hadn't I spotted him? And was it really just because a different light had been cast upon him, from a chandelier, a few candles, cultured friends, was that why I was wondering now if, when I'd nodded off on the train, I'd had my mouth open? Or why on earth I hadn't painted my toenails?

Claudia put her hand over Paddy's at the far end of the table. I don't lip-read as a rule, but this wasn't difficult. And there were tears in her eyes as she said it.

'It's lovely to see you.'

Paddy smiled back, equally warmly. 'It's lovely to see you too, Clauds.'

I sank into my wine, appalled.

CHAPTER 24

The following morning, having spent a blissful night in an incredibly comfortable double bed in a tremendously tasteful spare room that had been Cole-faxed up to the eyeballs, I awoke to my phone ringing. In my head it was still the middle of the night, the early hours at most, but there it was, vibrating away on the bedside table. I groped for it and answered groggily, eyes firmly shut. I rested my head back on the pillow again.

'Molly?'

'Mum?'

'Are you awake, my sweet?'

'Well, I am now.'

'Now darling, there's absolutely nothing to be alarmed about, so don't worry, but I'm afraid your father's had a bit of a turn.'

I flayed about a bit then managed to sit bolt upright in bed. 'What d'you mean, a turn?' I whispered. 'A stroke?'

'Good Lord no, nothing like that. Just a spot of exhaustion, I think. He was rather breathless last night when we went to bed, with a pain in his chest, and then this morning he was a tiny bit worse and said his heart was racing. So I called the doctor – well, Hugh, obviously, from next door – who came immediately. He said he'd been overdoing it for a man of his age and fitness and that he needed a few days in bed.'

'Oh. Right.' I felt my pulse rate slow down slightly. 'Nothing serious then?'

'Nothing at all, darling, but all my fault.' Her voice suddenly sounded small. A bit wretched. 'I've been a bloody idiot, Moll. I've been pushing him too hard. My stupid mid-life crisis. I should never have taken him to that festival, camping, at his age.'

'You weren't to know, Mum. It's not your fault.'

'It is, but I'll know next time. It was too hot and over-crowded for him and he got no sleep at all with all the noise and that terrible camp bed. But anyway, the thing is, darling, I don't think I can house-sit. He definitely needs to be here at home – not that he was coming anyway – but I don't want to leave him. Certainly not for the night.'

'No, quite right. Poor Dad. Give him my love.'

My mind was already whirring. Who could I ask? Tia? Too busy.

'So what I thought I'd do is pop in and out. Feed the animals, walk the dogs, shoot home, then pop back later.'

'Oh, would you, Mum? You're a star, thank you!'

'So that's what I did, early this morning – I got your text – knowing the dogs would want a pee. Only there's a young man there, Molly. In the house.'

I froze. Stared at the tasteful spriggy wallpaper opposite. Shit. Ted.

'Toxic Ted,' I breathed. 'Christ, Mum, I completely forgot! I left in a tearing hurry, all a bit of a blur. God – did he have anything on?'

'A dressing gown of Nico's but not much else.' I heard

her light a cigarette. Exhale breathily. 'I must say, he's frightfully attractive, darling. We had a bowl of cereal together in front of breakfast TV and I couldn't take my eyes off his cheekbones. You could pare cheese with them. Apparently he's a friend of Minna's.'

'Yes, he is, but – hang on – you left him there?'

'Well, it seemed rude to evict him.'

I shut my eyes. 'Mum, I'm so sorry, you're going to have to go back and get rid of him. Did he look – you know – settled?' I yelped. 'As if he was staying?'

'Well, I didn't really ask. I wasn't sure what the arrangement was. But don't worry, I'll pop back later and have a word. Is he Minna's young man? There didn't seem to be any sign of her.'

'No, she's in London, and no, he's not. She's got a new boyfriend, I think.'

'Oh? What happened with this one?' I could tell my mother had settled down in front of an already overflowing ashtray. 'Was it the sex? It often is.'

'No idea, but listen, Mum, that boy has to go, d'you understand? No more cosy bowls of cereal in front of Phillip Schofield in heaven knows what squalor.' I put a hand over my eyes. What had happened to my life? What would David say? What would my colleagues at Price Adamson say if they could see this crazy woman, chasing a document she may or may not have signed, leaving a house full of starving animals, towers of soap, strange men in dressing gowns . . . I shook my head, sent more love to my father, obtained further reassurance that he really was absolutely fine, and got off the phone. It could be worse, I told the Colefax wallpaper. Dad could be very ill. He wasn't, thank the Lord. Get a grip.

Paddy was already downstairs having a civilized breakfast of grapefruit and muesli when I appeared. There was no sign of his parents. His back was to me as he sat at a bar which divided the room. At my end, a state-of-the-art, chrome-encrusted and polished granite kitchen prevailed, whilst at the other, a plush sitting area with bright, Indian-themed sofas and scatter cushions, rugs on the floor and murals on the walls gave a relaxed, casual look. French windows opened on to a leafy walled enclosure scented with lilac and hyacinths, and classical music hummed softly in the background. The contrast to my own home could not have been more stark.

'Morning.' I slipped in beside him on a stool, noticing he'd yet again completed the crossword and probably read *The Times* from cover to cover.

He glanced up. 'Oh good, you're up.' He put the paper to one side and glanced at his watch, shooting up his cuff to do so, which was pressed, pale blue, and linked with gold. There was a tie, too, and smart chinos. I gaped, never having seen him in anything other than jeans and a sweater. Naturally the whole ensemble suited him hugely.

'You look, um, smart,' I said, managing to resist 'lovely'.

'Well, we're meeting Willem at eleven thirty, or at least I am, so I thought I'd better look the part. I need to get a move on, actually. Docklands, you say?'

'Er, yes, near the Tate Modern,' I said, feeling even more out of control than usual. 'Paddy, what exactly *is* the plan? Willem was full of nods and winks last night about how he owed Felix a little comeuppance – and you look like you're off to Lloyds to broker some deal – but I'm not entirely sure what he's up to.'

'Oh, it's very simple. Willem failed to authenticate a Degas watercolor Felix uncovered in Paris about five years ago, for the simple reason that it was an out-and-out bogus fake. So last year, in New York, Felix got a wealthy friend to out-bid Willem on a Renoir drawing he'd always wanted and which had finally come up for sale at Christie's. This is all part of the fun in the art world, Molly, they thrive on it. I only had to mention your little local difficulty with the very same man and Willem was all over it like a rash. He's delighted to come to our rescue.'

'So what's he going to do?'

'He's contacted Felix to say he'd like to look at a piece of sculpture in his son's collection – he couldn't say *his* collection; everyone knows Felix is a crap artist, apparently, but the son's not bad – with a view to buying it for a wealthy corporate client. He's told him the Royal Gulf Bank in Dubai are looking for something to go on a plinth in the middle of their foyer. We'll go over to his studio, become interested in more than just the one piece – down-right excited, in fact, about two or three – and keep him longer than he expected. We'll be a bit late arriving anyway, about twelve. He's probably meeting his father at one, and the hope is he'll leave us in there, poring over the sculptures – after all, he knows Willem – telling us to shut the door behind us.'

'Right. We? Us?'

'I'm the wealthy client.'

'You look quite rich, actually.' I admired the Church's brogues. 'And I suppose you could be foreign, you're quite dark.'

'Why, thank you, Molly.'

He held my eyes teasingly and I realized I didn't look remotely rich or exotic in my five-year-old Phase Eight summer dress.

'So I'm not coming.'

'We thought not.'

'Because I'd hardly pass as the wealthy wife?'

'No, because he'd recognize you,' he said patiently. I nodded.

'I'm still a bit sleepy,' I said carefully.

'Clearly,' he murmured, sipping his coffee.

'And if he decides to stand his father up? Ring and cancel him?'

He shrugged. 'That's a risk. But if he's anything like my parents, his father won't be glued to a mobile so it won't be that easy. Anyway, we'll see.'

'And when he's gone . . . you root around in his drawers and find the contract.'

'That's the plan.'

'It's a good one,' I said slowly. Again, I felt a certain indefinable sadness. Such a short time ago I'd been thoroughly overexcited to be in that very same house with the handsome Felix, and now I was hoodwinking him and ransacking his home. But needs must.

'And meanwhile, what do I do?'

He shrugged. 'Kick your heels here, I suppose. Mum's out at some arty charity event and Dad's gone to his office, so do whatever you like.'

'I'll stay here,' I said quickly, thinking I really would like to take a good look around, not least at this light, airy kitchen with its dresser full of crockery, but more to the point, photographs, popped in between those mugs and plates. Obviously I wouldn't be too intrusive. Obviously.

He shot his cuff up again. 'Right. I'm off now, actually. I promised to go and see someone first. Willem's picking me up from there.'

'Oh. Right.' I badly wanted to know. 'A client?' Lame, I know.

He laughed. 'Why would I have a client in London, Molly? A long-distance appointment? No, a friend.'

'Ah, OK.' Don't say it. Don't ask. Oh God, I was going to. 'Claudia?' I blurted.

He laughed again. 'Yes, OK, Claudia. We're having a coffee.'

'Right. She's very beautiful, Paddy.'

'She is.'

'And you were engaged, I gather.'

'You gather right.'

'And Paddy, can I just ask, I know it's none of my business, but—' Damn. He was answering his mobile, which had rung on about the second word of that sentence.

'Yes, that's it . . .' he was saying. 'Draycott Gardens, forty-eight . . . Well, I'm leaving here now, so I'll see you at about half eleven . . . OK.' He pocketed his phone, stood up and drained his coffee in one gulp.

'Gotta go. That was Willem. Make yourself at home, Molly. Help yourself to breakfast and anything else you want. There's orange juice in the fridge.'

He slipped into a dark linen jacket and I had a mad moment of wondering if he'd kiss my cheek, like a husband off to work, but of course he didn't, and in another moment, he was gone.

From the other end of the house the front door closed softly behind him with a hushed puff of air, not a clang and a rattle as mine had done in the days when it opened at all – it was currently jammed shut, warped by winter rain.

On an impulse I got to my feet and stole quickly to the front of the house, slipping into the lofty drawing room where we'd had coffee last night, darting to the window to watch him go. My eyes followed him down the street. A taxi appeared around the corner and Paddy's arm shot up in the air. As it drew to a halt and he went to get in, he must have had a sense he was being watched because he turned. I shot back behind the curtain, fist in mouth. Had he seen me? I hoped not. Really hoped not. I tiptoed back to the kitchen. But what was I *doing* acting like some adolescent schoolgirl?

Disappointingly, the adolescent activity continued. Having established that I really was alone and that a silent starched maid wasn't about to materialize enigmatically from the shadows, I set about casing the joint.

I picked up every single photograph in the kitchen and gazed avidly, my study forensic. The dresser, as hoped, proved fruitful. It yielded Paddy as a boy, with what looked like two younger sisters. I didn't know that. Why didn't I know that? But then again, why should I? One or two more of Paddy, mostly as I knew him today. The fridge revealed Paddy as a teenager, with his parents and sisters on a skiing holiday. I released this treasure from its magnet, drank it in then replaced it carefully, the magnet in exactly the same place. In the dining room, where I stole next, were two sets of wedding photos: both girls and their new husbands, Paddy smiling in the background.

Back in the drawing room Paddy was graduating, with a mortar board and a scroll. He looked young, sheepish, a bit scruffy, and God, *so* handsome. Then I found Paddy with a puppy. Then Paddy on a horse, out hunting. Then Paddy with Claudia. I plucked this jewel, this large, silver-framed treasure, from the far end of the drawing room at the back of a bank of photos on the grand piano. I gazed greedily. It had clearly been taken on holiday, Tuscany possibly: a stone farmhouse in the background plus some skinny cypress trees. In the foreground were the happy couple, who did indeed look blissful. They were laughing into the camera, arms around one another, Claudia's blonde hair billowing. What had gone wrong?

Well, I knew what had gone wrong, she'd balked at

deepest Herefordshire – and who can blame her, I had too – but then she'd come round. Was his pride really so colossal that he couldn't forgive her? Had he let her initial resistance stand in the way of marrying the girl he loved?

I thought of his anger when I'd failed to meet him for supper. Which had gone on for quite some time. His refusal to come and see my animals even months later, sending Mike, his then assistant, who would deliver my latest recalcitrant calf – in the days when I had a few cattle, which didn't last long on account of their inability to give birth without expensive veterinary assistance or, in the case of one pregnant cow, a tractor. On that occasion Paddy had had to come out: it had taken two of them to deliver her. Paddy had driven the tractor and I remembered him yelling at me to keep the rope taut, tied as it was to the calf's protruding feet, whilst Mike held the poor bellowing cow in the halter. Oh yes, we'd had some fun times. Most of them with Paddy looking like thunder. I stared at the happy photo. But surely no man was so proud that having had his ego dented thus, he'd let it stand in the way of his eventual happiness? It seemed Paddy Campbell might just be that man.

I replaced the frame thoughtfully. I wondered what he was saying to her now. *I've been a fool. Time spent alone and without you has made me realize that . . .* I caught my breath. I hoped not. I really hoped not. I gazed through the French windows to the leafy walled garden beyond, lost in meditative thought. Then I shook myself. Swallowed. I knew what I needed right now: a plan to make myself feel better, even if it was a flimsy one. I racked my brains for a moment. OK, this one was practically diaphanous, but it was nevertheless all I had, so it would have to do. I flew upstairs, grabbed my handbag then left the house, making sure I had the key.

I spent the next few hours in a very unfamiliar fashion. First I managed to secure a walk-in, as I now know it to be called, at Michael-John in Kensington High Street. There I had a wash and blow-dry. Then I had a leg wax in Valentino's opposite. Next I went to Zara and bought something totally unlike me, but oh so Claudia. It was in the palest pink silky material, a shift dress, summery, slight – so slight I shivered but, boy, it felt good – and I had my nails done too, what was left of them.

Obviously the whole thing cost a small fortune and I shut my eyes and prayed every time my debit card was sucked away, expecting 'transaction denied' with every nervous tap of the digits, but miraculously, it all went through smoothly. I then had a teeny-weeny lunch as befitted the teeny-weeny person I was about to become, shivering slightly, perched on a bench in Holland Park. It was a minuscule tub of sushi from M&S and naturally as I raised the first peck to my lips, a slimy slick of salmon slopped straight into the lap of my new dress. I limped to a handy water fountain and mopped it feverishly with a tissue which left a mark and some bobbles of tissue. No matter, I decided, it would dry, and I walked back to Essex Villas, shaking my dress periodically to air it.

By now it was about two o'clock but I'd deliberately left it late, not wanting to appear back at the homestead before Paddy. It wasn't that idle chit-chat with the Campbell parents should they materialize made me nervous – OK, it did a bit – it was more that I wanted to breeze in after him, look- ing great. Naturally I'd been anxiously checking my phone all morning, but to no avail. No message. Although this was understandable, I decided on reflection.

Paddy was not the sort of man to text blow-by-blow updates as I would – 'just arrived', 'plan in progress', 'going well' – no. Unlike me, he'd execute a plan, return and deliver a verdict in a concise, non-pejorative manner.

I'd already become far less nervous about the actual outcome of the plan and had barely given it a second thought this morning for two reasons. One was the pressing business at the nail bar and Simone's tutting over my disastrous cuticles, but the other was the fact that the more I thought about it, the more I was convinced I hadn't signed the document. I distinctly remembered resting my head on that glass coffee table and the pen slipping from my hand. It was odd how that had come back to me. Had I remembered it because I wanted to? I didn't think so. I felt it absolutely to be so.

I quickened my pace excitedly around the corner into Essex Villas, just as Paddy, a man I would never normally associate with taxis – always jeeps and tractors – stepped from what must have been one of many for him today. As he paid the driver, he did a double take.

'God, I almost didn't recognize you. What are you wearing?'

'What, this?'

'It looks like a nightie.'

'No, it's not a nightie.'

'Have you peed on it or something?'

'What?'

'There's a huge mark on your crotch. What's happened to your hair?'

'How d'you mean?'

'It looks like a helmet.'

'Oh. Must be the wind. Blown it straight.'

'Looks ridiculous. Anyway, let's go in, you'll freeze in that.'

I followed him up the path, thinking what a sickening

waste of two hundred pounds *that* had been, and wondered what was to follow.

In the black-and-white flagstone hall he shut the door behind us with that classy 'huff' and then, instead of filling me in, turned and carried on down to the kitchen in his clicky brogues without a word.

'Well?' I breathed, running after him. He filled the kettle, snapped it on then turned. Grinned.

'It worked. A treat.'

'Did it? Oh, *good!* ' I clapped my hands excitedly. 'Oh, *excellent.* I was convinced he'd smell a rat!'

'No, no rats. He fell for it hook, line and sinker. Took the bait about his son's highly acclaimed artwork, didn't stop for a moment to remember he'd shafted Willem a few years ago – greeted him like an old friend, in fact; presumably he shafts his friends every day – and couldn't hustle us into his studio quickly enough. Inside, all the lighting had been dropped and angled and positioned to make it look like an art gallery, and his son's works were dotted about on plinths he'd clearly brought in specially. There was nothing else in the room at all work-wise and all the blinds were closed. It was rather impressive, actually. His son's definitely got style.'

'Oh.' I felt momentarily sorry for Felix, so proud of his son.

'But all marked up ridiculously high. Willem says he's seen the son's work in Mount Street going for much less, but of course, had we been for real, Willem would be taking a commission, so that would have suited him too. And as a rich Arabian just flown in from Dubai, I wouldn't necessarily know. I was simply representing my sheik back home, and the corporate finance bank he owns.'

'Arabian. Golly, is that what you were pretending to be? Did you speak?'

'Not in English, because as Willem explained to Felix, I don't, only French as a second language, learned while studying at INSEAD. And I wore dark glasses too, even inside. We thought about going the whole hog with robes but decided I'd probably be more of a suited businessman. Also Willem thought he might get the giggles every time he looked at me.'

I snorted. 'God, I wish I'd been there. And he left you there? In the studio?'

'He did, eventually. We looked at everything in great detail, then prevaricated over the two most expensive pieces, me in French, Willem in German. It got later and later. Felix started hopping about from foot to foot and looking at his watch and tapping his phone and clearly getting no response from his father, and finally Willem said, "Do you have another appointment?" So Felix said, "No, it's only lunch with my father, he'll understand if I don't show up."

Willem looked shocked at this and translated for me, at which point I looked *really* shocked. I started to say a few things under my breath in my own tongue – I had an Arabic friend at university and obviously made it up too – and Willem looked agitated and nervous. He hastily explained to Felix that in my culture it would be unheard of to do what he had just suggested, at which point I looked downright disgusted and started to back away from his son's work.

Felix looked highly alarmed and said – no, no, quite right, he was off to meet his father right now. He wouldn't leave an old man waiting; he'd only been trying to let him know he'd be late. Would we kindly see ourselves out, he asked, and shut the door behind us, then let him know which piece we wanted? We agreed that of *course* we would and became all smiley again, inching forward towards the most expensive sculpture, which was under a light on a plinth. I got a tiny magnifying glass out and peered and Felix beamed and purred and backed out of the room, twisting his hands like Uriah Heep. We heard the front door shut behind him.'

'Oh – excellent!' I crowed, jumping up and down on the spot in my wet nightie with my poker-straight hair. 'So then you had a good look round?'

'We did. There's so little furniture in that place we found it almost immediately. It was in the top drawer of a bureau in the drawing room.'

'Splendid. And?'

'Yes, all very splendid, up until that point. After that it all went a bit tits up, Molly.'

I stared at him. Felt the blood drain from my face right down to my shoes. 'Shit. I signed it?'

He nodded. Reached in his inside jacket pocket and handed me a sheaf of papers. 'I'm afraid you did. You signed it.'

CHAPTER 25

$\mathcal{I}$ sat down heavily on a stool at the breakfast bar, the papers in my hand. There, sure enough, on the last page, right at the bottom on a dotted line in black ink, was my signature. Flowing rather confidently, actually: nothing equivocal about that. Bugger. I massaged my forehead furiously with my fingertips. I must have lost about three minutes of my life in that alcohol- or drug-fuelled haze. Three minutes when I lifted my head from the glass table, regrouped and, with a rush of blood to the head – possibly even another slug of wine – seized the pen and executed a flourishing autograph, before collapsing in a sozzled heap in Felix's arms, and thereafter his bed. And what *had* I signed, anyway? This wordy, lengthy document which went on forever. What was it all about?

'Have you read it?' I asked, feeling a bit sick.

'I have. In the taxi. Haven't you?'

My mind instinctively flew to the lie direct. But something in his steady dark gaze as I glanced up stopped me. 'Not . . . entirely. Not . . . terribly thoroughly, anyway. In fact – no.'

'You didn't read it before signing it?'

'I was drunk, Paddy. So drunk. What can I say?'

He didn't answer. Suddenly I felt unutterably stupid. There was nothing ditsy or charming or amusing about a woman of my age – a woman of any age – behaving like this. It was infantile. I was ashamed of myself, truly horrified. What must he think?

'Go on then,' I said as he sat down beside me. 'Tell me the worst. What have I done?'

He shrugged. 'Well, most of it is standard legalistic jargon which means nothing much at all really, just stating the bleeding obvious in terms of property law and no doubt there as padding to ensure you didn't wade through it and get to the nub of the matter.'

'Which is?' I said, my mouth drying.

'Which is . . .' he flipped over quite a few pages, 'on page seven. Paragraph five, second clause down. It reads: "I therefore affirm that I give license for Mr Robert Carrington to reside at said property, thirty-two Lastow Mews, until he chooses to relocate, or in the event of his death." '

I blinked. 'Oh, well, that's OK. No, that's fine, Paddy. That's what I was intending to do anyway. After all, it's only fair, he and Cuthbert were practically—'

'Wait,' he interrupted.

' "I also transfer rights of contract to the property to Robert Carrington henceforth, and thereafter on his death to his heirs in perpetuity." ' Paddy looked up.

I stared. 'Right. So that means I've . . .'

'Signed away the deeds.'

'To Felix.'

'Eventually, effectively to Felix, yes. Because of the transferral of contract.'

I swallowed. 'Bastard.'

'I agree.'

'He stitched me up.'

'Very tightly. In fact he put in an extra stitch towards the end just for good measure.' He cleared his throat. '"I therefore testify that the aforementioned transfer—"'

'OK,' I muttered, holding up my hand to stop him and shutting my eyes. 'Don't . . . go on. I get the picture.' I gulped.

Felt wretched. And very panicky. 'But – we can tear it up, can't we? Burn it? Then it doesn't exist.'

'This is a copy, Molly. I printed it on his scanner. I didn't take the original.'

'Why not?' I yelped.

'Because that would be stealing,' he said patiently.

'Yes, but—'

'And I have no doubt he's lodged another copy elsewhere anyway, with a lawyer, probably. He's not an idiot.'

'No. Right.' I felt a bit faint, licked my lips. 'He kept saying I could speak to his lawyer, give him a ring, he even gave me his card.'

'To embarrass you, no doubt. Make you feel guilty should you take him up on it.'

'Do you think the lawyer's dodgy too?'

'No, I doubt it, just a normal one, who will have no idea you've been coerced into signing this.'

'By foul means, with lashings of champagne – drugged, even, you thought.'

He shrugged. 'Perhaps. But it's too late to find out now.'

'Won't it be in my hair?'

'Only in films.'

'So it's my word against his? That he coerced me?'

'Yes.'

I nodded miserably. Stared down at the document in my hands. 'So . . . this is legal and binding?'

'I'm afraid so.'

'Felix said something about – if there was anything I didn't like in it, I could change it.'

'Bollocks you can. Don't be a fool, Moll.'

I nodded wordlessly. There were no words. That said it all. A fool. And I'd once been so smart. So . . . qualified. A good degree. A great job. Which I juggled with my family.

I wanted to tell him that I'd once headed up a team of eleven people, had my own department, made crucial executive decisions, even hired and fired. I'd read many contracts. Standard commercial contracts. What had happened to me?

Men had happened to me. Men had been my downfall, ruined my life, because I'd let them. First Henri, on the domestic front, and now Felix on the economic one. I'd signed away an inheritance worth, ooh, heavens . . . a great deal of money, anyway. I felt sick. I imagined the children's faces, Lucy's in particular. Nico's. And look at me now. In a stained, girly frock with a soggy patch on my crotch, a face full of slap and ridiculous teenage hair. Because of yet another man. Whose ex-girlfriend looked a bit like Sienna Miller. Who rocked this look, the one I was attempting, whilst I sank it. I took a deep breath: let it out shakily.

'Paddy, I'm just going to go up and get changed. I'll be down in a minute when I've given this some thought.'

He nodded, embarrassed, I thought. He got up to make himself a cup of coffee. I disappeared upstairs. In the spare room, I shed the dress, changed into a pair of jeans and a grey T-shirt I'd happily packed and a pair of trainers. Then I tied my hair back in a band and washed my face. I looked at myself for a long moment in the oval mirror perched on the beautiful chintzy, knick-knacky dressing table. I had a private word. Quite a long one. When I'd finished, I tidied the room and went downstairs with my laptop.

Paddy had already got his in front of him and was sitting at the bar, tapping away. I perched beside him and did my own research. We both came to the same conclusion at about the same moment. He turned to me.

'You're stuffed.'

'I know.'

'There are no loopholes in a contract like this. No escape clauses.'

'No.'

'Which means you only have one conceivable option.'

'Go and see Robert. Tell him what's happened.'

'Exactly.'

I gazed at Paddy. His eyes told me I must. That so much money said I must. My children said I must.

'The thing is, Paddy, I will go, but I have to tell you, I have a feeling it will break his heart.'

'You don't know this man, Molly. You don't know this family. They're nothing to you.'

'That's not true. He was Cuthbert's partner. And Cuthbert was family. David's family. All he had. And the thing is, he's a sweetie. A totally genuine sweetie. Which his son clearly isn't. And I'm about to tell him that. Spill the beans.'

'To which he'll say—'

'To which I'm almost certain he'll say, "I rescind this contract immediately, Molly. Override it. Reject all claim on your property. In fact I'm going to move out now. Go straight to Broadstairs." And he'll never, ever see his son again in the same light.'

'Because he's an honorable man.'

'Yes.'

'And if he is such an honorable, intelligent man, do you not think he knows already?'

'That his son's a shit?'

'Yes.'

I recalled Robert's haunted eyes not long ago, looking over my shoulder as he suggested I should be careful.

'Possibly. In some tiny corner of his soul. But it's one thing to have an inkling and another to have a bloody great light shone. This is like being woken up by the Gestapo.'

'I know,' Paddy said, but it was spoken dispassionately.

I closed my laptop. 'But I'll do it. Of course I'll do it. I'd be an idiot not to.'

He gave me those steady brown eyes again. 'Do you want me to come with you?'

'To check I go through with it?'

'No, for moral support.'

'Oh. Yes, please.'

And so he did. That very day. Although no rush, we decided. After all, Robert was lunching with his son. He might be a while. We'd go after a sandwich, which Paddy made me, cheese and pickle, and another cup of coffee. And a read of the papers in the garden, although I couldn't read anything. After that, we set off on foot. After all, it wasn't far, just one end of Kensington to the other.

We didn't talk much on the way. He probably thought I was thinking through what I was going to say, but I wasn't, actually. I knew what I'd say. The truth. Mum had at least taught me that. When in a very tight corner, a complete squeeze, it was the best option. The only option. No, I was thinking more about Robert's reaction. The liver-spotted hand going to his brow, quivering slightly. Having to sit down at the table in that now familiar kitchen. Looking brave. But maybe needing a lie-down too, when we'd gone. And then not telling anyone. Certainly not sharing it with friends. How it would age him. How he might not play bowls this week, at the Hurlingham. Make an excuse to his teammates. How all shocks and bumps bruised us, chipped away at us, but how it was harder to withstand them at that sort of age.

I remembered walking along the river with Felix, as he told me about his father's youth. Rather proudly, I recalled. Filling me in on all I didn't know about Robert and Cuthbert. About how Robert had been a soldier in the Grenadier Guards, on active service in Malaya, but also ceremonial duty at Buckingham Palace, changing the guard. 'All six foot four of him, plus a bearskin,' Felix had laughed, 'imagine!' I had imagined. Tall and very handsome, no doubt, but living a lie, as others did in those days.

How he must have suffocated his feelings. Denied them. Married. Had a child. But then, realizing he liked his comrades too much, he had left the army, Felix told me, and a couple of years later had bravely come out, because don't forget, it had only been legal for a few years then. And then telling his wife, Cynthia, who, to his astonishment, had not turned a hair, Felix said. Had suspected – known, even – all along, but had loved him anyway, always. From the moment she'd met him as a dashing young officer at some Chelsea party. And then had so generously left him, so he could pursue his own life, with Cuthbert, and his beloved son Felix, who, although his mother brought him up, in Hampstead, Robert had unlimited access to. Every day, if he liked. And who he was so close to. Particularly since Cynthia had died young, at only fifty-six, of cancer. Felix and Robert had really bonded after that.

I swallowed: watched my feet on the pavement in step with Paddy's. And I was about to blow all that careful love and trust that Robert had put in place for his son. Blow it out of the water, with a bloody great grenade. Show Felix up for what he really was. A fraudster.

When we reached the arch over the front of the cobbled mews, Paddy stopped. His eyes scanned the road. 'Good.'

'What?'

'Felix left for lunch in a black Golf, we saw it go from his house. I just wanted to check it wasn't here.'

'Oh. Right.'

Down we went, to the pink house at the bottom, on the right. I pressed the doorbell.

'Who shall I say you are?'

'A friend?'

'Yes, no, I just thought . . .'

'What?'

'I don't know.'

I didn't. And anyway, footsteps could be heard coming down the hall towards us so there was only time for me to arrange my features in an appropriately grave manner and await Robert's florid face creasing into a smile of welcome above an extravagantly bright cravat. Neither came to fruition. The door was opened by a lean, almost bony young man, his dark hair tied back in a ponytail. He had a sallow complexion and a rather guarded expression. He regarded us wordlessly.

'Oh,' I faltered. 'Hello. I was looking for Robert?'

'He's not here, I'm afraid. I'm his grandson. Can I help?'

Felix's son. The artist. But not like him at all, apart from the high cheekbones. And of course the eyes, I suddenly realized.

'May we come in a moment?' asked Paddy pleasantly, and rather boldly, I thought. 'We won't be a moment, and we could just as easily explain this to you as to your grandfather.'

This, to me, seemed like a gross miscalculation on Paddy's part. We knew Robert. Or I did. Knew he was a good egg. We didn't know this young man at all, and as Felix's son and the next heir, this could go badly wrong. But the ponytailed young man had shrugged and was holding open the door, and Paddy was already following him down the hall to the kitchen whilst I, unable to do otherwise, followed like jetsam in his wake.

'What's this all about?' asked the young man with understandable caution once we were in the kitchen. He plucked a piece of burnt toast from the toaster, which was smoking, and flung open the back door to let the fumes out.

Paddy explained, matter-of-factly and succinctly, as if he were merely outlining a recent business transaction between myself and his father. He told the tale in a methodical way which left nothing to the imagination, no embarrassing stone unturned, but at the same time gave plenty of credence to Felix in terms of a possible misunderstanding and therefore lack of culpability. There were no accusations, no suggestions of foul play, just puzzlement at the nature of the contract – which Paddy placed carefully on the table – in the light of my original agreement with Robert. He wondered if – 'I'm so sorry, what was your name?'

'Daniel.'

If Daniel would be able to shed any further light, because obviously we didn't want to upset his grandfather. It wasn't a threat, just a statement of fact. When Paddy got to the part about me being unable to remember if I'd signed it, and waking up in Felix's bed the following morning, I had to slide away my eyes, which up until then had been firmly on Daniel's green ones, to the floor. But when I glanced up, Daniel's expression hadn't changed. He remained inscrutable as he digested what he'd just been told: as I would, I decided, if I had the sangfroid, and if I'd been told something similar about my father. I wondered why Paddy thought it was OK to shock a son rather than a grandfather.

Yet, as Daniel perched on a stool at the breakfast bar and lit a cigarette, I could see that he was not shocked. What I couldn't work out was what his response might be. What excuse he would give, what character assassination he might make of me, to whom his eyes were turning in slight disgust (and who could blame him?): what form his mitigation on behalf of his father might take. When it came, it was blunt and to the point.

'I don't believe you,' he said. 'I mean, I believe what you,' he glanced at Paddy, 'have just told me, but I don't believe you didn't know what you were signing.' He looked at me. 'I believe you fell headlong for my dad, as many others have done before and many still will. I think he sold it to you on the basis that you'd live here together. I think – and I'm under no illusions here – that he gave you all sorts of promises and visions of the future, and that madly in love – and I use that word advisedly, it does send people bonkers – you agreed to anything he proposed, under the guise of it being what Cuthbert would have wanted. I think your conscience pricked you, too. There you were, a very recent heir with no previous knowledge of this family at all, helicoptering in, stealing the family silver. I think this compromise appealed to you. Made you feel better. Seduced by Dad's charm, you agreed he was right and signed the contract. Only afterwards, when he no doubt dumped you, did you turn into a woman scorned. So then you came round here with all your fury and your spokesperson friend, and your righteous indignation. That's what I think happened.'

He made it sound so plausible that I wondered for a crazy moment if that was indeed the case. Love was a kind of madness. But I knew I hadn't been that deranged. That was the fate of foolish old sugar daddies in a fable straight out of the *Daily Mail* and bore no relation to me.

'OK,' said Paddy, 'that's understandable. You're going to line up with your father in his camp. But we're not here to discover what you think, actually, we're here to outline what we will say to your grandfather, which frankly we'd rather not do.'

'Feel free. He'll say the same as me.'

'Like hell he will.' A woman's voice came from the garden. We all swung about. Through the open back door we saw a bicycle being flung on the grass, an open gate in the garden wall revealing its point of entry. Camilla came into the kitchen from outside. Her slight frame looked even smaller in oversized faded dungarees and a white vest, and her beautiful, heart-shaped face was etched with pain and misery. She ignored me and Paddy and crossed the room to square up to Daniel. Her bottom lip was quivering. 'Like hell.'

CHAPTER 26

*C*amilla kept her eyes firmly on Daniel's, almost daring them to look away. 'Come on, Dan.' Her voice was quiet. 'You know as well as I do something like this was bound to happen. Something had to give.'

It was as if we weren't there. She was addressing only the young man, inches away from him. Her face was older close up, I realized, with a faint fretwork of lines around the eyes and mouth. Still lovely, but not in the first flush of youth. Mid-thirties, maybe. She took one of Daniel's cigarettes from the island and lit it, which made the fine lines pucker even more. As she exhaled above his head, Daniel averted his gaze: it rested somewhere in the middle distance, somewhere beyond all of us. She turned. 'The only reason he's here,' she told Paddy, 'is to have his own vendetta with his father. Felix has been hiking his prices up to ridiculous levels. The Mount Street Gallery is very pissed off, isn't that right, Dan?'

'Leave it, Camilla,' Daniel muttered.

'No, I will not leave it. He jeopardizes your standing at the gallery by accumulating all the work they don't exhibit, all your old stuff – which by your own admission is not up to your recent standard – he inflates the prices exorbitantly to snare some Dutch dealer, and how d'you think that goes down with Pascal at Manon, who you're supposed to have such an exclusive relationship with? Just as I am supposed to have such an exclusive relationship with your father.'

For the first time she turned and looked at me, training her cool blue eyes in my direction. I felt myself shrink. 'Oh, don't worry, you're not the first, not by any means. Felix's love life is littered with women like you. I'm not a complete fool.'

I found my voice. 'I realize that now. At the time, I didn't even know you were together. I've been a complete idiot.'

'Women always are where he's concerned. And I've obviously been the biggest of all, so don't beat yourself up about it. But not any more. I've had it with him. I'm too sick and tired of the lies and the excuses and the constant need to kid myself. I'm sick of being a victim. Always looking, despite all the overwhelming evidence, for a reason to believe in Felix Carrington.'

She took another drag of her cigarette then stubbed it out savagely. Her chin wobbled. 'But you don't need to hear all this. I'll save it for when I see him. Just as Dan here, who came round with his own agenda, his own pent-up fury, will hopefully do the same. I'd like to think we've both come to the end of our respective tethers.'

She gave him a meaningful look but he didn't return it. 'Harder, I know, in his case. When it's blood. You don't want to believe your father is skimming a profit off your art, trying to steal a march on your talents.'

'He won't succeed,' said Paddy. 'That was a scam on the part of myself and a friend called Willem Brecht, the

Dutchman you referred to, to find the agreement Molly signed.'

He turned to Daniel. 'For what it's worth, he left us in his house so as not to stand up your grandfather.' That wasn't quite how Paddy had originally described it to me but I let it go, knowing he was being kind.

'And to be fair, he's always broke,' said Daniel quietly. 'He's had a run of bad luck with his work.'

'He's never had any good luck because he's not in any way, shape or form an artist of calibre,' said Camilla. 'Not like you. He's not even a respected critic any more; his judgment is questioned constantly. Look at that awards show he judged in Glasgow, overturned immediately by a committee at the College of Art following an appeal, and that fiasco in Milan.'

'So what are you saying, he's crap at what he does? So what? So are a lot of people, it's not a crime.'

'It's a crime if he's corrupt at what he does, too, Dan. And he is. In every sphere of his life. You heard the story they just told you, you know in your heart it's true.'

Daniel stared at a small space on the floor, a crack in the tiles, a million miles away. His shoulders were hunched. 'He wasn't always like that,' he said softly.

'I know!' she cried, her voice cracking with emotion. 'D'you think I don't know that? Why d'you think I fell in love with him? Why d'you think I've stayed with him all these years, not just because he's brilliant company and the best fun, but because I know there's a better person deep inside. But the much worse person has been creeping up and up and slowly suffocating that one for years now, and we're deluding ourselves if we don't recognize that.'

She turned swiftly to me. 'You've lost your driving license, haven't you?'

I blanched, wrong-footed. 'My . . . my driving license?'

339

'Yes, I found it in Felix's house. He probably meant to pop it back in your purse, but you woke up and he didn't get a chance.'

I stared at her. 'I have no idea what you're talking about.'

'Take a look.'

I rummaged in my bag. Found my purse. It wasn't there.

'And that's OK,' Camilla went on, 'because you'd have just been irritated when you eventually needed it, to hire a car abroad or something, and imagined you'd dropped it. You wouldn't think Felix would steal it while you were asleep and copy the signature.'

I felt my mouth fall open. 'Is that what . . . ?'

She shrugged. 'I don't know. But you don't remember signing that thing, do you?'

'No.'

'So maybe. I wouldn't put it past him.'

'Oh.' I put my hand over my mouth as I realized something. Removed it to speak. 'It had the flourish on the F of Faulkner. I haven't done that for years. I thought it was odd. It was an affectation I had when I was younger.'

'Here.' She opened a leather pouch slung around her waist and placed my license on the counter between us. Paddy put the document beside it; he flipped to the last page. The signatures were identical. Uncannily so.

'He'd have been able to do that,' said Daniel bitterly. 'He's a good draughtsman, good at copying. Look at that Sam Spencer he rattled off for Harry.'

'I know,' said Camilla shortly, shooting him a look. Clearly there were murkier depths we could dredge if we felt like it.

'So . . . does that make this null and void?' I asked.

'It certainly makes it open to rigorous legal investigation,' said Paddy. 'And by that I mean the police, rather than a lawyer.'

Camilla and Daniel both looked scared. 'Please. There's no need for that,' said Daniel nervously. 'We'll talk to him. I'm sure he just got . . . carried away.'

Paddy frowned and looked thoughtful.

Camilla's voice broke the silence. 'And actually, there really is no need for that, because what Felix doesn't realize is that there's another will. A more recent one.' She raised her chin. 'And after all, that's what this is all about, isn't it? Why you're here?'

We stared at her.

'What d'you mean, another will?' said Paddy. 'We didn't think there was a will at all, thought he'd died intestate?'

'Not a bit of it, there were two. Cuthbert knew what would happen, you see. He was a cunning old sod. And he loved a game. He left the first one very deliberately in the top righthand drawer of his bureau so that when Felix instantly searched the place – indecently quickly, I might add, hours after Cuthbert's death; I found him prowling around while Robert was still grief-stricken – he'd find it very quickly. And destroy it. But then be horrified to discover that the estate would go to a blood relative. Well, he was furious. And Cuthbert knew he'd be furious, absolutely livid, and that he'd get up to no good. Try to contest it, override it, take it to court and maybe even win. After all, some judges might look favorably on such a long relationship which, to all intents and purposes, was a marriage. On the other hand, some might have said – no, the law's the law. If there's no will, follow the bloodline. It stands. So it was a risk. But I can tell you now, Felix was definitely going to do it. He'd looked into it, seen a lawyer. But the problem was, it was expensive. So instead, when he met

Molly, he simply decided to seduce her. And get her to agree to something different.'

'Cuthbert didn't know that would happen, of course. What he did know, though, was that eventually there would be a catch in place. A comeuppance for Felix. He'd put it there. In his second will, which I found recently. He knew, you see, that only one person would eventually sort through his stuff, his papers. Me. Robert would just leave it and Felix wouldn't bother. So he knew that, sometime down the line, I'd find it. A more recent will. The one I was supposed to find. With a letter, to me. I'm not going to tell you what the letter said because it's very private. Cuthbert and I were very close. I'd worked for him for years and he was my friend. But suffice to say, he detailed pretty much exactly what would happen, the expense Felix would go to, the route he'd take towards the courts – oh, Cuthbert was enjoying himself immensely. He was a controlling old queen and he very much wanted to thwart Felix from beyond the grave. He must have disliked him very much,' she said sadly.

She swallowed, then went on. 'He said – he knew I loved Felix, but I would ruin my life if I stayed with him. This was his way of warning me off him. And my test, if you like, was my own morality. My own honesty. He asked me to produce the real will, the most recent one, to override the last one, and to put a stop to all Felix's shenanigans. I think he anticipated a good few months of legal fees and costs mounting up by this stage. How he must have rubbed his hands with glee,' she said bitterly.

'When was this?' I asked quietly.

'When did I find it? Oh, about a week ago. I didn't tell anyone, though. Because I wasn't sure what I was going to do. I still loved Felix very much. Probably still do. And producing this would ruin all his plans, all the ones I pretended not to know about. And it would most certainly be the end of us. Did I want that? Of course not.'

'But now?'

'Now . . . I've listened to what you've had to say,' she looked at Paddy, 'and I've believed it. If I'm in any way going to save my own soul and not continually be blind-sided by him, I have to show you.'

She walked through the middle of us and out of the kitchen towards the sitting room. The rest of us followed, not daring to utter a word in case she changed her mind. She hadn't taken it home or hidden it away somewhere. It was clearly exactly where she'd found it: right at the bottom of the last drawer of a tallboy, an exquisite piece of Georgian walnut furniture at the far end of the room over-looking the garden. The piece was stuffed, it seemed, with papers and photograph albums and years and years of history.

'For some reason I started at the bottom,' she told us, 'which Cuthbert probably wouldn't have anticipated.'

She knelt and pulled out the drawer, but it was so heavy, so overloaded, it stuck. Paddy crouched and helped her. Together they removed the entire drawer, crammed with paperwork, and set it on the Persian carpet. Camilla rummaged with her hand down at the left-hand side, delving right to the bottom. She produced an A4 manila envelope with her name, Camilla Bennett, in black ink. She fished inside and withdrew a folded piece of paper. She handed it to Paddy. 'Here.'

He took it over to the light of the window and opened it. I followed, looking around his shoulder. It was dated 14th December 2015. The first paragraph read:

This is the last will and testament of Cuthbert James Christo-pher Faulkner written to negate and supersede any other previous wills and testaments in my name, or any lodged with my lawyer, Piers Hamilton of Hamilton & Simpson Associates.

Paddy glanced at me. 'Couldn't be clearer.'

It was short. Written on only one page. Much shorter than I'd imagined a will to be. And it was to the point.

I hereby leave my estate, in its entirety, and in perpetuity, to my partner, Robert Angus Carrington, to be inherited on his death by my nearest relative, Molly Victoria Faulkner, wife of my deceased nephew, David Sinclair Faulkner. On no account is any part of my estate to be inherited by Robert Carrington's son, Felix Carrington.

'Oh!' I glanced up. 'But that's almost exactly . . .'

'What you had in mind,' finished Paddy.

'That Robert could live here until his death?' asked Daniel.

'Yes, she'd already told him that,' said Camilla. She looked at me gratefully. 'Which was very good of you. And Cuthbert hadn't anticipated that. Part of the leverage on me was obviously the fact that Robert wouldn't be entitled to live here. He knew I'd hate that, the cunning old bugger, and was forcing my hand, but you let me off that particular hook by being so magnanimous. I could have just let it go, much more easily.' She turned back to Paddy. 'Read the next bit.'

Paddy went on:

' *"On no account is Felix Carrington to inherit any antiques, paintings or furnishings in any sort of bequest from his father, on the latter's death."* '

A silence prevailed. I couldn't look at Daniel.

'That's it,' Paddy told us. 'Apart from a note to his lawyer at the bottom, directing him to one of his files.' He folded it up again.

Camilla cleared her throat. 'Right. Well, in fact I *am* going to read you part of the letter he wrote to me. The end of it, anyway.' She took a clearly much handled envelope from the bottom of the same manila envelope and removed the pages. She turned to the last one, gazed. Then she took a deep breath.

FINALLY, my dear Camilla, along with a great deal of doubtless irritating advice from an interfering old man – but please accept it in the spirit in which it's offered, with the best of intentions and the greatest affection – you will see that I've left you something else.

Another copy of my will. The first, Felix will have already destroyed. I left it prominently in the top right-hand drawer of my bureau with the passports and it will not have been to his liking. It has therefore been turned to dust and ashes in the fireplace. He will have found it within hours of my death whilst dear Robert was perhaps consumed with something other than money. This, therefore, is a second. Why didn't I lodge it with my lawyer, you might ask? To be found in the conventional manner? Like the one it overrides? Because I wanted you to find it. And to deliver it to Mr Piers Hamilton of Hamilton & Simpson. Or not, as the case may be. The decision rests with you.

Camilla, I have every faith that you will step up to the plate and do what is right, and in so doing, rid yourself of this pernicious man forever. Forgive me, for testing you thus, but you have been like a daughter to me and I see no alternative.

Your loving friend, Cuthbert

A SILENCE PREVAILED. Her face was pale and empty and very sad. So was Daniel's.

'Cuthbert knew Felix would never forgive you,' Paddy said gently.

'Yes.'

'And if we hadn't got involved . . . if events hadn't

unfolded the way they did, would you have delivered it to the lawyer?'

'I . . . don't know. I like to think I would.' She shrugged miserably. She looked tiny and lost in her enormous dungarees. 'Yes. Eventually. But it breaks my heart.'

'Mine too,' said Daniel bitterly. He reached for her hand and she clutched it. 'I'm gonna miss you so much, Cam.' They held on tight.

At that moment we heard the sound of the front door opening, and then Robert's voice, mid-flow, in the middle of a story. 'She's priceless, I can't tell you! Always lurking like that, talk about a curtain twitcher. Did you see her face? She monitors everyone who comes in and out of here, thinks I'm some kind of merry widower and is longing for me to come back in the small hours with a toy boy, which will thrill her beyond measure!'

Robert appeared in the sitting room, in the midst of the hushed gathering. He stopped short at the sight of us. He was wearing a biscuit-colored linen jacket, a pink shirt and an MCC tie. His face was flushed – almost matching his shirt – and still wreathed in delighted smiles. He did a mock recoil, rocking backwards on his heels.

'Hello, hello, what's this, a party?' he asked. He grinned amiably, glancing from face to face. Then he jerked his head backwards and cupped his mouth. 'Hey, we've busted a break-in!' he threw jokingly over his shoulder. After a moment, we heard the front door shut. Then, emerging into the room beside his father, with an equally flushed, post-lunch face, and wearing a dazzling peacock-blue shirt, came Felix.

CHAPTER 27

Felix looked stunned. He kept his cool but it was very much surface deep. 'What's this?' he said faux affably, but I could tell he was startled to see me. 'A house party?'

Suddenly he registered Paddy and looked completely taken aback, having last glimpsed this Arabian client in his own house not five hours ago, albeit in dark glasses. Felix blinked rapidly then came to.

'Mr Karimi, how lovely to see you again,' he murmured, stretching out his hand, his eyes wide with wonder.

Paddy gave him a long, speculative look and returned the handshake but ·not the greeting. The look spoke volumes: it told Felix, most eloquently, that Paddy was not Mr Karimi at all. You could see it register in Felix's lovely sea-green eyes; it ticked over in the tigerish depths. One by one, a few pennies began to drop into place. Amongst the rest of us, some other quick comprehension flickered, like a sparking element: a tacit agreement that this should not play out within Robert's earshot. The old man was still looking from face to face, his own a picture of amiable bafflement, awaiting enlightenment. Daniel was the most alive to the situation.

'Grandpa!' He kissed him. 'How lovely to see you. Listen, can I borrow you for a moment? There's a painting I want to show you in Rathbone's down the road, that's why I popped by. But I've been here ages and I badly need to get back to the studio.'

'My dear boy, of course! So sweet of you to wait. I'm afraid your father and I had a little digestif in the Garrick after lunch. What a treat, though, I'd love to see it. Funnily enough I was in there the other day and thought their latest show was right up your street. But tell me,' he broke off to glance around again, 'what are the rest of you doing here?' He blinked a bit.

'Thing is, I've got to show you now because I said I'd meet Pascal at four with a client. I've got literally five minutes.'

Robert turned back to his grandson. 'Hm? Oh, right you are, darling. Lead on. You can tell me about this little party on the way.'

Daniel put a guiding hand on his grandfather's elbow and propelled him door-wards. 'It's by a young Scottish artist I haven't come across before, Cuthbert would have loved him.'

'Excellent, splendid! How kind, Dan. Such a treat to see my grandson, I don't see nearly enough of you.'

We heard the front door open and then shut behind them. A silence fell on the remaining assembly. Felix looked from me to Paddy to Camilla, his face unattractively flushed from drink and anger now.

'What's this all about? Who the hell are you, anyway? Who is he, Camilla?'

'My name's Paddy Campbell and I'm a vet and Camilla knew nothing about this until just now.'

'Well, you're a bloody impostor, that's all I know, and a fraud. A complete fraud.' His eyes were bloodshot and furious. 'I'll get the police on to you.'

'I wouldn't do that if I were you,' said Paddy smoothly. 'They might have more questions for you than they do for me.'

'Oh really, such as? Camilla, what the hell's going on – and what the hell are *you* doing here?' He glared at me, then realized he was terribly fond of me and forced his face to soften into a smile. 'Molly?' he finished lamely.

'Oh, I just wondered if I could have my driving license back. I left it at your house. Or to be more precise, you took it.'

Felix's mouth opened.

'Felix, it's over,' Camilla said softly. 'I've told them everything.'

He stared at her for a long while. 'You don't *know* anything,' he said finally.

'Oh, I do. I know a great deal more than you imagine.' Her eyes told him that she did. They communed silently: years of lies and broken promises and manipulative games and so much damaging detritus seemed to be littered there. She went on quietly. 'I know, for instance, that you destroyed Cuthbert's will. But Felix, he left another one. For me to deliver to the lawyer, and then to Molly. I've short-circuited that process and given it to her.'

Felix stared some more. Eventually, he moved as if on automatic pilot towards the nearest sofa and sat down heavily. He bent his head and gazed between his knees: massaged his brow savagely with his fingertips.

'You wouldn't.'

'I have.'

'You're bluffing. There is no other will.'

Paddy produced it. He bent and displayed it briefly in front of Felix's nose then folded it up again. Felix looked up at us. His gaze rested on Camilla. He swallowed.

'You know what this means.'

'That it's the end of us, yes.'

'I didn't mean that. But yes, it is. More pertinently, though, you've ruined me, Camilla.'

'Ah yes, I see, more pertinently. So more importantly. But no, I didn't do that, Felix. You ruined yourself.'

There was a silence. His eyes traveled from her to Paddy. His face hardened. 'I knew there was something dodgy about you,' he said savagely. 'You didn't know enough about art, not a bloody thing. I'm not a complete fool.'

Paddy shrugged amiably, accepting this with equanimity.

'And you.' His lip curled as he regarded me.

I widened my eyes in mock disbelief. 'Me? But you were so enamored of me. So attracted.'

'Don't kid yourself.'

I gave him a steady look. 'None taken, Felix.'

'Camilla, if you think for one moment I slept with her – you know me better than that,' he pleaded.

'Oh, I do,' she agreed. She turned to me. 'You're too old for him. Felix doesn't like women of his own age, or even ten years younger. These days, even twenty,' she said bitterly. 'I knew he wouldn't have slept with you.'

'Of course I bloody didn't!'

'Well, that's a relief all round then, isn't it?' I said lightly. 'But I'm grateful to be enlightened because my own memory, what with everything you gave me,' I said pointedly, 'is a bit shaky.'

Paddy cleared his throat. 'We're done here, aren't we?' He looked at me, eyebrows raised. I nodded.

'Camilla,' he went on, 'we'll lodge this with Hamilton and Simpson, so they've got a copy. Best if we do it, though, don't you think?' Camilla nodded miserably, knowing what he meant by that. That she could still be coerced. 'I expect you'd like to be left alone,' Paddy went on gently. 'Unless . . .' he hesitated, glancing at Felix, who had his head in his hands now and was tugging at his hair.

'Yes. Please go. I'm fine. Really. I can be left alone with Felix. He's not a threat. Not a danger. Except to himself. He's just a bloody idiot.'

She sat down beside him on the sofa and put an arm around his shoulders. To my horror, I could see that his face was twisted with pain and that he was crying. I looked away.

'Not a word of this to Dad,' he managed to whisper, wiping his face with his sleeve. Camilla squeezed his shoulders in assent. 'Does Dan know?'

'Yes.'

Felix's face contorted again and a strangled sob escaped. Camilla put both arms around him and held him close. I could see her love for this complicated, failed, deeply flawed man was not going to disappear overnight. I saw the sorrow in her eyes. As we turned away and left them, I also realized that this could conceivably be just another episode in their tangled story. I hoped not. I hoped, somehow, that it could be the making of them.

For all my horror at what Felix had done, I knew too he'd been a desperate man, and desperation sometimes makes us do extraordinary things. Sometimes good, brave, heroic things; sometimes bad, small, corrupt things. It's all a question of temperament. Felix had seen his career and his limited talent, which he'd been frantically pushing uphill to preserve, disappearing down the plughole, and he'd panicked. He'd lunged the wrong way: done the wrong thing. He'd lit a match and thrown that will in the grate. In a matter of moments, he'd taken a road that he'd been building up to for years: one littered with plenty of indiscretions and tiny lies, but nothing on this scale. Having taken that road, his soul had shriveled and he'd plunged inexorably into a terrible web of deceit which had got just deeper and deeper.

I was reasonably certain Felix was not out-and-out bad, and that he woke in the small hours and considered what he'd done in a cold sweat. I certainly don't think his conscience remained untroubled; you could see that from his crumpled face just now. But having finally hit rock-bottom, as Felix surely had, and given that the game was up, might he decide to play it straight? Since there was no alternative? Might this be the catalyst the two of them needed to stay together, patch things up and live more real-istically, within Felix's means and talent? Start a new life? I voiced this to Paddy, breaking the silence as we walked down the cobbled mews together.

He shrugged. 'I doubt it, somehow. That's a nice fairy story, but it doesn't ring true. What – buy a country cottage somewhere, grow roses round the door and paint water-colors in the garden while Camilla cooks and sings in the kitchen?'

'Well, I—'

'No. I have a nasty feeling if she stuck by him and helped him back on his feet again he'd take advantage of some other situation. Take over her cleaning business or something. Run it into the ground. Employ illegal immi-grants on the basis that they were much cheaper. Ruin her. I hope she leaves him. She's a nice girl.'

'Oh. Yes. I see. My, how your mind runs, Paddy. On

such cynical lines. I hadn't thought of that.' I swallowed, realizing my motives for the fairy story were slightly disingenuous too, in that it would restore some faith in my own terrible judgement. 'On the other hand,' I went on as we passed under the arch at the end of the mews, 'I think she still loves him. And if he does forgive her for exposing the new will—'

'Because he's destitute and has no choice – incidentally, he's about to lose his house and studio, according to Willem. It's all mortgaged up to the hilt.'

'Right. Well, if he does, then, through expediency, forgive her, all Cuthbert's efforts will have been in vain. Because she's not over him, Paddy, you can see it in her eyes. The way she holds him. She knows exactly what he is and she'll have him anyway. Warts and all. I can tell.'

'Well, she's a fool,' said Paddy shortly.

I shrugged. 'Love is rather like that, though, isn't it?' I said as we crossed the main road.

'What?'

'Blind.'

'Look out!' He held my arm as a car whizzed past, missing us by inches. Paddy blinked. 'Well, you certainly are.'

As WE SAT, some time later, having a much needed drink outside a wine bar at the other end of Kensington, I realized he was on his phone a lot, which was unlike Paddy. I looked at him across the table from me, his beer hardly touched, unlike my gin and tonic. He was still dressed in the smart chinos, crisp blue shirt and suede loafers, and he had the effortless, urbane look of a man about town which he could clearly become in an instant. Not a chameleon, though, the genuine article. He was leaning back in his chair, his ankle resting on his knee as he tapped away, smiling slightly. Not work, I felt. Not with that smile. He was totally oblivious to me. Rude, actually.

'Claudia?' I enquired at last.

He glanced up. Raised his eyebrows. Then he registered. 'Oh. Sorry.' He put his phone away sheepishly and pulled his chair in politely. He smiled at me as one would a maiden aunt. 'What were you saying?'

I made myself smile. 'I just asked if that was Claudia. You seemed very intent.'

'Oh, yes. Well, you know.' He looked embarrassed, which again was unusual. He sipped his beer then turned and took the manila envelope from the pocket of his jacket, which was hanging on the back of his chair. 'D'you want to pop this round to the lawyer's now, Molly, before they shut?'

I blanched. 'Me?'

'Yes. And explain, within reason, what's happened? I mean, basically that another will has been found which is in accordance with your wishes anyway and gives Robert the right to live there for his lifetime.'

'Oh. Yes. Right. Sure.'

My heart plummeted right down to my boots. I'd thought he might come with me. After our drink. Thought we were in this together. Bonnie and Clyde. Thelma and Louise. Or Louis. Also, my mind wasn't on the house at all any more. Or Robert. Or sodding money, or anything else like that.

'I wonder if Felix will end up living there anyway. In the spare room,' Paddy mused. 'Wouldn't surprise me.'

'Me neither,' I managed, staring at him. God, what a fool I'd been. He'd been there. Right there. Under my nose. All those years.

'After all, he is his son.'

'Yup.'

'And although ownership eventually passes to you, whilst Robert's living there, it's no business of yours who he shares it with.'

'No, none at all.'

A silence ensued. Paddy sipped his beer. 'Go on then, Molly,' he said gently, this time more as one would to a six-year-old. 'It's round the corner, isn't it? Onslow Terrace, you said? I'll get this.'

'Oh. Yes. Right.' I got to my feet. 'Sure I can't . . .'

'No, no, my shout.'

Before I'd even turned to go, that bloody phone was out of his pocket again. I hesitated for a second then walked away. When I got to the corner of the street I turned back, he was still totally absorbed. On I went to the lawyers' office.

MR HAMILTON WAS UNAVAILABLE, in a meeting. But then, when I explained to the receptionist who I was and what it was about, suddenly he was available, and in I went. His face wore a tragic expression as he got to his feet from behind his leather-topped desk. We shook hands as I approached.

'Mrs Faulkner. I'm so sorry.'

I frowned. 'What d'you mean?'

'Well, I gather another will has been found, which contradicts a straight inheritance by you.'

'Oh, yes, but that's what I was going to do anyway. It's only fair.' I sat down heavily and handed it over to him blithely. I waited as he read it. He looked up. 'Well, it's legitimate. Legal and binding, if that's what you wanted to know.'

'No, not really. As I said, it's what I wanted. I'm just

355

lodging it here for safe-keeping, although I'll obviously take a copy.'

'Right.' He seemed nonplussed by my indifference. 'Well, I'll get Sandra to do that for you.' He glanced down at the paper again. Stared. 'Hang on. There is just one thing.' He turned to his computer. Tapped away. I waited. 'OK,' he said at length.

'OK what?' I asked.

'There is something . . . here,' he said slowly, still reading. 'A directive, to me, to one of Mr Faulkner's files, by way of this asterisk at the bottom. It points me to a clause which is commonplace in wills, and which allows the eventual recipient to bequeathe something within the house right now, during Mr Carrington's lifetime, to whosoever they choose.'

'Oh?'

'Yes, although Mr Faulkner does seem to have a specific person in mind, and a specific painting.' He scrolled down: read some more. 'It's by an artist called Fernand Léger. In a magical mystery tour kind of way, the clause suggests the recipient is a Miss Bennett.'

I stared. 'Camilla.'

'You know her?'

'Yes. And I agree. Camilla should have something.' In a way, I'd wondered why she hadn't been provided for. 'But . . . but why didn't Paddy – I mean, this friend of mine – spot that?'

'Because it's not written down. It's just a directive, to one of my files, which when I open it, says see clause twenty-six of transaction lodged on file of treaty of intent, and when I go to Mr Faulkner's file of treaty of intent . . .' he tapped away again, 'that's what it says.' He turned to me. 'If you hadn't brought it in, it wouldn't have been disclosed.'

'Oh. Right.'

He gave a wry smile. 'Some people very much like to leave complicated wills. It diverts them. To think they're still in control, still pulling the strings from – you know . . .'

'Beyond the grave. Yes. Well, it has a certain amusement factor, I must admit. To think of everyone running around in circles when you're not there.'

He grinned. 'Quite.' He leaned back in his chair, interlaced his fingers. 'But this is better than most. This is satisfyingly intricate, even for an old hand like me. He was an extraordinary man, you know, Mr Cuthbert Faulkner. Larger than life, certainly, colorful and exuberant – some would say outrageously so – but a man of extraordinary sensitivity and integrity too. Very much hidden depths.'

'Yes. I wish I'd known him.'

I stared past Mr Hamilton through the window behind him to the leafy square beyond, thinking of Camilla's small fortune. I didn't know who Fernand Léger was but I was pretty sure he could paint.

'I didn't even know it was in the house,' I said, meaning, I suppose, that I was rather surprised a certain person hadn't lifted it off the wall.

'Oh, it's not in the house. It's in a vault. I'll write to Miss Bennett now and say you thoroughly accord with Mr Faulkner's wishes, shall I?'

'Yes, please do. But . . . make it a very private letter. The most private.'

'Oh yes. I have strict instructions to do just that. Interesting, though, isn't it? That it's not a straight bequest. It's at your discretion. In your jurisdiction. He also wants it to be made clear to Miss Bennett that this is the case.'

'Right. And if I hadn't agreed? Could I have done that?'

'Oh yes. You had right of veto, could have removed the

clause. It might have gone to court, of course. She might have contested it, had she discovered, and it could have become unpleasant.'

'So . . . in a way he was testing me, too?'

Mr Hamilton regarded me kindly over his reading glasses. 'I believe so, yes.'

He returned to his computer, clearly intrigued. He patently wanted to peruse it all again, and I left him to it. As I got to my feet, the receptionist appeared with a copy of the will, which I put in my handbag. Then I went outside and down the steps into the sunshine. I paused for a moment. The shadows from the trees in the square opposite were long and thin as they cut across the pavement and I put my sunglasses on in defense against the low light.

As I turned and walked away I thought of many things. I thought about friendship, the sort Cuthbert and Camilla had, which was actually love. I thought about her never once saying a word about the contents of the will, about it all being left to me, even though, as we knew from Cuthbert's letter, she'd been like a daughter to him. She hadn't complained. I thought of her surprise and astonishment and joy when she eventually heard, which she would soon. Most of me hoped she'd make a new life for herself without Felix, as Paddy had strongly advocated, but a bit of me knew she wouldn't. I sighed. And then I thought about other friendships and other forms of love, and how, if one wasn't terribly careful, they could just slip through one's fingers: evaporate before one's very eyes.

CHAPTER 28

The peace of my Herefordshire farmhouse seemed a million miles from the shenanigans of London when, many hours later, having collected my car from the station, I pulled into the yard. It was late, nearly midnight, and I'd crept in without even alerting the dogs. I turned off the engine and let the blackness and the silence wash over me. The countrywoman I'd become knew that there was no real silence, though: a busily thriving universe was murmuring away out there, one of foxes creeping back to their lairs, badgers emerging from burrows and bat wings whispering down through dark corridors of trees.

It occurred to me that if there was an optimum time to return home, this was it. No ducks and chickens clamoring to be fed, no ill-disciplined dogs scratching their welcome on the side of the car, no children looking shirty and disgruntled. Yes, Re-Entry, as my friend Anna called it – two teenagers, husband on a short fuse and, like me, too many animals – was best done under the cover of darkness, so, for a moment, I sat there savoring it, and trying not to feel sad.

I hadn't seen any more of Paddy after that. He'd texted me to say he'd got things to do and would probably stay for the weekend in London since Poppy seemed to be holding the fort admirably back home. He hoped all had gone well at the lawyers' office and said that his mother knew I was popping by to collect my things. Right. Quite sort of . . . formal. And, unless I was being hypersensitive, a tiny bit pack-your-things-and-go. So I'd gone.

I'd popped round to Essex Villas for my bag. Paddy's mother had opened the door with another dazzling smile and another blast of Dior, wearing a beautiful floral dress. She'd been to the Royal Academy, she explained, to a private view, an exhibition of Monet's garden paintings, so she'd thought she'd look the part, but she wondered, rolling her eyes ironically down at her dress, if she didn't look too much like a herbaceous border? I assured her, laughing, that she didn't. She grinned and led me down the black-and-white hall to the kitchen, her heels clicking on the limestone. Then she embarked on a story about how, at the gallery, she'd been cornered by some frightfully familiar-looking old boy whose name she could *not* remember. In an attempt to jog her memory she'd ventured '. . . still doing the same old thing?' to which he'd replied, 'Yes, still King of Spain.'

'Can you imagine?' she shrieked, turning to me. 'It transpired we'd met in Madrid, at some art event Jack had got involved in. I'd sat *next* to him, for heaven's sake!'

I'd laughed along with her but as she reached for the coffee percolator my heart was sinking rapidly. Not only beautiful but a sense of humor, too, I thought with rising panic. If only this family were more dislikable.

'Luckily he roared,' she told me, eyes sparkling, 'and we had a terrific gas after that, but I mean honestly.'

She poured the recently brewed coffee into porcelain

mugs. She turned, smiled. 'My dear, you're not really off just yet, are you? Paddy says you are, but surely you've only just arrived?'

'I am, I'm afraid,' I said, perching on a stool and trying to keep a bright smile going. 'I've got stables to muck out and mouths to feed. Sadly the animals don't look after themselves.'

'I can believe it. I've only got a Shih Tzu but there never was a more demanding dog.' She stooped and gathered the ball of white fluff into her arms, kissing his nose. She regarded me kindly over the dog's head.

'And did you get what you wanted? What you came up here for?' she asked carefully.

'Up to a point,' I replied, equally carefully. She nodded. You see, the thing was, suddenly her son seemed the whole point. But obviously I couldn't say that. I took a deep breath. Said something different.

'Paddy's staying up here for the weekend, I gather.'

'Is he? Oh good. Well, that's news to me, but us mothers are always the last to know – why keep the catering corps in the loop?' She grinned. 'I expect he's got plans.'

'Yes, I – I think he's seeing Claudia.'

'Oh, I *am* pleased.' She beamed. 'We love Claudia, we'd adore to see more of her. Did you get to speak to her the other night?'

'Only very briefly. In the drawing room, over coffee.' I felt a bit sick. 'Um, Mrs Campbell—'

'Virginia, please!'

'Virginia, there's a train that leaves at four minutes past, so if you don't mind I think I'll leave this – it's a bit hot – and get my things.'

'Of course, of course! Golly, don't burn your mouth, for heaven's sake. Can I give you a lift or—'

'No, no, the tube's quicker, but that's such a kind offer. I really appreciate it and you've been simply marvelous to have me here.' Oh God, I was beginning to speak like her.

I slid off the stool at the marble-topped breakfast bar and slipped down the hall. Then I went up the stairs, two flights, three, to my room. When I came down with my bag I made a big show of being in a panicky rush, just popping my head around the kitchen door where she was sitting reading the newspaper, begging her not to see me out as she made to get up, thanking her again and saying that I really must fly. Then I left.

I shut the front door behind me – 'poof' – and walked quickly down the street. When I turned into the next road, I slowed. Right down. There was no real rush. My train wasn't for another twenty-five minutes. But I was protecting myself. I didn't want to spend any more time in Virginia's company. Didn't want to soak up any more of that gorgeous, loving, homey atmosphere than I could possibly help. I knew it wouldn't do me any good. Tempting, obviously, to be as greedy as possible: to drink in every minute detail about his life, ask about his sisters, their husbands, children perhaps, then relive it all on the train – but no. That way madness lay.

Instead, I made my way to Paddington, and drank heaps of coffee in Starbucks. Then I texted or rang the children ascertaining their whereabouts, and now, here I was, sitting in my yard under an inky, starless sky. Alone again, naturally. Who'd said that? Shakespeare? Oh. No. Leo Sayer. Right.

As I went inside, flicking on the kitchen light, a strange, eerie calm assaulted me. The dogs got up to greet me, but not in their usual wild manner, flinging themselves accusingly and demandingly against my legs, merely wagging their tails politely and returning to their baskets. The cat didn't dive-bomb me from the top of the cupboard where she slept from a position of insecurity and vigilance; she was asleep with the dogs in their basket. Were they drugged? I glanced around.

The kitchen was remarkably, uncharacteristically tidy. Oh my, Mum had done a good job. Dad was very much better, I knew that from her texts – a rest had indeed been the answer – but still. I hadn't expected any more than the animals being cared for; she had her own house to run. I went to the blackened window and turned on the outside light, illuminating the garden. The pink caravan was obviously shut up for the night, but the collapsible steps were down and the 'Open' sign hung on the door. When I'd spoken briefly to Nico from Starbucks, he'd said he thought Granny had managed to fit in a couple of clients.

'Hoodwinking the gullible as usual!' I'd joked, hoping for a comradely moment with my son, who was still sounding cool. But it had backfired.

'If Granny has a nice chat with some lonely old local who doesn't see a soul because he's on his tractor all week and his wife's died and he's feeling a bit low and he pays her ten quid to chatter away, so what? So what if she tells him it's all going to be fine and all sorts of lovely things are on the horizon and he goes away feeling better? What's wrong with that? What's the difference to talking to a counsellor? For a lot more money? In a far more depressing place, without Granny's charm and humor and music? What's the bloody difference, Mum?'

I couldn't tell him but I was taken aback. And I resolved not to be such a moralizing old cow in future. And when I saw her, to thank her profusely for everything she'd done. I felt ashamed. And a bit guilty too, about liking Paddy's elegant, fragrant, sophisticated mother so much.

No sign of Minna: she must have gone to bed. I

glanced up the stairs. Having got no response from her mobile, I'd texted Lucy, who'd said Minna had gone home, which had surprised me, so I'd rung. Obviously she hadn't answered the landline, but then my children didn't, on the basis that it wouldn't be for them, so why bother? It only involved the tedium of taking a message. Yes, she must be asleep, I decided, except . . . there was a light on through here.

I pushed through the sitting-room door and caught my breath. The room was empty but pristine. Low, subtle lamplight I didn't even know I possessed revealed a vacuumed and dusted sanctuary. There was a smell of beeswax in the air. Even the cushions were plumped. Cushions were never plumped in this house. The nasty stain on the carpet where it looked like someone had been battered to death but was in fact a whole bottle of red wine had disappeared, and the throws covering the threadbare sofas had been washed and ironed.

In a daze I followed the sound of music. Soft, low music that was coming from the old playroom beyond. I pushed through the door to behold Minna, at a table in the bay window, playing chess with Toxic Ted. I didn't know she could. Ted stood up when I came in.

'Hi, Mum.' Minna flushed a bit. 'You remember Ted?'

I took his hand as he proffered it. 'How could I forget?'

'Sorry about that, Mrs Faulkner.' He didn't do his usual charming grin but went a bit pink instead. 'I think I overdid it the night before with Nico and his mates.'

'These things happen,' I said, playing for time and crossing to close the curtains, which was about the only thing that hadn't been done in this room. It was otherwise immaculate. 'Did Granny do all this?' I asked Minna incredulously, looking around.

'No, Ted did it.'

Ted went even pinker and his brow furrowed. 'Hope you don't think it was cheeky, Mrs Faulkner. It's just I heard you had to be in London and that Minna's granddad was poorly and your mum seemed to have her hands full, so I thought I'd lend a hand.'

I stared at him. 'You did all this?'

'Yeah, I didn't stay or anything. I just came after work and did the animals for your mum and tidied the house and that. Gave the dogs a long walk to tire them out. The cat came too.'

'Yes, she . . . does that. Well I – I don't know what to say. I'll pay you, of course.'

'Oh no, I don't want that. Didn't do it for that. I did it for – well . . .' He tailed off. Minna was looking very dewy-eyed. Someone had to speak.

'Gosh, well, how incredibly kind. Thank you.' I wasn't going to overdo it, though. I gave him a bright smile. He took the cue.

'Yeah, well, I'd better go. It's late. See you, Minna. Mrs Faulkner.' He went towards the door and Minna went after him. A few minutes later she was back, glowing visibly, eyes bright.

I widened my eyes meaningfully at her. 'I thought he was a love rat? Thought you'd got him out of your system in London and were seeing other boys?'

'Is that what you wanted to think?'

'Well, I . . . what about Adam? I thought you liked him?'

'Adam was nice, but he was a bit dull. And persistent. And I've told Ted about him. I mean, we only dated, but I've told him.'

'Right.'

'Look, Mum, I know you're being protective, but you don't need to be, because you don't know everything. You think you do, but you don't. Ted and I were only ever having a thing. We weren't exclusive. He didn't screw me over.'

'I see.' No. Not a clue.

'But now we are. Exclusive.'

'Right.' Did we have that in our day, I wondered? Exclusive? Inclusive? Things? I think we just called it cheating or playing the field and merrily got on with it. There were more rules these days. In fact I'd say the young were more moral. More . . . responsible. Faithful. Perhaps because of social media. You couldn't get away with anything any more. Would be found out in moments. Yes, the courtship plates had shifted seismically, perhaps for the better.

Minna, I could see, though, was not keen to continue this line of sociological chat, or indeed any kind of chat for that matter. I knew the rules: the other, mother and daughter ones. If all was misery and despair my ear was needed every waking minute. But the moment all was rosy, I must disappear. Vanish. Become invisible. So I went to shut the chickens up. Although of course Ted had already done it, and when I came back, she'd gone to bed.

I turned out all the lights and went up myself, marveling at the piles of ironed clothes on the table on the landing and wondering if he'd tidied my bleeding knicker drawer. He hadn't. Hadn't been in my bedroom, which was as chaotic as I'd left it. He had tidied Nico's, though, but not Lucy's. I wandered around in a daze. Clean sparkling baths! Shiny taps! I stroked them, then wiped the fingermark away with my sleeve. I hadn't had a cleaner for two years. I had now. I peered in the loo. I wasn't convinced I could live with that blue water, but I wouldn't hurt his feelings and take the funny plastic thing out of the cistern. Just live with it, Molly. Blue toilet water is a small price to pay. Shattered, I went to bed.

THE FOLLOWING MORNING I very definitely overslept because when I awoke and went to the window to open the curtains, Moira Grundy was coming down the caravan steps, looking very pleased with herself. Ah. Good moment. I seized it. Throwing on some clothes, I went outside. The day was cooler than the preceding ones had been, perhaps heralding the end of the heatwave, but the bright blue sky highlighted the green of the garden beautifully. I hurried up the slope to the terraced lawn and mounted the steps. Inside the caravan I found Mum tidying up the predominately pink interior. Radio Two was on and she was humming away happily to Diana Ross, but not dressed as a gypsy, just in a patterned skirt and top. We hugged each other warmly and I thanked her for everything.

'Another satisfied customer?' I asked, nodding in the general direction of Moira's retreating back down the lane.

'Oh, very. She found her reading glasses last week as I told her she would. And she's getting on much better with her brother.'

'I thought she wanted him to move out?'

'She did, but she knows she'd miss him, so she's agreed not to mention the fact that he tries on all her clothes when she goes out. A bit of harmless fun is how I put it. And so what if he's getting his private part pierced? It's his private part, isn't it?'

I smiled. 'It is indeed, Mum.' Nico was right. She was more agony aunt than anything else. 'And what's in her stars for this week?'

'This week she's going to be reunited with an old

friend. I had Avril Hutchinson in yesterday and her sister's visiting from Glasgow on Tuesday, who I know Moira gets on very well with. They grew up next door to each other in the village, of course.'

She smoothed down the throw on the sofa then turned and beamed. 'I say, what d'you think of darling Ted? Isn't he something?'

'Well, he certainly seems to have undergone a miraculous transformation, that's what I came to ask you about.' I sat down at her table with its fringed cloth. 'What the hell's going on?'

'*Well*,' she said importantly, perching on a chair next to me and clasping her hands. 'All I know is I came back and found him here, as I told you, and then the next time I came, to tell him to vamoose like you said, it was as if Mary Poppins had been. I had mentioned I was up to my eyes with your dad – yes, right as rain –' she waved away my enquiry, 'doesn't want any more fuss and wishes I'd never mentioned it – and that what with business hotting up here, which it is, blimey, I had the entire village in yesterday – I might be a bit pushed, but I never expected him to jump into the breach like that. And did you notice all the soap had gone?'

'God, no, I didn't. But now you mention it . . . where is it?'

'In a loose box. And he walked Nutty for me to stretch the tendon. Mucked him out, too.'

'And it's all for Minna?'

'Totally. He came in here a couple of days ago and we had a nice chat – I didn't charge him, of course – and he said he'd been an idiot and he missed her. Said he'd lost her to London and the bright lights. He admitted he'd never been there in his life. He said that all the other girls

were nothing compared to her and he wondered if he'd
lost her for good.'

'And what did you say?'

'Well, obviously I read his palm.'

'Obviously.'

'And I said I could see calmer waters ahead, but only if he
really mended his ways. Put his philandering days behind
him. Then I furrowed my brow and asked if he knew anyone
called Adam. He said no, so I said I thought Minna might
and he went away in a bit of a lather. Then I rang Minna and
told her I'd dropped her in it but with very good reason, and
that *her* stars said she should stay up in town for another night,
have her highlights done, get a St Tropez tan, not answer her
phone, and sashay down here yesterday, which she did.'

'To play chess.'

'He's teaching her. His dad's a grandmaster.'

'Stop it!'

'Swear to God. Eileen Price told me. Don't be such a
snob, darling, you know nothing about his family.'

'True.' I narrowed my eyes thoughtfully. 'But one
swallow doesn't make a summer.'

'I agree, but it's a start. And he's got to be the most
delicious-looking young man for miles around, don't you
think? Have you ever seen such a specimen?'

'Who's a specimen?' said a familiar voice. We both
turned as Lucy put her head around the door. She looked
beautiful, blonde hair piled on her head in a messy bun,
her face lightly made up. She came up the steps, followed
by Robin, who looked tanned and well and was smiling
broadly.

'Oh! Darlings!' I got up to hug them both, as did Mum.
'What a surprise! I had no idea you were coming!'

'Bit of an impulse decision, to be honest, we haven't

actually been to bed,' said Lucy, rolling her eyes. I realized she was still in evening clothes, an old coat over the top. 'Robin heroically drove and I slept on the way. But who's the specimen?'

'Toxic Ted, who's undergone something of a dramatic sea change – I'll explain,' I said quickly, seeing her face darken. 'Only don't go in there as I did and question her about love rats and a new boyfriend in London. She doesn't need it from both of us.'

'Well, I certainly wouldn't do that, I do have some tact and subtlety. And actually today . . .' Her face lightened and a broad smile broke out like sunshine across her face. 'Today I'm prepared to love anyone. Even Toxic Ted.'

I suddenly realized her eyes were unnaturally bright and her cheeks were flushed.

'Why today . . . ?' I asked, floundering. She reached out her hand to Robin, beside her. He took it, beaming. They gazed at one another.

'Well, Robin wanted to ask you, but I said we weren't really that kind of family and that it would be fine if we did it together. It is fine, isn't it, Mum?' She turned to me. 'If he doesn't ask? If we just tell you' – she glanced up at him again – 'that we're going to get married!'

*A*s I told her, later, over champagne in the sitting room, I'd never seen her look happier or lovelier. We'd hugged and cried out there in the caravan – well, *I'd* cried, obviously – but such joyful tears, such overwhelming emotion, to see my darling daughter, my eldest girl, so obviously happy. Yes, they were young – or she was, Robin was five years older – but she knew he was right, I could tell. And he knew she was right, too. And they were very much in love.

'So why delay?' she asked brightly, waving her champagne glass about in the sitting room – immaculate, for once, thank God – where we'd all gathered around the bottle I'd thrust quickly in the freezer for two minutes and which Nico poured: yes, Nico arriving from Jake's in the nick of time, in his spluttering old Fiesta, chugging into the yard as we waved madly from the open window. 'Why wait any longer when we've been going out for years?'

'Why indeed,' I agreed, thinking she deserved this: this happiness, this security, this love, and that Robin was a good man. He'd give it to her in spades. And yes, she might well give him the runaround, I thought, looking at his adoring eyes as they shone down into hers, but I had a feeling he had a bit of steel to him too. I'd recently witnessed him simply ignore her when she went into a huff, something the rest of us found hard to do, always rising to the bait. It had worked a treat. She'd had to seek him out later, apologize, when she'd calmed down, which of course he'd given her time to do. No, he wouldn't be a pushover, but he'd deal with her intelligently. And now that he too felt secure in claiming her, his confidence would grow. Not that she needed dealing with, I thought guiltily, but – you know. You know your children. I sipped my champagne, still blinking my watery eyes a bit. I watched the happy couple chatting with Minna, Nico and Mum, discussing venues, dates.

'You must have it here,' Minna insisted. 'In the long meadow.'

'Oh, I intend to! I couldn't get married anywhere else. I want a proper country wedding, with bunting and orange blossom and hay bales – the whole bit. We won't have moved by then, will we, Mum? Late summer?'

'No I – hope not.' But everyone looked a bit sad suddenly, as if a damp tea towel had been thrown over proceedings.

'Well, if necessary we can always have it at Rutsham,' volunteered Robin.

'Oh yes, how lovely, Robin,' I said quickly. But I saw Lucy envisage this: Robin's grand ancestral home, with the mile-long drive, the imposing turrets – she'd shown me a picture – private chapel, too. With his parents at the helm instead of us. Charming, Lucy had said, but – you know. Quite grand.

'Or London,' she said quickly.

'Exactly,' I agreed, equally quickly, but we all took a

huge slug of champagne. Minna drained her glass in one and mine spilled and went down my chin.

It wasn't going to be easy, this move, I reflected, and the closer it got, the more difficult it would become. But then, nothing ever was, was it? Easy? Certainly in my life. It didn't help, of course, that it was the most glorious of days with the sun shining down on the buttercup meadow outside the bay window where we'd gathered, freckled with ewes and lambs, which was where she'd want to put the marquee, bunting fluttering, framed by the smoky blue hills beyond.

Buddy munched happily out there now in the paddock, avoiding the ragwort, which no matter how much I pulled it up, still sprouted away joyfully, and quite prettily, I thought. Shame it was poisonous. In the distance, last year's boy lambs grazed peacefully, bound for market soon, and quite rightly, someone had to keep this place afloat, but at the moment, they were sweetly oblivious to their fate and merely adding to the sylvan scene.

Where the land sloped gently up and away from the river towards the hills beyond, the grass was already too rich for the horses, too full of clover, and I resolved to move Tufty later, bring him in with a hay net. For the moment, though, his dear little white face and round tummy and gently floating mane and tail added a touch of nostalgia to the picture. I remembered Lucy as a little girl, bouncing around on his back, squealing with glee: Nico and Minna too. No, none of that helped either.

Lucy came across. 'I just want you to be happy too, Mum,' she said softly, perhaps seeing my face. She gave me a hug. 'It doesn't matter where I get married. Doesn't matter a bit. It's your life that needs sorting now.'

For some ridiculous reason I couldn't speak. I gave a quick nod and blinked some more.

'She needs a man,' put in Minna helpfully. Heroically, I managed a hollow laugh.

'I do *not* need a man.'

'Come on, Granny, what's in her stars?'

'Ooh, well, now you're talking,' began my mother enthusiastically, pausing to light a cigarette for extra oomph – an error. I seized my chance and raised my hand.

'Or not, Mother!'

'Oh, but darling, I was only going to—'

'I know you were, but this is Lucy's day, Lucy's and Robin's. And if you don't mind, we'll keep it that way and refrain from talking about me for a change.' It got the laugh I was hoping for and everyone fell to chattering about dresses and bridesmaids instead.

'Jake's uncle fancies you, Mum,' Nico told me, shuffling across. 'Jake told me.'

'Thank you, Nico,' I smiled. Then screwed up my nose as if considering. 'But not really.'

'And not just because you're the only single woman in the village, Jake said. Which you're not, obviously. There's Batty Brenda and Mrs Higginson at the butcher's.'

'Well, quite.'

'And now Jake's aunt's buggered off with Joe Sutcliffe, he's on his own. You'd have to get over his beer belly and his gambling habits – his aunt couldn't, obviously – but Jake said he'd happily buy you a port and lemon at the Nag's Head.'

'Thank you, darling, I'll bear that in mind.'

'Just – you know. To get you out a bit.'

'Except, I've been out rather a lot, recently, don't you think?' I grimaced. 'With mixed results. Now, a toast, don't you think?' I raised my glass.

'Oh yes, a toast!' agreed Mum, refilling everyone's glasses. I waited until everyone had a full one, and in a vivid moment, clear as day, had a vision of David doing this. It rocked me dramatically: almost took my breath away. But I powered on.

'To Lucy and Robin.'

'Lucy and Robin!' everyone roared and then there was lots of whooping and clapping and Minna, ever her mother's daughter, burst into tears. Then Mum rushed to the phone to ring Dad, shrieking about why she hadn't thought of doing it before, and then everyone proceeded to get really quite drunk and no one had had breakfast, so I went into the kitchen to rustle up some blotting paper.

It was as I was cracking eggs into a pan to scramble them, humming along happily to the radio, full of joy and warmth and champagne for Lucy, who I could see through the open door in the sitting room, laughing with Robin, one arm round her grandmother's shoulders, her eyes shining, when something else caught my eye. Not in the sitting room, but outside the kitchen window. I moved closer, eggshells in hand. Stared. Across the yard, the stable door was open. Nutty's. And I knew he'd been in there, I'd seen him earlier. He wasn't now. Where the hell was he?

In one fluid movement I'd abandoned the eggs and flown through the back door and across the yard. The stable was very definitely empty, just the shavings on the floor, a water bucket and a broody chicken sitting on some eggs in the corner. I spun about. Shit. Where the hell had he gone? Back to the fields for company, in the shape of Buddy or Tufty? Or Monty, perhaps, the goat, who he whinnied for most, stuck as he was all day, in splendid isolation, in his cell.

I raced to the paddock. But Monty had been put in with Buddy and the geese for company: he'd long ago forgotten Nutty, and there was no sign of his erstwhile friend clamoring to be let in at the gate, or even leaping it, as we now knew he could. Who did he whinny for next? Or what? Food, damn it. I caught my breath then ran like the blazes, back down the track, across the yard, and round the back of the stables to the feed shed. A large, dappled grey bottom blocked my entrance.

'*Nutty!*' I shrieked, squeezing past him, my cry jerking his head out of the feed bin. He started in surprise to see me. I stared into the bin. Empty. And I'd filled them all before I left, made sure the lids were on to stop the mice getting in. Empty, apart from a few . . . I reached in and pulled out the last remaining nuts, except they weren't nuts. Because this wasn't the pony nut bin. It was the sugar beet bin. Sugar beet, which had to be soaked, for twenty-four hours, in a bucket, or in this case, Quick Beet, for ten minutes. During which time it would swell to six times the size. I swung around to Nutty in horror. His replete, brown eyes gazed back.

'Oh God, Nutty, what have you done?' I whispered. 'You are going to explode. You are literally going to explode!'

I grabbed a head collar, shoved it on him and getting in front of his broad chest pushed him bodily, in reverse, out of the shed. My heart was racing as I turned and trotted him smartly back to his stable. At least he could move, that was something, but for how much longer? How long had he got?

With trembling fingers I pulled my mobile from my pocket and ran to the house. Obviously I had Paddy's number on speed dial but not Poppy's, and with him in London, I'd have to look it up. No point ringing the surgery, the receptionist was fierce and only took messages, never put you through to an actual vet. Poppy, Poppy . . . I riffled through my address book in the kitchen and was just punching in her mobile number when the children descended on me from the sitting room.

'What's wrong? Why did you charge out like that?'

'Nutty got into the feed bin. Eaten a ton of sugar beet.'

'Dry?' gasped Lucy.

'Yep.'

'Oh God, that was me!' breathed Minna, putting her hand to her mouth in horror. 'I put him away. I took him to his stable – didn't I bolt it properly?'

'I don't know, darling, all I know is he was out and – hello, Poppy?'

I turned away as Minna burst into tears. Mum went to comfort her as Nico muttered, 'Dickhead.'

'I didn't mean to! I didn't *mean* to, Nico!' she wailed.

I spun around, removing myself from the noise, putting my finger in my other ear. 'Poppy? It's Molly Faulkner here.' My breath was coming very fast but I knew I had to be clear. 'Nutty, my horse, has got in the feed bin and eaten dry sugar beet.'

There was a pause. 'How much?'

'A lot. I don't know exactly but I'm pretty sure the bin was full.'

'How long ago?'

'Just now. I've just dragged him away.'

'Quick Beet or twenty-four-hour?'

'Quick Beet.'

'Shit. I'm on my way. I'm at Baldwin's at the moment so I'll be five minutes. Keep him in his box and keep him standing up, Molly. Don't let him go down.'

'Right.'

She rang off and I fled outside. I could still hear Minna in hysterics behind me with Nico shouting at her, but Lucy and Robin were on my heels. When I raced into the stable, Nutty was in the far corner, looking rather less pleased with

377

himself than he had done a few minutes ago. His sides were heaving and he was sweating and pawing the ground.

'Quick, get a head collar on him. Poppy says he mustn't lie down.'

'Is she coming?' asked Lucy, flying to get one and quickly clipping it on him.

'Yes, five minutes, she's at Baldwin's.'

'Is it like colic? Keep him upright in case the gut twists?' asked Robin. I'd forgotten he hunted.

'Yes, although in this case, I don't know if it's the gut twisting or – shit, he's going down. Quick.'

Robin, Lucy and I jerked his head up and pushed him on to walk, pulling him round his stable.

'Should we take him out? Walk him in the yard?' Lucy asked as he snorted and rolled his eyes in alarm.

'Poppy said no. He's too strong, he might just pull away from us and go down. We just have to keep him moving in here.'

But Nutty was in trouble now: terrible trouble. Terror was in his wild eyes at what was happening to his insides which very recently had been so sated, so comfortable, so lip-smackingly fine. Now, all of a sudden, he was in tremendous pain and lying down seemed to him the obvious option.

'NO!' we shrieked as his front knees buckled. Robin gave him a sharp slap on the buttocks to jerk him on, his other hand pulling the head collar. 'Get on!' he roared as Nutty, bewildered, unbuckled his knees and staggered into a walk. 'Lucy, get behind him,' he ordered, 'I'll pull.'

Minna and Nico appeared at the stable door. Minna was in floods. 'I've killed him, haven't I?' she wailed. 'The sugar beet will swell and his insides will burst, won't they?'

'Of course not,' I told her.

'But where will it go to, all the food? It'll have no room,

it'll just swell and swell until it gets so massive his stomach will explode!'

'Shut up, Minna, you're not helping,' said Lucy as Nutty, panic in his eyes, tried to jerk the rope away and rear up simultaneously in fear, backing into the corner.

Robin held on valiantly. 'Easy boy! Easy there, walk on!' 'I can't bear it! I can't bear it!' Minna cried, tears streaming down her face.

'Take her away, Nico,' yelled Robin.

'Yeah, piss off, Minna, you're not helping,' snapped Nico.

'I can't, I have to be here with him, it's my fault!'

At that moment, in the unfolding, unhelpful cacophony surrounding poor Nutty's distress, Poppy's car was heard pulling into the yard. A car door slammed, then running footsteps.

'Oh, thank God,' I murmured as she appeared. I flew to open the stable door for her.

She came in with her bag and one look at Nutty told her all she needed to know. 'Right,' she said quickly. 'So what I've got to do, if you could keep him upright and as still as possible,' she was crouching and unpacking her bag as she spoke, 'is get this plastic tube down his throat.' She pulled out a long length of transparent flexible tubing from within. Robin was still valiantly wrestling with the snorting, stamping horse.

'What will that do, suck the food out?' I asked, flattening myself against the wall as Nutty and Robin surged past. Poppy was still searching for something else in her bag, riffling about. Paddy would have got the tube down by now.

'No, it's not the stomach that's the problem, it's the breathing. Everything swelling up to block the oesophagus.' She was approaching Nutty with one end of the tube but I noticed her hands were trembling a bit. Poppy was only young. Very much a new assistant. I wondered how long she'd been qualified. Now didn't seem quite the moment to ask. I caught Robin's eye; he'd also seen her approach somewhat hesitantly.

'Right, so we open his mouth and you shove it in, is that it?' he asked.

'That's it,' she agreed, as if we were just popping a little pill in his mouth, not a ruddy great tube, all the way down to his stomach.

It was a great deal easier said than done. By sticking his fingers in the corner of Nutty's mouth to open it – not easy, given that it was a moving, if not jerking target – Robin gave Poppy short but crucial opportunities, which Poppy somehow managed to bungle each time. She missed again, for the fourth time.

'Here, you do the mouth and I'll get the tube in,' said Robin, exasperated, as Nutty whinnied frantically.

In my peripheral vision, I could see Nico backing away. He'd have added a bit of muscle to hold the horse but this was not his sort of thing. But try as we would, Poppy, Lucy and I couldn't hold Nutty's head still enough so that Robin could get his mouth open with his tongue out of the way, and Nutty was getting more and more panic-stricken, whinnying and rearing as we grabbed and shouted, and he was a big horse.

'Oh, please let him be quick!' gasped Poppy as Nutty surged forward suddenly, barging the door with his chest and shooting the rope out of our hands.

'Do you mean to die? Let him be quick to die!' shrieked Minna, who, oh so helpfully, was still with us, albeit some yards from the stable, her hands over her wet face, or shoved up into her vertical hair.

'No, let him be quick getting here!' Poppy said breath-lessly, grabbing the head collar again. 'Paddy, I mean.'

'Paddy's coming?' I cried.

'Yes, I rang him, but he was over towards Ludlow, Barnacre Farm. But he's on his way.'

'But Paddy's in London!' I shouted above the whin-nying din.

'No, he came back yesterday, I wondered why you rang me.'

'Oh!' I breathed, confused, but heartily relieved. Paddy was coming – oh thank God. Surely he couldn't die if Paddy was here?

A cry went up from the yard as a car was heard and Minna ran to get him. We had a problem, though, because in that moment, Nutty had decided that he really would lie down, that it was the only way to relieve his terrible, searing pain, and his knees had gone and he was on his side, almost taking Lucy and me with him. In fact we were both on our knees.

'Oh!' We panicked, trying to stumble up.

'Get that horse on its feet,' commanded a steely, controlled voice as the stable went dark and the vet's form blocked the light.

'Paddy, we can't,' I gasped, 'he's too strong – oh Paddy, he's eaten sugar beet.'

'I know. Here, Robin, pull the rope hard and level while I get behind.'

Robin did as he was told as Paddy, with seemingly super-human strength, telling Lucy and me to do the same at the sides, got behind his buttocks and pushed like the blazes. Somehow, we got the poor thrashing horse to his feet.

'Did you give him a shot?' he asked Poppy.

'No!' she gasped. 'Oh – God, sorry, I just knew the tube had to——'

'Quite right, but this will help.'

In a seamless movement Paddy had opened his bag, taken an already loaded syringe and dexterously slotted it into Nutty's neck, pushing in the serum.

'To knock him out?' I breathed.

'Not completely, we need some compliance, but it'll sedate him a bit and hopefully calm him. Now, hold the other end of the tube, Poppy, and feed it in when I say.'

The tricky operation that four of us had been struggling with was completed in moments as Paddy held the head collar with one hand, opened Nutty's mouth and shoved the tube in with the other, and Poppy fed it through, noticeably calmer now. But Nutty's eyes had disappeared back into his head, no doubt in supreme discomfort, surely ten minutes into eating the food.

'Oh God, are we too late?' I gasped as we all propped him upright, his soaking sides heaving, his breathing filling the stable and going rickety rackety, like a pneumatic drill.

'We'll see. He may be too spent to accommodate the tube, we'll see.'

'Don't we have to get the food out of his stomach?'

'No, to be honest that's a myth. The stomach's so big it will stretch and accommodate the beet, and anyway, it'll empty into the intestines. No, it's choke that's the problem because he's bolted it, something's got stuck and we need to flush it out.' He was shooting a liquid through the tube now as he talked. Perhaps due to the tranquilizer, or perhaps Paddy's presence, Nutty seemed a bit calmer. His eyes were still white and rolled back, but he was quieter, and he seemed to be getting used to the tube. He was breathing more easily.

'I think we may have flushed it through,' Paddy said as

he held the tube with one hand and stroked Nutty's neck with the other. 'Think we might be clearing things, eh, mate?'

So it was not a substitute oesophagus to breathe through, it was to clear the obstruction. Poppy had got that wrong or got confused. But who could blame her? She was only young, and in the heat of the moment and with a thrashing horse, all foaming mouth and steely hooves – thank God we'd all avoided those, he'd lashed out a couple of times – who cared what the tube did? She'd had the right idea. None of us could really breathe as we watched Nutty intently, including Poppy, I know. *Please live, please live,* we all seemed to be willing him, as Paddy stroked and cooed in his ear, and suddenly, I knew he would. If Paddy stroked and cooed in my ear, I bloody would, too. Such tenderness. Such genuine concern. It made my eyes fill up, while Nutty's, so wild and panicked earlier, began to flicker and half close. His breathing became more regular, his sides heaved a little less. His head dropped right to his knees, but he didn't try to lie down. He just stood, nose almost on the shavings, recovering slowly, gathering strength. After a few minutes, I dared to say it.

'He's going to be OK, isn't he, Paddy?'

'Yep,' he agreed. 'I think he's out of the woods.'

'Oh, thank God!' gasped Minna, at the door, covering her mouth, her eyes wide and wet. I saw Poppy glance to the heavens and shut her eyes briefly. I put my arm around her shoulders and squeezed.

'Got that a bit wrong,' she gasped.

'No, you didn't,' said Paddy in that level, steady way. 'You got the treatment exactly right.'

'Not sure I'd have shot the fluid down.'

'But he'll make it, that's the important thing,' said Lucy, and Poppy glanced at her gratefully. 'Robin, you were brilliant,' Lucy added warmly. He had been brilliant. We wouldn't have kept him upright but for him; he'd have gone down a lot sooner.

'Well done, mate,' said Paddy, and Robin looked pleased. Paddy was a bit of a local hero round here, which I always laughed about, because let's face it, the competition for that title wasn't fierce.

'You know Nina Bartlett has your practice photo on her fridge, don't you?' I'd tease.

I wasn't laughing now. There was so much, *so* much, I wanted to ask him as we stood in that quiet, highly charged stable, watching Nutty recover. *Why are you here? Why aren't you in London? Is Claudia with you? Did she pack her bags that very second and is even now installed in your house with you?* That house. Paddy's darling little thatched white cottage, surrounded by lush water meadows. Was she even now unpacking her suitcase upstairs, throwing open the bedroom window to the buttercups, singing as the swallows swooped and soared in the sky, smoothing down the duvet, taking a look around her new surroundings, going out to pick some flowers for the side of the bed, suddenly a nature lover, a Damascene moment having taken place, together with a great surge of love?

Paddy was talking to me. Looking into my eyes with his steady brown ones and telling me about a new feeding regime. 'Nothing, obviously, for a while, but access to plenty of water. It'll need topping up regularly. And then tomorrow a little molasses but make it good and sloppy, and little and often, like a child. Not a proper feed. No hay yet. Take that net away.'

'Right.'

'And keep him in. Box rest for the next couple of days.'

'Will do.'

'But then he can go out in the paddock with Buddy, but

not over where Tufty is, it's too lush. He needs to come in, too.'

'Got it.'

Perhaps something more was in my eyes, because his face softened. 'Are you all right, Molly?'

I saw Lucy's head snap round at this change of tone. She glanced from me to him.

'Yes. Just a bit . . . all in.' I managed a wan smile.

'I can imagine. That was very traumatic.' He gave a sympathetic smile. Then he glanced at his watch. 'Well, I've got to get home now. I brought a friend down with me and I just need to see she's OK, but I'll be back later to check on him.'

I felt my face collapse. Knew my mouth had drooped dramatically too, like a child's. Like Nutty's head had to his knees. She *was* in his bedroom. She *was* smoothing down the white Egyptian cotton, watching the swallows.

'OK,' I managed. I couldn't do anything about the mouth.

'About six o'clock all right?'

I couldn't speak. Nodded miserably. 'Perfect,' I agreed eventually. 'Absolutely fine.'

Paddy and Poppy began to pack up their respective bags. Paddy was speaking encouragingly to her, I noticed, praising her. Lucy caught my eye sympathetically, perhaps with some insight. Minna wanted to stay with Nutty, even though Paddy had said he'd be fine. Nonetheless, she sat down in the corner of the stable, her back to the wall, hugging her knees. Nico sloped up, took a view and sloped away again. Lucy and Robin left to go back in the house, Lucy giving my shoulder a quick squeeze on the way out. I saw Mum open the back door for them.

Paddy and Poppy were still deep in conversation as they went on their way to their cars. I shut the stable door

385

behind me and followed them out. When Poppy had got into her car, having packed her stuff in her boot, Paddy gave her a pat on the back, then walked to his.

'Thanks, Paddy,' I said.

He turned back, surprised. 'Oh, no problem,' he said vaguely. 'All in a day's work.'

It was as if I were Jo Saunders at Baldwin's, or Jake's father with his herd of Friesians at Longmeadow. As if I were just another client. A box ticked. And a bit of a relief to be driving away from, if he was honest.

He eased his long legs into the open cab in one elegant motion. Then he turned the ignition and the engine roared into life. A few moments later, I watched his red pickup drive out through the gates with a lump in my throat. I saw it turn and go down the lane behind the hedge. I was still there a moment later, when it had disappeared.

CHAPTER 30

*P*addy texted me later to say that if it was all right, he wouldn't come by at six; he'd come round after dinner instead, at about ten. But no one needed to be there, he'd just pop his head into the stable. Check Nutty was OK. After dinner. I felt sick. Where? I wondered. Out in town? Or perhaps on the terrace in the garden, it was such a lovely evening. And who would cook? Could Paddy cook? I didn't know. Perhaps they'd do it together, laughing as they chopped vegetables, music in the background. I actually had to hold on to the sink and breathe in case I really did heave.

I determined to be there anyway at ten, when he called, to greet him, with a smile even bigger than Claudia's. And I'd be in the kitchen, not in the sitting room in front of the television where I usually was, and where I'd miss him and wouldn't see the car. I dressed carefully for the occasion. Obviously I didn't dress up, I dressed right down, but my jeans were skinny and clean – I washed and tumbled them quickly – and the sweater was new, a kind of loose, crochet, oatmeal affair, worn over one of Lucy's vests. Not much make-up, obviously, but a bit. Foundation to cover the brown sun marks and red spider veins, then a touch of pink lipstick. And a bit of eyeliner. Oh – and mascara, just on the top lashes. OK, a tiny bit on the bottom. I came downstairs. Lucy glanced up from the television in the playroom where she was lying on the sofa, her head in Robin's lap.

'Where are you going?' she asked in wonder.

'Nowhere.'

'Oh.'

Robin didn't notice, but Lucy's eyes followed me into the kitchen. I hoped she wouldn't come in. Ask questions. Diplomatically, she didn't, which was probably rather a bad sign. She'd already caught the mood in the stable and sensed the total lack of interest on his part and the blatant begging on mine. Luckily I had no other audience since Minna, having satisfied herself Nutty was fine, had walked to the pub to meet Ted, and Jake had sloped round here to see Nico. The pair of them were even now ensconced in his room upstairs, smoking God knows what. I quietly shut the kitchen door on the television. After a while, though, as I watched the clock creep up to ten, pretending to busy myself tidying the kitchen which couldn't be cleaner, Lucy came in. She went to the fridge for a bottle of wine.

'Who's this friend then?'

'Hmm?' I turned from the depths of the empty dishwasher, pretending I had no idea what she was talking about.

'The girl. The one who's staying with Paddy.'

I feigned surprise. 'Oh! That one. His girlfriend, I think.'

'Ah.' She regarded me sympathetically. Then she grinned. 'Good to let him know what he's missing, though, eh?' She looked me up and down.

I laughed heartily. 'Good heavens, no. I wasn't trying to do that! It's Paddy, for heaven's sake.'

My forced jollity faded as she left the room. I made myself a cup of tea then switched it to a glass of wine. Reapplied my lipstick and sat down. It was five minutes past ten. Suddenly I jumped up. To be found sitting at the kitchen table with a bottle of wine was not good. Instead I perched on it jauntily, swinging my legs, my eyes on the back door for his lights. When I saw them, I'd busy myself again, so I'd look – you know. Busy. But I didn't see them. And my eyes began to hurt with the staring. And then my mobile rang, making me leap, because it was in my jeans pocket on vibrate. It was him.

'Hello?' I breathed.

'Molly? You OK?'

I cleared my throat. 'Yes! Yes, sorry. I was . . . something went down the wrong way.'

'Oh, right. How is he?'

'Who?'

A pause. 'Nutty.'

'Oh! Yes. Fine. He's doing well. Had a drink and a poo, according to Minna.'

'Excellent. That's exactly what we need, some movement. Listen, I won't come then, if that's the case.' I could have kicked myself. 'Pete Bradman's got a rare breed calving at Longmeadow, it's one of his Shropshire Show girls. He's in a bit of a state, I ought to hold his hand.'

'Oh. Right.' I tried to keep the crushing disappointment from my voice. I licked my lips. 'It was only a tiny one.'

'What was?'

'The poo.'

Another pause. 'OK. But he's had a bowel movement, that's the important thing.'

'Yup.' I took a brave deep breath. 'So . . . maybe tomorrow?'

'Maybe, but if he's had a good night, you won't need me. It'll only add to your bill.'

'Yes. Yes, I see. Although . . . I'd quite like to be reassured.' I shut my eyes.

'Oh well, if I can, I'll pop in at the end of my rounds. Say about eight.'

'OK, great,' I breathed again. Like a teenager, with a date. 'Thanks, Paddy.'

I pocketed my phone, horribly disappointed. I gazed at the damp patch on the wall for a long time. Suddenly I had a thought. A rogue one. I crept upstairs to Nico's room, following the rhythm, which wasn't hard. The door was pulsating to the monotonous, thumping beat within. I knocked, but no one heard me, so I opened the door on the ghastly, smoke-filled, hormone-infested den. I didn't go inside, just put my head round the door. They were both sitting on the bed smoking, iPhones in hands. Nico looked horrified to see me. I ignored him.

'Jake – turn that thing down please, Nico.' I waited until Nico had obliged, looking incensed. 'Jake, I'm sorry to hear your dad's rare breed is in trouble.'

Jake gazed at me, uncomprehending, his habitual charm and manners for once deserting him.

'The one he won Gold with at the Shropshire Show? She's calving?' I said.

His eyes registered and he cleared his throat politely. 'She was, but she had it two weeks ago. Landed it safe and sound.'

I stared. 'Ah. Right. Good.'

Nico made the face of his tribe. The incredulous, screwed-up one that said he was frankly appalled, ashamed and furious. I shut the door. Stood a moment on the threshold as the thumping resumed. Right. Pure fiction. Complete and utter fabrication. To get back to his romantic lair. To make the evening last a little longer. And to deflect me. Feeling even sicker, I tottered into my bedroom on wedges I wouldn't usually wear at home and certainly not with jeans. I kicked them off, tore off the oatmeal affair which was deeply irritating because it caught on everything, and took everything else off. I went into my bathroom and ran a bath with very pursed lips, catching my reflection in the mirror above it. I looked very old. And because I was bending to turn the taps, very saggy. When I got into bed, I didn't sleep for ages. I stared wide-eyed into the night, feeling very alone.

The following day, Lucy and Robin drove off to Robin's parents in Wiltshire to spread the good news. We waved them goodbye with smiles and kisses and many hugs and good wishes to his parents. They sailed away in his silver convertible, the wind in Lucy's blonde hair. Minna, having satisfied herself that Nutty was indeed on the mend, went to Ted's house to have lunch with his family, who, it transpired, she'd never met before, whilst Nico and Jake set off for a few days' camping, drinking, head-banging and what-have-you, in Anglesey. The gnomic Derek joined them, having shuffled from his cottage across the fields. They dripped out of the house trailing bedding, booze, the contents of my larder, and a strange girl I'd never seen before with the unlikely name of Fuzzy.

'Mum, have we got a tent?' They were literally packing their stuff in the trunk of the car. Literally about to leave.

I remembered to count to ten before I spoke. 'What about the one Granny and Grandpa brought back? I thought Granny mended it?'

'Derek took it to Dale last week. It got nicked.'

Derek shrugged as if this were the tragic, occupational hazard of a festival-goer.

'Then no, we no longer have a tent. Why don't you get one from Derek's house?' I asked sweetly.

Derek looked alarmed. 'We don't have that type of thing.'

'Neither do we now, Derek. Jake?'

Jake smiled brightly. 'Yes, Molly?'

'Tent?'

'Fresh out, sadly.'

'Fuzzy?'

Fuzzy jumped, her heavily made-up eyes boggling, as if no one had ever asked her a civil question in her life.

'Wha'?' She looked terrified.

'Do you, by any chance, have a tent?'

'Nah,' she managed eventually, shaking her peroxide head vehemently.

'Right. Well, it looks as if you're spending a night under the stars.'

They all looked horrified, and it occurred to me that not one of their mothers gave a monkey's, but they'd assumed I'd fix it, because I always did, and I'd be uneasy if I didn't. My blood boiled as I whipped out my phone. I rang Tia, who couldn't oblige, then Anna, who agreed she had a four-man, and that they could pick it up on the way, as long as they promised to return it.

'Thanks, Mum,' said Nico, relieved.

'You don't bloody deserve it,' I told him. 'And if you don't drop it off on the way back, I will actually take your gun and shoot you through the kneecaps.'

'Yeah, yeah,' he said giving me an impish grin and a rather endearing squeeze of the shoulders. And actually, I knew he would return it, because Anna's husband, Jim, was quite scary. Something I clearly wasn't, from Derek's point of view. They piled into the car and spluttered out of the yard, bumper hanging off and wobbling. Another fox shot, I thought, watching them go. No problem too big. Just as long as it's not mine.

So that just left me. I went to see Nutty, who was looking much perkier. He gave me a friendly nudge with his mealy nose. I gave him another of his little-but-often sloppy feeds and went inside. Then I rang Peter and asked about the sale of the house, hoping he'd say it was all off. It wasn't. It was very much all on. The vendors were still frightfully keen, he said, and all being well, he reckoned I'd be exchanging next week, and quite possibly out in a couple of months. Did I have anywhere to live? he enquired.

'No! Not yet,' I said, panic rising inside me like a high-speed elevator. It went all the way to the top. 'It's been a bit – convoluted, the house in London.' God, the house in London. It seemed like a million years and a million miles away: totally out of my sphere of orbit. And my comfort zone, too, I thought with a frisson of fear as I put the phone down. Who was that ambitious woman with plans to sail confidently off to Harvey Nichols to purchase her Armani, then away to Ottathingy for lunch, before bridge parties with her pencil-thin, manicured, new best friends? What was wrong with my old ones? Would the new ones produce a tent at a moment's notice? I thought not. I thanked Peter tremulously then put down the phone.

Swallowing hard to stop the fear rising further, I took a pony halter from the hook behind the door and whistled to the dogs. The cat followed too, and out we went, across to the paddock and beyond. I folded my arms tightly against my chest in defense, holding myself together like a cracked old vase, hoping I wouldn't fall apart. As I went, I tried not to notice the shimmer of the rain which had fallen in the night and was cupped in the eyes of the ox-eye daisies. Or the way the stream glistened in the valley, the water so clear I could see every pebble on the bed as I went over the stepping stones to get Tufty. He came up to me with a whicker of pleasure and I stroked his dear old white nose and put his halter on. As I led him back towards the stream I tried not to remember the picnics the children and I had had down here, in the early days, in the immediate after-math of David's death. When I was trying very hard to make their lives as normal as possible, to be a great team – team was a word I used a lot in those days – and when Minna and Nico at least had believed in us as a slightly diminished family, even though Lucy had taken some coaxing.

I stood for a moment, on the brink of the stream, succumbing to the memories. I half shut my eyes and remembered the quad bike they'd roared around on so dangerously down here, me shrieking from a bedroom window for them to slow down. The cows who'd got bored and escaped as cows did, we learned, and who we used to meet in the lane, coming back on the school run. The chil-dren in hysterics, me frantic, as I stopped the car and we chased after them. The joy of all the chicken hatches at Easter in the barn, before the fox invariably got them all in the autumn. How we'd gradually got used to that. The way nature was: its peaks and troughs. But peaks, mostly, it seemed to me now, looking back as I obviously was, with slightly rose-tinted nostalgic spectacles.

What was I doing? What *was* I doing, I thought, in a moment of genuine horror, as Tufty, bored now with standing still, embarked on wading across the stream, the dogs swimming beside him. The cat and I used the step-ping stones and I held the end of Tufty's rope. Back in the yard, I popped him in the stable beside Nutty, who whinnied in delight. Then I turned and walked quickly across to the house, tears filling my eyes.

That evening, I knew he wouldn't come, so I didn't even bother. In fact I deliberately didn't put on a scrap of make-up and was back in my usual uniform of ill-fitting but comfy jeans and a well-worn sweater. Almost in defiance, really. It made me feel better, if no one else. I put a pan of water on to boil for some pasta so I'd get really fat and made a comforting cheesy sauce. Then I turned the television on to *Made in Chelsea*, which Minna watched avidly and I pretended to be above but was secretly fascinated by, and sat down as I waited for the water to boil. The front doorbell rang. Well, it wouldn't be Paddy, because he always came round the back. But when I went to answer it, there he was. Paddy Campbell. In a jacket and pressed shirt and those chinos again. I looked him up and down.

'Going out?'

'Hopefully,' he grinned.

'Oh. Right. So . . . you popped round to see how Nutty was on the way? Is that it? Is she in the car?' I peered around him. Couldn't see.

'Who?'

'Claudia.'

He laughed. 'Oh, no. She's not. Can I come in?' Confused, I stood back. He strode past me, still grinning.

I shut the front door and followed him through to the sitting room. He flopped down in an armchair, making himself very much at home. I stood over him. He looked around.

'You've tidied up.'

'It happens, occasionally.'

He nodded. There was a pause before he spoke. 'You fell for that, then.'

'Sorry?'

'The Claudia ruse. Actually, I knew you did, it was pretty to watch. Quite made my week.' I stared. 'Well, it was kind of payback time. You'd strung me along for so long.'

I crossed the room and perched on a sofa arm opposite, lost. 'Paddy . . . what are you saying . . . ?'

'Oh, she was a willing accomplice. Claudia. Thought it was a hoot. Likes you very much, by the way.'

I felt my mouth hang open. 'Are you saying . . . you set me up? Deliberately?'

'I believe I am.'

'No.'

'Yes.'

'I don't believe you.'

He shrugged. 'Up to you.'

'But that's . . . that's so duplicitous!'

Another shrug. 'Needs must. And I needed to. Quite hard to make you jealous in Herefordshire. Who should I take to the Pig and Whistle? Wendy Higgington? Tia?'

'Tia's lovely,' I said defensively, but automatically, my mind was whirring furiously elsewhere.

'She is. She's also married. Everyone's married.'

'Except us.'

'Yes.'

I lurched away from that, not meaning it to sound the way it had emerged. Went back to Claudia. 'But . . . you held hands, at dinner,' I whispered, leaning forward incredulously. 'I saw you.'

'Yes, I asked her to. Whispered in her ear that I very badly needed to make you jealous. Said that I'd tried everything else, and nothing had worked. We thought it worked a treat. You looked mighty distracted as you talked to Dad and Willem.'

'You bastard.' I stared, amazed. Licked my lips. Shook my head. 'The constant texting . . .'

'At the café? To Poppy. Trying to keep on top of things while I was away. She's frightfully young to be holding the fort. And then obviously I told you I was staying in London but got the next train down, the one after you.'

'But . . .' I shook my bewildered head again. 'Oh my God, so elaborate! Your mother! Saying she'd always liked Claudia, was so pleased to see you together again!' My heart was pounding in my ribcage.

He frowned. 'I doubt she'd say that. Or if she did, she'd mean as friends. No, no, Mum wasn't in on it. She was totally baffled when I took off back here, straight after you. But she does like Claudia, and hoped we'd be friends again one day. In fact she'd already had Clauds and Alberto round the week before, for drinks.'

'A-Alberto?'

'Her boyfriend. Fiancé, actually, they're getting married in September. He's a polo player. Argentinian. Couldn't come to our dinner, because he was playing a match in Brazil. Nice chap.'

Paddy's eyes were steady and watchful now: not so jocular.

I licked my lips which were extraordinarily dry. My head was trying to assimilate all this. 'Paddy, are you saying you concocted this whole elaborate charade over the last few days, just to make me jealous?'

'Well, it wasn't that elaborate. Just a few tiny white lies. And it was extremely interesting actually. I must do it more often. As an anthropological experiment it was fascinating.'

'I don't believe you. It's so unlike you.'

He swallowed. 'No, you're right. I hated it, if I'm honest.'

'No, but I don't believe . . .' I didn't know what I believed.

There was a silence. We stared at one another. It *was* so unlike him. He blinked first.

'Molly, I'm sorry,' he said abruptly, his face changing. It collapsed slightly. No longer remotely jocular or confident. 'I knew of no other way.' He got to his feet and walked to the window, his back to me. He thrust his hands in his pockets. 'And if you feel hoodwinked, or betrayed, I totally accept that it was bad form. I was joking about it being interesting. I didn't actually enjoy any of it.'

I stared at his back a long moment. At the blue linen, slightly creased from sitting in the car.

'But the thing is—' He turned, hesitated. 'The thing is, I did it because I wanted you to want me. Really want me. I could tell you were more interested, that the wind was turning, but I didn't want to be second, third or even fourth fiddle. Didn't want to be the backstop as in – oh well, my husband's dead, the Frenchman would never have worked out and Felix turned out to be a shit, but hey, there's always Paddy. I wanted you to want me like I've wanted you. For so long.' He looked down at the floor. When he eventually spoke his voice was quiet. 'I'm ashamed to say, I wanted it to hurt.'

I breathed in sharply at that. At length I spoke. 'It hurt,' I whispered.

He glanced up, hopeful. He looked like a boy suddenly. In that moment, I got a glimpse of a younger, more vulnerable man, not the proud, irascible Paddy Campbell I knew.

'Oh Paddy.' It escaped from me involuntarily, but it was full of everything I meant.

His face altered at my tone. He read my expression in an instant, and in another, his face cleared completely. He held out his arms and I walked into them. We held on tight. I could feel his heart pounding under his jacket and I'm quite sure he could feel mine too. The television was still blaring, but not as loudly as the pasta water, which could be heard boiling over, sizzling madly all over the hob in the kitchen. He released me and I fled to take it off the boil. I gave myself a moment in there in the kitchen to steady myself, hanging on to the Rayburn rail, but it didn't do any good. Every pulse was racing and my cheeks were burning, I knew.

When I came back he'd found the remote and snapped off the television, which was just as well, because as I'd left, Lucinda was telling Anton exactly why she'd slept with so many men. Paddy still had the slightly unsure look of a much younger, more insecure man. I loved him for it. For being reasonably certain he was home and dry, but still not entirely confident. And of course this sudden change of situation was very new to us. We'd had such a volatile relationship up to now.

'I booked that table again,' he told me, summoning up a flashing grin. 'The one at the Fox and Hounds.' He shrugged: suddenly looked a bit worried. 'Perhaps I shouldn't have. Perhaps it was a bad omen. You know, our last disastrous non-event.'

'Oh no!' I reassured him. 'I love the Fox and Hounds! Give me two minutes, literally, two minutes!' I beamed at him and actually thought my face would crack in half.

I raced upstairs in a blur: threw off my clothes and tossed them on the floor. Then I washed under my pits, blasted on some deodorant, threw on the skinny jeans and the oatmeal affair and the wedges and slapped on a bit of make-up. I barely looked in the mirror actually. I ran downstairs and followed him out through the front door, almost at a trot, to the car. Before you could say keen as mustard, I was in the passenger seat beside him. Not the red pickup truck, you understand, a proper car. A nice little low-slung affair with no roof, and although obviously I didn't look like Lucy, I didn't look like Mr Pritchard either. We beamed at one another under the inky night sky, the outside lights illuminating our faces. It looked very much as if his face might crack too.

Off we roared, the wind, for once, in *my* hair. And not to a little Italian tucked away down a side street in Ludlow where no one would see us – no, we were going to the pub. To the local. Where half the village went. As we sailed confidently into the car park, the Hobsons and the Burdetts were just getting out of their cars, greeting each other, no doubt bound for a couples supper.

This was very high stakes, I realized, as they turned, seeing us drive in. I wondered if Paddy had wanted that – wanted it to be all around the valley in moments. Maybe he did, because when he'd parked, and just before we got out of the car, he did a very un-Paddy like thing. He leaned across and took me in his arms and kissed me, really rather comprehensively, on the lips.

As he finally ran out of steam and released me, his breath as he held me close racing in my ear, mine no doubt in his – we weren't sixteen, after all – I knew there was no going back. And not just because the Hobsons and the Burdetts were nudging each other, bug-eyed, as they went into the pub, or because Bob Harris, as he came out of the public bar having downed his habitual two pints, was rooted to the spot, eyes on stalks. No. I knew there was no going back because for once, both my head and my heart were in accord, and they both said yes. I grinned at our audience as I hopped out of the car.

Almost took a bow. Then, unable to keep the ridiculous smile from my face, I took Paddy's hand as he held his out to me, and off we sailed. Confidently, heads high, to the cosy, packed little restaurant off the saloon bar, but luckily to a corner table, where we wouldn't be overheard, and where we could chatter away to our hearts' content, maybe even hold hands over coffee, but most definitely, for all the world to see.

THE OLD GIRL NETWORK

#1 bestselling author Catherine Alliott tells a hilarious story about the twists and turns of love, loyalty and getting mixed up in someone else's affairs.

Finding true love's a piece of cake - as long as you're looking for someone else's true love . . .

Polly McLaren is young, scatty and impossibly romantic. She works for an arrogant and demanding boss, and has a gorgeous if never-there-when-you-need-him boyfriend. But the day a handsome stranger recognizes her old school scarf, her life is knocked completely off kilter.

Adam is American, new to the country and begs Polly's help in finding his missing fiancé. Over dinner at the Savoy, she agrees - the girls of St Gertrude's look out for one another. However, the old-girl network turns out to be a spider's web of complications and deceit in which everyone and everything Polly cares about is soon hopelessly entangled.

The course of true love never did run smooth. But no one said anything about ruining your life over it. And it's not even Polly's true love . . .

'*Hilarious and full of surprises*' **Daily Telegraph**

For this and other books go to:

www.catherinealliott.US

OLIVIA'S LUCK

Catherine Alliott's brilliantly warm and funny take on taking control of your life, in *Olivia's Luck*.

'I don't care what color you paint the sodding hall. I'm leaving.'

When her husband Johnny suddenly walks out on ten years of marriage, their ten-year-old daughter and the crumbling house they're up to their eyeballs renovating, Olivia is at first totally devastated. How could he? How could she not have noticed his unhappiness?

But she's not one to weep for long.

Not when she's got three builders camped in her back garden, a neighbor with a never-ending supply of cast-off men she thinks Olivia would be drawn to and a daughter with her own firm views on . . . well, just about everything.

Will Johnny ever come back? And if he doesn't, will Olivia's luck ever change for the better?

'*Sensitive, funny and wonderfully well written*' **Daily Express**

Find 'Olivia's Luck' and other books by Catherine at:

www.catherinealliott.US

MY HUSBAND NEXT DOOR

Separated in every way but distance, Sebastian resides in an outhouse across the lawn from Ella's ramshackle farmhouse.

When Ella married the handsome, celebrated artist Sebastian Montclair at just nineteen she was madly in love. Now, those blissful years of marriage have turned into the very definition of an unconventional set-up.

With an ex-husband living under her nose and a home crowded by hostile teenaged children, gender-confused chickens - not to mention her hyper critical mother whose own marriage slips spectacularly off the rails -Ella finds comfort in the company of the very charming gardener, Ludo.

Then out of the blue Sebastian decides to move on, catching Ella horribly unawares. How much longer can she hide from what really destroyed her marriage . . . and the secret she continues to keep?

'I raced through it, completely gripped from start to finish' **Daily Mail**

'A captivating and heartwarming tale' **Closer**

For this and other books go to:

www.catherinealliott.US

WISH YOU WERE HERE

A hilarious, compulsively readable novel from the #1 bestseller Catherine Alliott

When Flora, James and their two teenage daughters are offered the holiday of a lifetime in a chateau in the South of France in return for one simple good deed, they jump at the chance to escape the confines of Clapham, the weight of the mortgage and anxieties over their future for a blissful break.

But Flora didn't anticipate a mysterious guest and a whole heap of family baggage coming along too.

And with James developing a schoolboy crush on a famous singer and Flora distracted by ghosts from her past, their dream holiday suddenly takes some very unexpected turns . . .

'A breezy, comic, summery romp that will appeal to fans of Jilly Cooper' **Sunday Mirror**

'A thoroughly engaging, entertaining read' **Daily Mail**

'While you'll probably be glad that you're not on this holiday with the Murray-Browns, make sure to take them on yours.' **Heat**

For this and other books by Catherine go to:

www.catherinealliott.US

A MARRIED MAN

'What could be nicer than living in the country?'

Lucy Fellowes is in a bind. She's a widow living in a pokey
London flat with two small boys and an erratic income. But
when her mother-in-law offers her a converted barn on the
family's estate - she knows it's a brilliant opportunity for her and
the kids. But there's a problem …

The estate is a shrine to Lucy's dead husband Ned. The whole
family has been unable to get over his death. If she's honest the
whole family is far from normal. And if Lucy is to accept this
offer she'll be putting herself completely in their incapable
hands.

Which leads to Lucy's other problem. Charlie - the only man
since Ned who she's had any feelings for - lives nearby. The
problem? He's already married . . .

'A joy . . . you're in for a treat' **Daily Express**

'I literally couldn't put this down.' **Time Out**

For this and other books go to:
www.catherinealliott.US

GOING TOO FAR

'You've gone all fat and complacent because you've got your man, haven't you?'

Polly Penhalligan is outraged at the suggestion that since getting married to Nick and settling into their beautiful manor farmhouse in Cornwall she has let herself go. But watching a lot of telly and gorging on biscuits, not getting dressed until lunchtime and waiting for pregnancy to strike are not the signs of someone living an active and fulfilled life. So Polly does something rash.

She allows her home to be used as a location for a TV advert. Having a glamorous film crew around will certainly put a bomb under the idyllic, rural life. Only perhaps she should have consulted Nick first.

Because before the cameras have even started to roll - and complete chaos descends on the farm - Polly's marriage has been turned upside down. This time she really has gone too far . . .

'Alliott's joie de vivre is irresistible' **Daily Mail**

For this and other books go to:

www.catherinealliott.US

ONE DAY IN MAY

One day in May, Hattie's life changes forever . . .

Hattie Carrington has good reason to be happy. Her antiques business is flourishing, her teenage son is settled at school and she's enjoying a fling with a sexy, younger man. But when work takes her back to the village of Little Crandon, heartbreaking memories of her first love surface. It seems that the secret affair with married politician Dominic Forbes, which changed the course of her life, just won't go away.

So when Hattie's bumps into Dominic's widow and his gorgeous younger brother, Hal, her world is turned upside down. Though she's still trying to hide from her mistakes, she knows that if she's ever to fall in love again she needs to be honest with others, and herself.

Can she admit what really happened with Dominic all those years ago? And, if so, is she ready for the consequences?

'Another charming tale of love and heartbreak from this wonderfully warm and witty author' **Woman**

For this and other books go to:

www.catherinealliott.US

NOT THAT KIND OF GIRL

A girl can get into all kinds of trouble just by going back to work . . .

Henrietta Tate gave up everything for her husband Marcus and their kids. But now that the children are away at school and she's rattling round their large country house all day she's feeling a little lost.

So when a friend puts her in touch with Laurie, a historian in need of a PA, Henrietta heads for London. Quickly, she throws herself into the job. Marcus is - of course - jealous of her spending so much time with her charming new boss. And soon enough her absence causes cracks to form in their marriage that just can't be papered over.

Then Rupert, a very old flame, reappears, and Henrietta suddenly finds herself torn between three men. How did this happen? She's not that kind of girl . . . is she?

'An addictive cocktail of wit, frivolity and madcap romance' **Time Out**

For this and other books go to:

www.catherinealliott.US

THE REAL THING

Every girl's got one - that old boyfriend they never quite fell out of love with . . .

Tessa Hamilton's thirty, with a lovely husband and home, two adorable kids, and not a care in the world. Sure her husband ogles the nanny more than she should allow. And keeping up with the Joneses is a full-time occupation. But she's settled and happy. No seven-year itch for Tessa.

Except at the back of her mind is Patrick Cameron. Gorgeous, moody, rebellious, he's the boy she met when she was seventeen. The boy her vicar father told her she couldn't see and who left to go to Italy to paint. The boy she's not heard from in twelve long years. And now he's back.

Questioning every choice, every decision she's made since Patrick left, Tessa is about to risk her family and everything she has become to find out whether she did the right thing first time round . . .

'*The writing is both intelligent and sparkling*' **Marian Keyes**

'*You're in for a treat*' **Daily Express**

For this and other books go to:
www.catherinealliott.US

THE WEDDING DAY

Annie O'Harran is getting married . . . all over again

A divorced, single mum, Annie is about to tie the knot with David. But there's a long summer to get through first. Annie's retreating to a lonely house in Cornwall, where she's planning to finish her book, spend time with her teenage daughter Flora and make last-minute wedding plans.

Annie should be so lucky.

As soon as Annie arrives, her competitive sister and her wild brood fetch up. And Annie's louche ex-husband and his latest squeeze keep dropping in. Plus there's the surprise American houseguest who can't help sharing his heartbreak.

Suddenly Annie's big day seems a long, long way off - and if she's not careful it might never happen at all

'Alliott's joie de vivre is irresistible' **Daily Mail**

'Possibly my favorite writer' **Marian Keyes**

For this and other books go to:

www.catherinealliott.US

ROSIE MEADOWS REGRETS

'Tell me, Alice, how does a girl go about getting a divorce these days?'

Three years ago Rosie walked blindly into marriage with Harry. They have precisely nothing in common except perhaps their little boy Ivo. Not that Harry pays him much attention, preferring to spend his time with his braying upper class friends.

But the night that Harry drunkenly does something unspeakable, Rosie decides he's got to go. In between fantasizing how she might bump him off, she takes the much more practical step of divorcing this blight on her and Ivo's lives.

However, when reality catches up with her darkest fantasies, Rosie realizes, at long last, that it is time she took charge of her life. There'll be no more regrets, and time, perhaps, for a little love.

'*Completely gripped from start to finish*' **Daily Mail**

'*An entertaining read*' **Daily Express**

For this and other books go to:

www.catherinealliott.US

THE SECRET LIFE EVIE HAMILTON

Evie Hamilton has a secret . . . one she doesn't even know about. Yet . . .

Evie's an Oxfordshire wife and mum who's biggest worry in life is whether or not she can fit in a manicure on her way to fetch her daughter from clarinet lessons. But she's blissfully unaware that her charmed and happy life is about to be turned upside-down.

For one sunny morning a letter lands on Evie's immaculate doormat. It's a bombshell, knocking her carefully arranged and managed world completely askew and it threatens to sabotage all she holds dear.

What will be left and what will change forever? Is Evie strong enough to fight for what she loves? Can her entire world really be as fragile as her best china?

'Classy, wonderfully gossipy and breathless' **Red**

'We defy you not to get caught up in Alliott's life-changing tale' **Heat**

For this and other books go to:

www.catherinealliott.US

A RURAL AFFAIR

'If I'm being totally honest I had fantasized about Phil dying.'

When Poppy Shilling's bike-besotted, Lycra-clad husband is killed in a freak accident, she can't help feeling a guilty sense of relief. For at long last she's released from a controlling and loveless marriage.

Throwing herself wholeheartedly into village life, she's determined to start over. And sure enough, everyone from Luke the sexy church organist to Bob the resident oddball, is taking note. Yet the one man Poppy can't take her eyes off seems tantalizingly out of reach - why won't he let go of his glamorous ex-wife?

But just as she's ready to dip her toes in the water, the discovery of a dark secret about her late husband shatters Poppy's confidence. Does she really have the courage to risk her heart again? Because Poppy wants a lot more than just a rural affair . . .

For this and other books go to:

www.CatherineAlliott.US

A CROWDED MARRIAGE

There isn't room in a marriage for three . . .

Painter Imogen is happily married to Alex, and together they have a son. But when their finances hit rock bottom, they're forced to accept Eleanor Latimer's offer of a rent-free cottage on her large country estate. If it was anyone else, Imogen would be beaming gratitude. Unfortunately, Eleanor just happens to be Alex's beautiful, rich and flirtatious ex.

And from the moment she steps inside Shepherd's Cottage, Imogen's life is in chaos. Coping with rude locals, murderous chickens, a maddening (if handsome) headmaster, mountains of manure, and visits from the infuriating vet, she has to face Eleanor, now a fixture at Alex's side.

Is Imogen losing Alex? Will her precious family be torn apart? And whose fault is it really - Eleanor's, Alex's or Imogen's?

For this and other books go to:

www.CatherineAlliott.US

A WRITER'S JOURNEY

Catherine Alliott has written fifteen bestselling novels and is translated into eighteen languages. She has sold over 3 million books worldwide. Catherine lives with her family in Hertfordshire, UK.

**Visit CatherineAlliott.US to sneak peek at
Catherine's other books including:
"About Last Night..."
"The Old Girl Network"
"Wish You Were Here"
"Olivia's Luck"
"One Day In May"**

'People often ask me if I always had a burning desire to be an author, and the honest answer is no, in fact it almost happened by accident.

I was working as a copy-writer in an ad agency and tired of writing blurb for soap powder, began writing a novel under the desk. I had no thought of publication, was just doing it to relieve the boredom, but I must say it was a bit of a shock when my boss walked in one day and said we're not sure you're entirely committed and gave me the sack!

Actually I think that galvanized me and I was determined to finish it. I did, but it took a while: I was working freelance, and then pregnant with my first child so it wasn't at the forefront of my mind.

When my son was born I discovered babies slept for great chunks of the day, so I revisited it, tapping it onto a computer my brother gave me. (The first draft was in long hand, I'm a complete Luddite by nature, and actually, still write my first draft into note books.)

My husband persuaded me to send it to an agent who took it - amazingly and then a few weeks later I had a publisher too. The Old Girl Network came out about a year later and the first time I saw it in a shop, I was so startled I ran out again!

I'm convinced it was easier back then to get published, these days it's far more competitive because there are so many girls doing it I'm glad I started early!

I've written a few more since then, but some things don't change: I still get a thrill when I see them around. I hope you enjoy the books, I certainly have a lot of fun writing them.'

facebook.com/AlliottCountry
www.catherinealliott.us
catherine@catherinealliott.us

Made in the USA
Middletown, DE
15 January 2021

31685678R00262